Praise for Margaret Daley
and her novels

"*Buried Secrets*…is a fun, adventurous tale with romance blended into each scene."
—*RT Book Reviews*

"*Christmas Bodyguard*…exemplifies the importance of a father's love in a girl's life while keeping the reader busy trying to figure out who the bad guy is."
—*RT Book Reviews*

"Action and intrigue start early on and will have the reader rooting for…justice to prevail."
—*RT Book Reviews* on *Guarding the Witness*

Praise for Vicki Hinze
and her novels

"Steady suspense keeps the reader guessing throughout, and the story behind the candy canes and their biblical connection is delightful."
—*RT Book Reviews* on *Christmas Countdown*

"Della's grief and guilt are skillfully conveyed and demonstrate the healing powers of finding faith."
—*RT Book Reviews* on *Survive the Night*

Margaret Daley, an award-winning author of ninety books (five million sold worldwide), has been married for over forty years and is a firm believer in romance and love. When she isn't traveling, she's writing love stories, often with a suspense thread, and corralling her three cats, who think they rule her household. To find out more about Margaret, visit her website at margaretdaley.com.

Vicki Hinze is an award-winning author of nearly thirty novels, four nonfiction books and hundreds of articles published in as many as sixty-three countries. She lives in Florida with her husband, near her children and grands, and she gets cranky if she must miss one of their ball games. Vicki loves to visit with readers and invites you to join her at vickihinze.com or on Facebook.

Christmas Stalking

Margaret Daley

&

Christmas Countdown

Vicki Hinze

✦ HARLEQUIN® LOVE INSPIRED® SUSPENSE

LOVE INSPIRED BOOKS

Recycling programs for this product may not exist in your area.

ISBN-13: 978-1-335-00540-3

Christmas Stalking and Christmas Countdown

Copyright © 2018 by Harlequin Books S.A.

The publisher acknowledges the copyright holders of the individual works as follows:

Christmas Stalking
Copyright © 2012 by Margaret Daley

Christmas Countdown
Copyright © 2012 by Vicki Hinze

CONTENTS

CHRISTMAS STALKING

Margaret Daley

To Shaun and Kim, my son and daughter-in-law

For if ye forgive men their trespasses,
your heavenly Father will also forgive you.
—*Matthew* 6:14

Chapter One

In the dark, Ellie St. James scanned the mountainous terrain out her bedroom window at her new client's home in Colorado, checking the shadows for any sign of trouble before she went to sleep. The large two-story house of redwood and glass blended in well with the rugged landscape seven thousand feet above sea level. Any other time she would appreciate the beauty, but she was here to protect Mrs. Rachel Winfield.

A faint sound punched through her musing. She whirled away from the window and snatched her gun off the bedside table a few feet from her. Fitting the weapon into her right palm and finding its weight comforting, she crept toward her door and eased it open to listen. None of the guard dogs were barking. Maybe she'd imagined the noise.

A creak, like a floorboard being stepped on, drifted up the stairs. Someone was ascending to the second floor. She and her employer were the only ones in the main house. She glanced at Mrs. Winfield's door two down from hers and noticed it was closed. Her client kept it that way only when she was in her bedroom.

So who was on the stairs? Had someone gotten past the dogs outside and the security system? And did that someone not care that he was being heard coming up the steps? Because he didn't intend to leave any witnesses?

The latest threat against Mrs. Winfield urged her into action. She slipped out of her room and into the shadows of the long hallway that led to the staircase. Having memorized all the floorboards that squeaked, Ellie avoided the left side of the corridor as she snuck forward—past Mrs. Winfield's door.

Another sound echoed through the hall. Whoever was on the steps was at the top. She increased her speed, probing every dark recess around her for any other persons. Near the wooden railing of the balcony that overlooked the front entrance, she found the light switch, planted her bare feet a foot apart, preparing herself to confront the intruder, and then flipped on the hall light.

Even though she expected the bright illumination, her eyes needed a few seconds to adjust to it. The large man before her lifted his hand to shield his eyes from the glare. Which gave Ellie the advantage.

"Don't move," she said in her toughest voice, a husky resonance she often used to her advantage.

The stranger dropped his hand to his side, his gray-blue eyes drilling into her then fixing on her Wilson combat aimed at his chest. Anger washed all surprise from his expression. "Who are you?" The question came out in a deep, booming voice, all the fury in his features reflected in it.

"You don't get to ask the questions. Who are—"

The click of the door opening to Mrs. Winfield's

bedroom slightly behind and to the left of Ellie halted her words as she shifted her attention for an instant to make sure the man didn't have an accomplice already with her client.

"Winnie, get back," the intruder yelled.

By the time Ellie's gaze reconnected with the man, he was charging toward her. She had less than a second to decide what to do. The use of her client's nickname caused Ellie to hesitate. In that moment the stranger barreled into her, slamming her into the hardwood floor. The impact jolted her, knocking the Wilson Combat from her hand. The thud of her weapon hitting the floor behind her barely registered as she lay pinned beneath two hundred pounds of solid muscle. Pressed into her, the man robbed her of a decent breath.

Her training flooded her with extra adrenaline. Before he could capture her arms, she brought them up and struck him on the sides of his head. His light-colored gaze widened at the blow. She latched onto his face, going for his eyes with her thumbs.

"Miss St. James, stop!" Mrs. Winfield's high-pitched voice cut into the battle between Ellie and her attacker.

The man shifted and clasped her wrists in a bone-crushing grip.

Ellie swung her attention from the brute on top of her to her employer standing over them with Ellie's gun in her quivering hand. Pointed at her!

"He's my grandson," Mrs. Winfield said. "Colt, get up. She can hardly breathe."

The man rolled off her, shaking his head as though his ears rang. After her attack they probably did.

Sitting up, he stared at his grandmother who still held the weapon. "Please give me the gun, Winnie."

His soft, calm words, interspersed with heavy pants, contradicted his earlier authoritative tone.

Ellie gulped in oxygen-rich breaths while he pushed to his feet and gently removed the weapon from Mrs. Winfield's hand. He dwarfed his petite grandmother by over a foot.

With her gun in his grasp, he stood next to her client and glared down at Ellie. "Now I would like an answer. Who are you?" Anger still coated each word.

She slowly rose from the floor. "Ellie St. James."

He put his arm around his grandmother, who stood there trembling, staring at Ellie as though she was trying to understand what had just happened. "What are you doing here, Miss St. James?" he asked.

With a shake of her head, Mrs. Winfield blinked then peered up at her grandson. "She's my new assistant."

"What in the world are you doing carrying a gun?"

His question thundered through the air, none of the gentle tone he'd used with his grandmother evident. He glared at her, his sharp gaze intent on Ellie's face. Although he'd lowered the gun, Ellie didn't think it would take much for him to aim it again. Fury was etched into his hard-planed face.

"My dear, why *do* you have a gun?"

Mrs. Winfield's light, musical voice finally pulled Ellie's attention from the man. Her employer had regained her regal bearing, her hands clasped together in front of her to control their trembling.

"I've lived alone for so long in a big city I've always had a gun for protection," Ellie finally answered.

Although Mrs. Winfield was her client—the person she'd been assigned to guard—the older woman didn't know it. Her lawyer and second-in-charge at Glamour Sensations, Harold Jefferson, had hired Guardians, Inc., to protect her. Ellie was undercover, posing as her new assistant. Her cover had her growing up in Chicago—the south side—and still living there. But in reality, at the first opportunity she'd had she'd hightailed it out of Chicago and enlisted in the army. When she'd left the military, she hadn't gone back home but instead she'd gone to Dallas to work for Guardians, Inc., and Kyra Morgan—now Kyra Hunt.

"You don't need a weapon now. This isn't a big city. I have security around the estate. You're safe. I prefer you do something with that gun. I don't like weapons." A gentle smile on her face, Mrs. Winfield moved toward her as though she were placating a gun-toting woman gone crazy.

Ellie didn't trust anyone's security enough to give up her gun, but she bit the inside of her cheeks to keep from voicing that thought. She would need to call Mr. Jefferson and see how he wanted to proceed. Ellie had wanted to tell Mrs. Winfield that her life was in danger, but he'd refused. Now something would have to give here.

"I'll take care of it, Winnie. I'll lock it in the safe until she can remove it from here." The grandson checked the Wilson Combat, slipped out the ammo clip and ejected the bullet in the chamber, then began to turn away.

"Wait. You can't—"

He peered over his shoulder, one brow arching. "I'm sure my grandmother will agree that this will have to be a condition of your continual employment. If I had any say in it, I'd send you packing tonight." He rubbed his ears. "They're still ringing. You have a mean punch. Where did you learn to take care of yourself?"

"A matter of survival in a tough neighborhood." That was true, but she'd also had additional training in the army.

"As my grandmother said, that isn't an issue here. We're on a side of a mountain miles away from the nearest town. No one bothers us up here."

If you only knew. "I'm licensed to carry—"

But Mrs. Winfield's grandson ignored her protest and descended the staircase.

Ellie rushed to the railing overlooking the downstairs entrance. Clutching the wood, she leaned over and said, "That's my weapon. I'll take care of it."

"That's okay. I'm taking care of it." Then he disappeared into the hallway that led to the office where the safe was.

"I certainly understand why you got scared." Mrs. Winfield approached her at the railing and patted her back. "I did when I heard the noise from you two in the hallway. I didn't know what was happening. I appreciate you being willing to protect me, but thank goodness, it wasn't necessary."

This time. Ellie swung around to face the older woman. "Yeah, but you never know."

"The Lord watches out for His children. I'm in the best care."

"I agree, but that doesn't mean we shouldn't be proactive, Mrs. Winfield," Ellie said, hoping to convince Mr. Jefferson to tell her about the threats tomorrow.

"Please call me Winnie. Christy, my previous assistant, did. I don't like standing on formality since you'll be helping me." She smiled. "Colt gave me that name years ago, and everyone calls me that now."

"Was he supposed to visit?"

"The last I heard he wasn't going to come back this year for Christmas. He probably heard my disappointment when we talked on the phone a few days ago. If I had known Colt was coming, I would have said something to you."

She'd read the dossier Kyra Hunt had given her on Colt Winfield, the only grandson Mrs. Winfield had. She should have recognized him, but with a beard and scruffy hair and disheveled clothes he'd looked like a bum who had wandered into the house intent on ill gains.

"He was supposed to be in the South Pacific on the research vessel through Christmas and the New Year." Mrs. Winfield gave Ellie a smile, her blue eyes sparkling. "Just like him to forget to tell me he was coming home after all for Christmas. Knowing him, it could be a surprise from the very beginning. He loves doing that kind of thing. Such a sweet grandson." She leaned close to Ellie to whisper the last because Colt Winfield was coming back up the steps.

"I wish that were the case, Winnie." Colt paused on the top stair. "But I need to get back to the *Kaleidoscope*. I managed to get a few days off before we start the next phase of our project, and I know how important it is to you that we have some time together at Christmas."

Great, he'll be leaving soon.

"Just a few days?" His grandmother's face fell, the shine in her eyes dimming. "I haven't seen you in months. Can't you take a couple of weeks out of your busy schedule to enjoy the holidays like we used to?"

Please don't, Ellie thought, rolling her shoulders to ease the ache from their tussle on the hardwood floor.

He came to the older woman and drew her into his embrace. "I wish I could. Maybe at the end of January. The government on the island is allowing a limited amount of time to explore the leeward side and the underwater caves."

Mrs. Winfield stepped away. "You aren't the only one on the research team. Let someone else do it for a while. You're one of three marine biologists. And the other two are married to each other. They get to spend Christmas together."

"I need to be there. Something is happening to the sea life in that part of the ocean. It's mutating over time. It's affected the seal population. You know how I feel about the environment and the oceans."

"Fine." Mrs. Winfield fluttered her hand in the air as she swept around and headed for the door to her bedroom. "I can't argue with you over something I taught you. Good night. I'll see you tomorrow morning. I hope you'll at least go for a power walk with Ellie and me. Seven o'clock sharp."

"Yes, Winnie. I've brought my running shoes. I figured you'd want me to."

When her employer shut the door to her room, Ellie immediately said, "I need my gun back."

"You do? What part of your duties as my grandmother's assistant requires you to have a gun?" His gaze skimmed down her length.

Ellie finally peered down at the clothes she wore—old sweats and a baggy T-shirt. With a glance at the mirror at the end of the hall, she noticed the wild disarray of her hair. She looked as scruffy as Colt Winfield. She certainly wouldn't appear to this man as a capable and efficient bodyguard. Or a woman who knew how to use a gun when she needed to. "Ask yourself. What if you had been a burglar? Would you have wanted me to let you rob the place or do worse?"

For half a moment he just stared at her, then he started chuckling. "Since I'm not and I'll be here for a few days, you'll be safe. Didn't you wonder why the three German shepherds didn't bark?"

"I know that dogs can be good for security purposes, but they can be taken out. It shouldn't be the only method a person uses." Which Mr. Jefferson was changing—just not fast enough for her liking. A new alarm system for the house would be in place by the end of the week. But even that didn't guarantee a person was totally safe. Hence the reason why Mr. Jefferson hired her to guard Mrs. Winfield—Winnie.

"So you decided to bring a gun."

"I'm very capable. I was in the army."

"Army? Even knowing that, I'm afraid, Miss St. James, we're not going to see eye to eye on this." He swiveled around and went to pick up a duffel bag by the steps. He hadn't had that when he'd first come upstairs. He must have brought it up when he put the gun in the safe. "Good night."

Ellie watched him stride down the corridor in the opposite direction of her bedroom. When he paused before a door at the far end, he slanted a look back at her. For a few seconds the corners of his mouth hitched up. He nodded his head once and then ducked inside.

She brought her hand up to comb her fingers through her hair and encountered a couple of tangles. "Ouch!"

Moving toward her bedroom, she kept her eye on his, half expecting him to pop back out with that gleam of humor dancing in his eyes. When he didn't, something akin to disappointment flowed through her until she shoved it away. She would have to call Mr. Jefferson to tell him that Colt was here. From what she'd read about the man he was smart, with a doctorate in marine biology as well as a degree in chemistry. Currently he worked on a research vessel as the head marine biologist for a think tank formed to preserve the world's oceans.

His grandmother hadn't ever questioned why Ellie was always around, even in her lab, but she had a feeling Colt would. Then he would demand an answer.

After traveling for almost twenty-four hours the day before, Colt dragged himself out of bed at a quarter to seven in his old room where he'd grown up. Winnie hadn't changed anything in here, and he doubted she ever would. She would always think of him as her little boy. Although Winnie was his grandmother, she'd raised him when his own mother had died from a massive infection shortly after he was born. Thinking of his past brought both heartache and joy. Heartache because he'd lost so many people he cared about. But he'd rather not dwell on his past. Besides, he had Winnie. She had given him so much.

After dressing in his sweats to power walk in the crisp December air in the Colorado mountains, he made his way toward the kitchen and the scent of coffee. Just its aroma made his body crave caffeine. He'd need it if he was going to keep up with Winnie. At seventy-three, she was an amazing woman, owner of Glamour Sensations and creator of both women's and men's fragrances. Not to mention her latest development—a line of antiaging products rumored to revolutionize the cosmetic industry. This had been a dream of Winnie and his granddad for fifteen years. Although his grandfather was dead, Winnie was close to completing their vision with the development of a cream that faded scars and lines as though they had never been there in the first place.

Clean-shaven, Colt came into the kitchen to find his grandmother and her new assistant sitting at the table drinking mugs of coffee. "I thought you would be gone for your power walk by now, leaving me with the whole pot of coffee."

His grandmother glanced at the clock on the wall. "As usual, ten minutes late. Did I not tell you we would have to wait on him, Ellie?"

The pretty assistant, dressed in a navy blue jogging suit with her long curly blond hair tamed into a ponytail, gave him a sugary sweet smile, a sparkle in her brown eyes. "I tried to talk her into leaving without you, but she insisted on waiting."

He made his way to his grandmother, kissed her cheek then headed for the pot to pour some coffee.

"You won't have time for that. I have a meeting with Harold at eight-thirty, and I'm sure he would want me to shower and change before we meet in the lab." Winnie rose and took a last swallow from her mug before setting it on the table. "You can have some later."

"What if I walk off the side of the mountain because I fell asleep?" He put his empty cup on the counter.

"Dear, if you manage to fall asleep while power walking with me, I'll be surprised. Besides, we're walking inside the fence. It would stop your fall."

"Your power walking is grueling." Taking up the rear, he followed the two women out onto the wooden deck along the back of the redwood and glass house that sat in a meadow with a high fence around the premises.

As though expecting Winnie at that time of the day, the three German shepherds sat near the door, their tails wagging. Rocket, the white one, barked his greeting.

His grandmother stooped over and patted each one, saying, "I've got a treat for you later today. A juicy bone. I know how much you like that."

Lady, the only female, nudged his grandmother's hand for more scratches behind the ear. Winnie laughed. "You always demand more attention than the boys here. They may be larger, but I have a feeling they do whatever you want."

Standing next to Ellie and watching the exchange between his grandmother and the guard dogs, Colt said, "My grandfather bought Rocket and Gabe to be company and guard the place seven years ago. He was very attached to them. Winnie went out and purchased Lady from the same trainer. She wanted female representation. They love staying outside, but whenever the weather gets bad, she brings them inside, even though they have a top-of-the-line dog structure."

"I've seen it. It isn't your ordinary doghouse. I thought it might be a storage shed until I saw them going in and out."

"That's because nothing is too good for her dogs.

When Granddad died, Winnie took over all three dogs' care with her caretaker's help."

When she finished greeting each pet, Winnie went through some stretches. "Colt, I don't want to hear any complaining on my walk. You're in perfectly good shape."

"I don't complain. I tease."

"I have a feeling you swim every day you have a chance on the job. Ellie, he can swim ten miles without tiring. Not to mention he can hold his breath underwater for two minutes. I think that's from growing up here in the mountains. Great lung capacity."

His grandmother's remark to her assistant slid his attention to the tall woman who lunged to the left then right. "So you're into power walking, too?"

Ellie brought her feet together, raised one leg behind her and clasped her ankle. "When I can get the chance, I usually jog, but I've been enjoying our early morning jaunts."

"Who did you work for before this?"

Pausing, she stretched her other leg. "A small company," she said finally.

Winnie didn't seem to notice the slight hesitation in Ellie's reply, but he did. Was something going on? When he got back from his power walk, he would catch Harold before he talked with Winnie. He didn't want to upset his grandmother unless there was a good reason, but who exactly was Ellie St. James? A woman who carried a gun and, based on last night, wasn't afraid to use it.

"I'm glad I caught you before you talked with Winnie." Ellie shut the library door after the lawyer entered.

"Ah, I see you've made good progress with Winnie," Harold Jefferson said. "She doesn't usually have someone call her Winnie unless she likes you."

"I think that's because she appreciated my attempt to protect her last night."

His eyebrows shot up. "Someone got in the house? Why didn't you call me?"

"Because it turned out to be her grandson."

His forehead wrinkled. "Colt's here?"

"Yes, for a few days. I thought he was an intruder and I pulled my gun on him in the upstairs hallway. Without her knowing why I'm here, she doesn't understand why I would have a gun. It's now sitting in her safe in her office. That ties my hands protecting her. She needs to be told."

"She will stress and shut down. She's under a tight deadline with this new product she's coming up with. That's why I'm here to talk to her about the publicity campaign now that her former assistant, Christy, has agreed to be the new face for the company."

"The Winnie I've seen this past week is tough when she needs to be."

"It's all a show. I've been through a lot with her. Years ago her company nearly fell apart because of her son's death. Then she had a heart attack ten years ago, and we went through another rough patch. That was followed by her husband passing away five Christmases ago. Finally she's close to going public with Glamour Sensations and offering stock as she brings out her new line, Endless Youth. She's been working toward this for years. She feels she needs to fulfill her late husband's vision for the business."

Ellie placed her hand on her waist, trying to control her frustration and impatience. "If she is dead, she won't be able to fulfill his vision."

"That's why you're here. To keep her alive. The fewer people who know someone has sent her threats the better. She *is* the company. The brains and creative force behind it. We need the infusion of money to make a successful campaign for the new products in the spring that will lead up to the unveiling of the signature cream next Christmas."

"If the company is going public, don't you have to disclose the threats?"

"Yes. When we reach that part of the process, we'll have to disclose the threats to the investment banker and lawyers. Fortunately, we have until right after Christmas to take care of the problem."

"I can't protect her without my weapon. It's that simple."

"What if we tell Colt and have him get the gun for you? She rarely goes into the safe. I imagine she's too busy in the lab downstairs."

Ellie looked out the floor-to-ceiling window across the back at the stand of pine trees. "Yes, but what if she does?"

She'd never liked the fact that Mrs. Winfield didn't know about the threats and the danger her life was in. The former assistant had given Mr. Jefferson each threatening letter. They had become more serious over the past month, and one also included a photo of Mrs. Winfield out power walking. That was when he had contacted Guardians, Inc. He was hoping nothing would come of the letters, but he knew he had to put some kind of protection in place. That was when Ellie had entered as the new assistant to replace Christy Boland, who was going to be the spokesperson for Glamour Sensations' Endless Youth line.

"On second thought, we probably shouldn't tell Colt. I don't want anyone else to know if possible. He might let something slip to his grandmother. It's probably better that he returns to the research ship." Mr. Jefferson snapped his fingers. "I've got it. I'll get you a gun to use. I can come back out here this afternoon with whatever you want. Maybe a smaller gun that you can keep concealed."

"Fine, unless I think there's a direct threat."

"I'm hoping I can catch the person behind the letters before then. The Bakersville police chief is working on the case personally, as well as a P.I. I hired. Winnie received another letter at headquarters yesterday."

"Another picture in it?"

"No, just threats of what the person is going to do to her."

Ellie thought of the sweet lady she'd spent the past week with—a woman who toiled long hours because she knew a lot of people who worked for her counted on her. "What in the world has she done to anger someone?"

"We're looking into disgruntled employees, but she was never directly responsible for firing anyone. If she had her way, everyone would still be working for her no matter if they didn't do their job. Thankfully I run that part of the business."

Ellie sighed. "I'll need you to bring me a Glock G27. It's smaller and easily concealed. It will have to do, even though I prefer my own weapon. At least you were able to get Winnie to stay and work from home this month. That will help the situation, but this home isn't secure."

"Is any place?"

"No, but there are some things we can do."

"Like what? I'm working on a better security system."

"That's good because the one she has is at least ten years old." Ellie paced the large room with bookcases full of books. "We could use bulletproof windows. Security guards to patrol the grounds and posted at the gate. Also cameras all over the house and the property being monitored 24/7."

"She won't go for anything else. She didn't even understand why I wanted to upgrade her security system. Told me the Lord was looking out for her and that's all she needs."

Ellie believed in the power of God, but Winnie was being naive. "What if someone gets to her? I've convinced her that I enjoy power walking, and she has graciously asked me to come with her, but she likes her independence. I'm running out of reasons to tag along with her when she leaves this house."

"It's only for a couple of more weeks at best. The P.I. on the case is tracking down some promising leads. If nothing changes after she has completed the last product for this new line, I'll tell her. She's fragile when she's in her creative mode. Easily distracted. Even Colt's visit will strain her schedule."

"And Christmas won't? I get the impression she enjoys the holiday." The wide-open space outside the window made her tense. Someone could be out there right now watching their every move.

"That's just a few days." Mr. Jefferson checked his

watch. "I'd better find Winnie. She starts to worry when people are late."

"I've noticed that."

"Five years ago next week, Thomas was on the way home from work and lost control of his car. It went off the cliff. The sheriff thought he'd fallen asleep at the wheel from reports by witnesses. So anytime someone is late she begins to think the worst." He covered the distance to the door. "I'll meet with Winnie in the lab then come back later with your gun."

"So let me get this straight. You don't want to tell Colt?" Another secret she would have to keep.

Looking back at her, Mr. Jefferson opened the door. "No, not right now."

"Not right now what?" Colt stepped into the entrance of the library.

Chapter Two

Mr. Jefferson waved his hand and passed Colt quickly in the hall. "I'll let Miss St. James tell you."

Ellie balled her hands at her sides. What was she supposed to tell Colt? Even worse, had he overheard anything they had been talking about? She started forward. "I'd better go and change for work."

He gripped her arm, halting her escape. "What aren't you telling me? Why were you and Harold talking in here?"

She schooled her expression into one of innocence. She would love to get her hands on Mr. Jefferson for putting her in this situation. "He wanted to know how my first week went with Winnie. Is there a reason we shouldn't talk? After all, he hired me."

"And how are you doing?" He stepped nearer until Ellie got a whiff of his coffee-laced breath. "Does he know about the gun?"

"Yes. I saw no reason not to tell him." Her heartbeat kicked up a notch. She moved back a few inches until her back encountered the wall behind her. "Your grandmother and I are getting along well. She's a special lady. Very talented. She's easy to talk to. To work for."

"Winnie?"

Hating the trapped feeling, she sidled away. "Who else are we talking about?"

"My grandmother is a private woman. She doesn't share much with anyone."

"I haven't found her that way. Maybe something has changed, since you've been gone for so long." There, she hoped that would keep Colt quiet and less curious about her relationship with Winnie. In some of her past jobs, she'd had to play a role, but it never was her favorite way to operate.

"Then maybe you can fill me in on what's going on with my grandmother."

"What we've talked about is private. If you want to know, go ask her." Before he could stop her again, she pivoted away and hurried down the hall to the foyer.

As she mounted the stairs to the second floor, she felt his eyes on her. It was so cold it reminded her of the icy mountain stream they'd passed on their walk today. Unable to shake loose of his frosty blue gaze, she felt the chill down to her bones.

After dinner that evening Ellie followed the small group to the den, a room with a roaring fire going in the fireplace and the dark rich wood of the mantel polished to a gleaming luster that reflected the lights. She sat on the plush, tan couch before a large glass-topped coffee table. In the middle an arrangement of sweet-smelling roses vied with the fireplace for attention. She'd quickly learned Bloomfield Flower Shop in the medium-size town at the foot of the mountain delivered a fresh bouquet twice weekly because Winnie loved looking at them in the evening. Their delicate aroma wafted up to Ellie and surrounded her in their fragrance. Since working for Winnie, she'd become attuned to the smell of things. Like breakfast in the morning or a fresh winter day with pine heavy in the air when they were power walking. Winnie always pointed out scents wherever she went.

Colt took a forest-green wingback chair across from her. She caught his glance lingering on her for a few extra seconds while the others settled into their seats. She pulled her gaze away to finish assessing the placement of everyone, along with all the exits. Harold took the other end of the couch she sat on while Winnie eased down between them. Christy Boland, the face of the new line, and her fiancé, Peter Tyler, a Bakersville dentist, occupied the love seat.

"I can't imagine living on a research vessel for months on end," Christy said, taking up the conversation started at the dinner table.

"I have to admit it does take getting used to. It was an opportunity I couldn't pass up. I don't even have a place of my own right now."

"You don't need one. You're always welcome here when you're in the country," Winnie told her grandson. "After all, you've done so much to help me with my new line, especially this last product, which will be the coup d'état."

"How so, Winnie? I don't remember doing that."

"Your research on certain sea life sparked a breakthrough for me on this project."

Colt tilted his head to the side. "Which one?"

Winnie smiled. "I'm not telling. Right now I'm the

only one who knows. It's all up here." She tapped the side of her temple. "But this will keep you busy for years, Christy. Harold isn't going to be able to count the money fast enough." Her grin grew. "At least that's what I predict. And all my predictions have been right in the past." She sat back and motioned the servers to bring in dessert.

Linda and Doug Miller, the middle-aged couple who lived on the property and took care of the house, carried in two trays, one with coffee and the other with finger sweets. Doug placed the coffee down in front of Winnie while his wife served the petite desserts to each person in the room.

"I will say I miss your cooking, Linda. No one on the vessel can cook like you." Colt selected four different sweets and put them on a small plate.

By the time the caretakers retreated to the kitchen ten minutes later, everyone had a cup of coffee and dessert.

Colt raised his cup in a toast. "To Christy. Congratulations again on becoming the face of Endless Youth. This is a big change for you from being Winnie's assistant to touring the country, your photo plastered everywhere."

"Yes. I haven't traveled like you have or Winnie. About as far as I've gone was Texas and California when Winnie did."

"That will definitely change, dear," Winnie said after taking a sip of her coffee. "I'm thrilled you agreed to do this. When you tested the product and it did such wonders for you, it became obvious you were perfect for this new job." She slid a glance toward Harold.

"Thankfully, Harold found a new assistant for me who is working out great."

All eyes turned to Ellie. Never wanting to be the focus of attention, she pressed herself into the couch until she felt the Glock in its holster digging into her back. Harold had brought the gun when he'd returned for dinner. Having it holstered under her jacket was a constant reminder she was on a job. "I appreciate you helping me, Christy. Answering my hundreds of questions."

Christy laughed. "I wish I had someone to answer my hundreds of questions. I've never been a model and don't know one. Poor Peter has to listen to all my questions."

"And I don't have any answers for her. Actually, she's been gone so much lately that I haven't had to listen to them." Peter covered Christy's hand that lay between them on the love seat. "I'm looking forward to some togetherness at Christmas."

Harold bent forward to pour himself some more coffee. "I just finalized some plans for Christy to start the filming of the first commercial in L.A. next week."

Christy glanced at Peter then Harold. "But I'll be here for Christmas Day, won't I? It'll be our first Christmas together."

"Yes, but since we're launching part of the line in February for Valentine's Day, your time will be very limited."

Peter picked up her hand and moved it to his lap. "We'll work out something," he said to Christy, his adoring look roping her full attention.

As Ellie listened to the conversation shift to the launch of Endless Youth, she decided to call Kyra, her employer, and have her look into everyone around Winnie, including Harold Jefferson, who ran the day-to-day operation of Glamour Sensations as the CFO. She'd learned quickly not to take anything for granted, even the person who hired her.

The threats against Rachel Winfield had started when news of Endless Youth leaked to the press. What was it about that product line that would make someone angry with Winnie? From what Ellie had learned, the development and testing didn't upset any environmental groups. So did Endless Youth have anything to do with the threats or was its development and launch just a coincidence? Maybe it was a rival cosmetic company. Was the industry that cutthroat? Did this involve an industrial spy?

She kneaded her hand along her nape, trying to unravel the knots twisting tighter in her neck. Finding the person behind the threats wasn't her priority—keeping Winnie alive and unharmed was. She needed to leave the rest to the police and Harold's P.I.

Colt entered the kitchen that gleamed with clean counters, any evidence of a dinner party gone, but the scent of the roast that Linda had cooked still lingered in the room. The Millers did wonders behind the scenes for Winnie and had worked for the family for ten years. He wasn't sure what his grandmother would do if they decided to look for another job. He didn't worry about Winnie with Linda and Doug taking care of the property and house.

He raided the refrigerator to make himself a sandwich with the leftover roast beef. After piling it between slices of Linda's homemade bread, he turned away from the counter ready to take a bite. But he halted abruptly when he noticed Ellie hovering in the entrance, watching him.

She blinked and averted her gaze. "I heard a noise and came to check it out. Winnie just went to bed."

"She stayed up later than usual, but then when Christy and Harold come to dinner, she usually does. That's the extent of her entertaining here."

"I can see that. She spends most of her day in the lab."

"My grandmother is one of the few people in the world who has a 'nose,' as they say in the perfume industry. She can distinguish different scents and has a knack for putting them together to complement each other. That comes easy for her. But this new product line is something else, more Granddad's pet project. I'll be glad when she finishes and doesn't have to work so much."

Ellie came into the room. "She's being taken care of. Linda makes sure she eats healthy. Harold doesn't let her worry about the running of Glamour Sensations, and I do all the little things she has allowed to mount up."

"So she can focus on Endless Youth. I can remember when Granddad was alive. Those two talked about the line back then. He had already started the research. Winnie is just finishing up what they began in earnest eight years ago. I think he pushed her to help her recover from her heart attack. She loves a good challenge." He held up his plate. "I can fix you one."

Her chuckles floated through the air. "I think I'll pass on that. I ate more tonight than I usually do."

He put his sandwich on the kitchen table and gestured at a chair beside him. "Join me. I hate eating alone. When you live on a small ship with fifteen others, you're rarely alone except in your tiny cabin. You would think I would cherish this time."

"You don't?" Ellie slid into the seat next to him.

He noticed she didn't wear any fragrance and wondered if Winnie would change that. "I'm used to it so it's strange when I'm not here. When I've come back here, I've felt the isolation I never felt while I was growing up here."

"Well, it won't feel isolated too much longer. Winnie has several evening events the closer we get to the holidays."

"Let me guess. Most of them have to do with the business."

"Yes, and she is the mistress of ceremony at the lighting of the Christmas tree in Bakersville in a few days. This year the town is naming the park after your grandparents."

"They've been trying to get her to light the Christmas tree for years. I'm glad she finally accepted."

A tiny frown made grooves between Ellie's eyebrows.

"You aren't?" Colt asked.

Her expression evened out. "I'm only concerned she doesn't wear herself out. She has the big gala for Endless Youth and Christy's introduction to the press a few days after that."

"Yeah, she's been trying to get me to stay an extra week."

"I can understand the demands of work."

"Is this job demanding to you? Is the isolation getting to you?"

"I love the isolation. Remember, I grew up in Chicago where everywhere I turned there were people."

"How did you find out about this job?"

Ellie rose. "I think I'll fix a cup of tea. Do you want any? Herbal, no caffeine." She walked to the cabinet where the tea was kept and withdrew a tin of lavender tea.

"No, thanks." He waited until she put the water on to boil then continued, "Harold said something about him finding you. How? Chicago is a far piece from here."

"Harold knew my former employer. She suggested me for the job."

"She let you go?"

"Not exactly. She knew how much I love the mountains and thought this would be perfect for me."

"What did you do at your former job?"

She laughed. "I feel I'm being interviewed again, but since I already have the job, that isn't it. So why the interest?"

"Because I love Winnie and have her best interest at heart."

Gripping the counter edge with both hands, Ellie lounged back, except that there was nothing casual about her stance. Something wasn't right. Colt lived in close quarters and had learned to read people accurately and quickly. It made his life much easier and calmer.

"What are you hiding, Ellie?"

Chapter Three

"What makes you think I'm hiding something?" Ellie busied herself pouring the hot water into a mug and dunking the tea bag.

"I get the feeling there's something in your past you don't like to talk about. If it wasn't that Harold is thorough when it comes to my grandmother, I would be concerned at your evasiveness."

"But Harold is thorough." She drew herself up straight, cupping her hands around the mug. "I didn't know full disclosure about all the details of my life was necessary for me to get this job. Winnie seems satisfied. Is this something we should bring up to her?" Lifting her chin, she clamped her jaws together to keep from saying anything else that would get her fired.

He dipped his head in a curt nod. "Duly noted. Winnie is a great judge of character."

Meaning he had his doubts? Pain shot down her neck from the tense set of her teeth grinding together. She strode to the table and took the chair across from him. Though she would rather drink her tea in peace, she knew escaping to her bedroom would only confirm that she had something to hide.

One of the reasons she liked being a bodyguard was that she could blend into the background. Most of her clients didn't engage her in casual conversation. But Winnie had been different, and it seemed to run in the family. She kept a lock on her past—a past she didn't want to take out and reexamine. No point in going over it.

"If you must know, the short version of my life so far is—"

"That's okay—"

"I grew up in Chicago," she interrupted, "in a part of town where I had to learn to take care of myself and stick up for my brother, too. People weren't kind to him. He had a mental disability and talked 'funny.' Their word, not mine. When I could get out of the neighborhood, I did." She sipped her tea, gripping the mug tighter to keep her hands steady.

"Where's your brother?"

"Dead." The word hung in the air between them for a long moment while Ellie relived the moment when Toby had slipped away from congestive heart failure.

"I'm sorry. I didn't mean to bring up something painful."

"What did you mean to do, then?"

"To make sure Winnie was in good hands."

She stared into his light, gray-blue eyes. "She's in good hands. When I do a job, I do it one hundred percent."

Another long silence stretched between them as she felt the probe of his gaze, seeking, reading between the lines.

"Did I pass?" She raised her cup and drank, relishing the warm, soothing tea.

"This wasn't a test."

"You could have fooled me." After she scooted back her chair, the scraping sound filling the kitchen, she pushed to her feet. "While I would love to continue this interrogation—I mean conversation—I'm tired and plan to go to bed. Good night."

She left the kitchen. Out in the hallway she paused, a hand braced on the wall as images of her twin brother washed through her mind—running from the neighborhood bullies, falling and scraping his palms and shins, crying because he didn't understand why they didn't like him. But the worst picture was of Toby on the floor of their small, dirty apartment, taking his last breath. He looked straight at her. She held him while they waited for the ambulance. A light brightened his eyes, and a peace she'd never seen fell over his face. Then he went limp as the sirens came down the street. She'd been thirteen.

Tears crowded her eyes. She squeezed them closed. This was why she never dwelled in the past. She did not shed tears—hadn't since she was thirteen.

She slowly crossed to the front door and checked to make sure it was locked and the antiquated security system was on. After Colt went to bed, she would make a more thorough check of the house before she slept. Until then she would prowl her bedroom, hating the situation she'd been placed in. This secrecy handicapped her doing her job.

Standing in the dark, Colt stared out his bedroom window at the yard in front of the house; the outdoor lights illuminated the circular drive. Usually by this time of year there was a lot of snow on the ground, but not so far this winter. Most Christmases as a child, he remembered it being white. This year he'd be in the middle of the Pacific Ocean with blue water as far as he could see. One morning at the beginning of the week, a day after he'd talked to Winnie, a strong urge had overcome him. He needed to see his grandmother if only for a short time. He couldn't shake the feeling all that day. By nighttime he'd made a reservation to fly back to Colorado.

He glanced at his bed. He needed to sleep. Wanted to sleep. But he couldn't. Winnie's new assistant plagued his thoughts. Something didn't fit. First, although she and Winnie seemed to get along great, Ellie wasn't his grandmother's usual type of assistant. Christy had fit the mold well for three years. Accommodating. Almost meek. A follower, not a leader.

But Ellie certainly wasn't meek. He rubbed his ear, recalling her defensive tactic last night. And accommodating? Hardly. He had thought for a minute that she was going to tackle him for her gun. But mostly she wasn't a follower. Although she'd done everything his grandmother had requested of her today, her mannerisms and actions spoke of a woman in command. A woman who wouldn't admit to a vulnerability.

A couple of hours ago, though, he'd seen a crack in her defenses when she'd talked about her childhood, her brother. That was what he couldn't get out of his mind. The glimpse of pain in her eyes he suspected she didn't realize she'd shown. Or maybe she did and couldn't control it because the hurt went so deep.

Staring at the play of light and dark surrounding the front of the house, Colt plowed his fingers through his hair. His skin felt as if he was swimming through a swarm of jellyfish, their tentacles grazing across his arms and legs, their touch sending pain through him.

Something wasn't right. He couldn't shake that feeling, just as he couldn't deny the need to come see Winnie a few days ago.

One of the German shepherds that guarded the property pranced across the drive and disappeared into the dark. Squinting, Colt tried to follow the dog's trek. Something white flashed out of the corner of his eye, so briefly he wasn't sure he'd seen anything. He shoved away from the window and headed for the door. He wasn't sure why. It was probably nothing. One of the guard dogs had white fur.

Still. He wanted to check.

A sound in the foyer caught Ellie's attention. She'd just checked that part of the house. Was Winnie up? Colt? She crept down the hallway toward the front entrance, pulling her gun from the holster under her large sweatshirt. She found Colt crossing the foyer to the exit.

Relieved it was only him, she stuck the borrowed gun back into its holster and entered the entry hall. "Is something wrong?"

With his hand reaching for the doorknob, Colt jerked and pivoted toward her. "What are you doing down here? I thought you went to bed."

"And I thought you did, too."

"I did. Couldn't sleep."

"So you're going for a walk dressed like that? Won't you get cold?" She gestured at his sweatpants, T-shirt and bare feet.

He peered down. "I thought I saw something outside." Taking a few steps toward her, he took in her similar attire except for her bulky sweatshirt to cover her weapon and her tennis shoes, in case she had to give chase. "I'm sure it was nothing now that I think about it. Probably one of the dogs. If anyone had been outside, they would be barking."

Unless they were taken out, she thought, recalling her words to Colt earlier. "Dogs aren't invulnerable."

He paused. "True. I'd better check on it."

"I can. I'm dressed for it."

"Yeah, I noticed your tennis shoes."

She started toward the front door. "I don't have slippers, and I'm not accustomed to the cold."

"But you're from Chicago," Colt said as she passed him.

"We are seven thousand feet up the side of a mountain in December, and, besides, I've never been accustomed to the cold, even being from Chicago." Glancing at the alarm system, she noticed he'd turned it off. She grasped the handle and opened the door. As she stepped out onto the front deck, Colt followed her. "I've got this." *Leave it to a pro.* The urge to say those words was strong, but she bit them back.

"You're kidding. I'm not letting you come out here alone. What if someone is here? Who do you take me for?"

"Someone who only has pants and a T-shirt on and no shoes, not even socks. That's who." She ground her teeth together, wanting to draw her gun as she checked the area out. But he was probably right about it being one of the dogs.

"I'm used to the cold. I'm coming. End of discussion." *Patience. I could use a dose of it, Lord.*

"Fine. Stay close behind me."

He chuckled in her ear. "Yeah, sure." Skirting

around her, he descended the steps, quickly heading into the wisps of fog snaking along the ground.

Where's a stun gun when I need one? Ellie hurried after Colt who moved quickly from the cold concrete drive to the warmer lawn. "Wait up."

He didn't slow his pace, but she caught up with him about ten yards from the house. When she glanced back and spied the unprotected place, lit with security lights, she clamped her hand around his arm.

He halted, his face unreadable in the shadows.

"Go back and make sure no one goes into the house. I'll finish checking out here." Her fingers itched to draw her gun, but Mr. Jefferson didn't want Colt to know why she was here.

"And leave you alone? This is my home, not yours. What kind of man would I be?"

"A smart one. What about leaving your grandmother alone?"

"Then you should go back and—"

Barking blasted the chilled air.

Ellie withdrew the Glock from its holster and started toward the sound to the left.

"Where did that come from?" Colt asked.

"Mr. Jefferson."

"Harold?"

"I'll explain later. Go back to the house, lock the door and don't let anyone in until I check out what caused the dog to bark. Do not follow me."

"Who are you?"

No more secrets—at least with Winnie's grandson. "A bodyguard hired to protect Winnie." She glanced over her shoulder to make sure no one was trying to get into the front of the house. "Go. Now."

In the cover of night that surrounded them, he stared at her, or at least she felt the drill of his gaze, then he whirled around and rushed back toward the deck. She moved toward where the sound had come from, retrieving her small pocket flashlight in case she needed it. Right now she let the half-moon and security lamps by the house light her path since it would be better if she didn't announce her approach if someone was inside the fence.

In the distance she heard the cry of a mountain lion. She'd seen evidence of a big cat on one of her daily power walks with Winnie. Was that what spooked the dog? She'd gone into enough situations with incomplete intel to know the heightened danger that could cause.

Her heart rate kicked up a notch as she drew closer to the perimeter on the west side of the house where the eight-foot chain-link fence was. Another roar split the air. Closer. The sound pumped more adrenaline through her body. Every nerve alert, she became hyperaware of her surroundings—a bird flying away to the right, the breeze rustling the evergreen foliage.

Away from the house the only illumination was the faint rays of the moon. Not enough. She switched on her flashlight and swept it across the area before her. Just outside a cut part of the fence, its glow fell upon the mountain lion, its big eyes glittering yellow in the dark. Her light captured the predator's menacing stance.

The rumble of a mountain lion nearby froze Colt as he mounted the last step to the front deck. He knew that sound from the many years he had lived here. He didn't know who Ellie St. James really was, how capable she was or why she would be protecting his grandmother, but he couldn't leave her out there to face a solitary predator by herself. No matter what she ordered him to do.

He rushed into the house to a storage closet where Winnie kept some of his possessions. He used to have a hunting rifle. Wrenching the door open, he clicked on the overhead light and stared at the mountain of boxes that he had stored there. He delved into the midst of the containers filled with his memories. Where was the gun?

Panic urged him deeper into the large, walk-in closet to the shelving in the back. There he saw something he could use. Not the rifle but a speargun, a weapon he was even more familiar with and actually quite good at using.

He snatched it up and raced toward the foyer, grabbing a flashlight on the way. Before leaving, he set the alarm, then locked the front door behind him. Another growl announced to anyone around that this was the big cat's territory and not to trespass.

As Colt ran toward the west side of the property, he hoped there weren't any trees the mountain lion could climb that allowed him access to the area inside the fence. Usually the eight-foot barrier kept dangerous animals out, but it had certainly sounded like it was close to the house, possibly inside the fence.

Then a yell pierced the night. "Get back. Get away."

Those words from Ellie prodded him even faster.

Ellie never took her eyes off the mountain lion. It was still on the other side of the fence with his head sticking through the part that had been cut and peeled back to allow something big—like a man—through the opening. She waved her arms around. She didn't want to shoot the animal because it was a beautiful creature. But she would if she had to.

Its snarls protested her order to leave.

Still it didn't move back. Its golden gaze seemed to assess its chances of leaping the four or five yards' distance between them.

Bracing herself, Ellie lifted her gun and shone her flashlight into its eyes. It continued to stare at her.

Behind her she heard something rushing toward her. Another mountain lion? But they were solitary animals that guarded their territory. One of the dogs? The one that had barked earlier? Where were the other two?

She was calculating her chances with the mountain lion, then the new threat, when she heard a war cry, a bloodcurdling sound. The mountain lion shifted its golden regard to her right for a few seconds, then stepped back out of the hole and sauntered away as though out for an evening stroll. Some of the tension siphoned from her.

She threw a glance over her shoulder and saw a light in the dark moving her way. Colt. An intruder wouldn't announce his presence with a flashlight or a war cry.

She spun around and started for him. "What are you doing? You were supposed to stay at the house." Her light found him in the night, carrying a speargun. "*This time* you need to stay here and guard this hole. I need to make sure Winnie is okay."

When she passed him, he clasped her arm and halted her progress. "Hold it. Winnie is fine. I set the alarm and locked the door. What's going on?"

She stared at his hand until he dropped his arm to his side. "Did you check on her?"

"Well, no. But we never went far from the house."

"I'm going to check on her, then I'll be back. Will you stay here and make sure the mountain lion doesn't come back? And this time stay where you're supposed to be. I could have shot you." She peered at his speargun. "A bit odd to be carrying around on dry land, but it should stop the cat if it returns. That is, if you can use it."

He pulled himself up straight. "I'm quite good with this. And it's very effective if you know what you're doing. Which I do." Each word was spoken with steely confidence.

"Good." She hurried away, at the moment her concern for Winnie's safety paramount.

What if this was all a diversion? What if someone got into the house when they weren't looking? Different scenarios bombarded her. All she knew was she had to lay eyes on Winnie to be reassured she was all right.

She unlocked the front door and immediately headed for the alarm to put in the code. Then she took the stairs two at a time. When she saw Winnie's door open, she finally breathed.

A strong scent of urine—probably the big cat's—pervaded the air as Colt neared the gap in the fence. He stuffed the flashlight through a chain-link hole, and its glow shone into the wooded area outside of Winnie's property. After leaning the speargun against the fence within his quick reach, he pulled the snipped sides back into place, enough that he hoped would discourage the mountain lion from plowing its way inside.

Then he examined the ground.

Footprints were barely visible on the dry ground, but about five or six feet away, tire impressions in the dead weeds and grass were clearer. Someone had pulled a vehicle up to the fence.

He swung around and swept his flashlight around his grandmother's property and then it hit him: Where were the dogs? Why weren't they over here?

Ellie entered Winnie's bedroom, her gun drawn but at her side in case the older woman was in the room unaware of what was transpiring outside. She didn't want to frighten her with a gun being waved in the air—not two nights in a row. Halting a few feet inside, Ellie stared at the messy covers spilling over onto the floor, the empty bed. As she raised her weapon, she circled the room, checking for her client. After opening the bathroom door, she noted the spacious area was empty.

As much as she would like to rush back outside and search the grounds for Winnie or any clue to her whereabouts, she had to check the house first.

As she started with the room next to Winnie's, prayers for the woman's safety flooded her thoughts. When she reached Colt's bedroom, she hesitated, feeling awkward to intrude on his privacy. But she had a job to do. She pushed open the door and looked inside. *This is ridiculous.* If the man had followed her orders, she wouldn't have to do this right now. She stepped inside and made a quick tour—noting his duffel bag on a chair, his shoes on the floor, keys and some change on the dresser, pictures on the wall from when he was young.

A picture of him coming out of the darkness with a speargun in his hand crowded into her thoughts. She shook the image from her mind and turned to leave.

"What are you doing in my grandson's room with a gun in your hand?"

Chapter Four

❦

"I was looking for you," Ellie said, putting the gun out of sight of Winnie in the doorway. "Someone has cut the fence and the guard dogs can't be found. I wanted to make sure you were all right." After picking up Colt's tennis shoes off the floor, she moved toward the exit.

"Where's my grandson? What are you doing with those shoes?" Winnie blocked her path.

"I'll explain everything after I call the sheriff and make sure Colt is okay. He's guarding the hole, making sure the mountain lion doesn't return. He's barefoot."

"The sheriff? A mountain lion? Colt barefoot in this weather? What in the world is going on?" What wrinkles Winnie had on her face deepened as she stepped to the side to allow Ellie to leave the room.

Ellie hurried toward the stairs, fishing for her cell in her pocket. At the top she paused and glanced at the older woman. "I'm going to set the alarm. Please stay inside."

Winnie opened her mouth but snapped it closed before saying anything.

Ellie rushed down the stairs while placing a call to

the sheriff's office outside Bakersville. After reporting what happened, she hit the buttons on the keypad to set the alarm and hastened outside.

The crisp night air burrowed through the sweatshirt, chilling her. The thought of Colt without shoes spurred her faster toward the fence line. When she arrived, he stood by the hole he'd partially closed, holding his spear gun while hugging his arms against his chest.

"I thought you could use these." She thrust his shoes at him, then shined her flashlight on the area beyond the fence.

"Thanks. I will never again leave the house in winter without my shoes on."

"Why did you?" She examined the set of tire tracks and boot prints, wishing it wasn't so dark.

"To protect you."

"Someone needs to protect you from yourself."

"You can't deny I helped you. Someone needed to guard this hole. Since you're back out here, I'm assuming Winnie is all right."

"Yes, and I called the sheriff's office." Ellie backed away, realizing there was nothing she could do until morning other than talk with the deputy who was on the way up the mountain. She had half a mind to call Harold Jefferson and wake him up with the news, but she would wait and give him a full report first thing in the morning. "Do you think there's anything at the house I can use to finish closing the bottom of this hole?"

"How about rope?" Colt started for his childhood home.

"That'll do." Ellie followed him. "I'm sure the mountain lion is long gone with all this activity, but I'll feel better when we have the hole completely closed."

"You don't think the person who cut the fence is inside here?"

"Probably not. Maybe the mountain lion scared him off or maybe his intent was to take the guard dogs. He could have tranquilized them. The ground looked like something was dragged toward the car."

"Why hurt the dogs?"

"It would take a while to get trained guard dogs to replace them. Maybe it was to scare Winnie like the threatening letters. When I find him, I'll ask him."

"When *you* find him? And what threatening letters?"

She reminded herself going after the person who was trying to harm Winnie wasn't her job. "I mean when the police find him, they'll ask him."

Colt unlocked the front door and hurried to the keypad to turn off the security system. Winnie sat on the third step on the staircase, her face tensed into a frown. She didn't move when both Colt and Ellie turned toward her.

"I need to check the house then I'll explain what's going on." She peered at Colt. "Would you stay here with your grandmother?"

He held up the speargun. "Yes. But the security system was on the whole time."

"This one can be circumvented quite easily if you know what you're doing. We have to assume whoever is after Winnie knows what he's doing," Ellie said in a low voice.

Winnie pushed to her feet. "Someone's after me? Who?"

Colt took a step toward his grandmother, glancing at Ellie. "I'll take care of her. Do what you need to do."

"What is going on, young man?" Winnie asked as Ellie hastened her exit.

As she went from room to room, she heard Colt trying to explain when he really didn't know much other than what she had told him. From her responses, Winnie was clearly not happy. Ellie decided not to wait until morning to call Harold.

"What's wrong?" the chief financial officer of Glamour Sensations asked the second he answered his phone.

After she explained what happened with the dogs and the fence, she said, "Not only does Colt know, but so does Winnie. I've called the sheriff's office, and one of the deputies is on his way."

"I'm calling Sheriff Quinn. Knowing him, he'll come, too. He lives halfway between Winnie's and Bakersville. It won't take him long to get there. I'll be there as fast as I can."

"You don't need to until tomorrow morning. After the sheriff leaves, I hope to get Winnie to go back to bed." She didn't want a three-ring circus at the house with so many people coming and going. That could be hard to secure.

"She won't do that. Maybe I should call her doctor, too."

"She seems okay." Ellie looked through the dining room into the living room where Colt had taken his grandmother. "She's sitting on the couch, listening to Colt."

"Fine. I won't call the doctor, but I'll be there soon."

Ellie pocketed her cell and made her way to the pair in the living room. "The house is clear."

Winnie shifted on the couch until her glare zeroed in on Ellie. "Who are you?"

"I told her you're here to protect her. That Harold hired you. But I don't know much more than that." Colt finally sat in the chair across from his grandmother.

With a sigh, Ellie sank onto the couch at the other end from Winnie. "I work for Guardians, Inc. It's a security company out of Dallas, staffed with female bodyguards. Mr. Jefferson came to my employer about his concerns that someone was threatening you. You have been receiving notes for the past six weeks, each one more threatening. He finally knew he had to do something when one included a photo of you on your power walk, dressed in what he discovered you'd worn the day before."

"Why didn't he come to me?" Winnie's mouth pinched into a frown.

"He's on his way, and he can answer that. I believe he thought it might interrupt your creative process and since the deadline is looming, he—"

"So that man kept it from me." Winnie surged to her feet. "I am not fragile like everyone thinks. Goodness me, I've been through enough and survived. That ought to give you all a hint at how tough I can be." She pivoted toward Ellie. "Is that why he neglected to tell me my new assistant was really a bodyguard?"

Ellie nodded. "I prefer full disclosure, but he was afraid of how—"

Winnie waved her quiet. "I know. I will take care of Harold. He promised my husband he would watch out for me, and he's taking his job way too seriously."

"Winnie, I don't know that he is." Colt leaned forward, clasping his hands and resting his elbows on his thighs. "Someone did cut the fence and the dogs are missing. Not one of them came up to us while we were outside. They always do."

Winnie blanched and eased down onto the couch. "So you really think there's a threat?" She looked from Colt to Ellie.

"Yes, especially after tonight." Ellie rose at the sound of the doorbell. "I'll get it."

She let the deputy and sheriff into the house. "I'm Ellie St. James. I was hired by Harold Jefferson to protect Mrs. Winfield."

Sheriff Quinn shook her hand. "Harold called me and told me. I understand the Bakersville police chief is looking into the matter of the threatening letters."

"Yes. I believe the person has upped his game. I haven't had a chance to search the whole property outside, but I feel the dogs have been taken. I did search the house and it's secured."

The sheriff turned to his deputy and said, "Take a look outside. Miss St. James, which part of the fence was cut?"

"The west side about halfway down."

"Let me know, Rod, when you're through checking the premises and the doghouse." Then to her, the sheriff asked, "Where's Winnie?"

"In the living room."

When the sheriff entered, Winnie smiled. "I'm so glad you're here, Bill. Did Ellie tell you what went on tonight?"

"Harold filled me in. It's a good thing Miss St. James and your grandson were here." The sheriff nodded toward Colt. "You couldn't have picked a better time to be home."

Winnie blew out an exasperated breath. "It would have been even better if they had clued me in on what was going on. Goodness, Bill, I've been out power walking. The man took a picture of me while I was."

"Maybe with all that has happened you should curtail that for the time being. It's gonna snow this weekend if the weather reports are correct." Sheriff Quinn sat on the couch where Ellie had been.

She assessed the law enforcement officer. He was probably in his early fifties but looked to be in excellent physical condition, well proportioned for his medium height with none of the potbelly she'd seen on others as they grew older and less active. She'd worked with her share of good ones and bad ones. From all of Harold's accounts, the sheriff fit into the good category. She hoped so because tonight the person after Winnie had stepped up his game.

She filled him in on what she'd seen outside. "Someone pulled a vehicle up to the fence recently. It rained hard a couple of days ago. The tracks could have been left maybe up to a day before, but they aren't deep enough for any longer than that. But I'm pretty sure it was this evening. We walk the perimeter every morning, and I haven't seen any evidence on the other side of the fence like what is there now. Also there are drag marks and a few paw prints beside those left by the mountain lion."

"So you think the tracks were made this evening?"

"Yes, Sheriff. That's the way it looks, but in the light of day we—you—might find more."

He smiled. "I'll take a look now. I've got a high-powered flashlight. I'll see where the tire tracks lead.

The west side of the fence isn't the closest to the road out front."

"But it's the most isolated," Colt interjected.

Sheriff Quinn headed for the foyer. "When he gets back I'm gonna leave Rod here. I'd like you to come with me, Miss St. James."

"Would you mind, Winnie?" Ellie asked her client, eager to go with the sheriff.

"No, go. I'll be well protected with Colt and the deputy."

As Ellie left, Colt told Winnie that he'd escort her to her bedroom. Ellie chuckled when the woman said, "Not on your life. I want to know what they find out there."

The doorbell sounded again while Ellie crossed the foyer. She'd relocked the door after the deputy had left. When she answered it, Harold stood there with the young officer.

He charged inside, slowing down only long enough to ask, "Where is she?"

"In the living room."

While he went to Winnie, the deputy came into the house. "I couldn't find any signs of the dogs. They're gone, Sheriff."

Quinn grumbled, his frown deepening. "Rod, stay with Mrs. Winfield." To Ellie, he said, "I don't like this. They were excellent, well-trained guard dogs."

"Yeah, that was the only part of the security here I liked." Ellie went ahead of the man onto the front deck.

"And possibly the only threat the person behind the letters needed to get rid of."

"Maybe. Something doesn't feel right."

"Any thoughts on what?"

"No. Just a vague feeling we're missing something." Ellie slipped into the sheriff's car.

As he drove to the road then toward the west part of the property, he said, "Harold told me the Bakersville police chief is looking into past employees. I can't believe one of them would be this angry with Winnie. She's the reason Bakersville is so prosperous. People around here love her."

"Someone doesn't. Maybe they aren't from around here. Maybe it's something we haven't thought about yet. Harold is having a private investigator look into Glamour Sensations' competition."

"Corporate sabotage?"

"It's a possibility. Winnie is the creative force behind the new line. From what I hear Endless Youth will change the playing field. It's not unheard of that a competitor will try to stop a product launch or beat a company to unveiling their own similar product."

"Mr. Winfield was the guy who talked me into running for sheriff twenty years ago. The best move I ever made. I owe the Winfield family a lot." He eased off the road and parked on the shoulder, directing a spotlight from his car toward the area where someone had driven off the highway and over the terrain toward the back of Winnie's property. "We'll go on foot from here."

Following the tire tracks led to the hole in the fence. Ellie knelt near the place where she'd seen the mountain lion's prints as well as smaller dog prints. No sign of blood or a struggle. When she had shined the light on the big cat earlier, she hadn't seen any evidence it had killed a dog. And she hadn't heard any noise to suggest that. So it meant the dogs had been taken recently by whoever drove the vehicle.

"These tire tracks look like they're from a truck or SUV. I'll have a cast made of them and see if we can narrow down the vehicle." The sheriff swung his high-powered light on the surrounding terrain. "These boot prints might help, too."

"It looks like about a size nine in men's shoes."

"Small man."

"Or a woman with large feet."

Ellie rose and searched the trees and brush. With some of the foliage gone because it was winter, she had a decent view. "No sign the dogs went that way."

"It doesn't look like it, but in the light of day we'll have better visibility and may find something. At the moment, though, I think the dogs were stolen. They're valuable. Maybe someone has kidnapped them."

"I don't think so. This is tied to the threats against Winnie somehow." Ellie ran her flashlight along the ground by the fence and caught sight of something neon green. She stooped and investigated closer. "Sheriff, I found something partially under this limb. I think it's from a dart gun. It would explain how he subdued the dogs so quickly."

The sheriff withdrew a small paper bag and gloves, then carefully picked up the long black dart with a sharp tip and a neon green cap on the opposite end. "Yup. I'll send this to the lab and see if there are any fingerprints on it. Hopefully they can tell us what was in the dart—poison or a knockout drug."

"At least there are a few pieces of evidence that might give you a lead."

As they walked back to the sheriff's car, Ellie kept sweeping her flashlight over the ground while Quinn scoured the terrain.

When he climbed into his patrol car, he said, "I have a friend who can repair the chain-link fence. I'll have him out here first thing in the morning. You don't want the return of the mountain lion."

"I'll be talking to Winnie and Harold about electrifying the fence and setting up a system to monitor the perimeter. If it hadn't been for the dogs, we might not have known about the hole in the fence for a while. That area is hidden by thick foliage from the house. We might not have seen it on our power walk in the morning, either."

"Yeah, she's definitely gonna have to beef up her security. She's been fortunate not to have problems in the past." As the sheriff returned to park in front of the main house, lights blazed from it. He chuckled. "She must have gone through and turned a light on in every downstairs room."

"I can't blame her. She all of a sudden realizes someone is after her."

Colt watched his grandmother as Harold explained his reasons for not letting her know what was going on with the letters. After he saw to Winnie, he was going to have a few words with Ellie and Harold. He should have been contacted right away when his grandmother first was threatened.

"The bottom line, Winnie, is that I didn't want you to worry about it when you have enough to deal with," Harold said.

Colt nearly laughed and pressed his lips together to keep from doing that. Harold was pulling out all the stops to persuade his grandmother not to be angry with him.

Her back stiff as a snowboard, Winnie narrowed her gaze on Harold, her hands clasped so tightly in her lap the tips of her fingers reddened. "I'm not a child, and you'd better remember that from now on, or no matter how long we have worked together, you'll be fired."

Harold swallowed hard. "My intentions were to protect you without worrying you. I have the police chief in Bakersville and a private investigator working on finding the person behind the letters."

"So you would never have told me if this hadn't happened. Was that your plan?"

Harold dropped his gaze to a spot on the carpet at his feet. Finally he nodded.

"I have to be able to trust you to inform me of *everything* that goes on at Glamour Sensations. Now I don't know if I can. What else are you keeping from me?" She lifted her chin and glared at her longtime friend.

Harold held up his hands, palms outward. "Nothing. But, Winnie, I promised Thomas I would look after you."

"I can look after myself. I have been for seventy-three years." Her rigid shoulders sagged a little.

Colt rose. "Winnie, let me escort you upstairs. We can hash this all out tomorrow."

She turned her glare on him. "Don't you start, young man. I don't need to be mollycoddled by you, too. I'll go to bed when I want to."

Harold interjected, "But you're starting the final tests tomorrow and—"

She swiveled her attention to him. "Losing a little sleep won't stop me from doing that. I'm not the fragile person you think I am. I want to hear what Sheriff

Quinn has to say about the situation before I retire for the night. Or I wouldn't sleep a wink."

Colt heard the deputy greeting someone in the foyer. "I think they've returned."

Not five seconds later Ellie and Quinn came into the living room. Colt couldn't read much into Ellie's bland expression, but the sheriff's indicated there were problems, which didn't surprise him given what had happened an hour ago.

Sheriff Quinn stood at the end of the coffee table and directed his attention to Winnie. "Your guard dogs were drugged and stolen. We found a dart they used and tire tracks where they came off the main road, probably in a good-size four-wheel drive. Can't tell if it was a truck or SUV yet. A cast of the tire tracks might narrow it down for us."

Colt's gaze latched onto Ellie. She focused on Winnie, too, except for a few seconds when she slid her attention to him. But her unreadable expression hadn't changed. He saw her military training in her bearing and the way she conducted herself. Ellie had certainly performed capably tonight, but what if the person after Winnie upped his tactics to more lethal ones?

When the sheriff finished his report, Winnie shook his hand. "Thank you, Sheriff Quinn. As usual you have done a thorough job. I want to be informed of any progress." She shifted toward Harold. "I want the Bakersville police chief and the private investigator you hired to be told that, too. No more secrets. Understood?" Her sizzling stare bore into the man.

Harold squirmed on the couch but locked stares with Winnie. "Yes, on one condition."

"You aren't in a place to dictate conditions to me.

For several weeks you have kept me in the dark about something that concerned me. Don't push me, Harold Jefferson."

The color leaked from Harold's face. "I won't," he bit out, his teeth snapping closed on the last word.

"Good, I'm glad we understand each other now. That goes for you, too, Ellie and Colt. Also, I don't want this common knowledge, and I certainly don't want anyone to know that Ellie is a bodyguard. She is my assistant."

"Agreed," Harold said quickly. "Sheriff, can you keep this quiet?"

"Yes. All my deputies need to know is that someone took your dogs. Nothing about the reason or who you are, Miss St. James. We'll play this down."

"I appreciate that. I don't want a media circus until I'm ready to unveil my new line, and then I want the focus on Endless Youth, not me."

The sheriff nodded toward Winnie. "We'll be leaving. I'm going to post Rod outside your house."

"You don't have to do that. I have the very capable Miss St. James." Winnie winked at Ellie.

"Humor me, ma'am, at least for tonight."

"Fine."

Colt hid his smile by lowering his head. His grandmother would have her way in the end. The deputy would be gone by the morning, but Colt planned to have some other security measures in place by tomorrow evening.

Harold stood. "I'll show you out, Sheriff, and give you the name of my P.I. working on the case."

"I'm sorry that Harold put you in the position he did. He told me you wanted to inform me from the first.

We'll proceed as usual, but my grandson will return your gun. I don't like weapons, so I'll ask you to keep it out of view." His grandmother struggled to her feet.

Colt rose quickly but didn't move toward Winnie. She would rebuke his offer to help, especially when he had made it obvious that he considered her fragile. In her mind she equated that to weak. His grandmother was anything but that. After all these years, Harold really didn't understand Winnie like Colt's grandfather had. If Harold had come to him, he would have told him his grandmother could handle anything.

He started toward the door when Winnie did.

She peered back at him. "Don't you buy into Harold's thinking I'm fragile. I hate that word. I am not going to break. Endless Youth was Thomas's project. I will complete it. I can find my own way to my bedroom. I have been doing that for years now."

Colt stopped and looked toward Ellie. Her mouth formed a thin line, but her eyes danced with merriment.

When Winnie left the room, Ellie took a seat on the couch. "I think she told you."

"It wasn't as bad as Harold got. He mismanaged this situation. All because he's in love with Winnie and doesn't really know her like he should."

"That's sad."

"I have a feeling my grandfather knew Harold has been in love with Winnie since the early days. That's why he asked Harold to watch out for her. He knew he would. But Harold envisions himself as her knight in shining armor coming to her rescue. My grandmother is not a damsel in distress."

"What happened when your grandfather died?"

"She did fall apart. She'd nursed him back to health

after his bout with cancer and was planning a month long vacation with him when he fell asleep behind the wheel and went off the mountain. For a short time, I saw her faith shattered. I was worried, but Harold was frantic and beside himself. He went into protective mode and hasn't let up since then."

Hearing footsteps nearing the doorway, Colt put his finger to his lips.

Harold came through the entrance, kneading his neck. "Winnie didn't even say good-night when she went upstairs. She really is mad at me."

"I'm afraid so." Colt waved his hand at the bouquet of flowers on the coffee table. "She isn't delicate like these roses. As soon as you accept that, you might have a chance with Winnie."

"A chance?" Harold opened his mouth to say more but clamped it shut.

Colt grinned. "Just so you know it, you have my blessing to court my grandmother. I've known for a long time how you felt about her, and once this line is out, she deserves something more than working all the time. She's been driving herself for the past few years."

"What makes you think…" Harold's fingers delved into his neat hairstyle, totally messing it up.

"Because I see how you look at her when she isn't looking."

Harold's face flushed a deep shade of red. "She thinks I'm too young for her."

"You're sixty-five. That's not too young." Colt settled into his chair again. "Sit. We need to talk about securing the house and grounds."

"You stole my line," Ellie said as she angled toward Harold at the other end of the couch. "You need to electrify the fence, put in a new security system *tomor-row* and, since she doesn't want people to know what is going on, at least replace the guard dogs. That may be the biggest challenge. They need to be here with a handler right away."

Colt spoke up. "I have a high school friend who trains dogs. I'll give Adam a call tomorrow. If he has a dog for us, he only lives in Denver so he should be able to help us right away." He leaned back, trying to relax his body after the tense-filled past hour.

"This place needs a minimum of two dogs. Three would be better." Ellie looked at Harold. "How about the security system? The one in place is old and can be circumvented."

"I'll have someone here tomorrow. With the right kind of monetary incentive, I'm sure they could start right away. Maybe tomorrow afternoon. They probably could take care of the fence, too." Harold glanced toward the entrance into the living room. "Do you think Winnie will forgive my judgment call on this?"

"Her faith is strong, and she believes in forgiveness. I wouldn't be surprised if she isn't fretting right now about who she has angered enough to do this to her. Knowing her, she'll be praying for that person, whereas I would like to get hold of him and…" Colt let his words fade into silence, curling and uncurling his fists.

They didn't need to know he struggled with forgiving someone who had wronged him. He still couldn't forgive his father for all but abandoning him and going his merry way, living it up as if he didn't have a son and responsibilities. Winnie forgave his dad a long time ago, but after his mother had died, Colt had needed his only parent, and he hadn't been there for him.

"Well," Harold said, slapping his hand on the arm of the couch and pushing up, "I'd better be going. We all have a lot to do tomorrow."

"I'll walk you to the door and lock up after you leave," Ellie said, trailing after him.

Quiet settled around Colt like a blanket of snow over the landscape. Resting his head on the back cushion, he relished the silence, realizing this was what he needed after months on a small ship with cramped quarters. As thoughts of his job weaved through his mind, he knew he had to make a decision. Stay until Winnie was safe or leave and let others protect his grandmother. There wasn't really a decision, not where Winnie was concerned.

A movement out of the corner of his eye seized his attention. Ellie paused in the entrance, leaning her shoulder against the doorjamb. "Have you warmed up yet?"

"Finally I've thawed out. I may be used to living here in the winter, but remind me never to go outside in winter without shoes."

"You seemed lost in thought. I want to assure you I will do everything to protect Winnie. In the short time I've gotten to know her, I see what a special lady she is." She crossed the room and took her seat again across from him.

"We probably should follow Harold's example and get some rest, but I'm so wired right now with all that's happened."

"I know what you mean. Your adrenaline shoots up and it takes a while to come down. But when it does, you'll fall into bed."

"I imagine with your job you've had quite a lot of experience with that. I can't say I have."

"One of the fringe benefits of being a bodyguard."

He laughed. "Never looked at it like that. How long have you been a bodyguard?"

"Three years. I started after I left the army."

"What did you do in the military?"

"For the last few years of my service I was in army intelligence."

"So that's where you learned your skills."

"Yes, it comes naturally to me now. Sometimes I only had myself to rely on when I was working alone in an isolated situation."

"Which I'm sure is classified top secret."

Her brown eyes lit with a gleam. "You know the cliché. If I told you, I'd have to kill you."

"I'm curious but not that curious. What made you go from army intelligence to being a bodyguard?" She intrigued him. It wasn't every day he met a woman who protected people for a living.

She shrugged. "It was my time to re-up, and I thought I would try something different. I had a friend who put me in touch with my employer. When I met Kyra, I knew this was what I wanted to do. I like protecting people who need it. I like the challenge in security."

"Why not police work?"

"I like to go different places. Kinda like you. I have a feeling you've seen a lot of the world through your work."

"Yes, and I've enjoyed it, but I've been on a ship a large part of that time."

"Tired of life on a boat?"

Am I? He hadn't stopped long enough to think about

it. "The past few years have been hectic but fulfilling. I've learned a lot about sea life aboard the *Kaleidoscope*. But if Winnie had her way, she'd want me to use my knowledge for Glamour Sensations. She tells me I've inherited her nose."

Ellie studied that part of his face and frowned. "I think you look more like your grandfather." She gestured toward the portrait over the mantel.

"But I have her supersensitive smelling ability," he said with a chuckle. "Every time I come home, I get the spiel about taking over the family business. But if she goes public, it won't be a family business anymore."

"How do you feel about that?"

"I don't know. It's good for the company, but it means we'll be in the big leagues and I don't know how Winnie will really like that. This is Harold's plan, and I understand why he is pushing to go public. The Endless Youth line will take us in a different direction. The expansion of the company will be good for this area."

Ellie tilted her head and smiled. "Do you realize you keep saying 'us' as though you are part of the company?"

"You'd make a good detective. Did you get your interview skills in the army?"

"I owe the army a lot, but I think I've always been nosy. It got me into trouble from time to time when I was growing up."

Colt yawned, the earlier adrenaline rush completely gone. "I guess that's my cue to get some sleep. Jet lag has definitely set in."

Ellie rose. "You've had two very hectic nights since you got here. This wasn't probably what you were expecting."

As he covered the distance to the foyer, he stifled another yawn before she thought it was her company. Because that was the furthest from the truth. If he wasn't so exhausted from months of nonstop work and traveling over a day to get home, he could spend hours trying to get to know Ellie St. James. And he had a feeling he wouldn't even begin to understand the woman.

He started up the stairs and she continued walking toward the dining room and kitchen area. "You're not coming upstairs?"

She peered back over her shoulder. "Not until I've checked the house again and made sure we're locked up as tight as we can be."

He rotated toward her. "Do you need company?"

Her chuckle peppered the air. "I've been doing this for a long time. It's second nature. Always know the terrain around you. In this case, this house. If I have to move around it in the dark, I need to know the layout."

"I never thought about that. I'm glad Winnie has you. See you bright and early tomorrow."

"Good night."

The smile that curved her lips zapped him. He mounted the stairs with that picture etched into his mind. He had grown up in this house. Could he move around it if the power went off and not run into every piece of furniture? Her skill set was very different from his. He could leave and be assured Winnie was in good hands.

That conclusion didn't set well with him. It niggled him as he got into bed, and it stayed with him all night.

After securing the house, Ellie ascended to the second floor. Walking toward her bedroom, she paused outside Winnie's room and pressed her ear against the door. Silence greeted her. She continued to hers two doors down. She couldn't shake the feeling they were vulnerable even with the deputy outside.

She immediately crossed the window that overlooked the front of the property. She studied the parked patrol car, glimpsing the man sitting in the front seat. She didn't leave her welfare or a client's to others. She hadn't vetted the deputy. She didn't even know him.

That thought clinched her decision. She went to her bed and gathered up a blanket and pillow then headed for the hallway. Outside Winnie's room, she spread her armload out on the floor then settled down for the night, fitting her gun close to her. This accommodation was four-star compared to some she'd had in the army.

She was a light sleeper, and anyone who wanted Winnie would have to go over her to get her client. She fell asleep with that knowledge.

Only to have someone jostle her shoulder hours later.

She gripped her gun. Her eyes inched open to find Colt stooping over her.

He leaned toward her ear and whispered, "I don't want to disturb Winnie, but Rod is gone. He's not in the car and hasn't been for a while now."

Chapter Five

Ellie was already on her feet, slipping on her shoes as she moved toward the stairs. "Stay here. It might be nothing but stretching his legs."

As she crept down the steps, avoiding the ones that creaked, only the light from the hallway illuminating her path, her eyes began to adjust to the darkness swallowing her at the bottom of the staircase. She saw the red glow on the security keypad across from her.

Before going outside to search for the deputy, she crept through the rooms on the first floor, using the moonlight streaming through the upper part of the windows that weren't draped. When she reached the kitchen, she had to switch on a light to inspect the area and check the back door.

When she returned to the foyer, she flipped on the light and punched the alarm off then went to the bottom of the steps. "Colt."

He appeared at the railing overlooking the foyer.

"I'm going outside and resetting the alarm. Don't leave there."

"You shouldn't go by yourself."

"I need you to stay there. Don't follow me. Understand?"

He nodded, but his jaw clamped in a hard line.

Ellie set the alarm, hurried toward the front door and slipped outside. She examined the patrol car, still empty. Rod's hat sat on the passenger's seat. That was the only evidence the man had been in the vehicle.

For the second time that night she made her way toward the west side of the property. Had the mountain lion returned and somehow got inside the fence? Earlier they had patched it the best they could. Now she noticed the rope they had tied across the opening had been cut and the fence had been parted again. Alert, she inspected the blackness beyond the property. Her eyes were fully adjusted to the dark, but a good pair of night-vision goggles would have been preferable. She swung around slowly, searching every tree and bush.

Something big lay on the ground near a group of firs. She snuck toward it. The closer she came the more sure she was that it was a body. From the size, probably a man. The body lay still, curled on his side, his face away from her. Was it the deputy? Was he dead?

Removing her small flashlight from her pocket, she increased her pace as well as her alertness in case this was a trap. Someone had cut those ropes.

The person on the ground groaned and rolled over. He tried to sit up and collapsed back. Another moan escaped him as Ellie reached his side.

"Rod? Are you okay?"

"Someone…hit me over the head." He lifted his hand to his hair and yelped when he touched his scalp. Blood covered his fingers.

"Why were you out here?"

"I heard something. I came to see what it was and found one of the dogs lying under the thick brush." He pointed beneath some large holly bushes. "The next thing I knew, I was hit and going down." He struggled to sit up.

Ellie helped him. "Take it easy. I'm phoning this in."

After she placed a call to the sheriff's office, Rod asked, "Is the dog gone?"

Using her small flashlight, Ellie inspected the bushes. "There's no dog here."

"There was a while ago. Its whimpering is what drew me."

"Whoever hit you must have taken the dog. The ropes on the fence were cut and the hole opened up again."

"They came back for the third dog?"

"I guess. Why do you say 'they'?"

"I don't know. It could have been one person or several. The dog weighed sixty or seventy pounds, so one person could have carried it, I guess."

"Or dragged it." She thought of the boot prints, about a size nine in a men's shoe, which meant probably a man of medium height or a large woman. "Can you walk back to the house?"

"Yes. I just need to take it slow."

Putting her arm around him, she assisted him to his feet. "Okay?"

"Yeah, except for a walloping headache."

She checked her watch. "Backup should be here soon."

"I didn't see that dog last night, but it was hidden by the holly bushes. I've got to admit I didn't think a dog was still here. I should have searched more thoroughly." He touched his forehead. "I've learned my lesson."

"It's only an hour or so to sunrise. We can search the whole grounds more thoroughly then."

"Why did whoever took the dogs come back for one of them? That was risky."

"Can't answer that." Although she had an idea. Last night Winnie had been extremely upset about the missing dogs. They had been special to her husband. So the person behind taking the animals might have had two reasons: to hurt the security around Winnie and to hurt her personally. "It does mean someone was watching the house for the right moment to come back."

"Except that I got to the dog before they could."

"It's looking that way."

The deputy gripped the railing as he mounted the steps to the front deck. "Does the sheriff know?"

"Probably."

Before she could unlock the door, Colt opened it. He took one look at Rod and stepped aside to let them inside. "What happened?"

Winnie hurried across the foyer, taking hold of the young man. "Come into the kitchen. Let me clean this gash."

"Ma'am, I'll be okay."

"Not until you see a doctor, and it still needs to be cleaned up. I have a first-aid kit in the kitchen." Winnie tugged the man forward.

Colt stood in Ellie's way. "What happened?"

She shut and locked the door, then faced him. "He heard a sound coming from the west side of the property and went to check it out. When he found one of your dogs on the ground under some bushes, he was hit over the head."

"One of our dogs wasn't taken?"

"It has been now, or at least I think it has. The dog was gone when I got there. The ropes were cut and the fence opened back up."

"Maybe there's another dog on the grounds?"

"In a couple of hours when it's daylight, we can search more thoroughly and see."

"We'd probably better go rescue Rod. My grandmother can get carried away with a cut or gash. Once she wrapped my calf for a small wound on the back. A bandage would have worked fine."

Ellie had taken a few steps when the doorbell rang. "I'll take care of this. It's probably the sheriff."

After looking through the peephole and seeing Sheriff Quinn, she opened the door. "The deputy should be all right, but he needs to be checked out at the hospital. He was hit over the head. Winnie is tending to him in the kitchen."

As they walked toward the room, Ellie explained where the deputy had been found and about the dog under the bushes.

Winnie glanced up when they entered. Frowning, she finished cleaning up the deputy's head wound. "Someone has stolen my dogs. Come on my property. Threatened me. And now hurt your deputy. I hardly see you, and in less than six hours you've been at my house twice. Neither a social call."

"I have one deputy outside right now and another on his way. Should be here any minute." He turned to Rod. "He can take you to the hospital. Get that head injury examined by the doc."

"Fine by me, but I want to work on this case. When this person came after me, he made it personal." Rod slowly stood and smiled at Winnie. "Thank you, ma'am, for seeing to me."

"Dear, I'm so sorry. You take care of yourself, and you're welcome back here anytime."

Before the sheriff followed his deputy from the room, he said, "If it's okay with you, Mrs. Winfield, I'd like to stay until sunrise and then thoroughly search the grounds."

"Of course. I'll get some coffee on and fix something for breakfast. I have a feeling we'll all need our energy for the day to come." Winnie washed her hands at the sink, then began making some coffee.

"I'll be back as soon as I see to Rod and post my other deputy. We need to discuss who would do this to you, Mrs. Winfield."

After the sheriff left, Winnie finished with the coffee. With her back to them, she grasped the counter on both sides of her and lowered her head.

"Winnie, are you okay?" Colt asked, coming to his grandmother's side and laying his hand on her shoulder.

The woman straightened from the counter, turned and inhaled a deep breath. "I will be once we find this person. If we get a ransom demand for the dogs, I'll pay it. I want them back. But what if…" Her bottom lip quivered, and she bit down on it.

"We'll do everything we can to get your pets back. I know how much they mean to you."

"I remember all the walks your granddad and I took with our dogs. It was our special time together. I think it was what helped me bounce back from my heart attack."

Colt embraced Winnie. "I'm not going back to the

ship until this whole situation is resolved. Your safety means everything to me."

Winnie's eyes glistened. "That means so much to me. You're my only family now."

Behind her Ellie heard footsteps approaching the kitchen. She turned around, her hand on her gun in case it wasn't the sheriff returning. But when he came into the room, she dropped her arm to her side.

"Just in time for some coffee, Sheriff." Winnie stepped away from Colt and busied herself taking four mugs from the cabinet. "If I remember correctly you take yours black."

"Yes, I sure do."

Winnie poured the brew into the mugs then passed them out. "I've been trying to think of anyone who would do this to me. I can't at the moment."

"Let's all sit and talk this out. Sometimes that helps."

Ellie took a chair next to Colt while Sheriff Quinn and Winnie sat across from her. "Who have you fired recently?" she asked.

"No one." Her eyebrows scrunched together. "Well, I haven't personally. Harold and the human resources department handle those kind of things. There are days I don't even go into the office. I prefer working here. That's why I have a fully stocked lab in the basement."

"So you can't think of any disgruntled employees?" The sheriff blew on his coffee then took a sip. "Let's say in the past year."

Her head down, Winnie massaged her fingertips into her forehead. "You need to get a list from Harold. There have only been a few people I know personally who have left the company in the past year or so."

"Who?" Sheriff Quinn withdrew a small pad along with a pen from his front shirt pocket.

"About a year ago one of the chemists working with me. I wasn't aware of this problem, but two different female employees in the lab accused him of sexual harassment. Glamour Sensations has always had a strict policy against it. Harold fired Dr. Ben Parker. He was difficult to work with but a brilliant chemist. When he came to me and complained, I supported Harold's decision. Frankly, I told him I was disappointed in him and…" Winnie averted her head and stared at the blinds over the window near the table.

"What else?" Colt slid his hand across the table and cupped his grandmother's.

"He said some ugly things to me, mostly directed at Harold and the company rather than at me. I will not repeat them." Squaring her shoulders, she lifted her chin.

The sheriff wrote down the man's name on the pad. "Okay, Winnie. We have one we can check on. Anyone else?"

"The only other who I had any contact with is the driver I used to have before my current one." She paused for a long moment. "I guess I was directly responsible for his dismissal. He came to work one day drunk. I knew he'd been having marital troubles so I was willing to give him a second chance. We all need those, but Harold was adamant that we don't. In the end I agreed with Harold."

"Harold was right. You can't be driven around by a person who has been drinking. What's his name?"

"Jerry Olson."

"Any more?" The sheriff took another drink of his coffee.

Winnie shook her head. "None. But there are a lot of departments I don't have any interaction with."

"How about someone who's been passed over for a raise or promotion?" Ellie cradled her mug between her cold hands. "This person doesn't necessarily have to be gone from the company."

"Well…" Winnie patted her hair down, her mouth pursed. "We did have several candidates to be the spokesperson for Endless Youth. Christy actually wasn't in the running. I'm the one who decided she would be perfect. She might not be considered beautiful by a model's standard, but she conveyed what I wanted to communicate to the everyday woman. There were two young women before Christy who were in the final running for the position. Mary Ann Witlock and Lara Ulrich. I suppose neither one was happy when they weren't picked. They don't work for Glamour Sensations. Lara Ulrich lives in Denver, and Mary Ann Witlock lives in Bakersville. Several members of her family work for Glamour Sensations, but she works as a waitress at the restaurant not far from the company's main office."

The sheriff jotted down the additional names. "If you think of anyone else, give me a call. I'll be meeting with Harold and the police chief in Bakersville to see who they're looking at."

"Have you all thought this could be simply a kidnapping of my dogs?" Winnie asked. "They are valuable. But even more so to me. Anyone who knows me knows that."

Ellie nodded. "True, but they're even more valuable to you because you care for them so much. That could be the reason the person decided to steal them."

She downed the last swallow of her coffee and went to get the pot and bring it back to the table. "Anyone else want some more?"

Colt held up his mug, as did the sheriff. Winnie shook her head.

The sheriff closed his notepad. "After I look around, I'll go back to the office and track down these people."

"How's an omelet for breakfast?" Winnie left her nearly untouched drink and crossed to the refrigerator.

"Wait until Linda comes to prepare breakfast." Colt pulled the blind to let in the soft light of dawn. "When she sees all the cars out front, she'll be here early."

"No, I need to keep busy. Besides, I don't get to cook like I used to. Thomas loved my omelets. Now to remember how to make them."

"I'll help."

Colt shifted his attention to Ellie. "You cook?"

"Yes, some. I have to eat so I learned how."

One of his eyebrow arched. "A bodyguard who can cook. A woman of many talents."

"I'd love your help," Winnie said. "Be useful, Colt, and take this cup of coffee to the deputy outside."

He passed Ellie as he left with a mug and whispered, "Watch her. She once almost set the kitchen on fire. That's why Granddad insisted she hire Linda to cook."

"I heard that, young man. At least I don't go outside barefoot in winter."

Ellie slanted a look toward Colt as he left. In the doorway he glanced back and locked gazes with her. Then he winked.

Heat scored Ellie's cheeks. She'd never been around a family like the Winfields. She would have loved having the caring and the give-and-take between her and her mother. What would it have been like to grow up in a loving family? She could only imagine.

Ellie watched the last workmen leave, the black iron gates at the end of the drive shutting closed after the truck passed through the entrance to the estate. The sun disappeared completely below the western mountains, throwing a few shadows across the landscape. She surveyed the nearly fortified property, her muscles still tense from all the activity that had occurred during the day.

"What do you think?" Colt asked, coming up behind her.

"I'd rather have been in the lab with Winnie than out here supervising."

"The sheriff put a deputy on the door to the lab. Your expertise was needed making sure everything went in correctly. Winnie needed her security system updated even without the threat to her."

"I agree. She thinks being isolated keeps her protected. On the contrary, that makes her more vulnerable." She threw him a grin. "I just hate it when I need to be in two places at once. But you're right. I needed to keep an eye on the workers and the job they were doing. After tomorrow I'll breathe even easier."

"When they mount the cameras and put in the monitoring station?"

"Yes. The only one up and running right now is at the front gate. I'm glad Winnie agreed to let us use that small room off the kitchen for the monitoring station. It's a good location. Even at night we'll be able to tell what is happening outside on the grounds."

"That would have been nice last night." Colt lounged against the railing, his gaze fixed on her.

The intensity in his look lured her nearer. It took all her willpower to stay where she was. "I'm hoping the electrified fence will keep people and large animals away. If someone tries to circumvent the power on the fence, the company monitoring it will notify the house. The jolt won't kill, but it will discourage someone or something from touching it."

"Tomorrow the two guard dogs from the trainer in Denver will arrive, but with the fence up and running and the new security system for the house, we should be all right."

He hadn't phrased it as a question, but his furrowed forehead indicated his lingering doubts. "No place can be one hundred percent safe, but this will be a vast improvement over yesterday. I wasn't sure how much they would accomplish today, but it helped that Winnie could afford to pay for a rush job."

"I got through to the *Kaleidoscope* and told them I have a family emergency. Just when you think you're indispensable, you find out they'll be all right without you. But then I figure you don't feel that way too much in your job. I know Winnie needs you. Yesterday proved that." He snapped his fingers. "I almost forgot. The sheriff called. He's on his way from Bakersville to give us an update on the people they're checking out."

"So he'll be here about the time Harold arrives. He wants us to have photos of the people Winnie mentioned and some he thought of. He wants us to convince Winnie not to attend the lighting of the Christmas tree in Bakersville tomorrow night."

Colt straightened, his movement bringing him a

step closer. "I'll give it my best shot, but I don't think Winnie will change her mind. Bakersville is honoring Granddad and her at the tree lighting for all the work they've done for the town. That's important to her. Bakersville has been her home a long time since she married my granddad and came to live here."

"As important as her life?"

"My grandmother can be a stubborn woman."

"Tell me about it. She didn't want the deputy in the basement. She thought he could sit in the kitchen where he would be more comfortable. I told her that workers will have to come down there and that I can't follow every worker around. The deputy stands at the door to her lab or inside with her."

"I know she balked at that. She doesn't even like me in there. Anybody in the lab is a distraction, and she is determined to complete the project in time. She believes it's tied to who is after her. She thinks it's a competitor."

"That's still a possibility. The P.I. is looking into that. Maybe Harold will have some information."

Colt nodded his head toward the gate. "That's his car now and it looks like the sheriff is behind him."

"Nothing is assured until I check the monitor," Ellie said as she hurried inside and to the small room off the kitchen.

She examined the TV that showed the feed from the front gate. Harold waved at the camera. After clicking him through, she observed the Lexus as it passed the lower camera that gave a view of anyone in the vehicle. It appeared Harold was alone. Then she did the same thing with the sheriff.

When she glanced up, Colt stood in the doorway,

his arms straight at his side while his gaze took in the bank of TV monitors. "We need someone to be in here 24/7 until this is over with."

"I agree, and I'm hoping you'll help me convince your grandmother of that in a few minutes."

"So you gathered the forces to help you?"

"Yes. She may be upset with Harold for not telling her sooner, but she trusts him. And she respects the sheriff."

"You are sly, Miss St. James, and I'm glad you are. In a week's time you have gotten to know Winnie well."

"I got a head start. On the plane ride here, I studied a file Harold provided me on her. From what he wrote, I could tell how much he cares about her. In army intelligence, I had to learn quick how to read people."

He closed the space between them. "That means you can't be fooled?"

"I'd be a fool to think that."

His chuckle resonated through the air. "Good answer. I like you, Ellie St. James."

The small room seemed to shrink as she looked at the dimple in his left cheek, the laugh lines at the corners of his eyes. She scrambled to form some kind of reply that would make sense. But as his soft gaze roamed over her features it left a tingling path where it touched as if he'd brushed his fingers over her face.

The doorbell sounded, breaking the mood.

"I'll get Winnie," he murmured in a husky voice.

She stepped to the side and rushed past him to the foyer. Her heartbeat pounded against her rib cage, and her breath was shallow as she peered through the peephole then opened the door to Harold and the sheriff.

"Colt's gone to get his grandmother," Ellie told them. "She wanted to be included in the update."

"How's she holding up?" Harold asked as they made their way into the living room.

"Fine, Harold." Winnie answered before Ellie could. "Worried? Is that why you didn't answer your private line today when I called?"

With his cheeks flushed, the CFO of Glamour Sensations faced Winnie coming down the hall. "I've been busy working with the police chief, to make sure we have a thorough list of people who could possibly be angry with you."

The older woman's usual warm blue eyes frosted. "I've always tried to treat people fairly. How many are we talking about?"

"Including the ones you gave the sheriff, in the past two years, ten."

Her taut bearing drooped a little. "That many? I've never intentionally hurt someone."

"It might not be you per se but your company. Tomorrow I'm going to look back five years."

"Why so far back?" Winnie looked from Harold to the sheriff, her delicate eyebrows crunching together.

"It's probably no one that far back, but I'd rather cover all our bases. It's better to be safe than—"

Winnie held up her hand. "Don't say it. It's been a long day. It was nearly impossible to think clearly with all the racket going on earlier. This may throw me behind a day or so. Give me the facts, and then I need to go back to the lab to finish up what should have been completed two hours ago." She came into the room as far as the wingback chair but remained standing behind it.

"Winnie, the workmen will be gone by midafternoon tomorrow. They're mounting cameras all over the estate and activating the monitoring system. The only one right now that works is the front gate." Ellie took a seat, hoping her client would follow suit. The pale cast to Winnie's face and her lackluster eyes worried Ellie.

Sheriff Quinn cleared his throat. "We've narrowed the list down to the three most likely with two maybes." He withdrew his pad. "The first one is Lara Ulrich. Although she lives in Denver, that's only an hour away, and she has been spotted in Bakersville this past month, visiting her mother. I discovered she's moving back home because she can't get enough work to support herself in Denver. Jerry Olson is working when he can but mostly he's living off his aunt, who is losing her patience with him. He's been vocal about you not giving him that second chance you're known for. The last is someone Harold brought to my attention. Steve Fairchild is back in town."

Winnie gasped.

Chapter Six

‿

Winnie leaned into the back of the chair, clutching it. "When?"

"A few weeks ago," Harold said, getting up and moving to Winnie.

Ellie glanced at Colt. A tic in his jaw twitched. She slid her hand to his on the couch and he swung his attention to her as she mouthed, "Who is that?"

He bent toward her and whispered, "She blamed him for causing Granddad's death."

"Why is this the first time I've heard about him?"

"Right after my grandfather died he left Bakersville to work overseas."

"Because I drove him out of town," Winnie said in a raw voice, finally taking a seat. "I said some horrible things to the man in public that I regretted when I came to my right mind." A sheen of tears shone in her eyes. "I wronged him and thought I would never have a chance to apologize. I must go see him."

"No." Colt's hand beneath Ellie's on the couch fisted. "Not when someone is after you. Not when that someone could be him."

Winnie stiffened, gripping both arms of the chair. "Young man, I will do what I have to. I will not let this wrong go on any longer. I need to apologize—in public. My words and actions were what caused people to make his life so miserable he left town. Wasn't it bad enough that Thomas had fired him that day he died?"

"I need you to tell me what happened." Ellie rose, her nerves jingling as if she felt they were close to an answer.

"Steve Fairchild messed up a huge account for Glamour Sensations. Thomas lost a lot of sleep over what to do about him. That day he fired Steve, Thomas stayed late trying to repair the damage the man had done to the company. I blamed Steve Fairchild for my husband falling asleep behind the wheel. That was grief talking. I now realize Thomas made the choice to drive home when he could have stayed at his office and slept on the couch."

Harold pounded the arm of his chair and sat forward. "Winnie, the man was at fault. We took a hard knock when that client walked away from our company. It took us a year to get back what we lost. You only said what half the town felt, and then on top of everything, he dared to come to Thomas's funeral. You were not in the wrong."

Winnie pressed her lips together. For a long moment silence filled the room. "This is the last I'm going to say on the subject. I owe the man an apology, and I intend to give it to him." She swept her attention to the sheriff. "What about Mary Ann Witlock?"

"I'm still looking for her. She's not been seen for a week. She told her neighbor she was going to Texas to see a boyfriend. That's all I've been able to find out so far."

"And you don't think Dr. Ben Parker is a threat?"

"No, he's in a nursing home in Denver."

"He is? Why?"

"He had a severe stroke. He can't walk and has trouble talking."

"Oh, dear. I need to add him to my prayer list."

"He wouldn't leave the young women in his lab alone," Harold muttered, scowling.

Winnie tilted up her chin. "That doesn't mean I shouldn't pray for him. You and I have never seen eye to eye on praying for people regardless."

Listening to the older woman gave Ellie something to think about. She was a Christian, but was her faith strong? Could she forgive her mother for her neglect or the bullies that made her brother's life miserable? She didn't know if she had that in her, especially when she remembered Toby coming home crying with a bloodied face.

"We'll continue to delve into these people's lives. I'm just glad the police chief is handling it quietly and personally," Harold said with a long sigh. "He's trying to track down how the letters came to your office. There was no postmark. He's reviewing security footage, but there are a lot of ways to put a letter in the interoffice mail at your company. Some of them aren't on the camera."

"Fine." Winnie slapped her hands on her thighs and started to push up from her seat. "I've got a few more hours of—"

"Grandma, we have something else we need to talk to you about." Colt's words stopped her.

Ellie noticed the woman's eyebrows shoot up.

"Grandma?" Winnie asked. "Is there something else serious you've been keeping from me? You never call me Grandma." Her gaze flitted from one person to the next.

Ellie approached Winnie. "I'm strongly recommending that you not go to the lighting of the Christmas tree tomorrow night."

"I'm going, so each of you better accept that. Knowing you, Harold, you've hired security. I wouldn't be surprised if every other person in the crowd was security. I won't let this person rob me of all my little pleasures." She stood, her arms stiff at her sides. "Just make sure they don't stand out."

Evidently Colt was not satisfied. "Grandma—"

"Don't 'Grandma' me. I will not give in to this person totally. I'm already practically a prisoner in this house, and after tomorrow, this place will be as secure as a prison." She marched toward the exit. "I'll be in my lab. Have Linda bring my dinner to me. I'm eating alone tonight."

Quiet ruled until the basement door slammed shut.

"That worked well," Colt mumbled and caught Ellie's look. "What do you suggest?"

"Short of locking her in her room, nothing. I'd say strengthen the security and pray. I won't leave her side. Harold, have you found a few people to monitor the TVs around the clock here at the house?"

"Yes. With the police chief and Sheriff Quinn's help, I have four who are willing to start tomorrow. One is a deputy and two are police officers. They need extra money. My fourth one is the retired police chief. He's bored and needs something to do. They will be discreet."

"Perfect." Although the police chief and sheriff vouched for the men, she would have her employer do a background check on them. She'd learned to double-check everything. "I'd like a list of their names."

The sheriff jotted them down on a piece of paper. "I personally know all these men, and they will do a good job."

"That's good. Did you discover what kind of vehicle could have left those tire tracks?"

"The tire is pretty common for a SUV, so probably not a truck."

"What was in the dart?" Ellie held her breath, hoping it wasn't a poison. Winnie still thought there was a chance to get her dogs back.

Sheriff Quinn rose. "A tranquilizer. We're checking vets and sources where it can be purchased. But that will take time."

Time we might not have.

After Ellie escorted the two men to the front door then locked it when they left, she turned to see Colt in the foyer, staring at her. The scent of roasted chicken spiced the air. Her stomach rumbled. "I just realized all I had today was breakfast."

"It looks like it will be just you and me tonight."

The sudden cozy picture of them sitting before a roaring fire sharing a delicious dinner stirred feelings deep inside her she'd fought to keep pushed down. She'd purposely picked this life as a bodyguard to help others but also to keep her distance from people. She was more of an observer, not a participant. When she had participated, she'd gotten hurt—first with her family and later when she became involved with Greg, a man she had dated seriously who had lied to her.

Colt walked toward her, a crooked grin on his face. "We have to eat. We might as well do it together and get to know each other. It looks like we'll be working together to protect Winnie."

"Working together? I don't think so. I'm the bodyguard, not you. You're her grandson. You are emotionally involved. That can lead to mistakes, problems."

He moved into her personal space, suddenly crowding her even though he was a couple of feet away. "Being emotionally involved will drive me to do what I need to protect my grandmother. Feelings aren't the enemy."

They aren't? Ellie had her doubts. She'd felt for her mother, her brother and Greg, and ended up hurt, a little bit of herself lost. "Feelings can get in the way of doing your job."

"It's dinner, Ellie. That's all. In the kitchen."

"I know that. I'm checking the house one more time, then I'll be in there to eat." She started to leave.

He stepped into her path. "I want to make it clear. I will be involved with guarding Winnie. That's not negotiable."

She met the hard, steely look in his eyes. "Everything is negotiable." Then she skirted around him and started her room-by-room search, testing the windows and looking in places a person could hide. She'd counted the workmen as they'd left, but she liked to double-check.

As she passed through the house, she placed a call to her employer. "I need you to investigate some law enforcement officers who are helping with monitoring the cameras I've had installed around the estate. The sheriff and police chief vetted them."

Kyra Hunt laughed. "But you don't know if you can trust them?"

"No. You taught me well. I can remember a certain police officer being dirty on a case you took."

"I've already looked into Sheriff Quinn and the police chief. Nothing I can find sends up a red flag."

Like the background checks Kyra did on Harold Jefferson, Linda and Doug Miller, and Christy Boland. She knew nothing was completely foolproof, but she would be a fool if she didn't have these background checks done on people who came in close contact with Winnie. After she gave the four names to Kyra, she said, "Also look into Colt Winfield. He came home unexpectedly and is now staying."

"Mrs. Winfield's grandson? Do you suspect him?"

"No, not really, but then I can't afford to be wrong."

"I'll get back to you with what I find."

When Ellie finished her call, she walked toward the kitchen, the strong aroma of spices and roast chicken making her mouth water.

"Linda, I'll take care of the dishes. Go home," Colt said as Ellie came into the room.

Linda nodded. "I imagine Doug is asleep. Today was an early one, and with all that's been going on, he didn't have much chance to even sit." She removed her apron and hung it up on a peg. "Winnie said she'll bring up her dinner tray later."

Ellie crossed to the back door and locked it after the housekeeper left. She watched out the window as the woman hurried across the yard toward the guesthouse where she and her husband lived. "I haven't had a chance to tell her today that any guests she has will have to go through me first. I'll do that first thing tomorrow." She pivoted, her gaze connecting with Colt's.

"We talked about it. She's fine meeting anyone she needs in town for the time being."

"Just so long as her car is inspected when she comes back."

Surprise flashed across her face. "You think Linda might be involved?"

"No, but what if someone managed to hide in her car? Then when she drove onto the property they would be inside without us knowing. It's necessary until we know how the new dogs are going to work out."

"You have to think of everything."

"My clients depend on it. As we speak, I'm having the men who are going to monitor the security system vetted by my employer. Nothing is foolproof, but there are some procedures I can put in place to make this house safer, so Winnie won't have to worry about walking around her own home. I've had everyone who comes into close contact with Winnie on a regular basis checked out."

"Harold?

"Yes, just because he hired me doesn't make him not a suspect."

"Me?" Colt pulled out a chair for her to sit in at the kitchen table set for two.

"Yes, even you."

"I'm her grandson!"

"I know, but some murders have been committed by family members."

He took the chair across from her. "Do you trust anyone?" he asked in a tightly controlled voice.

"I'm paid to distrust."

"How about when you aren't working? Do you go around distrusting everyone?"

"I trust God."

"No one else?"

Ellie picked up the fork and speared a slice of roasted chicken. Who did she trust? The list was short. "How about you? Who do you trust?"

His intense gaze snared hers. "I trust you to protect my grandmother."

"Then why are you wanting to do my job?"

"Because I trust myself to protect my grandmother, too. Isn't two better than one?"

"Not necessarily."

After he scooped some mashed potatoes onto his plate he passed her the bowl. "You never answered my question about who you trust."

"I know." Her hand gripping her fork tight, she dug into her dinner. His question disturbed her because she didn't have a ready answer—a list of family and friends she could say she trusted. Could she trust Colt?

The chilly temperature and the low clouds in the dark night promised snow when they arrived at the tree lighting. Ellie buttoned her short coat and checked her gun before she slid from the front passenger seat of the SUV. "Winnie, wait until I open your door."

While Colt exited the car, Ellie helped his grandmother from the backseat. The whole time Ellie scanned the crowd in the park next to City Hall, her senses alert for anything out of the ordinary. Lights blazed from the two-story building behind the tree and from the string of colored lights strung from pole to pole along the street, but too many of the townspeople were shrouded in darkness where the illumination didn't reach.

Ellie flanked Winnie on the right side while Colt took the left one. "Ready?" she asked.

"I see Harold waving to us from the platform near the Christmas tree." Colt guided his grandmother toward Glamour Sensations' CFO.

"No one said anything about you standing on a platform," Ellie said. The idea that Winnie would be up above the crowd—a better target—bothered Ellie. She continued her search of the faces in the mob, looking for any of the ones the police were looking into as the possible threat to Winnie.

"Oh, yes. I have to give a speech before I flip the switch. I'll keep it short, dear."

Ellie wasn't sure Winnie took the threat against her as seriously as she should. "How about you skip the speech and go straight to turning on the lights so we can leave?"

Winnie paused and shifted toward Ellie. "I've lived a long, good life. If I go to my maker tonight, then so be it."

"Winnie," Colt said in a sharp voice that reached the people around them. They all turned to watch them. Leaning toward his grandmother, he murmured, "I'm not ready to give you up. I'd care if something happened to you."

Winnie patted his arm. "I know. But I want you two to realize I have a peace about all of this. That doesn't mean I will fire Ellie—" she tossed a look toward Ellie "—because I won't give the person after me an easy target. But, as I'm sure she knows, there is only so much you all can do. The only one who can protect me is the Lord."

"But you know He uses others to do His bidding. I fall into that category. If I tell you to do something, just do it. No questions asked, okay?" Ellie wished she could get Winnie to take this whole situation more seriously.

"Yes, my dear."

"If I see a threat in the crowd, I'm going to get you out of here. Then later you can chalk it up to a crazy assistant getting overzealous in her job if you need to spin it for the press. Let's get this over with."

Up on the platform as Winnie approached the podium and the cheering crowd quieted, Colt whispered to Ellie, "You make this sound like we've come for a root canal."

"How about several? I don't like this at all." She gestured toward one area of the park that was particularly dark. "Why couldn't they have the lighting of the tree during the daytime?"

Her gaze latched onto a man in the front row reaching into his coat pocket. Ellie stiffened and put her hand into her own pocket, grasping her weapon. But the guy pulled out a cell and turned it off.

Five minutes later when Winnie completed her short speech thanking Bakersville for the honor to Thomas and her for naming the park after them, she stepped over to flip the first switch. Suddenly the lights went out in City Hall and the only ones that illuminated the area were the string of colorful lights along the streets and around the park. Next Winnie flipped the switch for the lights on the twelve-foot Christmas tree and their colorful glow lit the area.

"That's why it's at nighttime."

The tickle of Colt's whisper by her ear shot a bolt of awareness through Ellie. Her pulse rate accelerated, causing a flush of heat on her face. Someone in the crowd began singing "Joy to the World" and everyone joined in, including Colt and Winnie. Ellie sang but never took her attention from the people surrounding Winnie. Harold had said he would have people in plainclothes scattered throughout the attendees in addition to the police visible in the throng.

Ellie moved closer, intending to steer Winnie back to the SUV. But before she could grasp her elbow, women, men and children swamped Winnie.

"Thank you for what you've done for Bakersville," one lady said.

Another person shook Winnie's hand. "When the economy was down, you didn't lay off anyone at the company. We appreciate that."

After five long minutes of the same kind of praises, Ellie stepped to Winnie's right while Colt took up his position on the left.

Winnie grinned. "Thank you all. Bakersville is important to me. It's my home."

People parted to allow Winnie through the crowd. Suddenly a medium-built man stepped into Winnie's path. Ellie inched closer to Winnie while she gripped her weapon.

Winnie smiled. "I'm glad to see you, Mr. Fairchild. I heard you were in town."

"Yeah. Is there a problem with me being here?" He pulled himself up straight, his shoulders back.

"No, on the contrary, I meant it. I'm glad I ran into you." She raised her voice. "I wanted to apologize to you for my behavior right after Thomas died. I was wrong. I hope you'll accept my apology."

The man's mouth dropped open. The tension in his stance eased. "I—I—"

"I would certainly understand if you don't, but I hope you'll find it in your heart to—"

"I made mistakes, too," Steve Fairchild mumbled. Then he ducked his head and hurried off.

"Let's go, Winnie," Ellie said and guided her client toward the car.

The closer they got to the SUV the faster Ellie's pace became. Her nape tingled; her breath caught in her lungs. The person behind the threats was here somewhere—she felt it in her bones. Possibly Steve Fairchild, in spite of how the encounter had turned out. Not until Winnie was safe in the backseat and Colt was pulling out of the parking space did Ellie finally exhale.

"I thought that went very well, especially with Steve Fairchild, and nothing happened at the lighting of the tree," Winnie said from the backseat.

We're not at your house yet. Ellie kept that thought to herself, but her gaze continually swept the landscape and the road before and behind the SUV.

Winnie continued to comment on the event. "The Christmas tree this year was beautiful. Not that it isn't every year, but they seemed to have more decorations and lights on it. You were here last Christmas, Colt. Don't you think it was bigger and better?"

Ellie tossed a quick glance at Colt. In the beam of an oncoming car, she glimpsed his set jaw, his focus totally on the road ahead.

"I guess so. I never thought about it."

"Isn't that just like a man, Ellie?"

"Yes, but I've found a lot of people don't note their surroundings unless there's a reason." Ellie couldn't help but notice that Winnie hadn't said much on the ride down the mountain, but now she wanted to chit-chat. That was probably her nerves talking. "You'll be all right, Winnie. I won't let anything happen to you."

"I know that. I'm not worried."

"Then why are you talking so much?" Tension threaded through Colt's question.

"I'm relieved nothing happened and pleased by the kindness of the people of Bakersville. I even got my chance to apologize to Mr. Fairchild in public. I wish I could have stayed longer. I probably should call the mayor tomorrow and apologize that I couldn't linger at the end. I usually do."

Behind the SUV a car sped closer. Ellie couldn't tell the make of the vehicle from the glare of the headlights.

"I see it." Colt slowed down.

The car accelerated and passed them on a straight part of the winding road up the mountain. The Ford Focus increased its distance between them and disappeared around a curve. Ellie twisted to look behind them. A dark stretch of highway greeted her inspection.

She sat forward, her hand going to her gun. She took it out and laid it on her lap.

"Expecting trouble?" Colt asked.

Although it was dark inside the SUV, with only a few dashboard lights, Ellie felt the touch of his gaze when he turned his head toward her. "Always. That's what keeps me alert."

"Oh, my goodness, Ellie," Winnie exclaimed. "That would be hard to do all the time. When do you relax, my dear?"

"When I'm not working."

"I noticed you slept outside my bedroom again last night. You can't be getting rest."

Ellie looked back at Winnie. "Now that the security system is totally functioning and someone is monitoring it at night, I can go back to my room. But I'm a light sleeper on the job whether in a bed or on the floor in front of a door." After checking behind the SUV, she rotated forward. "You don't need to worry about me."

"Oh, but, my dear, I do. How do you think I'd feel if anything happened to you because of me?"

Again Colt and Ellie exchanged glances. She'd never had a client worry about her. If Harold hadn't hired her, she doubted Winnie would have, even knowing about the threatening letters. That thought chilled her. The woman would have been an easy target for anyone.

As the SUV approached the next S-curve, the one where Winnie's husband went off the cliff, Colt took it slow, leaning forward, intent on the road.

When they made it through without any problem, Winnie blew out a breath. "I hate that part of the road. If I could avoid it and get down the mountain, I would. That's a particularly dangerous curve."

"It's not much farther. Which is good since they're predicting snow tonight." Colt took the next curve.

Halfway through it Ellie saw the car parked across both lanes of the road. With no place to maneuver around it, Colt slammed on his brakes and Ellie braced for impact.

Chapter Seven

Ellie gasped as the brakes screamed and Colt struggled to keep the vehicle from swerving. She muttered a silent prayer just before they collided with the car across the road. The crashing sound reverberated through the SUV. The impact with the side of the Ford Focus jerked Ellie forward then threw her back. The safety belt cut into her chest, holding her against the seat.

"Are you okay?" Ellie fumbled with her buckle, released it and shoved open the door.

"Yes." Colt swiveled around to look at his grandmother.

"I'm fine," she said from the backseat.

Ellie panned the crash site as she hurried toward the car. She couldn't get to the driver's door because of the SUV so she rounded the back of the vehicle and opened the front passenger's door to look inside. Emptiness mocked her.

She straightened and turned to Colt. "Have Winnie stay inside."

Standing by his car, Colt nodded and went around to Winnie's side.

"No one is in the car. Call it in." Keeping vigilant, Ellie scanned the landscape and then made her way back to the SUV. She stood outside the vehicle.

"He said he was fifteen minutes away," Colt told her from the backseat where he sat next to his grandmother.

"Winnie, would you please get down," Ellie chided. "No sense giving anyone a target to shoot at."

"You think he's out there waiting to shoot me?"

Ellie looked around. "Could be. Someone drove this car here and left it across the road in just the right place for anyone coming around the curve to hit it. If this had been car trouble, where is the driver?"

"Walking to get help?" Winnie's voice quavered.

"But there's no reason to have it stalled across the road like this and not to leave the hazard lights flashing."

When Winnie scooted down on the floor, Colt hovered over her like a human shield.

"No, I'm not going to let you do that. I won't let you be killed in my place. Colt, sit back up."

"No. I won't make it easy for them."

"You're going back to your ship tomorrow." Anger weaved through Winnie's voice.

"We'll talk about this when we're safe at the house."

"Don't placate me. I'm your elder."

Ellie heard the back-and-forth between them and knew the fear they both were experiencing. She had a good douse of it herself. But she planted herself beside the back door, her gun raised against her chest. "Shh, you two. I need to listen."

Not another word came from inside the SUV. Ellie focused on the quiet, occasionally broken by a sound— something scurrying in the underbrush on the side of the road, a sizzling noise from under the hood, an owl's hoot. Finally a siren pierced the night. Its blare grew closer. Ellie smiled. She liked how Sheriff Quinn thought. Let whoever might be out here know that help was nearby. Through the trees on the cliff side, Ellie caught snatches of the red flashing lights as two patrol cars sped up the winding highway toward them. Help would be there in less than two minutes.

Even when the sheriff arrived at the wreck site, Ellie concentrated on her surroundings, not the patrol cars screeching to a halt and the doors slamming shut. Finally she slid a glance toward Sheriff Quinn marching toward her while three of his deputies fanned out.

"Is everyone all right?" The sheriff stopped, reaching out to open the back door.

"Yes, but I need to get Winnie to the estate." Ellie backed up against the SUV. "I don't think anyone is going to do anything now, but she isn't safe out here."

The sheriff pointed to his deputies. "One of you get behind that car. Let's see if we can push it out of the way. Wear gloves. We'll want to pull fingerprints off the steering wheel if possible. Someone left this baby out here." He waved his hand toward the car. "And I intend to find out who did this."

Colt climbed from the backseat, closing his grandmother inside and positioning his body at the door.

While the deputies moved the car off to the side of the road, the sheriff switched on his spotlight, sweeping the area. Ellie followed the beam, delving into the shadows for any sign of someone still hanging around.

Then the sheriff moved his car up along the SUV, rolled down the windows and said, "Winnie needs to get out on this side and into my car. If anyone was here, they'd be along the mountainside, not the cliff side of the highway. It's a sheer drop to the bottom."

"I'll take care of it," Ellie said to Colt. "When Winnie and I are in the sheriff's car, take the front seat."

Colt stepped to the side as Ellie slipped inside the backseat of the SUV, then he shut the door and resumed his position.

"Winnie, did you hear the sheriff?"

"It's hard not to. He was shouting."

"I'm going to follow you out of this car. We'll sit in the back of the patrol car."

"Do I hunch down in there, too?"

"It wouldn't hurt. We don't know what we're up against. Caution is always the best policy."

Winnie crawled across the floor to the other side of the backseat. She gripped the handle and pulled it down. "Here goes." The older woman scrambled out of the SUV and into the patrol car two feet away.

Ellie followed suit, and Colt jumped into the front.

The sheriff gunned his engine, maneuvering up the road with expert precision. "We had a report of a stolen Ford Focus from the parking lot near City Hall. A family came back from watching the tree lighting and found their car gone."

So someone had been at the celebration and decided not to go after Winnie in a crowd. Instead, he chose a dark, lonely stretch of road to cause a wreck. Was that someone Steve Fairchild? He had been at the tree lighting and he'd made a point to see Winnie. Was that his way of taunting her before he made his move?

If Colt hadn't been as alert as he had and his reflexes quick, the crash would have been a lot worse. Ellie peered at Winnie's face. She couldn't see the woman's expression, but she held her body rigid. Tension poured off Winnie.

Ellie felt a strong urge to comfort the woman. "You're almost home."

"Someone hates me that much. We could have gone off the road like…" Her voice melted into the silence.

"We'll find the person." Sheriff Quinn stopped at the main gate to the estate and peered back at Winnie. "This is my top priority. I'm leaving two deputies here, and I'm not going to take no for an answer."

Ellie pushed the remote button to allow them inside. As they headed for the main house, the two dogs followed the car as trained.

"Fine, whatever you think is best," Winnie said, the words laced with defeat.

Ellie covered Winnie's clasped hands in her lap. "If someone was trying to stir memories of your husband's wreck, then he would have picked the S-curve for it to happen. His intent would have been clear if he had done that. There still could be a logical explanation that has nothing to do with you. It could be kids joyriding who got scared and ditched the car."

"Do you really believe that?" Winnie asked, her hands tightening beneath Ellie's.

"It's a possibility. That's all I'm saying. Until I know for sure, I don't rule out anything." But something she said to Winnie nibbled at the edges of her mind. Was there a connection to Winnie's husband somehow? What if he didn't fall asleep at the wheel? What if it had been murder five years ago?

A couple of hours later, Ellie entered the kitchen where the sheriff and Colt sat at the table, drinking coffee and reviewing what had occurred.

"How's Winnie?" Colt walked to the carafe and poured Ellie a cup of the black brew.

She took a deep breath of the aroma. "She's bouncing back. I think the similarity to what happened to her husband is what got her more than anything."

"I agree. It worries me, too. A few threatening letters and cut-up pictures aren't nearly as menacing as trying to re-create the same kind of accident. My first instinct was to swerve and avoid the car. If I'd done that, we could have gone off the cliff." Colt slumped into his chair, releasing a sigh.

Ellie sat beside him. "That has me thinking, Sheriff. Your department handled Thomas Winfield's accident. Are you one hundred percent sure it was an accident?"

"Yes, as sure as you can be. When all this began with Winnie, I reviewed the file. Nothing to indicate he was forced off the road, no skid marks. The tire tracks on the shoulder of the road were from Thomas's car. No one else's. No stalled car like this evening. We checked for drinking and drugs, too. He had no alcohol or drugs in his system."

"He shouldn't have," Colt said. "Granddad didn't drink, and his medicine wouldn't have made him sleepy."

"I know, but there was a report of a car weaving over into the other lane a few miles from where the wreck occurred. The man who reported it honked and the driver of the other car swerved in time to miss him. That person watched that car drive off, and it was going straight, no more weaving. He called it in, anyway. His description wasn't detailed, but what he said did fit your grandfather's car."

"So you're saying in your opinion it was an accident?" Ellie took a large swallow of her coffee.

"Yes. Besides, nothing has happened in five years. Why something now? Why Winnie?"

Colt raked his fingers through his hair. "How in the world do you two sit calmly and talk about this kind of stuff?"

"Because it's good to talk about all the possibilities. Brainstorm theories." The sheriff stood. "Ellie, I'll take another look at the file, but I don't think there's a connection. While you were checking on Winnie, two of my deputies arrived after processing the scene of the wreck. The Ford Focus was towed, and we'll go over it, check for fingerprints in the front seat and door. Maybe something will turn up. Also the SUV was towed to the garage in town to be fixed. I'm posting one deputy inside at the front door and the other at the back. Don't want the two new dogs to mistake them for an intruder."

Ellie started to get up.

Sheriff Quinn waved her down. "I'll send the deputy in here and see myself out."

When he left, Colt looked at her. "Let's go into the den."

Too wired to go to sleep yet, she nodded, topped off her coffee and trailed after Colt.

In the den, he stoked the fire he'd made when they had first come home. Winnie had been cold and sat by it until she'd gone to bed. Ellie observed the strong breadth of his shoulders: his movements were precise, efficient, like the man. She liked what she saw.

When he sank onto the couch next to her, he picked

up his mug and sipped his coffee. "I never thought my brief vacation was going to turn out like this."

"I can imagine. No one plans for this."

He angled so he faced her, his arm slung along the back of the couch. "What if Harold hadn't acted quickly on those letters? What if Winnie's assistant hadn't alerted Harold about the threats? I know Winnie. She would have dismissed it. She wants to think the best of everyone. This could have been totally different, especially tonight."

"We can't think about the what-ifs. It's wasted energy."

"Which is precious right now. At least the house and grounds are secure. Winnie won't be happy seeing the deputies here tomorrow morning. She's worried the press will get hold of the fact that she's been threatened and make a big deal out of it. That could jeopardize the company going public. So far the people involved have remained quiet. That won't last long. I know Harold will have to notify certain people if nothing is solved by Christmas. Maybe that is the point of all of this."

"If the news does go public, that might actually help Winnie. Most of the people in this town love Winnie and will want to help her. Someone might come forward with information they don't realize could help the police find who is behind this."

"But rumors get started and get blown all out of portion, twisted around. It happened years ago when Granddad divorced his first wife. Not long after that he married Winnie. For a while people thought she had taken him away from his first wife, but that wasn't the case. It took years for her to correct those impressions. People had to get to know her to understand she would never come between a man and his wife. It hurt her enough that when I asked her about something I'd heard, she told me what happened."

"I know. I've seen similar cases on the national level, even ones I worked behind the scenes over in the Middle East. The truth often is twisted and blatantly altered."

His hand brushed against her shoulder. "So you see why she's trying to keep all this quiet. Already too many people know about it. I'm afraid she won't be able to. Which brings me to our next problem."

The feel of his fingertips touching her lightly sent her heart racing. His nearness robbed her of coherent thought for a few seconds until she forced herself to concentrate on what he was saying. "I'm afraid to ask what."

"You afraid? All I've seen is a woman cool under pressure."

"There's nothing wrong with being afraid. It keeps me on my toes."

"This Friday night is Glamour Sensations' Christmas Gala. I know my grandmother. Even with what happened tonight, she'll insist on going. She's supposed to introduce Christy as the face of Endless Youth and tease the press with what's going to come in February and the rest of next year."

"I was hoping she would decide not to go and let Harold take care of it."

"My grandmother has always been the spokesperson for the company. Any change will fuel speculation. Glamour Sensations will need the infusion of money by going public if we're to launch and produce the new line the way it should be. If she doesn't show up, some people will think she was badly injured in the wreck."

"Do you think that could be the reason for the wreck? Some competitor wanted to damage what the company is planning to do?"

"Could be." Colt scrubbed his hands down his face. "I wish I knew what was going on. It would make it easier to fight."

"Let me think about what we can do. I certainly don't want to drive to the gala."

"I doubt Winnie would, either, especially with the reminder of Granddad's accident. It took a long while to get over his death. Her heart attack didn't disrupt her life like his dying." He took her hands. "When this is all over with, Harold needs a raise for hiring you. Winnie trusts you. Maybe she'll listen to you about the gala."

"I'll do what I can. Meanwhile I have an idea about how to get her down this mountain without driving."

"How?"

"Use a helicopter. There's plenty of room for it to land in front of the house."

His eyes brightened and he squeezed her hands. "I like that. Winnie should agree, especially given the alternatives."

"I can talk to the sheriff tomorrow to see about who to hire in the area." Then she would have to vet the person in only a few days. But it could be done with her employer's assistance. "If there is no one in the area he'd recommend, we could check Denver or Colorado Springs."

Colt lifted one hand and cupped her face. "You're fantastic."

The gleam in his eyes nearly unraveled her resolve to keep her distance. When this was over with, she would move on to another job and he would return to his research vessel. She needed to remember that. But when his thumb caressed her cheek and he bent toward her, all determination fled in the wake of the soft look in his eyes, as though he saw her as a woman like no other. Special. To be cherished.

His lips whispered across hers before settling over them. He wound one arm around her and brought her close. Her stomach fluttered. Then he enveloped her in an embrace, plastering her against him as he deepened the kiss. Her world tilted. She could taste the coffee on his lips. She could smell his lime-scented aftershave. She could feel the hammering of his heartbeat. Heady sensations overwhelmed her, tempting her to disregard anything logical and totally give in to the feelings he stirred in her.

The realization frightened her more than facing a gunman. She wedged her hands up between them and pushed away from him. The second their mouths parted she missed the feel of his lips on hers. But common sense prevailed. She moved back, putting several feet between them.

"I know I shouldn't have kissed you," Colt said, "but I've wanted to since that first night when you attacked me in the hallway. I've never quite had that kind of homecoming before." One corner of his mouth quirked.

She rose, her legs shaky. "I need to check the house, then go to bed. There's still a lot to do tomorrow."

Before he said or did anything else, she spun on her heel and rushed toward the exit. She considered going outside for some fresh air but decided not to. Instead, she went through the house, making sure the place was secured. Heat blazed her cheeks. She'd wanted the kiss, even wished it could have continued. That would be dangerous, would complicate their situation. But she couldn't get the picture of them kissing out of her mind.

With his hands jammed into his pants' pockets, Colt stood in front of the fireplace in the den and stared at the yellow-orange flames. He'd blown it this evening. He'd had no intention of kissing Ellie, and yet he had. Against his better judgment. What kind of future could they have? He lived on a research vessel in the South Pacific. It wasn't as if he could even carry on a long-distance relationship with a woman. He'd learned from his past attempts at a relationship that he wanted a lasting one like his grandparents had had. Anything less than that wasn't acceptable.

Was that why he'd given up looking for someone? What kind of home could he give her? A berth on a ship? He didn't even call it home. This place on the side of a mountain would always be his home.

He heard her voice coming from the foyer. She said something to the deputy Colt couldn't make out. Peering at the mantel, decorated with garland and gold ribbon for the holidays, he glimpsed the Big Ben clock and the late hour. He needed to go to bed, but he waited until Ellie finished talking with the deputy. He gave her a chance to go upstairs before him because frankly he didn't know what to say to her.

He would have continued the kiss if she hadn't pulled away. His thoughts mocked his declaration to stay away from Ellie St. James, a woman who was fiercely independent and could take care of herself.

He'd always wanted someone who would need him. Someone to be an equal partner but rely on him, too.

After taking care of the fire, he moved toward the staircase. Coming home always made him reassess his life. Once he was back on the research vessel he would be fine—back on track with his career and goals.

A few days later Ellie waited for Colt and Winnie in the living room right before they were to leave for Glamour Sensations' Christmas Gala. Dressed in a long black silk gown with a slit up the right side and a gold lamé jacket that came down to the tops of her thighs, she felt uncomfortable. The only place she could put the smaller gun was in a beaded bag she would carry. After all, to the world she was Winnie's assistant, there to make things run smoothly for her employer.

A noise behind her drew her around to watch Colt enter wearing a black tuxedo. She'd only seen him in casual attire. The transformation to a sophisticated gentleman who moved in circles she didn't unless on the job only confirmed how different they were. Yes, he was working on a research ship, but he came from wealth and would inherit a great deal one day. She was from the wrong side of the tracks, a noncommissioned officer in the army for a time and now a woman whose job was to guard others.

He pulled on his cuffs then adjusted his tie. "It's been a while since I wore this. I was all thumbs tying this."

Ellie crossed to him and straightened the bow tie. "There. Perfect."

His smile reached deep into his eyes. "Sometimes I

think I need a keeper. I'm much more comfortable in a wet suit or bathing suit."

His remark tore down the barriers she was trying to erect between them. "Tell me about it. I don't like wearing heels. It's hard to run in them."

"Let's hope you don't have to do that tonight."

"I talked with the police chief and his men are in place as well as security from Glamour Sensations. They're checking everyone coming into the ballroom. Thankfully that doesn't seem as out of place as it would have years ago."

She should step away from him, but before she could, he took her hand and backed up a few feet to let his gaze roam leisurely down her length. When it returned to her face, he whistled.

"I like you in heels and that black dress."

She blushed—something she rarely did. "Neither conducive to my kind of work."

"I beg to differ. The bad guy will take one look at you and be so distracted he'll forget what mayhem he was plotting."

Ellie laughed. She would not let his smooth talking go to her head. Two different worlds, she reminded herself. She could see him running Glamour Sensations one day, especially when he told her yesterday he used to work at the company until he finished his college studies.

A loud whirring sound from the front lawn invaded the sudden quiet. She used that distraction to tug her hand free and go to the window. The helicopter landed as close to the house entrance as it could. The dogs barked at it even when the pilot turned it off. Doug

Miller called the two Rottweilers back. They obeyed instantly.

"Doug is great with the dogs."

"He was as excited as Granddad when he brought home Rocket and Gabe. Although I don't know if these new ones can ever replace the German shepherds in Doug's and Winnie's hearts. I was hoping we would get a ransom demand or someone would come forward."

"So did I with the nice reward Winnie offered." Ellie rotated from the window and caught sight of the older woman behind her grandson. "You look great, Winnie."

Dignified in a red crepe gown, she walked farther into the room. "I heard the helicopter. Probably our neighbors heard it, too. Never thought of using one to go to a ball."

"It's the modern-day version of Cinderella's coach." Colt offered his arm to his grandmother.

"In that case I fit the Fairy Godmother rather than Cinderella. That role needs to go to you, Ellie."

"Which leaves me as Prince Charming." He winked at Ellie.

Fairy tales were for dreamers, not her. Ellie skirted around the couple and headed for the foyer before she let the talk go to her head. "Well, our version of the story will be altered a tad bit. This Cinderella is taking her Fairy Godmother to the ball and sticking to her side. But I definitely like the idea of us leaving by midnight."

"I may have to go, but I don't have to stay that long."

Ellie stopped and hugged Winnie. "Those were the best words I've heard in a while."

"After dinner I'll make the announcements, stay for questions then leave. We should be home by eleven.

I know you aren't happy about me going to the gala, but I owe all the people who have worked years for my company. They'll benefit so much when we go public. A lot of employees will get stock in Glamour Sensations for their loyalty."

Ellie climbed into the helicopter last and searched the area. Where was the person after Winnie? Watching them here? Waiting for Winnie at the hotel or in the ballroom? She clutched her purse, feeling the outline of her gun. Was their security enough?

As employees and guests entered the ballroom, Winnie stood in a greeting line between Colt and Ellie, shaking everyone's hand and taking a moment to talk with each person attending the gala. At first Ellie wasn't thrilled with her client doing that, but it did give her a chance to assess each attendee.

When Christy moved in front of Winnie, her smile grew, and instead of shaking the woman's hand, Winnie enveloped her in a hug. "How was your trip to L.A. for the commercial?"

"A whirlwind. I never knew all that this position would involve. Peter picked me up from the airport late last night, and since I woke up this morning, I've been going nonstop. I'm going to cherish the time we sit down and have dinner tonight."

Winnie took Christy's fiancé's hand and shook it. "It's nice to see you again, Peter. Christy will be in town at least through Christmas. But afterward she'll be busy. I hope you can arrange some time to go with her on some of her trips. I never want to come between two people in love."

Dr. Tyler held Winnie's hand between his for a few

extra seconds. "When it's snowing here, I plan on being on that beach when Christy shoots her second commercial next month."

"Perfect solution. I love winter in Colorado, but that beach is beginning to sound good to these old bones."

"Tsk. Tsk. You don't look old at all. It must be your products you use. You should be your own spokesperson."

Colt leaned toward his grandmother. "I've been telling her that for years. She looks twenty years younger than she is. What woman her age wouldn't like to look as youthful?" He gave her a kiss on the cheek.

As Christy and Peter passed Ellie, she said, "You two are seated at the head table. There are place cards where you're to sit."

Peter nodded his head and escorted Christy toward the front of the room, which was decorated in silver and gold. Elegance came to mind as Ellie scanned the spacious area with lights glittering among the rich decor.

Thirty minutes and hundreds of guests later, Winnie greeted the last person. "Every year this event gets bigger."

"This year we have an extra dozen media people here, including our own film crew." Harold took Winnie's arm and started for the head table.

"I guess it's you and me." Colt fell into step next to Ellie, right behind Winnie. "Did you see anyone suspicious?"

"Actually several I'm going to keep an eye on. Did you realize Mary Ann Witlock's brother is here?" Ellie asked, recalling the photo she'd seen in connection with information on Mary Ann Witlock.

"Bob Witlock? He's worked at Glamour Sensations for years."

Winnie paused and turned back. "He's in marketing and agreed that Christy would be better than his younger sister for the position. Before I made the announcement, I talked to him. I wanted him to know first. For that matter, Jerry Olson's daughter works for Glamour Sensations and is here. She's married. I won't hold someone accountable for another's actions, even a close relative."

"Who is Jerry's daughter?" The reports from the sheriff hadn't said anything about that.

"They have been estranged for years, but it's Serena Pitman. She works in the research lab."

If she'd had the time she would have run her own investigation into each of the prime suspects with grudges against Winnie, but she couldn't do everything, which meant she had to rely on information garnered from reliable sources. Sometimes, though, those sources didn't give her everything she might need.

Winnie continued her trek toward the front of the room. Ellie racked her mind with all the guests who had passed before her, trying to remember who Serena Pitman was. Her visual memory was one of her assets. Face after face flitted through her thoughts until she latched onto the one that went with the name Serena Pitman. Red hair, almost orange, large brown eyes, freckles, petite. She searched the crowd of over two hundred until she found Serena at a table three away from the head one.

When Ellie sat down, her back to the stage, she faced the attendees with a clear view of Serena and her husband. The suspects the police had narrowed down as a viable possibility had not shown up—at least they hadn't come through the greeting line. The security and hotel staff were the only other people besides the guests, and she had made her rounds checking them when she had first arrived before the doors had been opened.

Sandwiched between Winnie and Colt, Ellie assessed each one sitting at the head table. Across from her sat Christy and Peter. Next to the couple was a reporter from the Associated Press and a fashion editor from one of the industry's leading magazines. A Denver newspaper editor of the lifestyle section and a Los Angeles TV show hostess took the last two seats. Harold took his place next to Winnie.

Halfway through the five-course dinner, Colt whispered into Ellie's ear, "Is something wrong with the food?"

"No, it's delicious. I'm not that hungry." Ellie pushed her medley of vegetables around on her plate while her gaze swept over the sea of people, most intent on eating their dinner.

"Everything is going all right."

She slanted a glance at Colt, said, "For the moment," then returned her attention to the crowd.

"Remember, you're Winnie's assistant."

"One who is keeping an eye on the event to make sure it's pulled off without a hitch."

The editor from the Denver newspaper looked right at Winnie and said, "I heard someone earlier talking about a wreck you were involved in. Is that why you arrived here in a helicopter?"

Winnie managed to smile as though nothing was wrong. "A minor collision. It didn't even set off the air bags. A car left stranded in the middle of the highway. Tell me how the drive from Denver was. It was snowing when we arrived."

The man chuckled. "This is Colorado in December. We better have snow or our resort areas will be hurting."

"You're so right, Marvin. Being stranded here isn't too much of a burden. Mountains. Snow. A pair of skis. What more could you ask for?" Winnie cut into her steak.

Harold winked at Winnie. "A warm fire."

"A hot tub," the TV hostess added.

"A snowmobile since I'm probably one of the rare Coloradoans who doesn't ski," Marvin tossed back with the others at the table throwing in other suggestions.

When the conversation started to die down again, Colt asked the Denver editor, "Do you think the Broncos will go all the way to the Super Bowl?"

Ellie bent toward him. "Good question. Football ought to keep the conversation away from the wreck," she whispered.

The mischievous grin on his face riveted her attention for a few long seconds before she averted her gaze and watched the people at the table.

By dessert the conversation morphed from sports to the latest bestsellers. As Peter expounded on a thriller he'd finished, Ellie half listened as she watched the various hotel staff place the peppermint cheesecake before the attendees around the room.

Four tables away Ellie spied a woman who looked vaguely familiar. Was she in one of the photos she'd seen over the past few days? She didn't want to leave Winnie to check the woman out, but she could send a security officer standing not far from her.

"Excuse me, Winnie," Ellie leaned closer to her and whispered, "I'll be right back. I need to talk to your head of security."

Winnie peered over her shoulder at the man at the bottom of the steps that led to the presentation platform. "A problem?"

"I want him to check someone for me. Probably nothing. Be right back."

"We'll be starting our program in ten minutes. The waiters are serving the dessert and coffee."

The head of Glamour Sensations' security met Ellie halfway. "Is there a problem?"

"The dark-haired woman on the serving staff at the table two from the left wall. She looks familiar. Check her out. See who she is and if she has the proper identification."

He nodded and started in that direction. The woman finished taking a dessert plate from a man, put it on a tray and headed quickly for one of the doors the servers were using. The security chief increased his pace. Ellie slowly walked back toward Winnie, scanning the rest of the room before returning to the woman. The dark-headed lady set the tray on a small table near the door then rushed toward the exit, shoving her way through a couple of waiters. The security chief and a police officer Ellie recognized gave chase.

A couple of guests rose, watching the incident unfold.

Ellie leaned down to Winnie. "You should think about leaving. I think the lady I spotted is who we're after."

Winnie turned her head so no one at the table could see her expression or hear her whisper, "I saw. If she's gone, she can't do anything. I'll start now and run through the program then we can leave."

"Did you recognize her?"

"I couldn't tell from this distance. My eyesight isn't as good as it once was."

"Okay. Then let's get this over with. I'll be right behind you."

Winnie was introducing Christy when the head of security came back into the ballroom. He shook his head and took up his post at the foot of the steps to the platform. Ellie noted that all the doors were covered so the woman couldn't return to disrupt the presentation.

Christy came up to stand by Winnie, their arms linked around each other as they faced the audience clapping and cheering. Behind the pair, the screen showed some of the Endless Youth products being released in February. At the height of the event the confetti guns shot off their loads to fill the room with red-and-green streamers. A festival atmosphere took hold of the crowd.

Through the celebration Ellie hovered near Winnie, fixing her full attention on the crowd. Not long and they would all be back in the helicopter returning to the estate. She would be glad when that happened.

Some colorful streamers landed near Ellie, followed by a glass vial that shattered when it hit the platform. A stinking smell wafted up to her. Coughing, Ellie immediately rushed to Winnie's side as more vials mixed in with the streamers smashed against the floor throughout the ballroom, saturating the place with an awful, nauseating stench. People panicked and fled for the doors. The gaiety evolved into pandemonium almost instantly.

Chapter Eight

❦

Over the screams and shouts, Colt hopped up onto the platform and reached Winnie's side just as Ellie tugged her toward the steps.

"We need to get out of here," she told them. "This would be a great time to strike in the midst of this chaos."

Colt wound his arm about his grandmother. Winnie faltered at the bottom of the stairs. He caught her at the same time Ellie turned and grabbed her, too. Their gazes met.

"We can get out this way." Ellie nodded toward a door behind the staging area. "It leads to an exit. All we have to do is get to the helicopter."

"But the announcement and celebration are ruined," Winnie mumbled, glancing back once before being ushered through the door and down a long hall.

His grandmother looked as if she were shell-shocked. He couldn't blame her. He, too, had hoped they could make it through the evening without incident.

"Once I get you home, I'll check to see what happened. Knowing the police chief and the sheriff, they are already on it." Ellie removed her gun from her purse.

The sight of the lethal weapon widened his grandmother's eyes at the same time the color drained from her face. He tightened his arms about her. She was a remarkable woman, but anyone could hit a wall and fall apart. He was afraid she was there.

At the door that led outside, Ellie held up her hand to stop them. "Wait. Let me check the area out." She searched the long hallway. "Be right back."

He looked over his shoulder at a few people rushing down the corridor toward the exit.

A couple of seconds later, Ellie returned. "Let's go. The helicopter is around the corner. People are pouring out of the hotel, but it's clear on this side."

"Not for long." Colt tossed his head toward the people coming down the hall.

With her hand on Winnie's right arm, Ellie led the way. She'd seen the pilot in the chopper and his instructions earlier were to start the engine the second he saw them approaching. Colt flanked his grandmother on the left and slightly behind her as though shielding her from anyone behind. Ellie did this as a job. He did it because he loved his grandmother enough to protect her with his life.

As she neared the front lawn of the hotel, Ellie slowed, panning the terrain for any sign of someone lying in wait. The woman who could have been behind what occurred in the ballroom might have planned the chaos so she could get to Winnie easier outside in the open. Ellie wouldn't allow that to happen.

Peering around the corner of the hotel, Ellie scoped

out the crowd emerging from the front entrance, many
with no coats on, who stood hugging themselves. The
biting cold penetrated the thin layer of her lamé jacket.
The people behind them in the hallway burst from the
exit, their loud voices charged with fear and speculation.

"Let's go." Ellie started across the snow-covered
ground.

A man hurried toward the helicopter as the blades
began to whir.

Her gaze glued to the exchange between the pilot
and the stranger, Ellie shortened her strides, waiting
to see what transpired. When the man ran back toward
the crowd, she increased her speed again. The sound
of sirens blasted the chilly air.

At the chopper Colt assisted Winnie up into it
while Ellie kept watch on the surroundings. After
Colt followed his grandmother into the helicopter, Ellie
climbed in and the pilot lifted off.

Over the whirring noise, Ellie spoke into her head-
set. "Who was that man?"

"Hotel security letting me know what happened in
the ballroom. I figured you'd be outside soon." The
pilot made a wide arc and headed toward the estate.

Ten minutes more. Ellie didn't let down her guard.
Sitting forward, she scanned the terrain below. A blanket of white carpeted the ground, lighting the landscape. A helicopter ride she'd taken during one of her
missions in the army flashed into her mind. Insurgents
on the ground had fired on it, wounding one person
in the backseat.

"Winnie, move as far over toward Colt as you can."

As her client did, Colt wrapped his arms around
her. Again trying to shield her as much as he could.

Nine minutes later the pilot brought the chopper down as close to the main house as possible. Ellie scrambled out and hurried to Winnie's side to help her. The second she placed her feet on the drive, Ellie shepherded the woman toward her front door while the dogs barked at the helicopter.

Colt gave a command, and they quieted. He came up behind Ellie as they mounted the steps to the deck. Doug threw open the front door, and Ellie whisked Winnie inside.

"The sheriff called and said he's on his way," the caretaker said. "He briefly told me what happened so I came over. I figured you'd be back soon."

Through the fear that marked Winnie's face, she smiled. "I can always count on you and Linda."

"She's in the kitchen preparing some coffee. She'll bring it into the den. I'll let the sheriff in when he's at the gate."

On the way to the den, Ellie paused in the doorway of the small control room. "Have you seen anything unusual?" she asked the ex-police chief who monitored the security feed.

"Nope. Quiet."

Ellie caught up with Winnie and Colt as they entered the den. While Ellie walked from window to window, drawing the drapes, her client collapsed onto the couch, sagging back, her eyes sliding closed.

"Winnie, are you all right?" Colt sat beside her.

"No. This has got to stop. Everything was ruined tonight. Poor Christy. This was her big debut, and some mean, vicious person destroyed her moment."

Ellie positioned herself in front of the fireplace close to Winnie but facing the only entrance into the room.

She still clutched her gun as though it were welded to her hand.

"I want to thank you for getting me out of there, Ellie. I'd still be standing on stage, stunned by the lengths a person will go to hurt another."

Ellie moved to the couch and sat on the other side of Winnie. Not until she took a seat did she relax her tightly bunched muscles. "I was only doing my job."

"You've done much more than that for me. The Lord sent you to me at this time." Winnie patted Colt's leg. "And you were there for me, too. I have truly been blessed having two people like you seeing to my welfare." Tears shone in her eyes.

Ellie thanked her. "I got a look at someone I suspect may be the one causing the trouble. Hopefully this might be over before Christmas. I'm still not sure from where I know that woman at the gala tonight, but when security approached, she ran. That's not the action of an innocent person." The sound of footsteps returned Ellie's attention to the door, her hand tensing again on her gun.

Linda entered with a tray of four mugs and a coffee-pot. "Doug let the sheriff in the front gate. He should be here any minute. After he arrives, we'll leave unless you need me for anything, Winnie."

She shook her head, a few strands escaping her usual neatly styled silver-gray bun at her nape. "You two are up late as it is. I'm glad you didn't go to the Christmas Gala. Not after what happened."

"Doug and I felt we needed to stay here and make sure nothing went wrong from this end. He patrolled the grounds with the dogs. You know how he is when it starts snowing. He'd rather be outside than in the house." Linda placed the tray on the table in front of the couch. "Do you want me to pour the coffee?"

Colt scooted forward. "I'll do it. Tell Doug thanks."

Doug appeared in the entrance with the sheriff. Linda crossed to them and left with her husband.

Sheriff Quinn grabbed the mug Colt held out to him. "It's getting cold outside."

Winnie didn't hesitate to ask her questions. "Bill, what happened? Is everyone all right? I'm assuming since I don't feel sick that what was released into the air wasn't poisonous."

"You're right, Winnie. Thankfully they were only stink bombs. The police are still trying to determine how many. There were five confetti guns, and it looks like each one shot at least one vial out of it. Maybe more."

"Any injuries with the stampede for the doors?" Ellie cradled her hot mug between her palms. She'd been caught up in a riot once and knew how easily people could get hurt when everyone was trying to flee a place.

"Right before I arrived, the police chief called to let me know he has access to the security feed at the hotel. He said so far it looks like ten injuries, mostly minor stuff. One woman is being sent to the hospital, but I don't think she will stay long."

"It could have been a lot worse." The firm line of Colt's jaw and the extra-precise way he set his mug down attested to his tightly controlled anger.

The sheriff looked at Ellie. "The police chief wants you to look at the tapes of the event. He understands from Glamour Sensations' security head that you think you recognized someone who fled out the staff door. We need to ID that person."

"Sure. I'll do anything I can, but I don't want to leave the estate. Not when Winnie is in danger."

"I thought you would say that. We'll have access to the tapes by computer. It'll be a good time for you all to look over the footage and see if anyone is out of place."

"Anything, even watching hours of tape," Colt said. "I want this to end. My grandmother has been through enough. All I can say is that I'm glad her last product development has been concluded."

"Hon, I'm fine, especially with you and Ellie here." She patted Colt's hand. "Dear, get my laptop from my lab downstairs, will you please?"

Right before he disappeared down the hall, Colt threw a look at Ellie while Winnie and the sheriff talked. In that moment Ellie saw how worried Colt was for his grandmother. Again, she found herself wishing she had that bond with someone.

Sheriff Quinn interrupted her thoughts. "The police are rounding up the staff to question them. If we could have a picture to show them, that will help."

Ellie closed her eyes and imagined the woman from across the ballroom. "She's about five feet six inches with long dark hair. I couldn't tell her eye color specifically, but I think a light color. She was dressed as a server—even had a name tag on like the others."

"I'll let the police chief know that. See if anyone is missing a uniform. If not, it could be one of their staff even if the person wasn't supposed to work that event. Did you see who Ellie is talking about?" he asked Winnie.

"No, sorry. I was trying to keep the conversation at

the table going in the right direction. As I suspected, a few rumors have been flying around. The AP reporter wanted confirmation the position of the stolen car indicated it was probably left deliberately, possibly to block our way home."

"Sheriff, did you find any fingerprints on the stalled car the other night?" Ellie leaned over, refilled her mug and poured some more coffee into Winnie's.

"The report came in. No fingerprints the owner couldn't verify weren't someone's who has been in the car lately. So no help there."

Colt came back into the den and handed the laptop to the sheriff to pull up the site with the security footage on it. When he had it, he turned it around and set it on the coffee table, then walked behind the couch to watch.

Sheriff Quinn pointed to a link. "Click on that."

Colt did and a scene from inside the ballroom popped up on the screen. They watched that angle, but Ellie couldn't find the woman or anyone else that appeared suspicious. Colt went to the next link and brought it up.

Ten minutes into it, Winnie yawned. "I'm sorry. I don't know if I can stay awake."

As her own adrenaline rush had subsided, obviously Winnie's had, too. Ellie was used to the ups and downs, but her client wasn't. "Sheriff, can she review it tomorrow morning? I may want to see them again, too."

"Sure." He turned to Winnie. "I can escort you to your room."

Colt paused the tape while Winnie struggled to her feet, sighed and stepped around her grandson. "No, you should stay. At least this person hasn't come into my home and threatened me. If I couldn't walk freely in my own house, I don't know what I would do."

When Winnie left, Ellie murmured, "I didn't have the heart to tell her there is no place one hundred percent secure."

Colt scooted over so the sheriff could sit on the couch. "You don't think it's safe here?"

"Basically it is, as much as it can be. Or I wouldn't let Winnie walk around by herself without me right there. But in any situation I've learned to be wary."

"On the research vessel we've had two run-ins with pirates in different locales, which keeps us on the watch wherever we go, but nothing like this." Colt clicked to continue viewing the security footage.

"It's sad," Ellie said, focusing again on the tape. "These kinds of things are what keep me in business."

"Pause it. That's her!" About an hour into the footage Ellie bolted forward, pointing at a dark-haired woman on the screen who was carrying a tray with coffeepots and a water pitcher. "The same height, hairstyle. Can we zoom in on her?"

Colt clicked several keys and moved in closer.

"That's who ran out of the ballroom when the security head made his way toward her. We need a still of that, and see if someone can make the photo clearer." Her image teased Ellie's thoughts.

"I'll see what I can do and bring it back to you tomorrow." Sheriff Quinn wrote down how far into that tape they were while Colt started the footage again.

On closer examination, Ellie saw surprise on the woman's face when she spied the two security men coming toward her. She glanced toward a table near the head table, then hurried toward the exit. "Back up. Who was she looking at?"

Colt found the spot and zeroed in on the table next to the one where they'd been sitting. "Take your pick who she's staring at."

"Maybe no one." The sheriff rose.

"Or maybe one of the people whose back isn't to the woman," Ellie said. "There are four men and three women. Is there any way we can find out who was sitting at the table? There were only a few tables reserved and that wasn't one of them."

"I'll see what I can find out tomorrow morning when I meet with the police chief. In the meantime, I'm leaving two deputies with you again. One is in the foyer. The other is driving up the mountain as we speak. Rod will let him in. We'll have a long day tomorrow so get some sleep. That's what I'm gonna do. I'm determined we'll find out who it is. We have a picture now. That's better than before."

"Sheriff, I love your optimism. I hope you're right. I could be home in time for Christmas." She walked with him out to the foyer where Rod stood.

"Where is home?"

"Dallas, when I'm between jobs."

"Family there?"

"No. It'll just be me, but my boss hosts Christmas dinner for anyone who's in town." Which was the closest she came to having a family during the holidays.

"I have a son coming in for Christmas with his three children. I can't wait to see them. It's been six months, and they grow up fast."

When Ellie returned to the den, Colt gathered up the closed laptop and bridged the distance between them.

"I heard what you said about Christmas. Do you think this will be over by then? That we'll have a peaceful Christmas?"

"I'm hoping. Winnie has been great dealing with what's been happening to her, but it's taking its toll."

"I'm glad she's finished in the lab. She doesn't have to worry about that at least."

"But that will mean she'll focus totally on what's happening. That may be worse."

"Then we'll have to create things for her to do. We haven't decorated the house like it has been in the past. Tons of decorations are still in storage in the basement."

Ellie couldn't remember decorating for Christmas in years, and even as a child, they often didn't have a tree. Her mother didn't care about the holiday, but Toby and she had tried to make their apartment festive. Then Toby had died and Ellie hadn't cared, either. "Sure, if it will help take Winnie's mind off the threats."

"Christmas is her favorite time of year. She's been so busy she's not had the time to do what she usually does. This will be perfect." Colt strode to the staircase with Ellie.

As she mounted the steps to the second floor, she wondered what a family Christmas was really like. At the top of the stairs, she looked around and started laughing. "I can't believe I walked all the way up here when I haven't checked the house yet."

"It must have been my charm and wit that rattled you."

"I hate to burst your bubble, Colt, but it's exhaustion." The sound of his chuckles sent a wave of warmth down her length.

"I'll put this laptop in my room and come with you. I wouldn't want you to fall asleep while making your rounds." He turned toward the right.

Ellie clasped his arm. "I'll be okay. I may be exhausted, but that doesn't mean I'll fall asleep."

He swung around. His gaze intent, he grazed his fingertips down her jaw. "What keeps you from sleeping?"

She shrugged one shoulder. "The usual. Worries."

"Winnie would tell you to turn them over to the Lord."

"What would you say?"

"Winnie is right, but I've always had trouble doing that. I still want to control things."

"Me, too. I know worrying is a waste of time and energy, but I've been doing it for so long, trying to control all aspects of my life, that I don't know how to give it totally to God."

"Practice."

"Have you ever practiced and practiced and never accomplished what you set out to do?"

"Not usually." He snapped his finger. "Except ballroom dancing. I have two left feet."

"I'll remember that if you ever ask me to dance." She took a step back. "Seriously, you don't need to come with me. At least one of us should get some sleep. I'm not going to bed until the second deputy arrives, anyway."

"I can keep you company if you like."

She would, but as she stared into his face, a face she'd looked forward to seeing each morning, she knew the danger in him staying up with her. Each day she was around him she liked him more and more. The way he loved his grandmother, handled a crisis—the way he kissed. "No, I'm not going to be long." She backed up until her heel encountered the edge of the staircase.

Like the first night they met, he moved with a quickness that surprised her, hooked his arm around her and tugged her to him. He planted a kiss on her lips that melted her resolve not to be around him. Then he parted, pivoted and started down the hallway. "Good night, Ellie. I'll see you in the morning."

Why did you do that? She wanted to shout the question at him but clamped together her tingling lips that still felt the remnants of his kiss. Coupled with her stomach fluttering and her heart beating rapidly, the sensations from that brief joining left their brand on her. She hurried down the stairs, sure the only reason she was attracted to the man was because it was that time of year when she yearned for a family, for a connectedness she'd never had except with her twin brother, Toby.

As Ellie went from room to room, making sure the house was secured, she forced her mind back to the case. She visualized the picture of the woman on the computer in her mind. She'd seen her before. By the time she reached her bedroom, she strode to the photos the sheriff had shown them of the possible suspects. She flipped through the pictures until she came upon Mary Ann Witlock. Covering up the woman's long blond hair, Ellie visualized her in a dark brown wig. And that's when she knew. Mary Ann was the bogus server at the gala tonight.

"Hot chocolate for everyone," Linda announced the next afternoon as she brought in a tray with the drinks and a plate of frosted Christmas sugar cookies.

For the past couple hours Ellie had been decorating a tree with Colt and Winnie and Harold and Christy. Now she climbed the ladder to place the star at the very top. When she descended to the floor, she viewed the ten-foot tree Doug and Colt had cut down that morning. The scent of pine hung in the air.

"This is turning into a party. I love it." Winnie backed away from the tree in the living room centered in front of the large picture window. "I might not be able to leave, but I appreciate you all coming here to help cheer up an old lady. This is just what I needed."

Colt slung his arm over his grandmother's shoulders. "Old? Did I hear you admit you're old? Who has stolen my grandmother?"

Winnie punched him playfully in the stomach. "I am seventy-three."

Colt arched a eyebrow. "So?"

"Okay, I admit I've let the threats get to me. But not anymore. The sheriff is closing in on the woman who, it looks like, has been behind everything."

"I can't believe Mary Ann is behind this. If I'd known what would happen, I'd have turned down the opportunity to be the spokesperson for Endless Youth." Christy took a mug of hot chocolate and a cookie off the tray. "I didn't realize she needed the money."

Winnie frowned. "Neither did I. If she had come to me, I would have loaned her the money."

"We don't know for sure it's her behind the threats," Harold said as he planted himself in a chair. "All we know is she was disguised last night as a server and then ran from security when approached."

"That's the action of a guilty person. And why was

she wearing a dark wig if she was innocent?" Linda asked as she left the room.

"What do you think, Ellie?" Winnie removed some tinsel from a box and passed it out.

"She needs money and lost a chance at making a lot. She is missing right now. The police went to her house and haven't been able to locate her. Maybe the search warrant will produce something more concrete." Ellie carefully draped a few strands of tinsel on a branch. Probably the person Mary Ann was looking at before fleeing the ballroom was her brother, sitting at the table next to them. When Winnie had identified him this morning on the video, that was at least one mystery taken care of. Sheriff Quinn was investigating Bob Witlock to make sure he had no involvement, but he didn't think the brother did because he and Mary Ann had been estranged for several years.

Colt came up beside Ellie. "At the rate you're going, Ellie, it'll be midnight before we finish decorating the tree. This is the way we do it." He took some of the tinsel and tossed it onto several limbs. "See? Effective and fast."

"But it's not neat."

"That's okay. It's fun, and our tree isn't what you would find in a magazine. It's full of our past—not fancy store-bought ornaments." Colt gave her some more tinsel. "Give it a try."

Ellie did and laughed when half ended up on the carpet. "There must be an art to it, and clearly I don't have the toss method down."

Colt stepped behind her and took her arm. "It's called losing a little control and just letting go at the right time," he whispered into her ear.

She was glad no one else could hear him; his words caused her pulse rate to accelerate.

As he brought her arm back then swung it forward, he murmured, "Let go."

In the second she did and the silvery strands landed on various branches haphazardly, but none on the floor, something inside her did let go. It had nothing to do with the activity. It had to do with the man so close to her his scent engulfed her. The brush of his breath against her neck warmed her.

Quickly she stepped away. "I have no idea when I'll use this new skill again, but thanks for showing me how to do it properly." She tore her gaze from his and swept it around the room, taking in the faces of the people, all of whom were watching them.

The chime of the doorbell cut through the silence that fell over the room. Ellie thrust the remaining tinsel into Colt's hands and hurried to answer the door. She'd let him get to her. Let him give her a little glimpse at what she was missing. And she became all soft.

She opened the door to allow the sheriff inside. "I hope you have good news for us. What did you find at Mary Ann's house?"

He faced her with a grim expression. "We found a lot of evidence that points to her being the person threatening Winnie—one letter Winnie received was on Mary Ann's computer, along with pictures of Winnie. There was also a suicide note from Mary Ann. When I turned the computer on, that was the first thing that came up."

"Suicide? You found her body?"

"No. No one has seen her since last night. The Bakersville police and my office are still searching for her.

There were also a couple of large dog crates in her garage and mud-caked boots, size nine men's shoes, although that isn't the size she wears. Also, there was a stack of unpaid bills on her kitchen table. She received a foreclosure notice a week ago."

"Winnie won't be safe until Mary Ann is found. I hope alive. But what about the dogs? If she took them, where are they?" Out of the corner of her eye she glimpsed Colt coming across the foyer toward them.

"Good question," the sheriff replied. "She could have gotten rid of them or sold them perhaps to someone not from around here. She needed money, so that would be my guess."

"So there's no telling where the dogs are, then?"

Colt stopped next to her. "Winnie was concerned something has happened."

"It has. It looks like Mary Ann is the person threatening Winnie, but she's disappeared." Ellie tried not to look at Colt directly in the eyes. Something had changed between them earlier in the living room, and she didn't know what to think or what to do about it.

"Which means Winnie is still in danger."

"Afraid so," the sheriff said, removing his hat and sliding the brim through his hands.

Winnie paused in the doorway into the living room. "Bill, why are you all standing out here? Come join us. Harold is here and Christy. Peter is coming after his last patient. We're getting ready for Christmas finally."

"I hate to intrude—"

"We've got hot chocolate and Christmas cookies."

"Well, in that case, I'll stay for a little while." The sheriff made his way toward Winnie, grinning from ear to ear. "Linda makes great cookies. I bought a box of them at the cookie sale at church."

"Why, Bill Quinn, I could have made them."

Both of his eyebrows rose. "Did you?"

Winnie giggled. "No, you're safe from my cooking. Why do you think I hired Linda in the first place?"

"Your husband insisted."

As the two entered the living room and their voices faded, Ellie hung back with Colt. "I wanted to let you know what the sheriff told me when they went to Mary Ann's house." After she explained what they found, she added, "There was a suicide note on her computer."

"But she wasn't there?"

"No. The woman isn't in her right mind. She's desperate. What she did last night is an act of a person falling apart. An act of revenge."

"And the dogs? Any idea where they are?"

"They're valuable dogs. No telling where they are now. She most likely sold them since she was in debt for thousands of dollars. The police chief is checking with the bank in Bakersville where Mary Ann had an account to see if she was paid a large amount of money lately."

"If that's the case, couldn't she take care of some of her debt, if not all?"

"I did some research on some of the suspects, and I remember she had extensive dental work six months ago. I saw a before and after picture. Her teeth and smile were perfect afterward. It made a big difference in her appearance. I wonder if she did that hoping she would get the spokesperson position for Endless Youth."

"If that were the case, I can see why Winnie wouldn't

hire her. She wouldn't want anyone who'd recently had work done to her face, even dental. The press could take it and focus on that rather than on Endless Youth. I've seen it before. Where the intended message is side-tracked by something that really had nothing to do with it."

"She had a huge dental bill and her waitress salary probably barely covered her necessities."

Winnie appeared in the living room entrance and peered at Colt. "We have guests. You two can talk after they leave. I imagine you're speculating about Mary Ann, and I would like to hear what you have to say. She needs our prayers, the troubled girl."

"Sorry, Winnie," Colt replied. "We didn't want to say anything in front of the others."

"It's only Christy and Harold. They're family. Oh, that reminds me. I've got to let the person monitoring the gate know to let Peter in when he arrives. I thought we'd have an early dinner before sending our guests down the mountain. And the sheriff is staying, too. It seems his office can run without him occasionally." Winnie hurried toward the monitoring room.

"Are you sure she is really seventy-three?" Ellie asked as she headed for the living room.

"That's what her birth certificate said. I saw it once before she whisked it away from me. That was when she wouldn't tell anyone her age."

"She should be the spokesperson for Endless Youth."

"You know Harold mentioned that to her, and she laughed in his face. I could never see my grandmother purposely putting herself in the public eye."

"Because of what happened when she married your grandfather?"

"Partly, and the fact that Winnie is really shy with most people."

"Shy? I don't see much evidence of that. Look at last night with the media before everything fell apart."

"She's learned to put on a front and can do it for short periods of time, but, believe me, the evening drained her emotionally beyond the threats and what happened with the stink bombs."

"No wonder I like her so much. She and I have a lot in common."

"I know. That's why I like you."

His words took flight in her heart until she shot them down. They didn't mean anything. Really.

Soft strains of Christmas music played in the background. The fire blazed in the hearth in the living room while the hundreds of lights strung around the tree and a lone lamp gave off the only illumination. Colt settled on the couch next to Winnie, with Harold at the other end. Ellie sat directly across from him. Cuddling as two people in love did, Christy and Peter shared an oversize lounge chair. Sheriff Quinn had left hours ago.

Cozy. Warm. Almost as if there had been no threats, no attempts on Winnie. Almost. But the thought had edged its way into Colt's mind throughout the day, souring a day meant to forget the incident at the gala and to focus on Christmas. Then he would look at Ellie and the outside world wouldn't mean anything.

Doug came into the room. "Before Linda and I leave, I thought I'd let you know that it has started snowing again. We're not supposed to get too much."

"Thank Linda for another wonderful dinner." Winnie set her coffee on a coaster on the table.

"We enjoyed sharing the celebration tonight with all of you, but I want to check on the dogs," Doug said. "We both hope they find this Mary Ann Witlock soon so this is all over with." After saying his goodbyes the caretaker left.

Colt had always felt his grandmother was in good hands with the couple who had become more a part of the family with each year. "I wish the sheriff would call us with some good news. Maybe Mary Ann fled the area."

"Sheriff Quinn said they checked the airports in the vicinity, but Mary Ann's car is gone so she might have. They have a multistate search out for the car." Ellie leaned back and crossed her long legs.

The movement drew Colt's attention, his eyes slowly making their way up her body to her face. The soft glow of the lighting in the room emphasized her beauty. What was it about Ellie that intrigued him? That she could take care of herself in just about any situation? He knew strong women, even worked with several on the research vessel, but other than respecting their intelligence, there was no draw for him—not like with Ellie.

"We all know there are plenty of places to hide in the mountains around here. Back roads to use." Peter shifted then circled his arm around Christy.

"Yeah, but it's winter and snow will make that more difficult," Harold said.

Peter came right back with, "We haven't had as much as usual so far this year. She may be long gone by now."

"True. And when you're desperate, you sometimes do things you wouldn't normally do." Ellie's gaze fixed on Colt as though there was a secret message behind her words.

"I know she was at Glamour Sensations a lot for the Endless Youth position, but she was always so quiet and reserved. I didn't really know her at all." Christy peered over her shoulder at Peter. "You did her dental work. Didn't you see her for a follow-up a few weeks ago? What do you think her frame of mind was like?"

"She was agitated. She asked me to extend the time she could pay off her bill. I did, but she still was upset when she left. If I'd thought she would commit suicide, I'd have said something, but..."

"Peter, we can't always tell what someone is thinking or is going to do. I know we all would have said something if we had known. I'm still praying the police will find her alive and hiding." Winnie's hand quivered as she brought her cup to her lips.

Colt slid his arm around his grandmother. "You'd be the first one to help her if you'd known. If she's found, I wouldn't be surprised if you pay for a good lawyer to defend her. That's one of the things I love about you."

A frown puckered Christy's forehead. "Can we change the subject? I don't want to spend any more time on this horrid situation. I feel bad enough about Mary Ann."

Winnie patted Colt's thigh, then smiled at Christy. "You're right. Let's talk about our plans for Christmas. Only three days away."

Ellie's cell rang. She looked at the number then rose, leaving the room. Colt heard her say Sheriff Quinn's name and followed her into the foyer.

As he neared her, she ended the call and lifted her gaze to his. "They found Mary Ann's body."

Chapter Nine

Ellie slipped her cell into her pocket. "Her body was found at the bottom of a cliff by cross-country skiers right before dark. Her car, parked near the top of the cliff, was found by a deputy a little later."

"Suicide?"

"That's what they think, but Sheriff Quinn will know more tomorrow after the medical examiner looks at the body and they have more time to thoroughly search the scene below and above. The preliminary processing supports a suicide, especially in light of her note and state of mind."

Colt blew out a long breath. "Then it's over with."

"It's looking that way."

"Let's go tell everyone." Colt held his hand out to her.

She took it, realizing by tomorrow or the following day she could be on her way back to Dallas. Just in time to spend a lonely Christmas at home. At least she'd have a few hours with Kyra and her husband on the twenty-fifth.

When they reentered the living room Colt sat next

to Winnie. "Ellie heard from the sheriff. They found Mary Ann's body at the bottom of a cliff. They think it was suicide but they'll make a ruling probably tomorrow."

"It's over. That's great." Standing at the fireplace, Harold dropped another log on the blaze. "The best news I've heard in a while."

"Harold! How can you say that? A young woman killed herself." Tears glittered on Winnie's bottom eyelashes.

The CFO flushed, redder than the flames behind him. "You're right. I was only thinking about you and your situation."

"She did try to kill you." Peter sat forward. "There are people last night who were hurt because of her rage. *You* could have been hurt in the stampede to leave. Or when you were outside. Surely the stink bombs were a ruse to get you outside."

Winnie pushed to her feet. "I don't care. I can't celebrate a woman's death."

Colt stood up beside her. "Grandma, I don't think Harold really meant that. He was just showing how happy he is that it's all over."

Harold crossed to Winnie and took her into his arms. "I'm sorry. I never meant to cause you any pain. Please forgive me."

She raised her chin and looked at him. "I know you didn't. I only wish I'd known what was going on in Mary Ann's head. I could have helped her."

Could she forgive like that? Ellie wondered. She still couldn't forgive her mother for her neglect as she and Toby grew up. If Toby hadn't had Ellie, he would have had no one to look out for him. He'd needed extra care, and their mother couldn't be bothered.

"I applaud you for wanting to help the woman, but she did try to hurt you." Peter shook his head slowly. "Aren't you just a little bit angry at her? That's a natural human response to someone who does something to you."

Winnie withdrew from Harold's embrace. "Did I ever feel anger toward the person behind the threats? Of course, I did. I'm no saint. But if I let that anger take over, I'm the one who is really hurt by it."

Peter snorted. "You're really hurt if they succeed in their plan. I'm sorry. I think people should be held accountable for what they do."

"I have to agree with Peter," Colt said. "Mary Ann had choices. I can't make excuses for what she put you through. I certainly won't celebrate her death, but I'm relieved it's over with. We can all have a normal Christmas." He looked from Winnie to Ellie.

Silence hovered over the group as his gaze drew her to him. Ellie gripped the back of a chair and remained still, finally averting her eyes.

"We'd better head home. I don't want to get caught out in a snowstorm." Peter rose right after Christy and put his arm around his fiancée. "Our time is limited since Christy found out she needed to go back to L.A. for a couple of days."

"Since when?" Winnie asked.

"Since last night." Harold kneaded her shoulder. "I forgot to tell you. I meant to first thing this afternoon, then we started decorating the tree. She is going to appear on *Starr's Take*. The talk show hostess felt bad about what happened last night and wants to highlight

Christy for a show at the first of the year. That is, if Christy will fly to L.A. tomorrow and tape the segment first thing the next day."

"I'll be back midafternoon Christmas Eve. I don't want to miss my first one with Peter." Christy clasped his hand. "We had plans, but he's been so good about it."

"Harold, I can't believe you didn't tell me the second you walked into my house," Winnie said.

"If you remember correctly, you dragged me over to the box of lights and told me to untangle them."

Winnie's eyes twinkled. "Oh, that's right. In that case, I know what it's like to be distracted. I've had my share of distractions these past few weeks. No more. I'm diving into Christmas. I might even persuade my grandson to go up to my cabin like we used to."

"Not unless the sheriff approves, Winnie." Harold gave her a kiss on the cheek and prepared to leave.

Winnie walked with Harold, Peter and Christy to the foyer while Colt stayed back, snatching Ellie as she started to follow his grandmother. "I can't believe this may be over."

"If it is tomorrow, when are you going back to your research vessel?"

"I'm definitely staying through Christmas now. I want to make sure Winnie is all right. She can beat herself up when she finds out someone is hurting and she didn't do anything about it. I don't want her to start blaming herself for not anticipating Mary Ann's reaction to not getting the job with Endless Youth."

"We can't control other people's reactions, only our own."

Winnie strode into the room. "You two don't have

to worry about me. I'm going to be fine, especially if I can spend some time at the cabin like we used to every Christmas."

"So you really are thinking about going up the mountain?" Colt asked.

"Yes, I know we spent the day decorating the house, but all of this has made me yearn for those simpler days. Thomas and I loved to escape life by going to the cabin."

"My fondest memories are of our Christmases spent there."

"So you'll agree to go?" Winnie picked up the coffee cups and put them on the tray Doug had left earlier.

"Yes."

Winnie looked up from the coffee table. "How about you, Ellie? I'd love for you to join us. You're part of the reason I'm safe and able to go to the cabin. It would be nice to share it with you."

"I hate to intrude—"

"Nonsense. I remember you saying that you don't have family to spend the holidays with. Consider us your family this year." Winnie started to lift the tray.

Colt hurried forward and took it from her. "I agree with Winnie. After all the time you've spent protecting her, let us show our appreciation. Please."

The look he gave Ellie warmed her insides. She wasn't quite ready yet to say goodbye to him or Winnie. Which, if she thought about it, was probably a mistake. Clearly she had feelings for them—and she didn't do emotions well. Still, maybe it was time just to do something impulsive. "I'll join you, if you're sure."

"Well, then it's settled. We'll go if the sheriff thinks it's okay." Winnie walked toward the hallway. "I'm suddenly tired. It's been quite a day—actually, quite a week."

After she left to retire for the night, Colt's gaze seized Ellie's, a smoldering glint in his gray-blue eyes. "What about you?"

"I'm surprised I'm not tired. Maybe I had one too many cups of coffee. Caffeine usually doesn't affect me, though."

"I'll be right back. I'm known around the *Kaleidoscope* as the night owl, the last to go to sleep and definitely not the first to wake up in the morning."

As Colt left with the tray, the warmth of the fire drew Ellie to the sofa nearest the fireplace. She decided that for a short time she was going to enjoy herself. Real life would return when she flew back to Dallas and took another assignment.

Settling herself on the couch, she lounged back, resting her head against the cushion. The faint sounds of "Silent Night" played in the background. She remembered a Christmas Eve service she went to years ago where at the end the lights were switched off and only candlelight glowed in the dark church. She reached over and shut off the lamp nearby, throwing the room in shadows with only the tree and fire for illumination.

With a sigh, she relaxed, though she knew she couldn't surrender her guard totally. Nothing was official concerning Mary Ann. The sheriff still had a few loose ends he wanted cleared up.

She heard Colt move across the room toward her. The air vibrated with his presence although he was quiet. The cushion gave in when he sat on the sofa only inches from her. His scent vied with the aromas of the fire and the pine tree.

"Ellie," he whispered as though he might wake her up if he spoke any louder.

"I can't fall asleep that fast." She opened her eyes and rolled her head to the side to look at him. "I was enjoying the sound of the music and the crackling of the fire."

"I can always leave you—"

She touched her fingertips to his lips. "Shh. The sound of your voice is even better. Tell me about what it was like growing up with Winnie. What happened to your parents?"

He leaned back, his arm up against hers. "I never really knew my mother. She died shortly after I was born. A massive infection. I guess my father tried to raise me—or more like a series of nannies did. One day when I was four Winnie showed up at the house and found the nanny drinking my dad's liquor. Winnie took me home with her, and I never left after that."

"What about your father?"

"I saw him occasionally when he wanted something from his parents. Mostly I just heard about his exploits from the servants or sometimes from the news. He played fast and furious. Never cared about the family business. One day he mixed drugs and alcohol, passed out and never woke up. Winnie told me he was mourning my mother's death. According to my grandmother, he loved her very much and fell apart when she died."

"How do you feel about your dad?"

Colt tensed, sitting up. "I hardly knew the man, so how can I answer that?"

"Truthfully. You might not have known him well, but that doesn't stop you from forming an opinion, having feelings about him."

For a long moment he sat quietly, his hands clasped together tightly, staring at the coffee table. "The truth is I don't have much feeling toward him at all. He was the man who happened to sire me, but he wasn't my father. My granddad filled that position in my life. The same with Winnie. She was my mother."

"Do you blame your mother for dying?"

He turned toward her, again not saying anything, but a war of emotions flitted across his features, everything from anger to surprise to sadness. "I never really thought about it, but I guess I do carry some anger toward her. But ultimately I'm sad I didn't get to know her. My grandmother told me wonderful stories about her."

"It sounds like Winnie and your granddad were here for you."

"Yes. That's why I feel like I'm letting Winnie down."

"How so?"

"I pursued my own interests and became a marine biologist, but there's a part of me that enjoys watching my grandmother create a product. I had a double major in chemistry and marine biology, but I went on to get my doctorate in marine biology because that interested me the most. I got the chemistry degree for my grandparents, but I did like the field."

"Then why did you become a marine biologist?"

"To see what I could accomplish alone, without the Winfield name." His mouth lifted in a lopsided grin. "How about you? What were your parents like?"

She'd wanted to get to know Colt better and should have realized he would want to do the same. "I don't talk about my childhood. It's behind me. Not something I care to revisit."

One of his eyebrows rose. "I should share my whole life story with you, but yours is off-limits?"

"I said I don't talk about it, but I'll make an exception with you."

"Why?"

"Because…" She didn't know how to say what she felt was developing between them because she had never been good at relationships. She was better as a loner, and her job made that easier.

"Because of what's happening between us?"

"What is that?" *Help me to understand.*

He shifted toward her, crowding her space. "I wish I knew. I do know I'm attracted to you. That if our circumstances were different, we could be friends—good friends. Maybe…" He swallowed hard.

"More?"

He nodded. "You feel it, too?"

"Yes. But you're right. Our lives are in different parts of the world and—"

He bent forward and kissed her hard, cutting off her words, robbing her of a decent breath. But she didn't care. She returned his kiss with her own fervent feelings. Intense, overwhelming. Threatening her emotionally.

She pulled back, one part of her not wanting to end the kiss, but the sensible part of her demanding she act now before she surrendered her heart to Colt. "You know, all this talk has worn me out. I'd better do my rounds then go to bed."

She got to her feet and put some space between them before he coaxed her to stay. He wouldn't have to say much. She skirted around the coffee table and started for the hallway.

"Ellie."

She turned toward him.

"I'm a good listener. When you want to talk about your parents, I'm here."

She strode across the foyer, making sure the alarm system was on and working. Then she began with the dining room, examining the windows to verify they were locked. Not many people had ever told her they would listen to her about her past, but then she'd rarely given anyone the chance. Colt was scaling the walls she kept up around herself. Was it time to let him in?

Late the next afternoon, not long before the sun went down, Ellie propped her shoulder against a post on the porch of the mountain cabin. The Winfield place was nothing like the image of a tiny log cabin she had in her mind. Though the bottom portion was made out of logs, the three-bedroom A-frame was huge and imposing. The smoke from the huge stone fireplace, its wisps entwining with the falling snow, scented the crisp air. A large mug with Linda's delicious hot chocolate, which she'd sent with them before they'd climbed into the four-wheel-drive Jeep and trekked up to the top of the mountain, warmed her bare hands.

The cabin door opened and closed. Colt came to stand beside her with his own drink. "It's beautiful up here. The view when it isn't snowing is breathtaking."

"Will this snow be a problem?"

"The weather report says this system should move out fairly fast. We'll probably get six or seven inches. Nothing we can't handle. But we have enough food for four or five days. We always come prepared with almost twice what we need and there are staples left up here. Doug and Linda use the cabin throughout the year."

"I was glad to see you had a landline. I knew the cell reception was nonexistent this far up the mountain. I don't want to be totally cut off from civilization."

"Mary Ann can't hurt Winnie anymore. The ME ruled it a suicide, and the sheriff couldn't find anything to indicate she wasn't working alone. Winnie is tickled they have a lead on where the dogs could have been sold."

"That'll be a nice Christmas present for Winnie if they find the dogs and they're back at the estate when she comes down off the mountain."

"If it's possible, Sheriff Quinn and Doug will make it happen."

"Winnie has a lot of people who care about her and watch out for her. That says a lot about her."

Colt's gaze snared hers. "How about you? You told me once your brother died when you were young. Do you have any more siblings?"

"Nope. It was just him and me. He was my twin."

"That had to be extra hard on you."

"Yes it was. He had a congenital heart defect that finally got the best of him."

"How old were you?"

"Thirteen."

"How were your parents?"

Suddenly the cold seemed to seep through the layers of clothing Ellie wore. She shivered, taking a large swallow of the now lukewarm chocolate. "I'd better go back inside before I freeze."

In the cabin, Winnie sat in a chair before the fire, knitting. Ellie stopped a few feet into the great room.

Winnie glanced up. "These past few years I haven't gotten to knit like I used to. I found my needles and some yarn and decided to see if I remembered how." A smile curved her mouth, her hands moving quickly.

"It looks like you remember."

"Yes. A nice surprise. The second I stepped inside the cabin I felt like a new woman. My product line is finished, at least for the time being, and the person after me has been found. I'd say that was a wonderful Christmas gift." She lifted the patch of yarn. "And now this. Have you ever knitted?"

Laughing, Ellie took the chair across from her. "I wouldn't be able to sit still long enough to do it. That's something I'll leave to others."

"I might just make this into a scarf for you. That way you won't forget me when you get back to Dallas and go onto another assignment."

"Forget you?" Ellie shook her head. "That's not gonna happen. You're an amazing woman."

A hint of red colored her cheeks. "Where's my grandson?"

"Communing with nature," Ellie said with a shrug.

"I'm glad you didn't change your mind about coming." Winnie paused and leaned toward her, lowering her voice. "I was sure you would."

"Why?"

"I saw you yesterday while we were decorating and celebrating. You weren't totally comfortable with the whole scene. I imagine since you go from one place to another because of your job, you don't do much for the holidays. Who did you spend Thanksgiving with this year?"

"No one. I microwaved a turkey dinner and celebrated alone. I have a standing invitation to Kyra's, but I hate always intruding on her and her husband. They're practically newlyweds."

"Kind of painful sometimes being around a couple deeply in love when you aren't."

"That's not it. I just…" *Just what?* she asked herself. In truth, Winnie was probably right. Kyra and Michael were always so good to include her in whatever they were doing, but she saw the looks exchanged between them—full of love that excluded everyone else in the room. She'd never had a man look at her like that—not even Greg, who she had thought she would marry one day. "It's not that I want a relationship, but there are times I get lonely."

"We all do. And why don't you want a relationship? You have a lot to offer a man."

Ellie peered at the front door, relieved it was still closed and Colt was outside. "I don't think I'd be very good at it. I've always depended on myself for everything."

"Everything? Not God a little bit?"

"Well, yes. I know He's there, but I'm not sure He's that interested in my day-to-day life."

"Oh, He is."

"Then where was He when I was growing up? Having to raise myself? Take care of my brother because our mother couldn't be bothered?" She finally said the questions that had plagued her ever since she gave herself to Christ.

"Look at the type of woman you've grown into. You're strong. You can take care of yourself. You help others have peace of mind when trouble happens in their life. I for one am thankful you came into my life.

Sadly, an easy road doesn't usually hone a person into what they need to be."

The door finally opened, and Colt hurried inside, stomping his feet. Snow covered his hair and coat. "I forgot something in the Jeep and went out to get it." After shrugging out of his heavy jacket, he put a sack on the table near the chair he settled into. "It's really snowing now. Too much more and we'll have white-out conditions."

"It sounds like the weatherman got it wrong." Ellie eyed the bag. "What did you forget?"

"A surprise."

"You know a bodyguard doesn't like surprises."

"This is a good one." He quirked a grin, his eyes sparkling. "You and Winnie have to wait until Christmas morning."

"It's a present? I didn't get you anything." An edge of panic invaded Ellie's voice. A gift from him made their…friendship even more personal.

"It's nothing. And I don't want anything. That's not why I'm giving you this."

Winnie laughed. "Ellie, enjoy it. Colt loves giving gifts. He's just like his grandfather. I used to be able to find out what it was before Colt gave it to me. But not anymore. He's gotten quite good at keeping a secret."

"So, Winnie, what are we having for dinner?" Colt combed his fingers through his wet hair.

Winnie gave him a look. "Are you suffering from hypothermia? You want *me* to fix dinner?"

Colt chuckled. "Not if I want to eat anything decent. I was teasing you. Ellie and I will cook dinner for you." He rose and offered Ellie his hand.

She took it and let him tug her up. "You do know I don't cook a lot for myself. I'm not home that much."

"But I cook. We all take turns on the ship, and if we weren't accomplished, we quickly learned or the rest of the crew threatened to toss us overboard."

Ellie examined the contents of the refrigerator. "Grilling is out," she said as she glanced back at Colt. "Which, by the way, I am good at. So I guess the steaks can wait for a less snowy day."

"From the looks of it outside, I don't know that's going to happen before we leave. We can use the broiler in the oven."

"So how are we going to get out of here if it snows that much?"

"We have a snowmobile in the shed out back and skis."

"Winnie skis?"

"She did when she was younger, but she'll use the snowmobile. How are you on skis?"

"Never tried it. I live in flat country."

"We have some cross-country skis. Flat country is fine for that."

"But the way down isn't flat. I might not make a pretty picture on skis, but I'll do what I have to." She took the meat out of the refrigerator. "Okay, steak it is. I can actually prepare them and put them in the broiler. So what are you gonna cook?"

His chuckle spiced the air. "I see how this is going to go. I'm going to do most of the work. I thought you said you could cook."

"Simple things like steaks. Let's say you're the head chef and I'm the assistant. Believe me, you all will be much better off."

"Well then, let's make this simple. Baked potatoes and a salad."

"I'm all for easy."

Surprisingly Ellie found they cooked well as a team, and by the time they sat down to eat she'd laughed more at the stories Colt told her about life on the research vessel than she had in a long time. Her jobs were serious and left little room for the lighter side of life.

"I'm glad you two talked me into coming up here," Ellie said when Winnie finished her blessing. "I've worked a lot in the past few years and have had little downtime. I needed this and didn't even realize it. No bad guys out there stalking a client. That's a nice feeling"

Winnie agreed. "That's how I'm looking at these next three days. A minivacation that I needed a lot. I'm too old to work as hard as I have been with Endless Youth. But it's mostly done, and I've accomplished what Thomas and I set out to do all those years ago. Once the company goes public, I'm stepping down as CEO of Glamour Sensations."

Colt dropped his fork on his plate. "You're finally retiring? I've been wanting you to slow down for years."

Winnie pursed her lips. "I would have if a certain young grandson had decided to use his degree in chemistry and come into the business. I figure Harold can take over the CEO position until he grooms someone for the job."

Ellie picked up on the sudden tension that thickened at the table between grandson and grandmother. She swallowed her bite of mushroom-covered steak and said, "What are you going to do with all your free time?"

"I won't completely turn the company over without keeping an eye on it. But I figure I could knit, read, wait for great-grandchildren."

Colt's eyes popped wide. "Winnie, now I know why you insisted on coming up here. Did you have something to do with all this snow, too? We won't be going anywhere until it stops. Visibility is limited."

His grandmother smiled. "I have a lot of skills, but controlling weather isn't one of them. I figured the circumstances were just right for me telling you this now rather than right before you go back to the *Kaleidoscope*. You'll inherit my shares in the company so you'll have a stake in it."

"What's this about great-grandchildren? This is the first time you've bought that up in a long time."

Winnie pointedly looked at Ellie before swinging her attention to Colt. "Just a little reminder. After all, I'm getting up there. These threats made me realize I won't be around forever. I need to make plans for the future."

Colt's eyebrows slashed downward, and he lowered his head, as though he was enthralled with cutting his steak.

"The threat is over and you should have many years before you, Winnie," Ellie said, trying to defuse the tension vibrating in the air.

"I'm planning on it, but it's in the Lord's hands."

The rest of the meal Winnie and Ellie mostly talked, with a few comments from Colt. What part of the conversation had upset him? Ellie wondered. The part about Harold becoming CEO or the great-grandchildren?

At the end Ellie rose. "I'll take care of the dishes.

That I know how to do at least. When I was first in the army I was on mess duty a lot."

"Colt will help you," Winnie offered. "You're our guest. We certainly can't let you do it alone."

As Ellie walked into the kitchen she heard Colt say in a strained voice, "I know what you're doing, and you need to stop it."

"Stop what? If you want, I'll help her."

The sugary sweet sound of Winnie's voice alerted Ellie to the fact that the woman was up to something, and she had a pretty good idea what it was. When Colt came into the small kitchen, his expression reflected his irritated mood toward his grandmother. Ellie worked beside him in silence for ten minutes.

As she washed the broiler pan, she asked, "What's going on with you and Winnie? Are you upset about her retiring and Harold taking over?" She didn't think that was it.

"I'm glad she's retiring, and Harold's a good man. Don't tell her, but lately I've been thinking about what I need to do. I don't see me living on a research vessel for years."

"So you might help with the company?"

"Maybe. I have an obligation that I need to finish first to the research team."

"Then what has you upset? And don't tell me you aren't. It's all over your face."

"She hasn't played the great-grandchildren card in ages. I thought she'd learned her lesson the last time."

"What lesson?"

"Come on. You're smart. Don't you see she's trying to play matchmaker with us?"

"It did cross my mind, but I think it's cute."

"Cute! The last time she did, I went out with the woman to make her happy. On the surface she seemed all right until we stopped dating and she began stalking me. That's one of the reasons I took the job on the *Kaleidoscope*. It's hard to stalk a person in the middle of the Pacific Ocean. It turns out I've enjoyed the work I'm doing and the woman went on to marry and move to New York, but Winnie isn't usually that far off reading people."

"We're all entitled to a mistake every once in a while. Besides, she had your best interests at heart—at least in her mind."

"I told the lady I wasn't interested in a serious relationship. She was and didn't understand why I wasn't. Hence the stalking to discover why she wasn't Mrs. Right."

"Don't worry. I don't stalk. I protect people from stalkers. And I'm not interested in a serious relationship, either. So you're perfectly safe. Your grandmother's wiles won't work on me." Ellie wiped down the sink. "So if you know that your grandmother has done that in the past, why did you talk me into coming this morning when I voiced an objection?"

He blew out a frustrated breath. "Because I like you. I've enjoyed getting to know you, and I didn't like the idea that you would spend Christmas alone."

"Oh, I see."

"Do you? Winnie needs to realize a man can have a friendship with a woman. She keeps insisting Harold is just a friend, so surely she can understand we can be friends."

Ellie laughed. "You don't have to convince me. Just Winnie."

"Yeah. Besides, after Christmas, I'll go back to *Kaleidoscope* and you'll go on another assignment. We'll probably be halfway around the world from each other."

"I agree. Forgive the cliché, but we're like two ships passing in the night."

"Exactly." He draped the dish towel over the handle on the oven. "And I think I'll go in there and explain it to her. Want to back me up?"

"Sure."

Colt stalked into the great room and found it empty. He turned in a full circle, his gaze falling on the knitting project in the basket by the chair his grandmother had been sitting in. His forehead crinkled, and he covered the distance to the hall, coming back almost immediately. "She went to bed. It's just you and me, and it's only nine o'clock."

"I think that was her intention."

"I know." A chuckle escaped Colt. "And I'll have a serious word with her tomorrow. In the meantime, want to play chess or checkers?"

"I can't play chess, so it has to be checkers."

Colt retrieved the board and game pieces and set it up at the table where they had eaten their dinner. "I'll have to teach you how to play chess. It's a strategy game. I have a feeling you'd be good at it."

"Maybe tomorrow. After the past few weeks, I don't want too tough a game to play tonight." Ellie took a chair across from him. "After an assignment I go through a mental and physical letdown, and after a particularly hard job, I almost shut down for a couple of days."

"Is this your way of telling me you're going to lounge around and do nothing but eat bonbons?"

"If you have any, I might. I like chocolate." Ellie moved her red checker forward.

"What else do you like?" Colt made his play, then looked up into her eyes, trapping her with the intensity in his gaze. Electrifying. Mesmerizing.

"Protecting people," she somehow managed to reply. "I really do like my work. Making sure a place is secure. Trying to figure out all the ways a person can get to another."

"I can understand liking your job. I like mine, too."

"What do you like about your job?"

"Finding unique species. Trying to preserve the ocean. The challenge of the job. That's probably what I like the most. I want a job that forces me beyond my comfort zone."

"We have a lot in common."

Colt answered her move by jumping her red checker. "You said you became a bodyguard because you want to help those who need protection. Why is that important to you?"

"King me," Ellie said when she slid her first red piece into his home base. "Because my twin was bullied. I wasn't going to allow that to happen to others if I could do something about it."

"He was but you weren't?"

"No. I had a rep for being tough and not taking anything from anyone."

He cocked his head to the side. "How did you get that reputation?"

"By standing up to the people who made fun of my brother. Toby was slow. He was the second twin. He became stuck in the birth canal and was deprived of oxygen, which caused some medical and mental problems."

"When did you start championing him like that?"

"When we started school. Kindergarten."

"What did your parents think?"

Ellie looked at the board and made a move without thinking it through. With his next turn, Colt jumped her pieces until she had to crown his black checker.

"Obviously the subject of your parents isn't one of your favorites," he said. "Like me."

Ellie swallowed the tightness in her throat. Recalling her past never sat well with her. "No. I never knew my father. He left my mother when Toby and I were born. He never once tried to get in touch with us. And for different reasons from your dad, my mother was less than stellar in the parent department. I basically raised Toby and myself. I didn't have grandparents like yours."

"So you and I have another thing in common."

There was something about Colt that drew her. She hadn't wanted to admit that to herself, but she couldn't avoid it any longer. They were alike in a lot of ways even though their backgrounds were very different. He came from wealth and was college educated. She'd graduated from high school and had been educated on the job in the army.

Ten minutes later Colt won the checkers game. She wanted to think it was because her mind hadn't been on the game, but that wasn't true. He was good and she wasn't. She hadn't played since she was a kid and the old man next door used to challenge her. She hadn't won then, either, but she had enjoyed her neighbor's conversation about the different places she could see around the world. So when the U.S. Army recruiter came to her school, she'd thought it would be a good way to go different places.

"Another game?" Colt asked.

"No, one beating in a night is enough. My ego can only take so much."

He threw back his head and laughed. "I have a feeling your ego is just fine."

"Okay, I hate to admit that Winnie has the right idea about going to bed early. What's even nicer is that I don't have to walk through the house and check to make sure we are locked up tight. No one in their right mind would come out on a night like this." Ellie made her way to the window and opened the blinds to look at the heavy snow coming down.

"Near blizzard conditions," Colt said close to her ear.

The tickle of his breath on her nape zipped through her, but she stayed still. There was nothing stopping her from turning around and kissing him. No job. No threats against Winnie. This was her time that she'd chosen to spend with Winnie and Colt. His presence so near to her tingled her nerve endings and charged her, demanding she put aside her exhaustion and give in to the feelings bombarding her from all sides.

"Yes, I haven't seen this much snow in a while." Her reply ended in a breathless rush.

"It makes this cabin feel even cozier." His soft, whispered words caressed her neck.

She tensed, trying to keep herself from leaning back against him.

"Relax. We'll be perfectly fine in here. If we need rescuing, people know where we are and will come when we don't show up the day after Christmas."

His teasing tone coaxed the tension from her. She closed the blind and swung around at the same time she stepped away. "I think I can survive being snow-bound in a large, warm cabin with enough food for a week. My boss doesn't expect me to come into the office until the day after New Year's."

"I wish I could say the same thing. I have to get back to the ship."

His comment reminded her of their differences. She was a bodyguard. He worked on a vessel in the middle of the Pacific Ocean. Not conducive to a relationship. "Good night, Colt."

"Coward."

"Oh, you think?" She'd been accused of being many things. Being a coward wasn't one of them.

"When it gets personal, you leave."

"That's what this is?" She drew a circle in the air to indicate where they were standing.

He moved to the side, sweeping his arm across his body. "Good night, Ellie. We'll continue our conversation tomorrow when you're rested."

On her way to her bedroom, the searing heat of his gaze drilled into her back. Every inch of her was aware of the man she'd wanted to kiss but didn't. It was better this way. Now she only had a few more days and she could escape to Dallas.

Ellie hurriedly changed into her sweatpants and large T-shirt then fell into bed. She expected sleep to come quickly. But she couldn't stop thinking about Colt. At some point she must have gone to sleep because the next thing she realized a boom shook the cabin, sending her flying out of bed.

Chapter Ten

Ellie fumbled in the dark for her gun she kept on the nightstand out of habit. When her fingers clasped around it, she raced into the hallway at the same time Colt came out of his bedroom.

"Check on Winnie," she said and hurried into the great room. The cabin seemed intact, but when she peered toward the large window that overlooked the front of the place, she saw an orange-yellow glow through the slats in the blinds as though the sun had set in the yard. She yanked open the door, a blast of cold rushing in while flames engulfed the Jeep nearby in the still-falling snow.

Gun up, she moved out onto the porch. When she stepped into the snow blown up against the cabin, she glanced down and realized she had no shoes on. In spite of the biting cold battering her, she scanned the white terrain. Although night, it was light and eerie. The storm had died down some but still raged, as did the fire where the Jeep was.

From behind a hand clamped on her shoulder. She jerked around, her gun automatically coming up.

Colt's eyes grew round, his hand falling back to his side.

"Don't ever come up behind me like that, especially after something like this." Using her weapon, she gestured toward the flames. "I could have shot you."

With her toes freezing and the sensation spreading up her legs, she hotfooted it into the cabin and shut the door, locking it. "How's Winnie?"

"I'm fine."

Ellie glanced over Colt's shoulder. Winnie hovered near the hallway, wrapped in a quilt. "You know what this means."

She nodded. "Mary Ann didn't send those threats."

"Possibly. Or someone was working with her and maybe killed her to keep her quiet. It's possible to make a murder look like suicide. That's what the police wanted to determine when her body was discovered."

"The Jeep couldn't have exploded on its own?" Winnie came farther into the room.

"Not likely."

Colt parted a few slats on the blinds and peeked outside. "The fire is dying down with all the snow falling, and the wind has, too. We need to call the sheriff."

Ellie marched to the phone and picked it up. "No dial tone. This is definitely not an accident."

"So we're trapped in this cabin with no way to get help." Colt strode into the kitchen and peered out the window. "I see nothing on this side."

Ellie checked the other sides of the cabin, calling out from her bedroom, "Clear here." *For the time being.*

"What do we do? Who is behind this?" Winnie's voice quavered.

Ellie reentered the great room. "At the moment the

who isn't important. We need to come up with a plan. If he blew up the Jeep, he could try something with the cabin and we can't guard all four sides 24/7. He might have destroyed the Jeep to get us out of the house."

"How can we leave?" Winnie pulled the blanket closer to her.

"The snow is starting to let up," Colt said. "Maybe I could make it down the mountain and get help. You could stay here with Winnie and guard her. I know these mountains and have the best chance of getting out of here."

Ellie faced Colt. "How are you going to walk out of here? Over a foot of snow was dumped on us in the past twelve hours."

"We have snowshoes I can use. Or I'll get to the snowmobile in the shed and use that."

"What if he's out there waiting to shoot anyone who leaves?" This was a situation where she wished she were two people and could stay and protect but also go and get help.

He clasped her arms. "I've fought off pirates. I can do this. Besides, the visibility isn't good because it's still night and snowing."

"Exactly. It won't be good for you, either." Thinking about what could happen to him knotted her stomach.

"But I know this area well. I doubt the person out there does. This is Winfield land. Not much else is up here. This isn't debatable. I'm going. You're staying." A determined expression carved harsh lines into his face.

She nodded. She didn't like the plan, but they didn't have a choice.

Colt started for his bedroom.

Winnie stepped into his path. "Colt, don't do this.

I don't like you being a target for this person. You're my only family left."

"I have to go. I'm taking Granddad's handgun with me." He looked back at Ellie. "I'm leaving his rifle in case you need it."

"Fine. Bring it out here with ammunition. I'll keep you covered for as long as I can." The helplessness Ellie experienced festered inside her. Protection was her job, not his.

Winnie turned large eyes on Ellie as Colt disappeared down the hallway. "I'm glad Thomas taught Colt to shoot. At that time it was for him to protect himself if he came upon a bear or cougar in these mountains—not a person bent on killing me."

"You won't die as long as I have a breath in me." Ellie's hands curled into fists.

Nor Colt. I won't let him die, either. He means too much to me. That realization stunned her for a moment, then because she had no choice, she shoved it into the background. She couldn't risk her emotions getting in the way of whatever she had to do.

When he reemerged from the hallway, dressed in a heavy overcoat and wool beanie, carrying snowshoes, thick gloves, goggles and the rifle, he thrust the latter into Ellie's hand then dug for a box of shells and laid them on a nearby table. "More ammunition is on top of my bureau."

He put on his goggles, wrapped a scarf around his neck and lower face, donned his snowshoes and gloves, then eased the back door open. Cracking a window that overlooked the back of the cabin, she took up guard as Colt trudged his way toward the shed two hundred feet away.

Her nerves taut, she shouldered the rifle, poised to fire if she needed to. Ellie scoped the terrain for anything that moved. All was still. Not even the branches of the pine trees swayed from wind now.

"What's happening? I don't hear the snowmobile," Winnie said behind Ellie.

"Nothing. He's inside the shed." *But is he safe?* What if the assailant was waiting for him? Ellie couldn't leave Winnie. That might be what the person wanted. But what if Colt needed—

The side door to the shed opened, and Colt hurried back toward the house, his gaze scanning the area.

"What happened?" Ellie asked at the same time Winnie did when Colt reentered the cabin.

"The snowmobile won't start. Someone disabled it."

"Are you sure? Does it have gas?"

"There's a hole in the tank. The gas leaked out all over the ground. The ski equipment and anything else we might use to leave here is gone. He's cut us off."

Trapped. She'd been trapped before and gotten out. She would this time, too, with both Colt and Winnie. "Okay. For the time being let's fortify the cabin, find places to watch our surroundings while we figure out what we should do."

"I still think I should try leaving here on foot," Colt insisted.

"Maybe. What's up in the loft?" Ellie pointed to a narrow staircase.

"Storage mostly, but it might be a better vantage place to watch the area from," Colt said.

"I'm going to fix some coffee. We need to stay alert. I don't think there's going to be any more sleep tonight."

"Thanks, Winnie. I could use a whole pot." Colt kissed his grandmother on the check.

When she left, Ellie moved toward the stairs. "Keep an eye on her while I look at the loft."

Colt stepped closer and whispered, "Ellie, I don't think Winnie could make it out of here, so all three of us going is not an option. She might have power walked around the perimeter of the estate, but sloshing through the deep snow even with snowshoes is totally different. It's exhausting after a few hundred yards. And snowshoeing can be treacherous going downhill over rough terrain, especially with her weak knees. Not to mention leaving her exposed for the person to shoot."

"And you don't think you'll be."

"What's the alternative? Waiting until we're missed? That could be days. No telling what would happen in that time."

"I'll be back down in a few minutes. Check the windows and doors to make sure they're locked. Put some heavy furniture up against the two doors. Shutter the windows we won't use for a lookout."

"What are you two whispering about?" Poised in the entrance into the kitchen, Winnie planted her fists on her waist. "If you're worried about me, let me inform you I'll do what I have to. I won't let this person win. Any planning and discussions need to include me. Understand?"

Ellie exchanged a glance with Colt before he pivoted and headed toward his grandmother, saying, "We were just discussing our options."

Ellie clambered up the stairs. The whole loft was one large room with boxes and pieces of furniture stored along the walls. Two big windows overlooked the west and east part of the landscape. One person with little effort could keep an eye on over half the terrain. That could leave Winnie and Colt covering the north and south. That might work. But then as she started back down the stairs, questions and doubts began tumbling through her mind like a skier who lost her balance going down a mountain.

The scent of coffee lured her toward the kitchen. She poured a mug and joined Winnie in the great room before the dying fire. She gave the older woman a smile, hoping to cajole one from her.

But Winnie's frown deepened. "I've been trying to figure out who would go to such lengths to get me. I honestly can't imagine anything I've done to cause this kind of hatred. I feel so helpless."

Ellie remembered that exact feeling a little while ago. It never sat well with her. "I've been thinking."

Colt suddenly came from the hallway with his arms full of warm clothing, snowshoes and other items. "If we need to leave suddenly, I want this on hand. I'm separating it into piles for each of us."

"I say we have two options. All of us leave and try to make it down the mountain. Or I go by myself and bring help back." Ellie sat on the edge of the sofa, every sense attuned to her surroundings.

"Those aren't two options in my opinion," Colt said. "I'm going it alone. I can move fast. I should be able to get back with help by dark if I leave right away. The best place for me to try and get to is the estate. I think that's the best—"

"No, Colt. You're not going by yourself. I won't have you get killed because of me. There is a third option.

We stay here. That's what I want." Winnie pinched her lips together and pointedly looked at each one of them.

Colt surged to his feet. "Sorry. I love you, Winnie, but the longer we spread this out the more this person has a chance to accomplish what he wants to do. Kill you and in the process take us all out."

"I agree with Colt about us all waiting, but I'd rather be the one going for help. I know how to avoid being a human target. I was trained in that."

"Winnie is your client and first priority."

"I know. That's the dilemma I—"

Thump!

"What was that?" Ellie rose and started for the window by the front door. She motioned Colt to check the back area.

Again she heard the sound—like something striking the side of the cabin. Ellie parted the blinds to peer outside. Nothing unusual but the sight of the charred Jeep.

Thump!

"That's coming from the north side." Colt rushed down the hallway.

Ellie helped Winnie to her feet and followed him. "Do you see anything?"

He whirled from the window. "We've got to get out of here. He's firing flaming arrows at the cabin."

Ellie stared out at the evergreen forest, which afforded a lot of cover along the north area of the property. Another arrow rocketed toward the cabin, landing on the roof. "He's burning us out. Either we leave or die in a fire."

Colt ushered them out of the room. "Let's go. If we can get away, I think I know a place you two can hide.

It's defensible, only one way in. We need to dress as warm as possible."

"He's on the north side. We'll use the window facing south to get out of here. He can't watch all four sides at once."

Winnie halted before her pile of garments. "Unless there is more than one."

"We have to take our chances and pray the Lord protects us." Ellie quickly dressed, then stuffed useful items into a backpack—flashlights, a blanket, matches, weapons, some bottled water and food.

"He'll be able to track us, but the cave system isn't too far away and it's beginning to snow again. I hope the conditions worsen after we get to the cave. The way I have to go is down. I can do that even in less-than-favorable visibility." Colt prepared his backpack then slung it over one shoulder.

The noise of the arrows hitting the cabin increased. The scent of smoke drifted to Ellie as they hurried into the laundry room. A three-by-three window four feet off the floor beckoned her. She pulled a chair to it and opened their escape route. A blast of cold air and snow invaded the warmth of the small room.

Ellie stuck her head out the opening. It was at least six feet to the ground. "I'll go first, then you, Winnie. Colt can help lower you to me."

After tossing her backpack out the hole, Ellie leaped up and shimmied through the small space, diving head-first and tucking into a ball. The snow cushioned her tumble to the ground. She bounced up and positioned herself to guide Winnie, breaking her fall. While Colt wiggled through the opening and followed Ellie's example, she and Winnie put on their snowshoes. Colt donned his as fast as he could.

The thumping sound thundered through the air.

Winnie started to say something. Ellie put her finger up to her mouth. Colt's grandmother nodded that she understood.

Colt pointed in the direction he would take, then set out in a slow pace with Winnie mirroring his steps, then Ellie. The less snow they disturbed the faster the falling flakes would cover their tracks.

When Colt reached the edge of the forest that surrounded the cabin, Ellie paused and glanced back. The stench of smoke hung in the air, but she couldn't see any wisps of it coming from the cabin because of the heavy snowfall. Even the indentations they'd made were filling in, though still evident.

Then the sound of the arrows striking the cabin stopped. Ellie searched the white landscape but saw no sign of the assailant. She turned forward and hurried as fast as she could to catch up with Colt and Winnie.

Fifteen minutes later, the wind began whipping through the trees, bringing biting cold to penetrate their layers of clothing. Even with so little skin exposed to the chill, Ellie shivered and gritted her teeth to keep them from chattering.

A cracking noise reverberated through the forest, followed by a crash to their left. Ellie looked up at the snow-and ice-burdened limbs on the pines and realized the danger of being beneath the heavy-laden branches. Winnie barely picked up each foot as she moved forward. Her pace slowed even more.

When Winnie stumbled and fell, Ellie whispered, "Colt," and rushed toward the woman.

The wind whisked his name away. He kept trudging forward.

"Colt," she said a little louder as she bent over to help Winnie to her feet, one snowshoe coming off.

He glanced back, saw his grandmother down and retraced his steps as quickly as he could. He assisted Winnie to her feet while Ellie knelt and tied the snowshoe back on Winnie's foot. Snow-covered, the older woman shook.

Another crack, like a gun going off, resonated in the air. A pine branch snapped above them and plunged toward them. Ellie dove into both Colt and Winnie, sending them flying to the side. The limb struck the ground a foot away from them.

Dazed, Winnie lay in the snow, then pain flashed across her face.

"What's wrong, Winnie?" Ellie asked, pushing up onto her hands and knees next to the woman.

"I think I did something to my ankle," she murmured, her voice barely audible over the howl of the wind through the trees.

Colt knelt next to Winnie. "I'll carry you the rest of the way. The cave isn't far."

"I'm so sorry, Winnie." Ellie peered at the large branch on the ground.

"Don't you apologize. I could have been hurt a lot worse if that had fallen on me."

While Colt scooped up his grandmother, Ellie used her knife to cut a small branch off the big one. She used the pine to smooth out the snow behind them as much as possible and hide their tracks.

Ten minutes later, Colt mounted a rocky surface, went around a large boulder and stooped to enter a cave. Ellie stayed back to clear away their steps as much as possible, then went inside the dark cavern, reaching for her flashlight to illuminate the area. A damp, musky odor prevailed.

Colt set his grandmother on the floor, took a blanket out of his backpack and spread it out, then moved Winnie to it. Kneeling, he removed the boot from the injured foot and examined it. "The ankle's starting to swell. I don't think it's broken. But a doctor will have to look at it when we get home. The faster I leave, the faster you'll get the medical care you need."

Ellie slung her backpack to the ground near Winnie and sat on it. "We'll be fine. I'll make Winnie comfortable then stand guard near the entrance."

"I should be back before dark. If I can get to the house, I can get help. It's a little out of the way, but I think it would save time in the long run. I know I can find help there." Colt started to stand.

Winnie grabbed his arm. "I love you. Don't you dare take any more risks than you absolutely have to. If you have to take your time to be safe, then you've got to do that."

"Yes, ma'am." He kissed her forehead. "I have a good reason to make it safely down the mountain."

Ellie rose and walked with him a few feet. "Ditto what your grandmother said. I have food and water. We have a couple of blankets. We'll be fine." She tied his scarf, which had come loose, back around his neck. Suddenly emotions jammed her throat. She knew the dangers in store for Colt. Not just the rough terrain in a snowstorm but a maniac bent on killing them.

He clasped her glove-covered hands and bent his head toward hers. A smile graced his mouth right before his lips grazed across hers once then twice. Then he kissed her fully. She returned it with all her needs and concerns pouring into the connection that sprang up between them.

In a raw whisper, she said against his mouth, "Don't you dare get hurt. We have things to talk about when this is over."

"If I hadn't been motivated before, I am now." He gave her a quick peck on her lips then departed, striding toward the cave entrance.

Ellie watched him vanish around the corner, then went back to Winnie to make sure she was comfortable before she stood guard at the mouth of the cavern.

"He'll be all right," Winnie assured her. "He knows these mountains well. Hopefully better than whoever is after me."

Ellie nodded at Winnie, remembering the grin Colt gave her before kissing her. The memory warmed her cold insides. "Yes. After all, he's fought off pirates before."

Winnie chuckled.

The warmth died out when a gunshot blasted the air and the mountain over them rumbled.

Chapter Eleven

Colt exited the cave, scanning the terrain for any sign of their assailant. Through the curtain of snow falling a movement caught his full attention. Suddenly a shadow rose from behind a rock and aimed a rifle at him. Colt dove for cover as the white-camouflaged figure got off a shot, the bullet ricocheting off the stone surface behind him.

A noise rocked the ground—like a huge wave hitting shore in a thunderstorm. Colt had only heard that sound one other time, right before tons of snow crashed down the mountain, plowing through the forest, leaving nothing behind in its wake.

The entrance of the cave a few feet away was his only chance. He scrambled toward it as rock, snow and ice began pelting him.

Winnie went white. "An avalanche!"

Ellie hurried toward the entrance. "Stay put," she said, realizing Winnie didn't have a choice.

As she rounded the bend in the stone corridor, she saw Colt plunge toward the cave, then a wall of white swallowed him up. The force of the avalanche sent a swell of snow mushrooming into the cavern.

When the rumbling stopped, snow totally blocked the cave entrance and she couldn't see Colt. She rushed to the last place he'd been and began digging with her hands. Cold and wet invaded the warmth of her gloves, leaving her hands freezing. She didn't care. Nor did she care Winnie and she were trapped. She had to find Colt.

Please, Lord, let me find him. Please.

Over and over those words zoomed through her mind. But all she uncovered was more snow.

Stunned, with limited oxygen, Colt tried to unfurl his body so he could use his hands to dig his way out before he lost consciousness. But the snow encased him in a cold coffin. He had a small pocket of air, but it wouldn't last long. He finally dislodged his arm from beneath him and reached it toward the direction of the cave, but he could move it only a few inches.

Lord, help me. Winnie and Ellie are in danger.

"I'm in here," he called out, hoping that Ellie was free on the other side.

"Colt!"

The sound of Ellie's voice gave him hope she could dig him out before he ran out of oxygen. "I'm here."

"I can hear you, Colt. Hang on."

He focused on those words and tried to calm his rapid heartbeat, to even his breathing in order to preserve his air. A peace settled around him as if God enclosed him in an embrace.

"Ellie, what happened?" Winnie called out. "It sounded like an avalanche."

"It was. I'm assessing our situation." Ellie kept digging near the area where she'd heard Colt and prayed he wasn't buried too deeply.

If he was almost to the entrance of the cave, he would have been sheltered from the worst of the avalanche. Concerned for Colt, she hadn't thought about their situation till now. They were trapped in the cave. It would be days before a search party was sent out, and then would the rescuers even realize they were trapped in the cavern? And if they did, would it be in time? She had a couple of water bottles and a little food, but what worried her the most was the cold. A chill infused every crevice of the cave.

Although tired from shoveling the snow with her hands, she didn't dare take a break. "Colt, are you there?"

"Yes," his faint response came back and a surge of adrenaline pumped energy through her body.

Her hand broke through the snow and touched him, and relief trembled down her length. She doubled her attack as though sand was running out of an hourglass and she only had seconds left to free him. Soon his arm was revealed. He wiggled it to let her know he was okay. She kept going, uncovering more of him until he could assist her.

When he escaped the mound of snow, Ellie helped him to stand, then engulfed him in her arms. "Are you all right? Hurt anywhere?"

"I feel like an elephant—no, several—sat on me, but other than that, I'm in one piece."

She leaned back to look into his dear face, one she had thought she would never see again. "I heard a gunshot then the rumble of the avalanche. What happened?"

"Our assailant found us and shot at me when I came out of the cave. That must have triggered the avalanche. I dove back into the cave. He might not have been so fortunate."

"Then he could be buried under tons of snow?"

"It'll depend on where he was and how fast he reacted, but it's definitely a possibility."

"Come on. Winnie is worried." Ellie grasped his gloved hand in hers and relished the connection. She'd almost lost him. That thought forced her to acknowledge her growing feelings toward Colt. There was no time to dwell on them now, but she would have to in the future. Every day she was with him, the stronger those feelings grew.

Winnie's face lit up when she saw Colt. "You're alive."

"Yes, thanks to Ellie." He slanted a look at her before stooping by Winnie. "Are you doing okay?"

"Now I am. What happened?"

As Colt told his grandmother, her face hardened more and more into a scowl.

"I hope he's trapped in the avalanche," Winnie blurted out at the end. "Evil begets evil."

One of Colt's eyebrows lifted. "No forgiveness for the man?"

Winnie pursed her mouth. "I'm working on it, but his actions are making it very hard. It's one thing to go after me, but he was trying to kill you. He needs to be stopped, and if the avalanche did it, so be it."

Ellie sat, her legs trembling from exhaustion. "We need to come up with a plan to get out of here. Colt, you said there's only one way into this cave. You've explored this place completely?"

"There's another way in that is blocked on the other side. This system goes through the mountain we are on."

"What do you mean by blocked?"

"Years ago there was a rockslide. There's an opening, but it isn't big. I'm not sure I can fit through it. For all I know the rocks may have shifted and closed it completely off."

"Or opened it up some more. Would the assailant know about the back way into this cave?" Ellie slid her glance to Winnie, who pulled the blanket around herself, her lips quivering.

"Unless you're really familiar with the area, you wouldn't know about it. Like I said, this is Winfield property."

"Let's hope he isn't because I don't think we can wait around to see if anyone finds us and digs us out."

"Agreed."

"Winnie, if Colt and I help you, do you think you can make it through the cave to the other side?"

She lifted her chin. "Don't you two worry about me. I'll do what I have to. If I can't make it, you can leave me and come back to get me after you find a way out."

"We can't leave you alone." Colt wrapped his arms around his grandmother.

"I'm not afraid. The Lord will be with me."

"It may not be an issue if I can carry you."

Ellie gathered up all the backpacks and supplies and led the way Colt told her to go while he carried his grandmother in his arms. Dripping water and their breathing were the only sounds in the cavern. The chill burrowed into Ellie's bones the deeper they went into the heart of the mountain.

"How long ago were you last here?" Ellie asked as the passage became narrower and shorter.

"At least ten years ago."

Ellie glanced back at Colt. Winnie's head was cushioned against his shoulder, her eyes closed. "Was there any crawling involved?"

He nodded. "Come to think of it, the cave gets tight in one area."

When Ellie reached a fork in the cave system, she stopped. "Which way?"

Colt shut his eyes, his forehead wrinkled. "I think to the right. This probably isn't the time to tell you I'm lousy with telling you the difference in right or left."

"There's no good time to tell me that," she said. "I could go a ways and see what I find."

"No, we'll stay together. If it's the way, you'd have to track back." Colt shifted Winnie some in his embrace and winced.

"Are you all right?"

"I hurt my arm when the whole mountain came down on me."

"Just your arm? Let's take a rest, eat something and drink some water."

"We should keep going."

"Our bodies need the rest, food and water." Ellie plopped the backpacks down on the stone floor and helped Colt lower his grandmother onto a blanket.

"You two don't have to stop for me," Winnie murmured, pain etched into her features.

"We're stopping for all of us." Ellie delved into her backpack and found the granola bars and a bottle of water. "It may be freezing, but we still have to keep ourselves hydrated."

"Just a short break." Colt removed his gloves and rubbed his left arm.

Shivering, Winnie took the first sip of water then passed it to Ellie. When she gave it to Colt, the touch of his cold fingers against hers fastened her attention on him. In the dim lighting his light blue eyes looked dark. Shadows played across his strong jaw. But the sear of his gaze warmed her as though she sat in front of a flaming blaze.

"I wonder if the cabin caught fire." Colt bit into his granola bar.

"If it did, maybe someone will see the smoke and investigate. They might be concerned about a forest fire." Winnie began unlacing the shoe she had put back on when they'd started the journey through the cave.

"Maybe, but we're isolated up here and the conditions down the mountain might be worse than up here." He popped the last bite into his mouth.

Winnie took off her boot to reveal a swollen ankle, worse than before. "I can't wear this anymore. It's killing my foot. Oh, dear, that was a poor choice of words."

"But true. I've had a sprained ankle, and it does hurt to wear close-fitting shoes." Ellie unwound her scarf and wrapped it around Winnie's foot.

"I can't take your scarf. You need it."

"Nonsense, you need it more than me. One layer of socks isn't warm enough. I find feet, head and hands get cold faster than other parts of your body. If you keep them covered it helps you feel warmer."

Winnie smiled, but the gesture didn't stay on her

face more than a second. "I can hardly keep my eyes open."

"Then keep them closed. I'm carrying you, anyway." Colt rose. "Ready."

"Are you sure?" Ellie mouthed the question to Colt, touching his hurt arm.

He nodded.

"If the cabin is gone, I won't get to see what you brought in the sack for me and Ellie." Winnie snuggled close to Colt's body.

"What if it isn't burned down?"

Ellie replied, "I think you should tell us, anyway. Don't you, Winnie?"

"Yes."

He exaggerated a sigh, but the corners of his mouth quirked up, his left dimple appearing in his cheek. "Doug carved a German shepherd like Lady for me to give to you, Winnie, and I found my mom's locket in my belongings in the closet when I put my speargun back." His gaze fastened onto Ellie. "I hope you'll accept it."

Her throat closed, emotions she couldn't express rushing to the surface. "I shouldn't. It's your mother's."

"She'd want you to have it. You've gone above and beyond your duties as a bodyguard."

"I totally agree, Colt," Winnie said. "I hope you'll accept it, Ellie, if it didn't burn."

"I'd be honored," she murmured.

Colt cleared his throat. "We'd better get going."

As Ellie continued their trek, the ceiling dropped more until Colt had to bend over while carrying his grandmother through the passage. When Ellie peered at the pair, she noticed Colt's back kept scraping the roof of the cave. Strain marked his features as he struggled to stay on his feet with Winnie in his arms. Ellie rounded a corner in the passageway and came to a stop.

"Does this look familiar, because if it doesn't maybe we should try the other path?" Ellie waved her hand ahead of them at a tunnel about four feet wide and three feet tall.

Colt paused behind her and put his grandmother on the floor. "Yes. I'd forgotten I had to crawl part of the way toward the end. I've been in a lot of caves through the years. They kind of all run together."

"Let me wait here while you two check it out," Winnie said. "I'll be fine. I can catch a catnap. If it turns out to be a way out, you can come back for me. If it doesn't, then we don't have to try and get me through there."

"I don't want to leave—"

"Ellie, we're trapped in a cave with a mound of snow standing between us and the person after me. I think I'll be perfectly safe here by myself."

"I'll go alone, and if it's the way out, I'll come back and get both of you." Colt moved toward the narrow passageway. "Rest, Winnie. It's not far from here so I shouldn't be gone long."

Ellie helped make Winnie more comfortable. Since this ordeal had started, she had appeared to age a couple of years. Ellie was concerned about her. Winnie had been working so hard the past year on the Endless Youth products and then to have to run for her life... It might be too much for even a tough lady like her.

Although her eyes were closed, Winnie huddled in the blanket up against Ellie and said, "Since this began I've been thanking God for sending you to me. Now I'm thanking you for staying for Christmas. I doubt it's your idea of how to celebrate Christmas, but I'm mighty grateful you're here, and if I'm not mistaken, so is my grandson."

"Here we are trapped in a cave and you're match-making."

"You can't blame a grandmother for trying. I've got a captive audience," Winnie said with a chuckle, some of her fight surfacing.

"I like Colt." *A lot.*

"What I've seen makes me think it's more than just like. Or is that wishful thinking on my part?"

Ellie opened her mouth to say, "Yes," but the word wouldn't come out because it wasn't the truth. "No, there is more, but Winnie, I just don't see how…" She didn't know how to explain her mixed-up feelings even to herself, let alone someone else.

"I know you both have separate lives, but even when two people live in the same town and their lives mesh together, a relationship can be hard. Colt needs someone like you in his life."

"You're right about the hurdles between us."

"Thomas and I had hurdles, too, but we overcame them. He'd just divorced his wife a couple of months before we started dating, but we'd known each other and worked together for several years. People took our openly dating as a sign we'd been having an affair while he was married, especially his ex-wife. She made our lives unbearable for a while, then thankfully she decided to move away and we began to have a normal relationship. Thomas was a wonderful stepfather to my son. In fact, he adopted him when we got married."

Marrying. Having a relationship. Where does that fit in my life? She'd spent her years just trying to survive and have a life with meaning. Her work and faith had given her that. But if she gave in to her feelings concerning Colt, everything would change. So much of her life had been one change after another and she had needed some stability, which her vision for her life had given her—until now.

The passageway narrowed even more. Colt flattened himself and pulled his body through the stone-cold corridor. Although pain stabbed his left bicep, he kept going because a freezing wind whipped by him, indicating there was a way out of the cave up ahead. Reaching forward to grasp something to help him slither through the tunnel, he clutched air. Nothing. He focused the small flashlight on the spot in front of him and saw a drop-off.

Dragging himself to the edge of the opening of the passageway, he stared down at a black hole where the floor of the cavern should be. Across from him, not thirty feet away, light streamed into the darkness. He swung his flashlight toward the area and saw the rocks he remembered piled up where the second cave entrance used to be.

So close with a thirty-foot gap between him and freedom.

"What's keeping Colt? He should have been back by now." Winnie's teeth chattered.

Ellie rubbed her gloved hands up and down Winnie's arms. "It might have been farther than he thought. It hasn't been that long." She infused an upbeat tone into her voice because she knew the cold was getting to Winnie. "Tell me some more about your marriage to Thomas. It sounds like you two were very happy."

"Don't get me wrong. We had our problems, especially concerning Colt's father, but we always managed to work them out. As long as we had each other, we felt we could deal with anything."

"That's nice. No wonder you're a romantic at heart."

"Me? What gave you that idea?"

"Oh, the flowers in your house, a tradition your husband started and you continued. The way you talk about Thomas. But mostly some of the products your company sells with names like Only Her and Only Him."

"You aren't a romantic?"

"Never had time for romance in my life."

"Why not?"

Ellie ended up telling a second person about her childhood. "What is it about a Winfield demanding to know stuff I've never shared with others?"

"It's our charm." Winnie grinned, a sparkle in her eyes for the first time since they'd started on this trek hours ago. "That and we care. People sense that about us. Hard to resist."

"That could be it."

A sound behind Ellie turned her in the direction of the tunnel. Colt crawled out of the hole, his features set in grim determination.

"Something wrong?" she asked.

He shook his head. "The tunnel is narrower than I remember, but if I can get through, you two can. Anyone larger than me won't, though. When I reached the other end, there is a sheer drop-off at the opening that wasn't there before, but the hole in the cavern is only four feet deep. I'll be able to lower myself to the floor and make my way to the entrance. It's still partially blocked. I may have to move a few rocks, but I'll be able to get through the hole."

"So bring back some skinny people to help us," Ellie said.

He laughed, then gathered what he was going to take with him—snowshoes, gun, tinted goggles. "I'll keep that in mind. Stay here. It's warmer in this cavern than the other one."

At the entrance to the tunnel, Ellie placed her hand on his arm.

He turned toward her.

"Keep safe. If an avalanche happened once, it can again."

His smile began as a twinkle in his eyes and spread to transform his earlier serious expression. "I like this role of knight in shining armor."

"Well, in that case, here's a token of my appreciation." She produced his scarf he'd left on the floor and put it around his neck. "It's cold out there."

"It's cold in here."

"True, but not as much wind." Her gaze linked with his. "I mean it. Don't take any unnecessary risks."

"Then it's okay to take necessary risks?"

"I'll be praying."

"Me, too, Colt," Winnie said from where she was sitting against the wall of the cave.

Colt stepped around Ellie, made his way to his grandmother, whispered something to her then kissed her on the head.

When he returned to Ellie, he caught her hands and brought them up between them, inching toward her until they touched. "I probably won't be back for a while."

"I know."

He leaned down and claimed her mouth in a kiss that rocked Ellie to her core, mocking her intention of keeping herself apart from him. It was so hard when he was storming every defense she put up to keep people away.

He pulled back, stared at her for a long moment then ducked down and disappeared into the tunnel. She watched him crawl toward the exit, his light fading. *What if I never see him again?* Her heart lurched at that thought.

Lord, keep him safe. Please. You're in control.

Although the temptation was great to check out the front of the cave and the cabin, Colt couldn't. That would eat into time he didn't have if he was going to get help back up the mountain before dark. He didn't know how long Winnie could last in this freezing weather. She had never tolerated the cold like he and his grand-dad had.

When he wiggled himself through the opening in the cave, he emerged into more falling snow, but at least it wasn't coming down too hard. Actually the snow could work to his advantage by covering his tracks if the assailant was still alive and out there waiting.

The scent of smoke hovered in the air. He looked in the direction of the cabin but couldn't see any flames. A dense cloud cover hung low over the area.

In his mind he plotted the trail he would take to the estate. Once there, he could use the phone and call for help. Then he and Doug could start up the mountain even before a rescue team could form and make it up to the cave.

Hours later, only a short distance from the house, Colt pushed himself faster. It would be dark before he could get back up the mountain if he didn't move more quickly. Although his legs shook with fatigue, he put one foot in front of the other, sometimes dragging himself out of a hole when he sank too far into the snow. But once he made it over the last ridge he would nearly be home. That thought urged him to pick up speed yet again.

When he put his foot down in front of him, the snow gave away, sending him tumbling down the incline. When he rolled to the bottom, he crashed into a pine tree, knocking the breath from him. Snow crusted him from head to foot. He wiped it away from his goggles and saw two snow boots planted apart. His gaze traveled upward past two legs and a heavy coat to a face covered in a white ski mask.

"Do you think Colt is all right? What if the bad guy didn't get caught in the avalanche and was waiting for him? I can't lose my grandson." Winnie took a sip from the bottle of water then passed it to Ellie.

"Colt can take care of himself." She prayed she was right.

"I know. I shouldn't worry. It does no good but get me upset."

"In a perfect world we wouldn't worry." Ellie worried, too. So many things could go wrong.

"We're safe in here while he's—"

A roar split the air, sending goose bumps flashing up Ellie's body.

Winnie's eyes grew round and huge. "That's—that's a…" She gulped, the color washing from her face.

"A bear. Nearby."

"In this cave!" Winnie sat up straight, the blanket falling away from her. "What's it doing in here?"

"It's a cave and wintertime. Hibernating?" Ellie quickly gathered up all their belongings and stuffed them into one of the backpacks.

"What do we do?" Winnie asked at the same time another deep growl echoed through the cave.

"Get out of here."

"How? It sounds like it's coming down the passage-way we used."

"We're going through the tunnel. Chances are it can't get through there. It's probably still fat since it's only December." Ellie felt for her gun at her hip. "If I have to, I will shoot it. Do you think you can crawl through the tunnel?"

"If I have to, I will."

Ellie helped Winnie to her feet, then supported most of her weight as the woman hopped toward the escape route. "You go first. I'm going in backward so if the bear follows, I can take care of it. From what Colt said, there is no room to turn around. Okay?"

Taking one of the flashlights, Winnie knelt before the entrance and began crawling forward. Ellie backed into the tunnel, pulling the backpack after her. Through the opening she glimpsed a brown bear loping into the area where they had been, sniffing the air. It released another roar, lumbered to the hole and stuck its head inside.

Colt started to spring up when a shovel crashed down on top of him, glancing off his head and striking his shoulder. His ears rang. The whole world spun for a few seconds. The man lifted the weapon again. Colt dropped back to the ground and rolled hard into the man. The action sent a wave of dizziness through Colt, but toppled his assailant to the snow.

Facedown, Colt fumbled in his coat pocket for his gun, fighting the whirling sensation attacking his mind. Before he could pull it out, his attacker whacked the shovel across his back. Again, pain shot through his body. Someone yelled right before blackness swallowed him up.

"That's the bear!" Winnie said behind Ellie in the tunnel.

"A big one thankfully. I don't think it can get in here. Keep moving as fast as you can just in case."

Keeping her eye on the bear and her gun aimed at it, Ellie listened to Winnie's struggles as she made her way. Ellie didn't want to go any farther until she knew what the bear was going to do. Even if the animal tried to fit into the narrow passage, it wouldn't be able to do much. She calmed her speeding heartbeat.

Wiping first one sweating hand then the other against her coat, she locked gazes with the beast, giving it the most intimidating glare she could muster. "I'm not letting you pass. Don't make me hurt you." A fierce strength coated each word.

The bear released another growl. Its long teeth ridiculed her statements. The animal pushed forward a few inches but didn't go any farther because the walls sloped inward at that point. Finally it gave one last glower then backed out of the entrance into the tunnel.

"There's a really narrow part," Winnie said behind her.

When the bear disappeared from her view, Ellie scooted backward toward the other end. Sounds of the animal drifted to her, but it hadn't returned to the tunnel. A chill pervaded the passage, especially the closer she came to the exit. The thought that it was even colder than where they had been worried Ellie. Winnie needed medical attention and warmth. Ellie couldn't give her either.

"Colt." A familiar male voice filtered into Colt's pain-riddled mind.

The first sensation Colt experienced besides the drumming throb against his skull was the chill penetrating through his clothing. He opened his eyes to find someone kneeling next to him. With his cheek pressed against the snow, frigid, biting, Colt fought the urge to surrender again to the darkness.

"Colt, I was checking the grounds when I heard a noise and looked up the rise. I saw someone attacking you."

Relief that it was Doug pushed Colt to keep himself as alert as possible. Winnie and Ellie were depending on him. Moaning, he lifted his head and regretted it instantly. The world tilted before him. He closed his eyes, but it still swirled. He didn't have time for this. He forced down the nausea churning his stomach and slowly he rolled to face upward. Snowflakes pelted him, but the storm had lessened. Which meant whoever attacked him could possibly find the other entrance into the cave because his footprints weren't totally covered by the falling snow.

"Winnie and Ellie are trapped in the cave system

near the cabin, the one I told you about." Somehow he strung together a sentence that made sense.

Doug looked up at the mountain. "That's the way your attacker fled."

Colt struggled to prop himself up on his elbows, searching for the tracks the man made. If he moved slowly, the world didn't spin too much. "I was coming to the house to call for help. There was an avalanche and it blocked the front of the cave. I used the back way in on the other side of the mountain. It's blocked, but I managed to remove a few rocks and wiggle out of the opening."

"Let's get you to the house and call 911, then I'll go up there."

"No, you go back. We're almost into cell range. Alert the sheriff then follow my tracks. I have to go. If that man finds Winnie and Ellie, he'll kill them. He tried to burn the cabin down."

"But wasn't Mary Ann Witlock the one threatening Winnie?"

"Maybe this guy was helping her."

Taking it slow, Colt tucked his legs under him then pushed himself to stand. Doug hurried to assist him. Colt's body protested with his every move, but he managed to remain upright. Then he put one foot in front of the other and started up the mountain, following his assailant's tracks.

He glanced back at Doug and the man was almost to the fence line at the estate. Help wouldn't be too far behind, but Colt had to quicken his pace if he was going to stop the attacker from harming Winnie and Ellie.

I need Your help, Lord. I can't do this without You. Anything is possible with You.

* * *

While Winnie stayed on the ledge at the tunnel, Ellie lowered herself over the cave shelf, clinging to a protruding rock. When her feet touched the floor, she let go of the stone, then positioned herself near the wall.

"Okay, Winnie. I'm going to guide you down and hold you so you don't put any weight on your bad foot."

"I still hear the bear. Do you think it can get through that tunnel?"

"No. It's angry we got away. Come on. We'll find a place to settle down and wait for Colt where we can also keep an eye on the tunnel."

After Winnie made it to the floor of the cavern, Ellie swung her light around to find the best place to wait. Puddles of icy water littered the area. Wind blew through the opening.

"The good news is that the water isn't totally frozen so the temperature isn't much below freezing."

Winnie snorted. "Tell that to my body."

Ellie pointed to a place a few feet away. "It's dry there and it looks like it'll shelter us from the wind. And I can see the tunnel."

Shielded from the wind slipping through the opening, Ellie cocooned Winnie in as much warmth as possible. She even used the backpack for her to sit on. "There. Now it's just a matter of a couple of hours. Everything will be over."

"No, it won't. We don't know who is after me. Who might have worked with Mary Ann?"

"I know we looked into her background and no one stood out. She didn't have a boyfriend, and the couple of members of her family who worked for Glamour Sensations didn't have much to do with her."

"One of the reasons I didn't pick her to be the spokesperson for Endless Youth was the way she always came across as though she were ten or fifteen years older than she was. An old soul but not in a good way. Weary. Unhappy. That wasn't the image I wanted to project for this line. Christy is the opposite of that. Young at heart although she is thirty-two. I didn't want a woman who was too young, but I wanted one who had an exuberance in spirit about her. I was so happy when Christy started dating Peter. She'd been engaged once before, and he was killed in a motorcycle accident." Winnie hugged her arms against her chest.

Ellie needed to keep her talking about anything but the situation they were in. "I understand that Christy became engaged to Peter right after you chose her as the spokesperson. Will that interfere in your advertising plans for the product?"

"No, Peter assured me he would do whatever Christy needed. He's been a great support for her. I was surprised at how fast he moved. They'd only been dating a couple of months. I think secretly—although he would never admit it—that he was afraid once the world saw her another man would snatch her right up. Men and claiming their territory." Winnie chuckled. "But I can't complain. Thomas was just like Peter. We only dated a few months, too. Of course, we worked together for a while before that."

"They know a good woman when they see her," Ellie said over the howl of the wind, its force increasing through the cave.

"Yes, and I'm hoping my grandson follows in his granddad's footsteps."

Even in the shadows created by the dim light, Ellie

could see Winnie's gleaming eyes. "I have a very persuasive boss who has tried her best to fix me up with a couple of men she knows in Dallas. So far I've not succumbed to her tactics."

"Colt needs someone like you."

"I refuse to say anything to that. I'm sure there is a better subject than my love life."

Winnie's forehead crinkled. "You know, I've been thinking. Not many people knew we were coming up here. We really didn't make the final decision until we talked with the sheriff yesterday. Remember?"

"Yes. We were having a late breakfast. But only Linda was in the room besides the sheriff and us."

Winnie gasped. "It couldn't be Linda, Doug or the sheriff."

A sound above Winnie drew Ellie's gaze. On top of the ledge stood a man dressed in white wearing a white ski mask with a gun aimed at Winnie.

Chapter Twelve

"Who are you?" Ellie asked the man on the ledge.

He cackled. "I'm not telling you. You two can die wondering who I am, especially after all the trouble you've put me through today."

"Why me?" Winnie lifted her face toward her assailant. "What have I done to you?"

"You continually have ruined my life," he said in a voice roughened as if he disguised it.

"I couldn't have. I haven't done that to anyone. I would know about it."

"Well, obviously you don't," the man shouted, his gun wavering as anger poured off him.

Ellie glanced at her gun lying on the ground next to her. She gauged her chances of grabbing it and getting a shot off before he did.

"Don't think about it. I'd have Winnie dead before you could aim the gun."

The voice, although muffled by the ski mask some, sounded familiar to Ellie. She'd heard him before—recently. Could it be Doug? The sheriff?

"Why me?" Winnie asked the gunman. "Don't you

want me to know why you're killing me? What satisfaction can you have in that if I don't know why, especially if I wronged you as you say?" A mocking tone inched into Winnie's voice.

Ellie needed to keep the man talking. "As far as we know you're a maniac who belongs in a mental—"

His harsh laugh cut off the rest of her sentence. "Colt isn't coming to your rescue. I left him for dead and followed his trail to you two. How accommodating he was to show me where you all were."

No, Colt can't be dead. He's psyching me out. Trying to rattle me.

"I guess you should know why, Winnie." He said her name slowly, bitterness dripping from it. "You stole my father from my mother."

Winnie gasped.

"If you hadn't come along, my parents would have gotten back together. I would have had a father who would acknowledge me. Instead, he wouldn't have anything to do with me. You poisoned him. You kept him from me."

"Thomas didn't have a child. Thomas couldn't have one."

"Liar!"

"The doctors told Thomas it was impossible, and we never could have children." The pain in Winnie's voice was reflected in her expression, too.

"I am Thomas Winfield's son. My mama showed me my birth certificate. It was right there on the paper. There wasn't a day that went by that I wasn't reminded I wasn't good enough to be a Winfield. He discarded my mother and me like we were trash."

"Are you talking about Clare, Thomas's first wife?"

"Yes. He decided to divorce her for you."

"No, he didn't. We didn't start dating until after the divorce."

"That's not what my mama told me. Why in the world would I believe you? My father wasn't the only one you took away from me. Everything I wanted you came after. Well, not anymore. I'm putting an end to you." He lowered the gun a few inches and pointed it right at Winnie's heart.

Ellie yanked Winnie toward her at the same time a shot rang out in the cave. Snatching her weapon from the floor, she raised it toward their attacker while putting herself in between Winnie and the man. But Ellie didn't get off a shot. Instead, his arm fell to his side, the gun dropping from his fingers. It bounced on the stone surface, going off, the bullet lodging in the wall. Blood spread outward on the white jacket he wore as he crumbled to the ground.

As Ellie scrambled up, she glimpsed Colt diving through the hole and springing to his feet, his gun pointed at their assailant.

"Ellie, Winnie, are you two all right?"

"Yes," they both answered at the same time.

Ellie swiveled toward Winnie. "Are you really okay?"

She nodded. "At least I'm not cold anymore. Fear will do that to you."

Ellie headed up the sloping side to the ledge above Winnie and joined Colt as he knelt next to the gunman. He removed the man's goggles then his white ski mask to reveal Peter Tyler, blinking his eyes at the light she shone on his face.

Ellie stared at the glittering Christmas tree in the living room at Winnie's house. Although it was Christmas Day, there had been nothing calm and peaceful so far. Winnie had spent time with Christy, consoling her over her fiancé. Harold and Colt had been behind closed doors a good part of the morning, then Colt insisted Winnie rest before the sheriff came this afternoon. He had an update on what Peter Tyler had said after he came out of surgery to repair his shoulder where Colt had shot him. Colt and Doug had gone up to the cabin to see what was left of the place. Colt had wanted her to come, but she'd felt she needed to stay with Winnie. After what had occurred with Mary Ann, she wasn't quite ready to relinquish her bodyguard duties with Winnie until she had reassurances from the sheriff.

Then she would return to Dallas. And try to put her life back together. She finally could admit to herself that she loved Colt, but how could she really be sure? Even if she was, that didn't mean he cared about her or that they should be together. He lived on a research vessel in the middle of the ocean. She could never imagine herself living like that.

When the doorbell rang, she hurried across the foyer to answer it. Stepping to the side, she let the sheriff into the house. "I hope you're here to tell us good news."

"Yes," he said as Winnie descended the stairs and Colt came from the kitchen.

"Would you like anything to drink? We have some cookies, too." Winnie gestured toward the living room.

"Nope. Just as soon as we talk, I'm heading home. My son and grandchildren are there waiting for me so they can open presents. I haven't quite had a Christmas like this year in—well, never." Sheriff Quinn stood in front of the fireplace, warming himself. "I came right from the hospital after interviewing Peter. I laid it on the line. We have him dead to rights on three counts of attempted murder, arson and a number of other charges. I told him the judge would look kindly toward him if we didn't have to drag this out in a lengthy trial. He told me what happened."

Winnie frowned. "What was his involvement with Mary Ann?"

Colt hung back by the entrance into the living room, leaning against the wall, his arms folded over his chest. Ellie glanced toward him, but his expression was unreadable, his gaze fixed on his grandmother.

"He encouraged her to act on her feelings and gave her suggestions. When she was his patient, they got acquainted. He listened to her when she ranted about not getting the spokesperson job, then began planting seeds in her mind about how she had not been treated fairly. The threatening letters were Mary Ann's doing and the stink bombs at the Christmas Gala. He helped her kidnap the dogs because he told her that she could get some good money for them and get back at Winnie."

"Your lead didn't pan out about the dogs. Does he know where they are?" Colt asked, coming farther into the room and sitting next to Winnie.

"Yes, because he connected her with the person who took them to sell in Denver. The police there are paying that gentleman a visit today before he gets rid of them. You should have your dogs home by tomorrow."

"Unless someone bought them for a Christmas gift." Exhaustion still clung to Winnie's face, especially her eyes.

"Then we'll track each purchase."

"Winnie, they're alive. That's good news." Colt took her hand in his.

"So Peter Tyler was responsible in part about the dogs. How about the car left in the middle of the road the night of the Christmas tree lighting?" she asked.

"That was him. He didn't care whether you went off the cliff like Thomas or got upset by the similarities between the two events."

Winnie sat forward. "Wait. He didn't have anything to do with Thomas's accident, did he?"

"No, at least that's what he said, and all the evidence still points to an accident, Winnie. He wasn't even living here at that time. He moved back not long after he saw in the newspaper about Thomas dying. His mother had passed away a few months before your husband. According to Peter, she was still brokenhearted after all the years they were divorced. She fed Peter a lot of garbage about you coming between her and Thomas. I told him that wasn't the case. You two worked in the lab together, but so did my mother and she said it was hogwash what Thomas's ex-wife was saying."

Winnie smiled, and even her eyes sparkled with the gesture. "Your mom is a good friend."

"She sends her regards from sunny Florida. I can't get her back here in the winter. Too cold."

Winnie laughed. "I heartily agree with her. I may go visit her and warm these cold bones."

"We didn't make the final decision to go to the cabin until you told us it was safe. How did Peter know we were there?" Ellie asked Sheriff Quinn.

"He knew there was a chance, based on the talk the night before. He planned ahead, staying in a small cabin not far from you on the Henderson property.

Then he came back to watch and see if you went."
The sheriff held his hands out over the fire and rubbed
them together.

Ellie liked seeing Winnie's smile and hearing her
laugh. The past weeks' ordeal had taken a toll on the
woman. After the doctor at the house had checked out
Winnie, she'd slept for twelve hours last night. Winnie
had insisted Colt go to the hospital and have some X-
rays on his arm. Ellie had taken him but little was said.
In fact, Colt dozed on the trip to the hospital where the
doctor told him he would be sore for a while, but he
hadn't fractured his arm. Colt had also suffered a mild
concussion, but he'd refused to stay overnight.

"Winnie, you could always return with me to the
Kaleidoscope. We're in warm waters. In the South Pacific, it's summer right now."

"Not if I have to live on a boat."

Colt smiled. "It's a ship."

"Not big enough for me. You know I can't swim.
You didn't get the swimming gene from me."

"Speaking of genes. Is Peter my uncle?"

Winnie shuddered. "Good grief, no. I don't know
who his father is, but Thomas was sterile. For some
reason she used Thomas to blame all her woes on. I
guess that was easier for her than changing."

"I'm heading home to salvage a little bit of Christmas with my family." The sheriff crossed the room to
the foyer, and Colt walked with him to the front door.

Winnie pinned Ellie with an assessing look. "You've
been quiet. I imagine you're glad this is over with about
as much as I am."

"I'm usually like this when a job is finished. It takes
me days to come down from the stress. How's Christy?

She looked much better after she talked with you this morning."

"At first she wanted to step down from being the spokesperson for Endless Youth, but I talked her out of that. I told her she's not responsible for other people's actions. She isn't to blame for Peter or Mary Ann. Christy told me she talked with Peter before he went into surgery. What sent Peter over the edge was that Christy got the job that would demand a lot of her time—time away from him. He came to Bakersville after years of being told I was the one who caused all the trouble for him and his mother. He struggled to make it through school and has a huge debt from college loans he's still paying back. He saw the money he thought he should rightly have as Thomas's only living son. It festered inside him. The trigger was Christy getting the job and getting all the attention. But it was Peter's problem, not hers."

"Can you forgive Peter for what he did?"

"Probably when I recover from the effects of yesterday. Hanging on to the anger will only hurt me in the long run. Look what happened to Peter and his mother when they held on to their anger."

Listening to Winnie's reasonable explanation of why she would forgive Peter made Ellie think about her mother. She hadn't talked to her in years, and that had always bothered her. Maybe she should call her tonight and wish her a merry Christmas.

Colt reentered the living room. "I'm glad this is all wrapped up. I got a message from the *Kaleidoscope*. Doug gave it to me this morning. I'm needed back there to finish up a study we've been running on the seal population in the area where we're anchored."

"When?" Winnie rose.

"Day after tomorrow. I want to make sure you're all right and things are really settled after what's happened."

"At least we have a little more time together. I think I'll take my second nap today. See you two at dinner."

After Winnie left, Colt took the couch across from Ellie. He stared at the fire for a long moment before looking at her. "One thing my grandmother isn't is subtle. For being tired, she can move awfully fast."

"I think she's still trying to process it all. Having not just one but two people angry with you to the point they wanted to harm you is hard on even the toughest person. Imagine Peter's mother lying to him for all those years."

"It just makes me realize how fortunate I've been to have Winnie and my granddad to raise me."

"I'm going to call my mother tonight. It's about time I did. I don't expect warm fuzzies, but I need to take the first step to try and mend our relationship. She's all the family I have. I see the relationship you have with Winnie, and although we'll probably never have that kind, we can at least have a civil one."

"You get a chance to do that. I don't have that. My father is dead."

"You can forgive him in your heart. That's what is important."

"You're right." Colt stood and bridged the distance between them. "Speaking of relationships, what are we going to do about us?"

"Nothing."

He clasped her hands and hauled her up against him. "You can't deny we have a connection."

"No, I can't. But this isn't real. This whole situation heightened all our senses. I've seen it before with others and their relationships didn't last. You and I live very differently. I couldn't live on a research vessel even if it's classified a ship. I need space. I would go crazy. How could a relationship last with you in the Pacific Ocean and me flying all over the world for my job? I think we should cut our losses and go our separate ways."

"How do you feel about me? Forget about what you just said. All the logical, rational reasons we shouldn't be together." He placed his hand over her heart. "How do you feel in there?"

"I love you, but it isn't enough. A lasting relationship is much more than love. We haven't had any time to think about our feelings. We've been on a roller-coaster ride since you arrived."

He framed her face. "I love you, Ellie. I don't want to let you go. I realized that when I was trying to get back to you and Winnie in the cave. I thought I was going to lose you when I saw Peter pointing the gun at you."

His declaration made her hesitate, her resolve wavering. Finally she murmured, "Someone has to be the logical, rational one. I guess I'm that one. I need time to figure out what I want. You need time. You have a job that needs you right now and so do I."

He bent toward her and kissed her. All the sensations he could produce in her flooded her, making her want to take a risk. When he pulled back, sanity returned to Ellie.

"Why not give the *Kaleidoscope* a chance? You might like it."

She shook her head.

"No, I'm leaving tomorrow morning to return to Dallas. Maybe sometime in the future we'll meet again under less stressful circumstances."

He released a long breath. "You're right. These past few weeks have been unreal. Reality is our everyday lives. Will you promise me one thing?"

"Maybe."

He chuckled. "Why am I not surprised you said that? Where's the trust?"

"That's just the point. I don't trust easily and these new feelings could all vanish with time."

"Winnie will be having an Endless Youth gala to launch the new line on Valentine's Day. In spite of what happened the last time, she'll be having it at the same hotel that evening. Come back. Meet me there if you think we have a chance at what we started here. That's seven weeks away."

"I promise I'll think long and hard on it."

"You do that," he said. "And I hope I'll see you then."

Colt stood at the double doors into the hotel ball-room on Valentine's Day. The event was in full swing. Laughter floated to him. A sense of celebration dominated the atmosphere of the Endless Youth gala. The music, soft and romantic, filled the room. Couples, dressed in tuxedos and gowns, whirled around the dance floor to the strains of a waltz.

None of the gaiety meant anything to him.

The ball was halfway over. Ellie wasn't here. She wasn't coming.

"Colt, why aren't you dancing?"

He forced a smile for his grandmother, but inside his heart was breaking. "You sent Ellie the invitation?"

"For the third time, yes, and I know she received it."

"I gave her the space she wanted."

"Then you've done what you can. Have faith in what you feel, what you two shared at Christmas. I saw how she felt about you. Give her time to work it out. Why don't you dance with your favorite grandmother?"

"You're my *only* grandmother."

"True."

"You know dancing isn't my thing. Harold is so much better than me, and he is your date for tonight."

"Just because Harold and I are dating doesn't mean I should neglect my grandson." She laughed, a sound Colt loved to hear from his grandmother. "I can't believe I'm dating again. I thought that would never happen after Thomas."

"Why not? You're seventy-three years *young*."

"You're right." Winnie held her hand out to Colt.

He threw a last glance over his shoulder at the hotel lobby. No Ellie. After three days on the *Kaleidoscope* he'd known what he'd felt for her was the marrying kind of love. There was no thrill and excitement in his job. He wanted to share his life with Ellie. He'd completed his research project and resigned. It was time for him to put down roots. Alone, if not with Ellie.

He whisked his grandmother out onto the dance floor and somehow managed to sweep Winnie around the ballroom to some love song without stepping on her foot or stumbling.

Then he saw her, dressed in a long red gown, across the room in the entrance to the ballroom. Ellie had come. He came to a standstill. Their gazes linked together, and his heart began pounding against his chest.

"Go to her," Winnie whispered, backing away from him.

Colt headed toward Ellie at the same time she did. They met on the edge of the dance floor. He was sure he had some silly grin on his face, but Ellie's smile encompassed her whole face in radiance.

"You look beautiful. Want to dance?" He offered her his hand.

She clasped it and came effortlessly into his embrace. The feel of her against him felt so right.

"I'm sorry I was late. My flight was delayed then we had to change planes and—"

He stopped her words with a kiss. When he drew back and began to move about the floor, he said, "You're here. That's all that's important."

They flowed as one through the crowd of dancers. All he could do was stare at her. He never wanted to take his eyes off her again.

"Seven weeks was too long to be apart. When I returned to the *Kaleidoscope,* my life wasn't the same. I wanted different things. I love you, Ellie."

"The same for me. I went back to Dallas. I even went on an assignment in Rome. I love Rome. I stayed a few days after my job was finished, but Rome wasn't the same without you. I tried to talk myself out of my feelings, but I couldn't, not in seven weeks. That's when I knew I had to see you again. Be with you."

The music stopped. Colt grabbed her hand and hurried off the dance floor out into the lobby. He found a private alcove and pulled her back into his arms.

"I want to be with you, too," he said.

"Our jobs—"

He put two fingers over her lips, the feel of them against his skin everything he remembered. Warm. Soft. Her. "I resigned from the *Kaleidoscope*. I'm slowly going to take over for Winnie. She wants to retire completely in a year or so. She says she's ready to lie around and eat bonbons."

Ellie laughed. "That'll be the day. She'll hole herself in her lab in the basement and create some other sensational product."

"As the soon-to-be CEO of Glamour Sensations, I'm hoping she will. What would you say if we hired you as the head of our security? The company is growing. I need someone with more experience than our current guy. Security will become more important than ever before. And there will still be some travel involved so you won't always be confined to here."

She snuggled closer. "I like being confined to here if you're here, too."

"Right by your side. I hope as your husband." Then he kissed her with every emotion he'd held in check for the past seven weeks without her.

"I think I can accommodate that."

* * * * *

Dear Reader,

Christmas Stalking is the fourth in my Guardians, Inc. series, where the women and men are both equally strong characters who know how to deal with dangerous situations. I've had readers write to me about how much they enjoy seeing a woman play a tough role and still be soft and vulnerable enough to fall in love. I have two more books coming in this series for Love Inspired Suspense. Look for them in the future.

I love hearing from readers. You can contact me at margaretdaley@gmail.com. You can also learn more about my books at www.margaretdaley.com. I have a newsletter that you can sign up for on my website.

Best wishes,

Margaret Daley

CHRISTMAS COUNTDOWN

Vicki Hinze

To Dawn Woodhams,
an admirable heroine very much like Maggie.
With love and wishes for much joy and many...
blessings,
Vicki

Greater love hath no man than this,
that a man lay down his life for his friends.
—*John* 15:13

Chapter One

Something wasn't right.

Alert and armed, Maggie Mason moved from room to room. Outwardly nothing appeared to be wrong. The house was chilly and quiet, silent in the way a house is on a cold December night when you're in it alone. Yet the awareness that something was off prodded her honed instincts. You didn't work in her field, much less enjoy her success, and not hone your instincts or fail to respect them. No one was inside the house with her; she'd have picked up on that immediately. Yet some nebulous alert had triggered her internal alarm. She couldn't explain it. She just felt it.

Knew it.

Feared it.

And she'd learned the hard way to never ignore internal warnings.

Controlling her breathing, deliberately working to slow her racing heart, she circled back to the kitchen, clicked on her flashlight and followed her emergency plan, taking the worn wooden stairs down to the basement. An unadvertised and unmentioned feature in the basement sold her on renting the Decatur, Illinois, home just days ago. It wasn't in the best neighborhood, but she'd lived in far worse, and it had that nondescript look about it—not too nice, not too dumpy—where she could fade into obscurity.

Obscurity was essential.

With it and any luck, she wouldn't have to move again for a couple of months. Oh, how she yearned for a little luck.

In the past three years, her record for staying put, hospital and recovery time aside, was two months, fourteen days, seven hours and twelve minutes. This basement's special feature could help buy her a little more time here and help her break her record. At least, she dared to hope it could.

Please, God. I'm so tired of running.

A knot rose in her throat. She swallowed it down and stepped off the bottom stair onto the cracked concrete floor. The twenty-by-twenty open area billed as a basement storage room was inky dark—no electricity, no windows, and only one door at the top of the stairs she'd just descended…or so it appeared until further inspection.

Sweeping the beam of light corner to corner on the floor, she checked the dull coating of dust for new footprints but spotted none, then lifted the beam up the walls, casting light on the thin cobwebs clinging to the corners at the ceiling and on the floor joists overhead. The webs glistened but remained intact.

A little reassured, she eased her finger on the trigger of her weapon and took a steadying breath to work the hitch from her chest. The basement clearly had been abandoned for a long time, yet it didn't smell musty or dank. Odd, with the occasional water stain in the pink fiberglass insulation stuffed between the wall studs. The stains spoke of past leaks now repaired, but the absence of a musty scent had first alerted her that more than met the eye was in this basement.

Following the flashlight beam, she moved across the empty expanse to the back wall, where a tall and rickety wooden shelving unit stood in the corner. Battered and worn, it, too, wore a layer of dust she'd been careful not to disturb. She checked each shelf. No smears or swipes marring its dull surface. Here, too, the dust remained undisturbed.

Stretching on tiptoes, she reached between the top and second shelves and tapped seeking fingertips along the rough wooden back wall. They snagged metal. A flathead bolt. Inching her nails under its edge, she pulled the bolt out and then slid the entire shelving unit sideways. Gliders bore its weight, but it moved in jerked spurts.

In the wall where the unit had stood, an opening appeared: a low, narrow passageway.

At one time, that passageway likely had been used as an emergency exit for a drug dealer—she'd seen a number of those in neighborhoods such as this during her time as a normal, active FBI profiler—but the rental agent hadn't mentioned the passageway at all. When he'd left her to explore, she'd found it on her own, though she hadn't mentioned finding it to him, either. If he'd known, he'd have disclosed it. For her own safety, the fewer who knew the better.

Bending low to keep from cracking her head against the wooden-beam reinforcements holding back the earth inside the tunnel, she focused her flashlight's beam down the passage and then followed it to its abrupt end at a heavy metal grate. The first thing she'd done when she moved in was to replace the grate lock with one of her own. She peered through the lacy metal outside into the backs of thick, squat bushes. The grate couldn't be seen from the yard. It took knowing it was there behind the bushes to find it.

She carefully checked the grate's internal perimeter. The chewing gum embedded with a single strand of hair she'd pressed on each of the four corners remained untouched and in place. Peering outside again, she scanned the dirt behind the bushes and spotted the heavy-duty string she'd strung ankle-high. Unmoved. Nothing disrupted the smooth dirt, and the stones she'd arranged in a distinct pattern were exactly where she'd put them.

Her escape route was intact.

Yet her internal alarm didn't shut off. It continued to pound its warning in time with the fast beats of her heart.

You've been running too long, Maggie.

She had. And paranoia was setting in. Chiding herself, she made her way back upstairs then bolted the basement door, slamming home both original dead bolts and the one she'd installed the night she'd moved in. *Three days and counting...*

Breathing easier, she tucked her weapon into the holster at the back of her jeans' waistband and shifted her focus to the barren kitchen. A familiar ache settled in her chest. It lacked any of the warmth or comfort of generations of family use. The kitchen on the ranch in North Bay, Florida, on the other hand, held a lot of history. Most of her history. It was and always had been home. Her big brother, Paul, still lived there, but for now, home and North Bay were off-limits to her. If Gary Crawford had anything to say about it, both would remain off-limits to her for the rest of her life, which he had every intention of ending as soon as possible.

Resentment and bitterness welled up from deep inside and soured her stomach.

No, don't do it, Maggie. Don't. Think about something else.

She looked at the kitchen table. Its once-white enamel top was chipped and yellowed and worn slick but the table was still sturdy, and currently nearly buried under the stewed makings of a gingerbread house. Christmas was just weeks away—the fourth in a row she'd spend alone—but she'd kept the gingerbread house family tradition for the past three, and she would keep it for this one, too. It wasn't much, but when you had nothing, it was, well, *something*.

Running was never easy. But holidays were hardest.

Her eyes burned. She blinked fast and snipped the corner of a Ziploc bag, inserted the plastic piping tip and seated it, then spooned icing into the bag. At home, Paul had always stuffed the icing bag. She'd put the gumdrops on the house, sprinkle nuts around the base and position the candy canes to frame the front door.

A smile curved her lips. From the time she'd had to tiptoe to reach the tabletop, Paul had fawned over her perfectly positioning each gumdrop. Every girl should be so lucky as to have a brother like him. She sniffed and checked her watch—four ten. He was late calling her, but just ten minutes. Not yet worrisomely late.

Snagging an apple, she took a crunchy bite, discovered she was starved and scarfed it down, then tossed the core into the trash can under the sink and rinsed her hands, careful not to bump the cup filled with her best artist's paintbrushes beside the tap. She gave them a longing look. *Security first. Then the gingerbread house. Then landscapes.* "Just a little longer," she told the red cup of brushes. "Tomorrow night, I paint. Maybe that sunset in Lafitte, Louisiana." The fall of dusk and the fading light on the bayou had been stunning…

Finally at five fifteen her cell phone rang.

Brushing at an errant lock of long reddish-blond hair clinging to her cheek, she primed to give Paul a hard time for calling late and checked caller ID. It was Ian. At first, he was her brother's good friend from the military, a physician and husband to Maggie's now-deceased friend, Beth. Now Ian was an investigator at Lost, Inc. And while due to Beth's murder he'd pushed most people away, he and Maggie remained close. But why was he calling now? Was something wrong with Paul?

Don't jump to conclusions. You've got enough trouble without borrowing more. "Ian, how are you?"

"Hi, Maggie. Paul's out of pocket and I promised him I'd check in on you. Sorry I'm late. Got tied up with a client. You okay?"

"For the moment." Trying not to be disappointed Ian called her as a favor, she pulled out a chair at the table. It scudded across the wooden floor. "Where's Paul?" Her brother rarely missed an appointed call with her. "He's okay, isn't—"

"He's fine. He and Della are on their way to her stepgrandmother's." Ian sounded excited.

"Did he propose to her or something?" Maggie snitched a red gumdrop. Paul hadn't told her, so she doubted it, but with the move, she had been out of touch the better part of two weeks.

"I think that might be the reason for the trip. She's Della's closest relative."

Paul would ask *somebody's* permission first, so it fit. He'd loved Della Jackson for two years, but she'd only recently allowed herself to love anyone. Thank goodness, she'd chosen Paul. He deserved the best, and Maggie prayed every day he got it. "I hope it is."

"Either way, they're happy and celebrating."

"If he hasn't proposed yet, what are they celebrating?"

"The hunt is over, Maggie." Intense emotion thickened Ian's deep voice.

Over. She tensed, afraid to hope. "They've caught Gary Crawford?" Surely she'd have heard through FBI channels—

"No. No, I'm sorry." Ian let out a powerful sigh, clearly rebuking himself for raising and then dashing her hopes. "They caught Della's stalker."

Disappointment fell to confusion. "It wasn't Crawford?" Maggie crunched a crisp piece of gingerbread between her forefinger and thumb. The entire task force agreed the stalker had to be Crawford. "You're sure?"

"Positive. It was Jeff Jackson, Della's ex. They had a personal encounter, and police nailed him with hard evidence."

"Personal encounter?" Sounded dangerous. She knew just how dangerous close encounters with Crawford could be, and how good he was at setting up others to take blame for his actions. Had he done that in this case? He'd nearly killed her with a car bomb in Utah. The shrapnel did what was expected to be permanent injury to her leg. Months in the hospital, multiple surgeries and more months of physical therapy, where she'd worked to the point of exhaustion to recover—her survival required mobility. She had ninety percent success in function of her leg as opposed to the forty-five percent the doctors originally estimated. Now there was another *personal encounter*? Elated and deflated simultaneously, Maggie pressed her elbow on the table and braced her head in her hand. "Paul and Della weren't hurt—"

"No, they're fine. They're great. I told you they're celebrating."

Life. They were living a life without being hunted down like animals. Living and laughing and loving… Maggie's eyes burned again, and again she blinked hard. She wanted those things for Paul, of course. Problem was, she wanted them for herself, too.

Pipe dream.

Definitely a pipe dream, and it would be so long as Gary Crawford drew breath.

She turned her mind and focused on letting gladness fill her heart. "I'm happy for them." So it was Jeff Jackson, not Gary Crawford. "They have to be breathing a lot easier."

"Paul won't breathe easy until you come home."

Guilt speared her. She stared sightlessly at the white stove top. Home. Safety. Security. The beloved ranch she'd grown up on, the rescue animals Paul had taken in for her, the friends she'd known her whole life, the smell of the pines and the feel of the grass and sandy beach under her feet at the little creek. Longing burned her stomach and left it hollow. More than anything she wanted to go home. Well, more than anything except not to ever again endanger those she loved. Her throat thick, she swallowed. "I wish I could, but I can't, Ian. You know why."

A year ago in Utah, Crawford had nearly killed both Paul and her in an act of revenge against her. He was a serial killer. A very bright one who had murdered four women and she'd been called in to profile him. She'd picked up things others had missed, giving the task force needed insights that brought them too close to capturing him, and he resented it enough to want her dead. Crawford willingly used those she loved as bait to get to her. If Paul hadn't forgotten his phone and gone back to get it and she hadn't started her car using the remote, he would have succeeded. It'd taken her six months to recuperate and get out from under intense medical care. No way was she exposing Paul to that again. Her heart couldn't take the trauma or bear the guilt.

"How's your leg?" Ian asked. "Doing the exercises like you're supposed to?"

She smiled. "Yes, and with the move, a lot more." Since his wife's—her friend's—murder three years ago, he and Maggie had supported each other long-distance. Little happened in either's life that the other wasn't aware of—her job status aside. That she couldn't share. "How's Uncle Warny?"

"He wants you to come home, too."

"You're as bad as Paul with the guilt trips, Ian Crane. You know Crawford is still after me. I can't come home, so quit."

"I know why you *think* you can't come home. You're protecting everybody else. But, Maggie, think about it. Paul and I and everyone at Lost, Inc., are ex-military and investigative specialists. We can protect ourselves, and we can help protect you."

Her childhood friend Madison McKay, a POW sacrificed to avert an international incident, had escaped and returned home to start the agency for the sole purpose of helping others who were lost find their way home. "You can't. Crawford proved that in Utah. But I know you, and I know Paul. This is about you two wanting to protect me." Paul had always protected her and, since Beth's passing while Ian was still active duty in the military and deployed to Afghanistan, he wanted to protect *everybody.*

"You can't run forever, Maggie."

She squeezed her eyes shut. "Not running doesn't work. If I come home, it means everyone I care about spends every moment looking back over his or her shoulder, and I worry nonstop when and where and whom Crawford is going to strike next. All of you deserve better. This is my problem. I'll deal with it."

"Will you just let me say what I have to say? I know you're tired of hearing it, but I'm not going to make the same old argument—I promise."

Ian was a former flight surgeon. After Beth's death, he left both medicine and the military and went to work at Lost, Inc., as an investigator. Paul, a former special operations officer, now worked as a veterans' advocate. Both men had special skills and abilities and could help her, and they wanted to, yet didn't they realize that's exactly why she couldn't endanger them? If she lost them, she lost everything. She could talk freely with

Ian in ways she couldn't talk with Paul, who'd been more parent than brother to her for her whole life. She couldn't lose either of them, and Crawford would use that. Still, Ian needed to have his say. "Go ahead."

"You really can't run forever. Crawford only has to be right once. You have to be right every single time. One mistake…" A hard edge nicked his voice. "We've seen what one mistake can do." He paused, no doubt to give her time to remember—not that she needed it. Who could forget?

"Think about something else, too," Ian went on. "Della didn't run and it worked out. She's not a prisoner anymore. She's free, Maggie. I want you to be free, too."

A hard lump crept higher, swelling in her throat. She grabbed a soda from the fridge and shut the door with her hip. "I'm seriously happy it worked out for her, but Jeff Jackson isn't a mastermind serial killer. Gary Crawford is." Maggie popped the top on the can. A swooshed gush of compressed air rushed out. "He's killed four women—that we know of—and he's determined to kill me."

"Which is exactly why you should come home. Maggie, listen to me. Please. Let us help you. We *can* help." He rushed his words as if afraid he wouldn't get them spoken before she tuned him out. "Paul and Della teamed up with the staff at Lost, Inc., and we won. If we did it for Della, we can do it for you. We're trained for this. We *can* do it."

Her heart ached. For three years, Ian had been struggling to care about something. The grief of losing Beth had tried its best to rob the joy of life from him. Maggie had refused to let it. Now he had that same desolate tone about her and her situation. Not good, that. Yet he had a point. Madison McKay, the owner of Lost, Inc., had been Maggie's friend since birth. They'd grown up together. The others at Lost, Inc., were newcomers Maggie didn't know well, but for Paul, they would put their lives on the line and protect her. Maybe together, all of them could battle Crawford and win.

Temptation bit her hard. She resisted it, and it bit her again. Harder. She could go home. Be with her family, her friends, Ian. No more holidays alone. No more running, always being on guard, always looking back, worrying about every move, every action. *Peace. Calm. Safety.* It would be so easy to say yes. So easy…

And so wrong.

No. No, she couldn't do it. Not and watch Gary Crawford murder them for sport, to terrify her, and just to show her he could. The entire FBI hadn't been able to protect her, which had driven her undercover, relying on them only for ancillary support. No. So long as she could stay a step ahead of him, she had to keep trying to face him alone. He wasn't killing other women while tied up chasing her. She couldn't forget that. If a time came when she couldn't do it and putting them in jeopardy by asking for their help was an essential last resort to her survival, then she'd seek their help. Yet Crawford now seemed to know whatever the FBI did, and considering that, her survival odds would be better with her friends and family to protect her. But she could risk their help only as an essential last resort.

Who are you kidding? Could you jeopardize them even then, Maggie? Well, could you?

Her hand shook. She wasn't sure. But Ian needed that reassurance. He needed her promise.

"Did you hear me, Maggie?"

"I heard you." She shoved at the gumdrops, pushing them in place on the gingerbread house.

He sighed. "The reward for being great at your job shouldn't be a penalty that robs you of a life."

"My former job." After the Utah bombing, she'd publicly retired from the FBI and gone undercover. Officially and on paper, she wasn't profiling anymore, just painting landscapes. They'd hoped that would get Crawford off her back. It hadn't made any difference to him. She'd homed in on things in his first four murders that others had missed. Things that brought her and the FBI task force close to his door, and he resented it enough to vow he wouldn't rest until he'd killed her. He had made serious efforts to make good on his word. And she'd vowed to find him first and had made serious efforts to make good on *her* word. The net effect was that sometimes she was the cat and sometimes she was the mouse. If she could just peg the significance of his black rose, she'd win this test of wills and skills between them. She knew she would. It had to be key.

He'd given a black rose to only one living victim—his second. And twice, he'd left a black rose for Maggie. Both times, she'd known he was close and had retreated to regroup. But even now she didn't understand the stealth message in that flower. Why would a man bent on killing you telegraph that he'd located you? Why did he kill and then deliver a dozen Black Beauty roses to his victim after burial? She just didn't get it, and until she did, she was stuck in the cat-and-mouse maze, matching wits with a skilled serial killer so accomplished he terrified seasoned pros.

"Your former job." Ian sighed. "It's nearly Christmas, Maggie. I don't want to spend another one knowing you're alone and Paul and your uncle Warny are looking across the table at your empty chair. And you and me talking while we eat just isn't the same. You know Warny would love you being home for Christmas."

Warny. She imagined her elderly uncle, wearing his overalls, his flannel shirts, his baseball cap and the ever-present red-and-white bandanna half hanging out of his back pocket. Her resolve drained, weakening. She wanted to go home. She wanted to sit in her chair and live her life with her family. She wanted to not run, not live with a knot of fear in her stomach all the time. To never again get another phone call from that twisted killer where all he did was taunt her, flaunting it that he was the cat and she the mouse. Chills ran up and down her arms, her back. She wanted to be normal again, and Ian offered it to her. The problem was, in accepting it she could be signing his death warrant. That shored up her thready resolve and gave her the strength and courage to turn her back on what she wanted and opt for what was right.

Tears flowed down her cheeks and regret dampened her tone. "I'd love nothing more, but you know… I can't." She gulped in air. "I'll call soon."

Before Ian could tempt her more, she hung up the phone. Sitting alone at the table, she stared at the lopsided gingerbread house and wept until dark.

He'd pushed her too hard.

Maggie had ended their call abruptly and too soon. His fault. Why had he pushed so hard? *Why?*

Ian sat in his lamp-lit living room and reread Maggie's note. She'd saved it as a draft in their joint email account—they never sent anything to avoid being traced—nearly a week ago, and he'd rather have talked to her a while longer, but the note would have to do.

On the move again. Will let you know when I've landed. Ian, it means so much to me to be able to write you. I have to watch what I say to Paul because, well, he's my big brother, and if he knew how close Crawford has come to getting me lately, he'd lose his mind.

Did you get the photo I uploaded? What do you think of the new look? Hair's still long, but red. Well, reddish. Isn't it wild?

Thanksgiving was awful and the Christmas countdown has begun. Holidays are the loneliest days now. Watching others with their families... I can hardly stand it. I'm happy for them, but sad for me. I hate being isolated but, as you so often say, things are what they are. At least once every season, I indulge in a blowout pity party. An unfettered squalling session where I shovel in an entire quart of Ben & Jerry's Chocolate Fudge Brownie ice cream during a two-hour bath immersed in bubbles using hot water with zero regard for neighbors sharing the water heater. It's just total self-indulgence and me. (I'll rent a house this time to not inconvenience anyone else. With luck, I'll get to stay in it until after Christmas.)

Binging doesn't help and afterward, I feel guilty for being a hot-water hog, sick from eating too many sweets, and my head hurts for a full day from crying. It's ridiculous, and every time I ask why I do that to myself, but next holiday season, I do it again. Too, I confess that even a self-indulgent blowout pity party without someone there to hold you and tell you not to worry, that things will be all right, makes you feel even more alone. This Christmas I'm going to try to skip it. I've been praying on it for weeks already, but I don't know if my heart is in the right place. My main reason is that I don't need the added stress. Do you think God will be sympathetic to that and help me? I can't do it on my own, so I hope He is and does.

What will you be doing? I need to hear something normal. You know how fish-out-of-water I feel when I move. I need grounding, and I'm counting on you. Don't you feel lucky?
Love,
Maggie

A lump rose in Ian's throat. She'd now moved and he still hadn't responded to the note. He couldn't. He didn't have the heart to answer her email draft with a reply draft telling her he felt every bit as lonely and isolated as she did. Or that he'd be spending the holiday at home alone, indulging in his own pity party sans the ice cream and bubble bath. He'd be teetering on the edge of the depression abyss and rereading her cards and email drafts to pull him back to solid ground.

She'd fuss at him for wasting his life in self-imposed isolation when she craved company. Worse, she'd cry. He didn't have to see her to know it. Maggie Mason was a strong but tenderhearted woman, and him doing what he did on holidays would strum her fragile strings. She rarely cried, but she would over that and the idea that he'd put Maggie in tears after all she'd been through and was still going through... he couldn't stand it.

Yet after that botched phone call, he had to answer her with *something*. Tell her *something* to lift her spirits. Moving to a new place was hard on her, and she'd had a rash of moves in the past year. Crawford was figuring out how her mind worked, and that made an already dangerous situation even more so for her. She needed to come home, where he and Paul could help her. Ian swept an unsteady hand across his forehead. It was worse than that. When Maggie admitted she was struggling, she was *really* struggling. He'd never known such a steely, courageous woman. Beth had been no slouch, but during his deployment to Afghanistan, she'd leaned hard on Maggie, and Maggie had been there for her, just as she had been there for him since Beth's death.

And her devotion to others was repaid with Gary Crawford stealing her life.

Anger simmered in Ian. Maggie deserved better. So much better...and so much more. If Ian still prayed, he'd pray for Maggie. For something to happen so Crawford couldn't hunt or hurt her ever again. He swiped a damp hand along his jean-clad thigh. But he didn't pray anymore. He hadn't since Beth's murder. And unless her murderer was found, convicted and justice prevailed, he doubted he'd ever pray again.

He'd done his part, going to Afghanistan and doctoring the sick and wounded. Not once had he asked God to spare his life. Not once. All he'd asked was that God protect his wife. But He hadn't. Ian had been in a war zone, but Beth had been murdered in her own home. The police figured it was some drug addict who knew Ian was a doctor, looking for painkillers.

He'd loved, honored and cherished, but he'd failed to protect her.

Guilt clawed his insides raw. Staring at his reflection in the glossy wooden tabletop beside his easy chair, he gave in to regret, suffered the hopelessness and helplessness for a long minute. Then, teetering at the edge of the abyss, he sought solace by lifting the worn page and reading Maggie's note yet again.

Love, Maggie. His heart hitched. She did deserve better and more, and though he felt totally incapable of giving her either, she was counting on him. She'd chosen him as her confidant. His best was pathetic, paltry. Man, he wished she had made a wiser choice. But she hadn't. She'd chosen him, no doubt due to her relationship with Beth, and he owed her. He'd give her all he had. "Okay, Doc," he told himself. "Rise to the occasion. Put your heart into it."

Fear rippled up his back, tingled in the roof of his mouth. He'd failed Beth and barely survived it. He couldn't fail Maggie, too. Yet putting his heart into anything was a tall order. The urge to shrink away hit him hard. His every instinct said backing away was right, smart and necessary to him making it through another day. Opening your heart led to unspeakable pain, and he'd already had his share and more. Still, he couldn't shrink away or turn his back. He couldn't. This was Maggie.

She always remembered him—his birthday, Christmas, the anniversary of Beth's death. Maggie talked him through the hardest times of his life and never missed a chance to congratulate or encourage him. The wear on her often-read cards and printed email drafts proved how sorely he needed what she freely gave him and how heavily he relied on her. Wasn't *she* the lucky one?

He took a sip of the cool coffee in his cup then set it back onto the stone coaster. Maggie needed him. She'd faithfully been there for Beth and him. Now he had to be there for her.

"Think, Ian. Think." Still blanking out on what to say, he pushed himself hard then harder. More than three years had passed since Beth died, and losing her remained an open wound that kept him nearly emotionally paralyzed. Anyone else in a similar circumstance to Maggie he'd refer to Madison McKay or Paul, but this time that wasn't an option. Maggie couldn't be totally open with Madison, a lifelong friend, or her brother.

You're too messed up. You'd die for her, yeah. But give her anything with emotion, and actually live? No way. You're DOA, Doc.

Fear twisted like a knife inside him. His hand shook. He could be DOA, but he had to try. Desperate, he whispered, "God, don't You dare let her down. She still believes in You."

God likely would take care of Maggie. He had kept her alive so far. But would He? And could Ian give her what she needed? Truth was truth, and he couldn't survive that kind of failure, or the guilt that came with it, twice.

Mess up, and you're down for the count.

"Don't tempt me," he told himself. Death was easy. Living was tough.

The doorbell rang.

Ian set aside Maggie's note and hauled himself out of his chair. General Talbot and Colonel Dayton had arrived to watch the ball game. It was a tradition they'd begun when Ian worked at the base on active duty, before he'd gone to Afghanistan. After Beth's death and his return home, he'd tried to nix the get-togethers but the commanders, under the guise of being supportive, refused to let him, so he tolerated it.

There had been a security breach at the Nest, the top secret military facility hidden deep within the wooded confines of the base under Talbot and Dayton's command. Considering that they were looking at Ian and everyone else at Lost, Inc., the investigative firm he'd worked at since leaving active duty, for someone to blame for that breach to protect their careers and pending promotions, now wasn't a good time to alienate the commanders.

Resigned, Ian opened the door.

One week later...

The doorbell rang.

Maggie's heart slammed against her ribs. She sat straight up in bed, snagged her weapon from under her pillow and crammed her flashlight into the pocket of her jeans. She hadn't gone to bed in PJs in three years, but always slept fully dressed, prepared for nights with an incident like this.

Hyperalert, she listened for the bell to chime again. It didn't. She hadn't dreamed it. She never slept soundly at night; if anything, she just dozed. Crawford attacked at night. The ring was real—and unexpected. The only person in Decatur who knew her at all was the rental agent, and there was no reason he'd be ringing her bell at midnight.

Midnight. Exactly, according to the red numerals on her bedside clock. *The precise time Crawford had killed his first four victims.*

Her skin crawled and her heart raced even faster. He couldn't have found her already. He couldn't have. It'd been only ten days…

She firmly gripped her weapon, swiped back the covers and then crept silently in the dark. Scraping her back against the wall, she inched down the hallway, not daring to turn on her flashlight. The house had to appear unchanged from outside. Otherwise, whoever was out there would know she was inside. *Keep them guessing, Maggie.*

She scanned ceiling to floor. *Second bedroom… clear.* She skirted the landscape painting of the Louisiana bayou at sunset, and then moved on, the rough wall snagging her blouse at her back, abrading her skin. *Bathroom…clear.* Moving again, she listened intently for the slightest creak or groan, for any sense of movement or odd sound.

Nothing. She checked the windows then the front door, avoiding the peephole. As a profiler, she'd read way too many reports of people checking peeps and meeting with a bullet or a rammed sharp object. Instead she peeked out at the edge of the window beside the door, through the tiny gap between window casing and miniblind. *Nothing.*

No one standing on her porch. No light or darkness

rupturing the soft amber rays and shadows cast by the streetlamp. No extra car at the curb or vehicle out of place. Nothing as it hadn't been for the past nine nights.

Stretching, she clasped a small mirror from a table beside the sofa and lifted it at an angle near the window to view the running length of the porch. *Rocker...unmoved. Planter...unmoved. Nothing at waist level obstructing her view.* Her hand not quite steady, she tilted the mirror down to reflect the porch floor and stilled.

What was that?

A dark clump lay on the welcome mat in front of the door. Straining, she made out the shape.

A black rose.

Her heart stopped then shot off like a launched rocket, shoving adrenaline through her veins that gushed and pounded in her ears. She jerked away from the window, fear churning in her stomach, turning the taste in her mouth bitter.

Her cell phone vibrated in its case clipped at her waist. She didn't recognize the number, let it go to voice mail, then checked the message.

"You can run. You cannot hide."

A distinct click ended the call.

He'd found her.

Maggie Mason had gotten careless.

Her running again hadn't surprised him. Without intercession, she'd already have been nailed. Neglecting to change phones before arriving in her new location...well, that was a rookie mistake she'd regret—and one he hadn't failed to exploit. Why a nonrookie of her caliber had made that mistake intrigued him. She was a formidable adversary and a beautiful woman. The sales clerk remembered her. They always remembered beautiful women. Getting her new number had been sinfully easy. He hadn't needed to go that route, of course, but doing so gave him more options in his backup plans. He'd long ago learned the value of backup plans.

The temperature had dropped at least twenty degrees since nightfall, into the teens. His arms and legs long since numb, he tucked his phone back in his pocket then slid the zipper and risked bending sideward from the tree just far enough to glance across the street. By now she'd surely seen the gift he'd left on her front porch.

His nose was running. He swiped at it, mask to sleeve, not daring to sniff. Her neighbor two doors down had a dog. The last thing he needed was for the mutt to start barking and rouse the whole neighborhood. The cold had frozen his skin and the swipe set it to burning. The wind sliced right through him, making his eyes water and the cold seep straight into his bones, but the prospect of winning his prize kept him plenty warm.

He waited fifteen minutes. Saw no signs of her stirring inside the house. No light came on, no movement at the windows, no lifting of the garage door signaling her getting into her car and beating a hasty retreat.

Staying put, eh?

Not a smart move for a very smart woman. But with the way this operation had developed, a lucky break for him.

He checked the street—silent and still—then peered through the darkness and stubbed branches of trees that had lost too many leaves for his liking. Still no movement in the house.

Well, if she wasn't coming out to her car so he could handle this in her garage, that left him no choice but to go in.

He crouched low and slithered down the shrubs, pausing near a large oak. Its low-slung limb bent double, nearly scraping the ground. It would give him cover to get closer to the house before exposing himself out in the open. The woman was a marksman. He couldn't afford to forget that.

Scrape.

Metal. Where had the scraping noise come from? Echoing through the trees, he couldn't peg the source, but instinct told him it was from her house. He stilled. Shallowed his breath behind the black stocking mask that left open only slits for his mouth and eyes. Ran a visual perimeter scan, checking her neighbors, but saw nothing amiss. Wind brushing a tree limb against a metal gutter? *Likely.* The mutt down the street hadn't alerted. Had to be something typical or he'd be yelping. Idiot dog had barked at his own shadow most of last night during his reconnaissance here. His owner had come outside twice to check things out. Fortunately, he never intended to act last night. But tonight he didn't want anyone seeing or hearing anything. When they found her body, he wanted nothing reported—just the entire neighborhood to be rocked and in total shock that while they'd slept, a murder had occurred right under their noses.

He took a step away from the tree, tripped over an exposed root. Pain shot through his frozen toes and he clenched his teeth and looked down to his neon blue shoe.

She'd pay for that.

Scrape.

There it was again. Distinct—and definitely metal.

She'd never just come out. Maggie Mason was far too clever for that. She'd lay some kind of trap for him going in. Unfortunately, in her line of work, she'd been exposed to many possibilities from which to choose. He shifted his vantage point, moving farther down the fence to get a better view of the backyard. The row of squat bushes along the back of the house shimmered. *Wind?* He scanned the clapboard. Solid. No door. Probably a raccoon. He'd spotted two last night, one in her yard, one next door. He waited a full minute…then another, but the metal scraping didn't repeat a third time.

He crept silently down the fence, tree to tree, crossing the outer edge of the backyard to the far side of the lot, then worked his way up the fence on the side of the house. The back door was metal.

His stomach sank. Had she slipped past him? No. No way. Her car hadn't moved—he'd had his eye on the garage door the entire time. She couldn't very well walk out of here in the dead of night.

Moving stealthily, bush to tree to bush, he made his way closer to the door. She was in there. She had to be in there.

The only way Maggie Mason would be leaving this house was toes-up in a body bag.

Chapter Two

Facedown in the dirt behind the bushes, Maggie watched him make his way around the perimeter of the yard until the house blocked him from sight. He was going for the door. She released the heavy string tied to the back screen door that she'd tugged to create the scraping sound, and then ran under the cover of the trees. Charging the stacked wood, she climbed, hopped the fence and then ran full out, cutting across lawns and between homes, not daring to pause to glance back.

Three blocks over, she spotted the junkyard. Her lungs burned, threatening to explode, and her leg, though stronger, was still weak from the Utah incident, and it throbbed. Snagging the key from under the fender of a clunker, she hopped in and then cranked the engine. Was he already following her?

Scared to death, she dumped her emergency bag into the passenger's seat, her weapon within reach on the console, and then cut across the parking lot to the T-street intersection. Scanning, she spotted no other cars, no one walking. Easing on the gas to minimize spewing gravel and leaving a calling card on the direction she was taking, she pulled out and reported a prowler to the local police, then followed the map she'd committed to memory to hit Highway 51 South.

All the way to Macon, she kept one eye firmly on the rearview, but spotted no signs of him behind her. Right before the exit, she retrieved an unused prepaid cell from her emergency pack and called in. "This is Sparrow," she said and then went through the positive identification ritual with an unidentified woman whose voice she didn't recognize. "Tell Henry I'm on my way and let the task force know."

"Already? It hasn't even been two weeks this time."

Like she didn't know that? "Already." Seeing the neon sign, she ended the call then pulled into the all-night gas station the agency had arranged. The man on duty watched her pull in and frowned. Word had already come down to him from on high.

She parked the clunker away from the street and grabbed her bag.

"He found you."

"Yeah." She dropped a key to the clunker in Henry's hand. "And he could be on my heels, so…"

"Key's on the board." Henry nodded to the near wall inside. "Red Honda out back."

"Thanks, Henry."

"I'm so sorry, Sparrow."

"Yeah." She nodded. "Me, too." She moved quickly inside, grabbed the key and then walked straight through to the back door. The red Honda was parked nose-out next to the building in deep shadows. She jumped inside, locked the doors, pulled on a wig that made her a brunette and then headed back down 51 South.

The agency assisted her, planting cars and other things she needed along her path, but neither it nor its field agents could protect her. Oh, the task force did what it could, but if it couldn't catch Crawford for the killings, it couldn't prevent him from killing her. The team knew it. The agency knew it. She knew it. *What are you going to do, Maggie?*

What was she going to do? He'd not only found her, but he'd meant to kill her. Tonight. Crawford had tired of the cat-and-mouse game, and he was done playing. Now he wanted her dead and out of the way.

Had he just been playing with her all this time? Could he have killed her at any time he wanted?

The more she thought about it, the more she believed that's exactly what he'd been doing. She couldn't protect herself. And now that he had decided to end the game, she had two choices: one. Get help. Two. Die.

She didn't want to die.

Glancing at the amber dash clock, she fretted over her choices. And that this attack signaled he was itching to kill again. She and her death didn't count. He was ready to resume killing his regular victims. She was just an obstacle he wanted out of his way for fear she'd catch him. Yet she had kept him otherwise occupied longer than anyone believed she could. Three years, nearly four. Still, that he was eager to resume his killing spree made her sick inside. He had a two-week span at Christmas every year that set everyone at the agency on edge, worrying that he would kill, shocked and grateful when he didn't. Why he always murdered his victims during those two specific weeks remained a mystery, though Maggie suspicioned they had something to do with his mother. What exactly, she didn't know. But tenuous threads led to her.

Maggie glanced at her watch. Nearly 1:00 a.m. She needed a sounding board. She needed Ian. Fishing her phone from her bag, she punched the second number on speed dial.

On the third ring, a drowsy Ian answered. "Crane."

The urge to cry slammed into Maggie. She didn't dare to give in to it. "Ian, it's me."

"Maggie?" Surprise flooded his voice. "Are you okay?"

"So far." She swallowed hard, speeding up to pass a slow-moving SUV in the left lane. In bits and spurts, she shared what had happened, and then said, "I thought I could do it, Ian. But I can't. This time, I had no idea he was even close until I saw the rose on the porch." She couldn't count a weird feeling something was wrong. That wasn't enough to qualify. Bitterness set in. "I should go back and shoot him." She considered it.

"He was going to kill me. He's already killed four women. I love life and preserve it whenever possible, but it's him or me, and I can't run anymore." Her chin quivered. She clamped it.

"You saw him?" Ian asked, shocked. "He was that close?"

"It was too dark to see his face, but it was Crawford. He was going into my house when I got away. Tonight was going to be the night."

Ian sucked in a sharp breath. "Why didn't you shoot him?"

She swallowed hard. "You know why." The same

God that made her made Crawford. She'd do it if she had to, but she prayed every day of her life that she wouldn't have to take that step. It'd change her forever, and oh, but she feared that change.

"I do." He sighed. "But you better accept that you might not be able to escape."

"If I can't, then I'll do what I have to do."

"Are you safe now?"

"I think so." Instinctively, she checked the rearview mirror but didn't see anyone tagging her in the light traffic. "I've switched cars twice since escaping."

"Maggie, him getting this close this fast…it's time to accept help. He will kill you."

"I know. I think he's been playing me, letting me think I was staying ahead of him when he's known my every move. How, I have no idea. But it's a bad sign." A chill had her skin crawling. "He's ready to move on."

"You think he'll stop coming after you?"

"No." She didn't. "I think he's eager to kill me so he can resume his regular murders unhampered." *You can run. You cannot hide.* His words echoed through her mind. "It's time."

"Time for what?"

"For him to kill again." Her breath stuttered. "He's been dormant while he's been occupied with me—at least, as far as we can tell. But if he repeats past patterns, before the end of December, he'll kill again." All four murders had been a week either side of Christmas.

"That's all the more reason to come home and let me help. Maybe if he can't get to you, then whomever he's targeted to be this Christmas's victim will survive."

That thought struck home. Yet another countered it. "To get to me, he'll kill everyone around me." Ian. Paul and Della. Uncle Warny. Probably even Jake, Paul's Rottweiler.

"He could try," Ian conceded. "But we're all trained and we've dealt with killers before. All of us, Maggie. Paul and Della, Madison and Grant and Jimmy." He reeled off the names of everyone on the staff at Lost, Inc. "I don't know about Mrs. Renault, but frankly, I wouldn't test her. The woman has a steel backbone and titanium nerves."

She did. Madison's assistant was more than capable of handling herself. She'd had to be. Her husband had been the commander of the base until his death, which meant she'd had to fend for herself against some very real enemies who considered the commander's wife a plum target. Still, this wasn't a garden-variety killer. This was Crawford. It was nearly impossible to defend against Crawford. "No one has faced a killer like him, Ian."

"We've faced ones a lot like him."

By the tone of Ian's voice, she knew he wasn't softening his words for her sake or straying from the truth. Paul had never told her that. Common sense said in their military experience, Paul and those at Lost, Inc., went after terrorists, but a serial killer of Crawford's caliber? "Really?"

"We got a mix of sociopaths and psychopaths along with the brainwashed and fanatics, Maggie. But it's a moot point anyway. We're your last resort."

Last resort. The very words she'd thought herself to signal that her survival depended on accepting outside help. She wrestled the pros and cons and ended up staring into the bleak depths of fact: on her own, she was as good as dead. *Last resort.* It had to be a sign.

Her mind settled. "I'm driving straight through. Don't call Paul. He'll freak out until I walk through the door. Let him and Della have their trip to her step-grandmother's."

Ian didn't acknowledge her response, likely because he intended to call Paul anyway, but he did ask a question. "How did Crawford find you?"

"I don't know." She'd been so careful. So methodical and cautious in preparing the house, stacking the wood to climb the fence, stashing her backup vehicles—everything. Her palm went damp and the phone grew slick. *The phone.* Surprise streaked through her chest. "Oh, Ian. It's my fault."

"Why?"

"I bought the new phones at the same time I got to my new house." He'd been in hot pursuit of her when she'd left her last one, and rather than buying multiple phones at different locations, she'd cut down on stops by buying several phones at once. It'd been a busy store, but apparently not busy enough that the clerk had forgotten her.

He groaned. "Take out the battery."

Even turned off, a phone with a battery in it could be tracked. "I know." *Shouldn't have cut corners. Should have made the stops.* She rapped the heel of her hand on the steering wheel.

"Do it now, Maggie—and call me as soon as you can after you replace it."

"I will." She ended the call, then unsnapped the back and removed the battery. Likely Crawford knew exactly where she was until the moment the battery hit the console. "Stupid mistake." Cracking the heel of her hand against the steering wheel, she said it again. Twice.

Spotting a blue truck behind her, she punched the gas pedal and sped up, eager to put as much distance as possible between her and where she'd been when she'd disabled the phone.

Her eyes gritty and burning, she checked the highway sign. Still north of Nashville and still pitch-dark. Oh, but she looked forward to dawn.

A few miles later, she checked the dash clock—after three in the morning. It felt like a lifetime since the doorbell had awakened her. She was exhausted and yet running on so much adrenaline, even if she were in a position to sleep, she wouldn't be able to do it. The blue truck she'd been watching moved up, now one car behind her. Had there been a blue truck in her neighborhood?

She mentally went down the block for the hundredth time, but she couldn't recall one. Still, the truck's sole occupant—gauging by height in the driver's seat, a man—hung close, watching her.

No one could positively identify Crawford. She had never seen his face, either—he'd always worn a mask, just as he had in her backyard earlier that night. Was he driving the truck? Or maybe the driver was some unsuspecting minion he'd hired? The man could be anyone. Worse, anyone could be Gary Crawford.

She slowed down, trying to nudge him into passing her. He hesitated then pulled alongside and stared at her through the window, his face lit up by his eerie green dash lights. She didn't recognize him. Couldn't recall running into him at a gas station or the grocery store or anywhere else. Henry might have alerted the bureau she'd picked up the car. The driver could be one of theirs, but he didn't signal he was an agent riding shotgun for added protection. Was he Crawford? Her skin crawled. *Stop it, Maggie.*

She did need to stop it. Things were bad enough. The man could be an unrelated outsider, but he kept pace and stared too hard for too long to be up to anything but no good. Maybe a guy bent on preying on a woman traveling alone in the wee hours before dawn. Unfortunately, she'd run into that kind of thing enough times to have lost count.

If he were Crawford, odds favored him pulling alongside her just long enough to fire a bullet into her car. When Crawford was done with the game, he was done. That left the second option—a predator seeking prey. She knew how to deal with predators. Reaching to the console, she lifted her weapon and propped it on her hand gripping the steering wheel. The steel glinted in her amber dash lights.

Shock widened the truck driver's eyes. He floored his accelerator. The engine whined, kicked in. The truck belched black smoke, and he sped off into the night.

Shaking and clammy, fighting that same need to scrub herself from head to toe she always felt on a close call with Crawford, she put the gun back down on the console. Soon she'd be in Nashville. The sun would be up; she'd stop and get a phone, and then call Ian.

She hated to admit, even to herself, just how badly she needed to hear his voice.

Where was Maggie's last note?

Ian felt certain he'd left it on the table next to his easy chair. He'd been reading it before Talbot and Dayton came over to watch the game. But he couldn't find it now.

Returning to the kitchen, he paced the hardwood

floor between it and the den, watching the clock just as he'd been watching it for the past three hours, waiting for Maggie to call back. Hoping Crawford wasn't following her. That he hadn't found her through her phone locator. That he wasn't ten minutes behind her on the highway.

He poured himself yet another cup of coffee and fought his conscience. The battle raged. Torn between calling and not calling Paul. Paul should know. He really should know...

But she'd specifically told Ian not to call her brother. Specifically.

You've got to do something.

Ian paused, leaned against the breakfast bar. Do something. Like what?

Get her home faster and out of Crawford's reach.

He could do that. General Talbot and Colonel Dayton were in Nashville. He could have her meet them at the airport. They'd bring her home.

They're going to blame someone for the security breach.

They were. But Maggie hadn't been in North Bay. She couldn't be a target for leaking word about the Nest. She didn't even know the secret facility existed.

He paced some more, arguing both sides with himself, and got nowhere. Finally, he gave in and called Paul. If he did ask Talbot and Dayton for help, he couldn't do it without Paul's blessing. With his connections, he could know reasons for doing it or, equally important, for not doing it. Stretching, Ian grabbed the phone.

"Ian, it's me."

"Thank heaven." The relief in his voice turned hard. "It's nearly seven o'clock, Maggie. I expected you to call hours ago. The things I've been seeing in my head—"

Sitting in the Walmart parking lot, she glanced in the rearview and didn't immediately recognize the woman reflected in the mirror as herself. Short brown wig, sunglasses and bright red lipstick. *Ugh!* "Sorry. I just got the new phone." Not that changing phones would stop Crawford. It hadn't stopped him so far. Somehow he still managed to track her. *How? An agency leak? A leak on her military consults?* The entire task force had tried to find out, but no one had found a thing… yet. TV shows made it all look so simple, but in real life, everything didn't wrap up all nice and neat, tied with a pretty bow. More's the pity.

"Are you all right? Being followed?"

"Tired but fine, and I haven't picked up on anyone following me."

"Where are you?"

She sipped from a large cup of steaming-hot coffee before answering. "About an hour out of Nashville." Clarkston, Tennessee, actually, but it was safest not to be too specific. "I'm driving straight through, so I should be in about four this afternoon. Maybe a little later if I get too tired." She was eager to get there, but not eager enough to endanger others on the road.

"You can't make that drive on no sleep."

"He won't be far behind me, Ian. I don't have any choice."

"Actually, you do. Just get to the Nashville airport, last depot in the terminal."

"I can't fly. He'll be watching, and even if he doesn't make the plane and jeopardize the other passengers, he'll be waiting when I step off. I don't know how he manages, but I've tried that before, and it just doesn't—"

"You're taking a private flight home on a military plane. My old commander, General Talbot, and his assistant, Colonel Dayton, have been in Nashville for a summit. They're ready to head back, just holding the flight until you get there."

Relief washed through her and she smiled. "You've been busy."

"If you recall, Paul, Della and Madison once worked for them, too."

"Yes, but they didn't call the general, did they? My guess is Mrs. Renault did." Madison's assistant. The widow of the man General Talbot replaced.

"Talbot wouldn't dream of refusing her anything."

Maggie's mind might be numb, but Ian was thinking. *Clever.* "He's been in love with her for years—well, since she's been widowed." He'd lost his own wife a decade ago.

"I've heard that, too," Ian agreed. "Which is why I suggested she be the one to call him."

Maggie laughed. "You are sly, Ian Crane. I can't say I've noticed that about you before, but I appreciate it now." She got back on the interstate and headed to Nashville. "Do you have net access? I need to give you my new number."

"This one isn't it?"

"No, I'll ditch this phone as soon as we hang up. You know where I'll be leaving the number." Their email drafts account. It was their strongest secure communication link. "When you call me back, use a throwaway phone. If Crawford found me through my phone once, he can do it again—and he'll know who I've talked with, too."

"Has he traced your calls before?"

"Regularly." She blended into traffic and set the cruise control.

"That's no small thing, Maggie. How does he get access?"

"If I knew the answer to that, I'd find him long before he got close to me." The wig itched. She tried to ignore it. Took another sip of coffee.

"Paul doesn't know about Crawford tracing your calls, does he?"

He'd lose his mind worrying about her. "No, he doesn't." She put her cup back into its holder. "So let me guess. You held out until five o'clock, then called him, right?"

Silence.

He'd called Paul, all right. The lack of an immediate denial proved it. "Ian?"

His sigh crackled static. "I held out until five fifteen."

She smiled again, checked her mirrors. "I love it that you're predictable." She did. It made her feel secure, steady, to know what to expect. "Did he go postal?"

"Not postal, no. But he is plenty worried. He saved postal for when he called back."

"About what?"

"To tell me he was snowed in and couldn't get out. Then he definitely went postal."

Postal, and then some. Ian's tone made that evident. "I'm glad he's snowed in, and I hope it holds. I want him and Della safe." She shuddered. "This time Crawford got way too close, Ian. I'm still shaking inside. If

I hadn't strung a string to the side door to open as a diversion, I seriously doubt I would have gotten past him this time."

"I know you. You prepared. I suspect it took everything you did to get past him, not one thing."

True. "Well, my everything really wasn't enough. I got lucky." Bumping the bushes. Crawford had stopped and stared right at her. She'd been terrified he was going to come right at her and she'd have to shoot him. Maybe she should have, but killing a human being— even one as twisted as Crawford—was reserved as a last resort.

Something had made him dismiss the shimmering bushes. What, she had no idea. "Things just as easily could have gone the other way." That truth left her chilled. She bumped the heater up a notch.

"Well, I'm glad they didn't."

So was she. Traffic was picking up. Getting close to Nashville, but also morning go-to-work traffic. "I'd better let you go so you can get ready for work. Will you be all right today, after me keeping you up all night?"

"I'm fine." He paused, and then added, "I don't sleep much anyway, and I thought we'd talk until you got on the plane."

He didn't want to break the connection. Her chest went warm in a way it shouldn't. The last thing either of them needed was a relationship complication. They were friends. Special friends—you can't trudge through grief and despair and terror as they had and not be—but just friends. "It's half an hour away."

"Yeah, it is."

Supporting her. She started to check her thoughts,

but they tumbled out of her mouth anyway. "I appreciate you, Ian."

"Yeah? Then take pity and stop scaring me, Maggie."

The truth set in and her smile faded. "I expect it's going to get a lot scarier before it gets better. You know I'm right about that."

"Yes."

"He'll keep coming until one of us is dead."

"I know."

"Others could get hurt."

"Yes."

"You could get hurt. If you want to back off, I wouldn't blame you." If she could back off, she might.

"No way. I'm here for you."

"Ian, seriously." She lifted a hand from the steering wheel and flexed her stiff fingers. "I'm touched, but I don't want you to feel you have to put yourself in Crawford's line of fire. You don't." That's the last place she wanted anyone.

"Drop it, Maggie. You're there, I'm there, end of story."

Quite a distance to go for even a special friend. Was that a blessing or a curse? She couldn't be sure, but she prayed after all he'd been through with Beth, their friendship would be a blessing to him. Crawford was the curse.

He's going to kill you or make you kill him.

Her chest went tight. All her muscles contracted at once, and the urge to give in to despair or scream dueled inside her. She gave in to neither, and instead said, "We know how this is going to end. I wish... I hate..." She couldn't make herself say it. "Never mind."

"The idea of killing anyone?"

"Yes." She swallowed hard. "But he won't stop, and I don't want to die."

"I know." Ian sighed. "It's a hard road, but it will sort out. Sometimes we have to do things we don't want to do. We don't have to like them, but we do have to do them. You know that better than anyone."

Undercover, trapped in Crawford's cat-and-mouse maze for over three years, yes, she knew it. She moved over into the left lane, passed a green Avalon, then eased back into the right lane and tapped off her blinker with her pinky. "You know what scares me the most?"

"What?"

"It's shameful. I—I... No, I can't say it. I don't want you to know I'm that awful a person."

"You're a good person. Now tell me." He sniffed. "We talk freely, remember?"

She dropped her voice. "What scares me most is I want him dead. Not in jail. Not injured. Dead. I feel awful about that, but it's the only way I know he'll ever leave me alone and stop killing."

"It's hard to imagine you wouldn't want him dead. His death is your only shot for any kind of life, much less peace."

"But it's horrible to want anyone dead."

"Ah, faith. You're worried about the conflict between your beliefs and actions, and living with what you do that God won't approve, right?" He sighed. "I understand, but if you don't stop him, he will keep killing other people. In or out of jail, Gary Crawford is going to murder. Don't you think God considers that?"

"I'm betting my eternity on it. But still, Ian. Wanting someone to die? I'm judging. That's not God's way."

Shame slithered over her. "He's got to be so disappointed in me."

"If He is, you're in line behind me. We're not on speaking terms, as you know. But I still expect He's proud of you. Pretty courageous, using yourself to draw Crawford's fire to keep him from killing others—especially after he nearly killed you." Ian paused, waiting and maybe hoping she'd deny it, but she couldn't. That's exactly what she'd been doing with this self-imposed exile. Finally, Ian went on. "God surely wants you safe. Self-defense is self-defense."

"I don't remember seeing that written behind 'Thou shall not kill.'"

"Oh, please. Don't tell me you think God expects you to stand still and let someone else kill you. There are plenty of instances where God created circumstances and conditions to protect His own on the battlefield. If this isn't a battle, I don't know what is."

She hadn't thought of her situation that way, but Ian was right. Four soldiers sounding like an army... "How do you know this is a situation where I'm supposed to battle and defend myself?" That had perplexed her for a long time and had been the focus of many prayers during this ordeal.

"I know because God loves you."

"But He loves Crawford, too." She was too tied up in knots for this conversation now.

"You're really muddled about this."

"I am. I'm having a hard, hard time with it, Ian."

"I wish I could be more reassuring. I do believe God understands, and if it's kill or be killed, He'll understand that, too."

"I hope so."

"Maybe when you get home, you can talk to the pastor. Surely he can walk you through it."

"I can't talk to him about this. It—it's horrifying to admit you want someone else dead."

"Crawford isn't just someone. He's a cold-blooded killer who's murdered four women and is bent on killing you so he can kill even more."

She shouldn't ask. Shouldn't, but she was going to do it. "Will you come with me—to talk to the pastor?"

"Oh, Maggie, don't ask me to do that." He groaned. "You know I don't go to church anymore."

He was still angry with God for not sparing Beth. Still outraged that while he was serving to protect, his own wife was murdered and God had let it happen. Disappointment rippled through her. She'd hoped... Never mind what she'd hoped. She had no business hoping that anyway. They were friends and neither of them could afford to forget it or to ever expect anything more. Between Beth and Crawford, it just couldn't happen. Not now, not ever. "You won't come with me, then?" Why had she asked that? What was wrong with her?

Fatigue. Had to be that she was so tired and scared and her defenses were down and her confidence at being able to protect herself lay tattered not on the floor but under it.

Ian blew out a sigh so strong she felt it on her end of the phone. "All right, I'll come with you."

She sank her teeth into her lower lip. "Thank you, Ian. Now, get over to the store, get a throwaway phone and then call me back."

"I'm going, but we'll talk on the way."

Touched, Maggie repeated herself. Special man. Special friend. "I'm grateful for you, Ian."

"Only when you're getting your way."

"You think?"

"I know."

She laughed, lush and deep.

On his way to the store, he caught her up on all the latest news in North Bay, and on his way home, he shared all the latest news about Lost, Inc. Madison was on a Christmas cruise, Jimmy had flown to Bainbridge Island off the coast of Washington and Mrs. Renault was at a resort in the Carolinas until after New Year's Day. He expected they'd all head home to assist on the Crawford case.

Maggie hoped not. She whispered a quick prayer to keep them in place and listened to Ian talk about his agreeing to hold down the fort at the office this holiday season.

"So it's you and me."

"Until they can get back here, yes. Oh, and your uncle Warny."

Who was bat-blind, nearly as lame as Thunder, her favorite rescue horse at the ranch, and quick on the trigger anyway. Maybe coming home wasn't such a good idea. She'd have to watch over Uncle Warny, too...

Certainty filled her. Going home was important. She couldn't explain it, but she sensed it. Maybe it was a deep longing for home, or a divine nudging. Whatever it was, it was there and she would heed it and pray hard for the best.

From the sounds coming through the phone, Ian pulled the truck into the garage and closed the door while filling Maggie in on Madison's new love/hate relationship with Grant Deaver.

"I don't know him."

"He's a former OSI officer. Just separated from the military and Madison snagged him."

"Ah. Well, I'm glad someone's finally gotten her attention." Truthfully, getting it wasn't hard—Madison noticed everything and always had—it was keeping it.

"He's got her attention, all right. She doesn't trust him, but anytime the two of them are in the same room, sparks between them fly."

"That kind of attention's got to be making Madison crazy." Maggie had never known her to associate with people she couldn't trust. But chemistry on top of that? Definitely personal…and very interesting.

"Actually, I think she likes it. He's a challenge," Ian said then corrected himself. "Well, he's clearly crazy about her, so it isn't that he's a challenge, it's whether or not she should trust him that makes him challenging."

"Why shouldn't she trust him?"

"I told you he just left active duty. He was stationed at the base and there's been a bit of an incident. I can't get into details."

Madison had been a POW. Her military days weren't fond memories. "She's strong and smart. She'll work through it."

"She will," Ian said. "Not that I like seeing her off balance, but it's entertaining to watch. I've never seen her like this with anyone."

"I don't think I have, either." A green sedan passed another vehicle and two cars back tucked into Maggie's lane. From the tag, the same green sedan that had been parked nose-to-nose and three cars down the row from her at Walmart.

Ian talked on.

Maggie focused on the sedan. She passed a white Volvo, then sped up and passed a blue Ford.

The green sedan followed and kept pace.

"Ian," she interrupted. "I've picked up a tail. Green sedan." She reeled off the tag number from memory. "One person in the car. Male. About forty-five. Dark hair, sunglasses. Can't make out anything else."

"Where are you?"

"Coming up on the airport exit."

"Traffic heavy?"

"Not too bad."

"Floor it."

Maggie stomped the pedal, stayed in the center lane and honked at the car in front of her to move over.

The driver did, but glared at her. She pushed the pedal harder, wove lane to lane between cars.

The sedan did, too.

"He's definitely following me." She stayed in the center lane, spotted the sign—a quarter mile to the airport exit. Her nerves drummed a wicked beat. She was going way too fast. Way too fast for him to expect her to exit. She jerked the wheel to the left, passed a pickup and then whipped in too close in front of an eighteen-wheeler. He slammed on his brakes. At the last minute, she hit the exit ramp, her brakes churning smoke the entire way down the circular off-ramp.

The truck blocked the sedan. He couldn't see her or make the exit. That could buy her a few minutes. Not many, but a few.

"You okay?" Ian sounded worried, fearful.

"So far. He couldn't turn. But I don't know how far it is to the next exit. I might have a minute, maybe a little more. I just don't know."

"Was the guy Crawford?"

"I don't know. I've never seen his face—just the mask. But he was definitely tagging me."

"Get to the cargo terminal, Maggie."

She sped the entire way, stuffed her weapon into her bag, abandoned the car in short-term parking and then ran full out the entire way into the terminal.

Colonel Dayton stood in uniform just inside, waiting for her. His sunglasses shaded his eyes. He whipped them off. "You all right, Maggie?"

A stitch in her side, she pressed a hand over it. "He's right on my heels."

"Let's move." He reached for her bag. "I thought you were blonde."

"I am." She hesitated, still breathless. "I'm also armed."

He smiled. "I'd be surprised if you weren't." He motioned with his fingers to pass the bag. "I'm already cleared."

Maggie half tossed it to him. "Hurry."

Within minutes they were on the C-17 and Colonel Dayton was passing her over to General Talbot.

Tall and lean, he was a little grayer than she recalled but still had the same kind eyes. She'd first met the base commander years ago when everyone had gathered at Beth and Ian's for a Super Bowl party, and he always attended community events. Maggie shook his hand. "It's good to see you, General." She smiled. "Thanks for rescuing me."

"Mrs. Renault said it was a matter of life and death."

"I'm sorry to say, she's right."

"Gary Crawford?" His graying brows lifted high on his forehead.

She nodded, not at all surprised he knew. After Utah, everyone did. That story was too big to be suppressed, and the media had had a field day with it for weeks. So the general clearly hadn't pressed Mrs. Renault for an explanation and Mrs. Renault clearly hadn't offered him one. Interesting. Why hadn't he pressed her? Odd. But then, maybe not so odd. Few pressed Mrs. Renault. She had an impeccable reputation and a very long history with these people.

Colonel Dayton stowed Maggie's bag in the overhead compartment next to one already there. "I can't believe Crawford hasn't been caught. He's been after you—how long?"

"Nearly four years." She could tell him down to the minute, but being specific made others uncomfortable.

The general frowned. "Sooner or later, he'll slip up. They always do." He pointed to a seat. "Buckle up and let's get out of here before he thinks to take out the plane."

She sat down and buckled up. "He'd never expect me to be on a military flight. I've totally avoided planes since a little incident in El Paso."

"Why?" The general buckled in. "Seems it'd be the most efficient way to move long distances quickly and get lost."

She smoothed her hair back from her face. "He threatened to take hostages and kill a passenger a minute until I turned myself in to him. We got lucky that time. Trying it again, knowing what he'd do...it's just not right."

Admiration lit in his eyes. "War makes for hard decisions we'd rather not have to make."

"Yes, it does." She stifled a yawn behind her hand. "Sorry. I haven't slept in a couple days. It's always like that when I move."

"You move a lot, don't you?"

"Unfortunately." He seemed gentle, which seemed at odds with his position. But maybe because of his position he could afford to be gentle.

"Are you hungry?" Dayton asked.

Her stomach hadn't stopped shaking. Until it did, she'd be crazy to mix flying and putting anything in it. "Not really."

"Rest then," the general said. "You'll feel better after a nap."

"Thank you. I really appreciate this."

The general nodded, opened a file and began reading.

The minute the plane lifted off, Maggie settled back and closed her eyes, sleeping soundly for the first time in a week.

The next thing she knew, someone was shaking her shoulder. "Miss Mason?" Another gentle shake. "Maggie?"

She startled awake, grabbed for the hand.

"It's okay. You're safe."

Wild-eyed, her heart racing, she struggled to focus and saw Colonel Dayton's stern, tanned face. Her hand went to her chest. "Sorry."

His voice gentled. "I'm used to it. Happens a lot in those returning from combat zones."

She nodded. "I guess it is similar…except I'm nearly sure my combat zone will be following me home."

"If we can help…" the general started.

"Thank you." She straightened. They were on the ground. The plane had landed, taxied and stopped near the terminal.

Dayton frowned. "I hated to wake you, but there's a man pounding the ramp, eager to see you."

She glanced out the window and saw Ian. "How did he get out there?"

"I took care of that." The general smiled. "Seems like a little thing, but I know it's not—not to him, and I suspect, not to you."

Touched by his thoughtfulness, Maggie smiled. "Thank you, General."

Colonel Dayton stretched into the overhead and grabbed her bag. He unzipped a side pocket in her bag and removed her weapon. "You can get this back on the other side of the terminal."

She nodded.

He grabbed the zipper on the second bag and tugged. Maggie spotted something bright blue. He dropped the gun inside and closed the zipper.

Unbuckling, she stood up and covertly stretched, stiff from head to toe.

General Talbot reached for the bag with her weapon. "Best let me carry that."

"Yes, sir." Dayton passed it to him.

"Ready, Maggie?" the general asked.

She smiled. "Ready." She nodded and sized up Dayton yet again. He seemed uptight and proper, all business. Not like the type of man who'd ever wear neon blue aquatic shoes.

Chapter Three

"Ian." Maggie ran into his open arms, sagged against him, relieved to finally be in a place she felt safe and secure. "I can't believe I'm really here."

He let out a sigh of pure relief. "Me, either. The elephant's off my chest and I can breathe again."

She pulled back, smiled at him. He looked the same. Still tall and fit and handsome, and dressed in khaki slacks and a cream-colored fleece-lined jacket that fit him and his personality. His face was tanned, a little leaner and more honed, but his eyes were still that fascinating blue and, if a little duller for the pain he'd endured, the sparkle she'd seen when they first met still shone in them. "You look…terrific."

He smiled. "I'd say you do, too, but I hate the wig and you've lost too much weight. Your uncle Warny is going to chew on you for that."

She laughed. "I can't say I care for the wig, either, and you know I always drop ten pounds when I have to move more than once in a short time." She shrugged. "You do what you have to do when things are as they are, but you also pay a price."

Dayton cleared his throat. "I'll meet you on the other side with your package." He nodded toward the terminal.

Ian and he shook hands. "Thanks a lot for bringing her home."

While Maggie thanked the general, Dayton lowered his voice to talk to Ian, but Maggie still caught his words. "Stay on your toes. Paul, too. A man driving the vehicle Maggie identified as the one following her hit the terminal not five minutes behind her. The FBI suspects Crawford hired him to tag her and refused to let us intercept him. I guess they're hoping he'll lead them to Crawford. You know he'll beeline it down here."

Keeping the news that Paul was away to himself, Ian sobered. "We'll be ready."

"She's exhibiting symptoms of PTSD," Dayton added, making no attempt to shield his voice from her. "You might watch that, too."

Ian nodded, looked over at her. She gave him a shaky smile. "I'm okay. Really. I just haven't slept much in a while."

"Well, let's get you home and remedy that." Ian guided her through the terminal. The general passed the bag off to Dayton, who followed her and Ian outside.

He transferred the weapon. "There you go."

She looked up at him and smiled. "Thank you again—for everything, Colonel." It felt kind of nice to have someone concerned about her when it wasn't a blood or friendship obligation. She'd forgotten how that felt.

"Sure thing. Give Paul my regards."

Something in his tone rang insincere and sent a chill through her. She brushed it off, blamed it on exhaustion. The man had been nothing but good and kind to her.

Ian led the way to his Ford Expedition. It was white, trimmed in gold around the fenders and bottom, and was even greater-looking than in the photos. He opened the passenger door.

Maggie stepped onto the running board and then slid into the creamy leather seat. Ian walked around to the driver's side and got inside. "Nice," she told him. "The photos didn't do it justice." She inhaled. "Don't you love that new-car smell?"

He keyed the engine. "It's more vehicle than I need most of the time, but it's versatile. I'm enjoying it."

She smiled. Ian Crane was an SUV nut. A really picky one, and she had the email drafts of his notes and photos to prove it. He'd shopped for months, picking out this vehicle, playing with options until he'd found exactly what he wanted. "Right."

He grinned. "Okay, I love it."

"Better." Honesty was essential. She bared her soul to this man, and she couldn't do that unless he was just as honest with her. Lowering her sunglasses from their perch atop her head, she seated them on her nose to shade her eyes. The sun was blinding.

They left short-term parking and headed north of town, toward the ranch. It was hard to believe—to even imagine—but in half an hour, she'd be home. *Home*...

Ian glanced her way. "How long do you think you've got before Crawford shows up?"

Didn't she wish she knew? "I hope a good while. North Bay is the last place he'd expect me to come.

I haven't dared to even visit since Utah." When he'd blown up her car and nearly killed Paul and her, she'd decided the risks to others were too great. She couldn't lead him to Paul's doorstep.

"I know and I'm sure he does, too." Ian cast her a worried, sidelong look. "But is it the first place he'll look?"

Had he done so before? A shiver coursed through her. "I don't know. He had to know I was on that plane."

"Possible, but doubtful. The military wouldn't disclose it. But someone who saw you in the terminal could." Ian shifted on his seat. "You should be okay at the ranch. Paul and your uncle Warny beefed up security during the ordeal with Della's stalker."

"Seriously? I didn't think that was possible."

"Every inch of the entire ranch is now under camera surveillance." He adjusted the heater.

Paul was a security specialist. He took the skills he'd acquired while in Special Operations and expanded them when he'd left the military. Honestly, after Utah, he'd gone a little security nuts, trying to entice her to come home and stay. "If he's added biometric scanning to get from the living room to the kitchen, I'm going to say he's gone too far. This side of that, I'm good with all the help I can get."

Worry flashed through Ian's eyes. He reached over and clasped her hand.

She wasn't expecting it and his touch surprised her. But, oh, it felt good to have someone hold your hand when you were scared. She gave his fingers a gentle squeeze, rested their linked hands and laced fingers on his thigh. "Thank you, Ian."

"What for?"

A little choked up, she buried it and swallowed hard. Emotions were one thing she couldn't afford—and hadn't been able to afford for a long time now. They clouded judgment, muddying your thinking. They made you even more vulnerable, and those were dangerous luxuries. "Being there for me."

"That's a given. As much as you did for Beth… how could I not be there for you?" He grunted. "And for me. Since Beth's death, I've been half out of my mind, trying to find out…" He stopped, sighed. "I don't know how I'd have gotten through these three years without you."

So he was doing this for Beth and because he felt he owed Maggie. Her heart sank, though it had no right to. He'd never led her to believe there was anything more between them—and there shouldn't be. In Crawford's eyes, that'd paint a bull's-eye on Ian's forehead.

"You really okay?" He stopped at a traffic light then headed north, away from town and toward the ranch.

"I'm fine." She forced herself to smile…and again questioned the wisdom of coming home. "It's just not the homecoming I've dreamed about with Paul not here."

"He'll get home as soon as the weather lets up and he can." Ian glanced over. "Until then, you're stuck with me." His eyes twinkled. "Lucky you."

"Yeah." She smiled. "Lucky me."

The reunion was sweet.

Uncle Warny sat in his usual chair, his glasses tucked into his red flannel shirt pocket, smiling at Maggie through red-rimmed, tear-blurred eyes with his arms stretched wide.

She flew into them, felt them close around her.

"Oh, Maggie girl, I'm so glad you're home safe." His huge body trembled.

"I missed you." She stroked his face.

"'Course you did. I'm a charming fellow."

She smiled. "I saw on the way in you've been exercising Thunder. He's moving a lot better." When she'd left here, he'd barely been able to move.

"We muddle along together. He likes his walks by ten every morning or he stiffens up." Uncle Warny chuckled. "Me, too."

"He's your favorite."

"They're all my favorite, but Thunder's special." His eyes twinkled mischief. "Like Paul."

She leaned close. "Don't you tease me, old man. I'm your favorite, and you know it."

"'Course you are, sweet pea."

"I'm sniffing blackmail fodder," Ian said, smiling. "Not telling Paul… It's going to cost you, Maggie."

"I'll pay, but I have to say I'm disappointed in you, Ian Crane. I can't believe you'd break my brother's heart. He needs to be *somebody's* favorite." She tried but couldn't quite get a teasing tone in her voice. Not when she'd felt that way her whole life. Their parents sure hadn't done much to make either of them feel loved. But Uncle Warny…he was their blessing.

"Della's got Paul covered now, Maggie girl." Uncle Warny sent her a satisfied look. "That woman's positively moonstruck over your brother." He rubbed his neck. "About time, eh?"

Past time. Way past time. "Glad to hear it, but it proves I need you more, so I'm your favorite." They'd competed in play forever, and she only realized then how much she'd missed it. That was the thing about being alone. There was nobody and nothing to keep you grounded. To Paul and Uncle Warny—to Ian to an extent—she mattered.

"Absolutely." Warny belly-laughed.

Maggie twitched her nose at him and snitched another hug. "It smells like heaven in here." She motioned for Jake, the black Rottweiler waiting patiently for his turn and her attention, and ruffled his scruff. "Hey, boy. I'm glad to see you, too." His tail wagged furiously fast, smacking the leg of her jeans. She scratched his ears and looked over at her uncle. "You learned how to cook?"

"Naw, Della packed the freezer with all kinds of stuff before she and Paul headed out to her step-grandma's." He lifted a sheepish shoulder. "She worries about me." And that she did clearly pleased him. "This one is roast, rosemary potatoes and glazed baby carrots—but it won't be ready for an hour and fifteen minutes. Then I have a peach pie to put in the oven."

"She made pie, too?" Maggie smiled. She'd talked to Della many times, and Paul being happy told her all she really needed to know, but that she'd opened her heart to their uncle, too...well, Della Jackson's stock rose from higher to highest in Maggie's book.

"Yep, a couple of 'em. She sure can cook." Warny looked at Maggie's eyes, homing in on the dark circles. "Have a nap, or go get your feet in the grass." He glanced over at Ian. "She ain't gonna feel like she's really home until she gets her own dirt under her feet."

Ian smiled. "She's notorious for that."

She was? "Did Paul tell you that?" She hadn't told him.

"Madison via Mrs. Renault." Ian crossed his arms.

Madison did know Maggie well, but how had Mrs. Renault discovered that? What was Maggie thinking; Mrs. Renault knew everything about everyone. "Walk with me."

Warny sent him a sly nod to keep close watch. Ian nodded back. "A short walk, Maggie. You need to rest."

"I slept the entire flight." She urged him around the table and toward the back door. "Come on, Jake."

He jumped to his feet and, nails clicking on the tile floor, got there first and nosed the glass.

"Some things never change." Nose prints. Maggie laughed. "Open it up, lazy bones," she told the dog. "You know how to do it."

Jake batted the doorknob, and then pushed the door open.

On the back porch, she ditched her shoes and took off down the steps and across the lawn in bare feet.

Ian caught up with her. "Madison meant that literally—your bare feet in the dirt? In December?"

"After being in Illinois, it feels warm here." Maggie smiled but there was sorrow in it. "It's grass, actually, not the dirt. It's the land I need to feel under my feet."

"It's home." He stuffed a hand into his slacks pocket.

"Yes." She laced their arms. "You ever go home?" He and Beth had been from Texas, a little town just outside of Corpus Christi.

"Home's not there anymore. Mom and Dad are gone now, and so is Beth. There's nothing left to go home to."

"Did you sell the place?" His family had a thousand acres of prime farmland. He was an only child, so she assumed it was his now.

"Leasing it out." He shrugged. "Truth is, I can't go

there, Maggie. I tried once, right after I got out of the military, but there're too many memories."

Maggie clasped his hand. "I can see where that would be really hard. But sometimes remembering is all you've got. They're kind of still with you then, if only in your heart and mind." He, Beth and Maggie had shared so many moments that she'd held on to while on the run. Picnics, lazy days at the beach. Sometimes Maggie would bring a date, sometimes not. They were close in the way friends who are open and honest with each other are…and then Beth had been killed and Ian had come home to mourn. Maggie had mourned with him, and their friendship had grown stronger, their bond forged to a depth only shared grief can forge.

"Maybe one day that'll feel good. But it doesn't yet."

He didn't say it. He didn't have to. Maggie knew. After Beth's murder was solved, then maybe he'd want to remember. Until then it wasn't comforting, it was haunting. How she wished she could make that easier for him, but she couldn't. He had to come to terms with that and with his anger at God over it in his own time and in his own way. Yet she could be there for him. Listen. Support. Do the things those who shared grief do for each other. It didn't seem like enough, but it was all there was. "Things happen in their own time."

"Yeah."

They walked along the fence toward the creek. The air was nippy, but crisp and clean. And the soft sounds of crunching leaves and running water at the creek soothed her, a tranquil balm to her weary soul.

Ian plucked up a broken twig from the ground. "The truth is, I'm stuck."

"Stuck?"

He tried to smile but it didn't touch his eyes. "Never mind. With all you've got going on, now isn't the time. I was being selfish."

Walking alongside, she patted his forearm. "Friends don't wait for the right time. Too often there isn't one. They talk when the need arises."

He glanced over at her, then out to the trees. "You know, even when you couldn't be here, you've been my main supporter." He grinned. "Does that make sense?"

"Perfect sense." The cards and email drafts. "I feel the same way." A soft hoot floated on the breeze and she smiled over at him. "Look. An owl." She lifted her chin toward a tall oak. "These woods used to be full of them." She'd heard them mostly at night, but occasionally during the day. "I wonder if they still are."

"Warny would know."

He would. "Owls always sound lonely, don't they?"

"I hadn't thought about it. Don't hear many of them in town."

"So what has you stuck?"

"Not now. You're tired." He patted her arm, still looped with his. "Let's just walk."

"Not finding Beth's murderer yet?" Maggie speculated, ignoring him. Innately, she sensed what he most needed to talk through was what he was most reluctant to discuss. That was generally always Beth's murder.

"How do you do that?"

Logic, pure and simple. "It's a woman thing." She wrinkled her nose at him. "So am I right?"

"Yeah, that's it," he confessed. "I'm feeling pretty hopeless. I mean, I try to stay focused on things not happening in my time but in God's perfect time."

"I thought you didn't pray anymore."

"I don't. But that doesn't mean I don't believe in Him. I'm just ticked off and disappointed. He let me down."

"So you're angry with God."

"Furious." His eyes glittered. "Sometimes so furious I can barely breathe."

A common reaction to the murder of a loved one. Some worked through it, some stayed angry with God forever. Her chest tightened. The thought of Ian being lost like that, not having the comfort of faith to help him through this, hurt her. It would break Beth's heart, too. "I can see why you'd feel that way…for a time."

"It is what it is. Beth's dead. I'm not."

Survivor's guilt. *Wretched mess.* Later would be soon enough to tackle the spiritual challenges. For now, Ian needed to vent. "So no new leads?"

He nodded that there hadn't been. "No. Nothing new for a full year."

No way could he keep the pain of that truth out of his voice. He didn't bother to try. Not with Maggie. She'd know anyway, so it was just as well. Still, it made her feel special that he'd be open with her. He wasn't that way with the team at Lost, Inc. Madison had told Maggie so a hundred times. "I've studied all the documents, Ian."

He shot her a stunned look. "All of them?"

She nodded, stepped around a stump and over its exposed roots.

"How did you get them?" Even he hadn't had access to everything.

"I could tell you but then I'd have to kill you." She gave him a toothy grin.

He dragged in a sharp breath. "You're still active."

It wasn't a question and she didn't insult him by deny-ing it. He stopped cold. "Maggie, tell me I'm wrong. Tell me you're not still active."

She shrugged.

"What are you doing?" The truth dawned in his eyes. "You have been Crawford bait. I suspected it when you didn't deny it, but I can't believe you're ac-tive and the agency has allowed it?" He dragged a hand through his hair. "Oh, good grief. They've had you undercover." A vein in his neck bulged and his face flamed red. "What are those fools thinking?"

To avoid confirming or denying, she bent and picked up a dried twig, slung it across the field between them and the edge of the woods toward the creek. "He hasn't killed anyone else."

"Because he's been laser-focused on killing you." Ian frowned. "Does Paul know this?"

"I'm not confirming anything, but if I were still ac-tive and undercover, no one could know. So of course Paul wouldn't know."

"Don't insult me. You're active and undercover. Of course you are. Why doesn't Paul know? He should know."

"He'd interfere. After Utah, he'd remove me from the situation if he had to go to the media and spill his guts to do it. He can't know anything, and you will not tell him."

She gave him *the* look, and he glared right back at her. "But, Maggie…"

She softened her voice. "You will not tell him, Ian. There are other lives at risk."

"Crawford's future victims." Ian's jaw clamped and he squeezed his eyes shut a long second. When he re-opened them, accusation burned in their depths. "You didn't just come home so we could help protect you."

"Actually I did. I can't handle him alone anymore." Had she ever been able to handle him, or had that been an illusion? Her uncertainty blew holes in her confidence.

"Don't lie to me."

"I don't lie, Ian Crane." The wind caught her hair. She swiped the long strands of it back from her face. Her nose was cold from the nip in the air, her fingertips, too, but the grass under her feet made up for it. "You know how these things work. It was job essential. And this is confidential—all of it, and I mean it, Ian. If you tell Paul a thing, I'm leaving, and I'll do the best I can on my own."

"He'll kill you." Ian cut to the chase.

"Paul won't kill me."

"Not Paul—though he'll likely want to. Crawford. You came home for help, but not to deter him from hunting for you. You expect him to come after you."

"I stayed away to protect my family. That's the whole truth." She lifted a hand. "It didn't work. By his own words, anytime Crawford loses me, he will come after Paul." She paused and let that fact settle in. "There's only one way I'll ever be free of him and know he isn't killing again." She let him see the truth in her eyes.

"Then why didn't you shoot him in your backyard in Illinois?"

"Spiritually, I couldn't justify it so long as I thought I could get away from him. When I picked up his tail on the way to the airport, I had to accept that I couldn't."

Acceptance hadn't come easily, and it wasn't painless. But she'd made peace with it.

"So you came here—" The truth dawned. Ian frowned, his shock in every tense line in his face. "Maggie, no. You can't mean—"

"I came home to confront him. On my turf. On my terms. With help I trust."

"I wanted you here, but I didn't know that you were set up as bait for him." Ian pressed a hand to his stomach as if he'd been sucker punched to the gut. "The FBI sanctioned all of this?"

"After he found me in Illinois, well, we don't have a lot of options." She toed the grass, sought comfort in it. "Actually, we have one—this one. Crawford will kill again in the next two weeks, Ian. We're in his habitual countdown to Christmas. What else am I supposed to do?"

"You could really quit." He frowned. "Does Crawford know you're still active? Is that why he won't leave you alone?"

"I tried quitting. Publicly, I quit after Utah. I've been covert the entire time since I got off medical leave. But me quitting didn't stop him." Her bitterness about that put a sharp edge in her tone. "A few honchos at work, the task force members and now you are the only people who know I'm still FBI." She stared off into the deepening shadows in the woods. "From everything we can tell, Crawford bought into the public resignation due to the permanent damage to my leg—at the time, my recovery wasn't expected, if you recall."

"It's a miracle you've got as much mobility as you do."

"Almost a hundred percent. I've worked hard at it." She had been motivated and diligent.

"So Crawford thinks you're an artist and he's still after you."

She nodded. "There's been nothing to lead him to any other conclusion. Whether or not I was still an agent didn't matter to him. I got too close to him and he resents it. I was supposed to die in Utah and I had the audacity to live. He won't forgive me for that, or forget it."

"I know that's why he's still after you—because he failed to kill you." A wrinkle formed between Ian's eyebrows. "But why do you have to die before he can continue his killing spree?"

"Because he knows that with or without the FBI I'm going to try to stop him, and I see things others don't. That rattles him."

Ian dragged a hand through his hair and raised his voice. "So you're active, and when he isn't after you, you're still consulting with the task force and you're after him. Now you turn the tables and— Maggie, I urged you to come home, but I think I was wrong. In North Bay, you're a sitting duck. You'll be slivering your focus between keeping yourself safe and everyone else. You know everyone in town."

She did. Everyone who'd been here any length of time, and he had a point. But having help to face Crawford balanced the added risks. "I'm a sitting duck regardless of where I am. It's taken me a while to accept that, but it's true." She took in a deep breath. "Isn't being a sitting duck on my home ground, which has the best security money can buy, surrounded by people who love and help me, better than being a sitting duck on the run without security or help?"

Ian tossed the twig toward the woods. Jake took off

like a shot after it. "I talked you into coming home, but it'd be better to be out of it altogether."

"Told you. I tried that." She slapped at her thigh. The muscle was stiffening up. "It didn't work, and I have the scars to prove it. So does Paul."

"I don't like any of this."

He wouldn't tell Paul, but he wasn't comfortable with the situation. How uncomfortable was he? Did she need to worry? "But you will support me, right?"

He glared at her, hesitated a long minute. "Yes, of course." He frowned and held it so she couldn't miss it. "But if you get yourself killed, I'm not forgiving you, Maggie, and I mean it. I'll throw rocks at your grave every day."

"That's fair." It'd probably be good aggression therapy for him. "I'll do my best not to put you through that." She looped their arms again and they walked back toward the house, Maggie leaning on him. All the activity and hours of driving, sitting had her knee stiff.

In the kitchen, Ian turned to her, his expression at odds with his tone. "I'm going to head home. You be careful, and if you need me, call."

Maggie shoved her hair back from her shoulder. "Ian, don't you even think about leaving," she said before thinking. She'd just assumed with Paul away he would stay at the ranch with Uncle Warny in the barn apartment. "Um, we've got a Monopoly match set for after dinner and you're my best hope against the Monopoly King."

Ian chuckled. "Jake?"

"No, me," Warny grumbled. "Don't let these overalls fool you, son. I've got a knack when it comes to real estate."

Maggie guffawed. "I'll say. In four years, you've nearly tripled my holdings."

"Woulda done better if the market hadn't crashed and you hadn't made me help—"

"I'm not complaining." She cut him off. "I'm thrilled with what you've done." She turned to Ian. "You will stay, won't you, Ian?"

"Actually," Warny said, "I'd be obliged if you'd stay out here until Paul gets back…just in case."

Ian looked at Maggie.

She nodded. "Please. I know it's a huge inconvenience, but—"

"It's not inconvenient at all. I didn't want to shove my way in, but I wasn't going home, Maggie."

"What were you going to do?"

"Hang close and keep an eye out."

Watch over her.

"I'm glad to hear it," Warny said. "If that varmint Crawford comes sniffing around, between you, me, Jake and Maggie, he'll be sorry he did."

He just might. "Thank you, Ian." Maggie beamed, happy from the heart out. Finally, she was home.

"Uncle Warny," Maggie complained. "You can't buy Marvin Gardens. I always buy the yellow ones."

He glared at her over the tops of his glasses. "I can buy whatever's for sale…especially when you buy Park Place right out from under me."

Ian didn't dare laugh. "At least you two are landing on properties. All I seem to hit are railroads, utilities and that pay-taxes thing."

"No justice," Maggie said.

His gaze locked with Maggie's. She looked happy,

and he felt less worried about her being here since Warny had walked him through the security system. If Crawford did show up, he wouldn't find attacking her easy—at least, not at the ranch. But that Ian worried about her, the way he worried about her, concerned him. It wasn't the worry of a friend but of a man who cared deeply for a special woman. He didn't have the right to worry about anyone like that.

Maggie rolled the dice and moved the thimble three places, to just visiting the jail. "Ian, you have to spend Christmas with us."

Warny winced. Ian understood why. Paul had invited Ian out every year since Beth's death. But he just couldn't celebrate holidays and there was little sense in dragging others down with him, so he opted to stay home alone. "I don't think—"

Maggie put a hand atop his on the table. "It's a great idea and it'll make me very happy. I've spent too many holidays alone, and I suspect you have, too. I want everyone important to me here. So, please, say yes. If not for yourself, then for me. Because I need it."

How did he refuse a frank plea like that? From anyone else, he'd have found a way. But from Maggie? He couldn't do it, of course, yet he couldn't make himself refuse her. "I'll think about it."

"Think all you like, my friend," Maggie said. "But Christmas Day, when the turkey hits the table, your backside better be in that seat or I'm going to cry my eyes out because it's not." She rarely cried, but the threat was extremely effective with Paul, Uncle Warny and Ian. None of them knew what to do with a crying woman but were wise enough to want to avoid one. She blew out a sigh. "First time I'm home for Christmas in four years, and you'll make me cry all day. I can't believe it."

Ian frowned at her. "That's blackmail, Maggie."

She walked her glass to the sink, filled it with tap water and then took a long drink. "Yep, sure is."

He looked at Warny for reinforcement, but got a grunt. "Don't look at me. You ever seen her cry? I seen it once or twice, though it's been a spell. I still remember it and I'm telling you straight-out, I can't handle it. Never could." Warny let out a sigh that heaved his shoulders. "It's pretty bad, son. Probably easier on you to just show up." He scratched at the back of his neck. "Definitely easier on me."

Maggie brushed a hand across her mouth to hide a smile. "Paul and Della want a happy Christmas, too."

"You're dragging them into this?"

"Do I need to?"

She had him. Either he capitulated or all of them would have a miserable Christmas and it would be Ian's fault. "I haven't seen this side of you before, Maggie. I can't say I like it."

"Me either, but drastic measures are required. Indulge me, okay?" She gave him her most sincere look and dragged a chip through a bowl of onion dip. "You being here makes me happy. Is it so wrong for me to want to be happy? It's been…a long time." Truer words couldn't be spoken.

If he had any sense, he'd go home and forget this day, and especially this night, ever happened. Being here with her and Warny was bittersweet. Wonderful, but it awakened a sense of longing and belonging in him. Made him acutely aware of the strength and acceptance in family, and how much he missed it. He'd forget the sparks that even a simple glance between them ignited. The smell of her hair, the feel of her hugging him, him holding her. The sound of her soft laughter and the serenity in her quiet stillness. He'd forget that when they'd walked the ranch, she'd patted his arm and reached for his hand and paused at the creek to dip her bare toes in the water. It was cold, but she'd had to feel the earth and water of home under her feet. He'd forget all that and her circumstances—if he had sense.

But all of those things bypassed sense and rendered her unforgettable. Every one of them had her knocking not only at the walls of his mind but also at the walls surrounding his heart. He *should* refuse…but this was Maggie. Maggie, who sent him cards on his birthday and at Christmas and Easter. Who not once had forgotten to call on the anniversary of Beth's death to talk him through what would have been merciless, guilt-ridden nights. Maggie, whose notes he'd read so often they were creased and whose conversations he'd played and replayed in his mind to conquer those lonely, hopeless times that plagued him. He couldn't refuse Maggie.

And yet for all those reasons, he shouldn't accept. He wanted her happy but, failing Beth, her murder still unsolved…he had no right to move on with his life. He had enough to regret.

He opened his mouth to inform her that her attempted blackmail had failed, but before he uttered the first sound, the phone rang.

"I've got it." Warny eagerly slid back his chair and snagged the phone from the kitchen counter. "Hello."

He listened for a long moment, his expression sobering, his body tensing. He stuffed a hand into the pocket of his overalls. It was fisted. Ian glanced at Maggie, and one look at her warned him she hadn't missed a thing.

"We'll be all right, Paul," Warny said, then added, "No need. He's sitting at the kitchen table, losing his shirt in a game of Monopoly. I've already asked him. Okay, then. I'll ask him again from you."

Ian homed in. Paul wanted something from him.

"Yes, she's here." Warny glanced at Maggie. "She had a nap on the flight in, but she's got circles the size of black holes under her eyes. Says she's fine, but she likely hadn't slept worth a flip for a week or more, and she's too skinny. Twenty pounds, at least. You do your best, son." Warny hung up the phone and returned to the table.

"What's wrong?" Maggie asked before Ian could. "That was Paul. I know it was."

"It was, and calm down. He and Della are fine. They're just socked in for a couple days. Half the country's immobile due to weather." Warny looked at Ian. "I tried to tell him you'd already agreed to stay put here, but he wasn't in much of a listening mood. He asked if you'd stay on the ranch and help Maggie and me in case Crawford shows up."

Ian had seen the weather report and planned for this in case he was asked. "Suitcase is in the car."

"You knew?"

"In here or out there," Ian said. "I wasn't going to leave you, Maggie. Especially with Paul being away."

She smiled. "Thank you."

He smiled back. "You're welcome."

"You ready to haggle a little over Park Place now?" Warny asked.

The next ten minutes were some of the most intense negotiations Ian had ever witnessed, and they still weren't resolved.

The phone rang. "You two settle this," he said. "I'll get it."

He grabbed the phone from the kitchen counter. "Hello."

"Ian. Ian, can you hear me?"

Madison. His boss and Maggie's lifelong friend. "I hear you." Tons of background noise competed with her voice. "What's up?"

For the next fifteen minutes, she told him, and he grew more and more concerned. By the time the call ended, he had forgotten all about the Monopoly game.

So had Maggie and Warny. He set the phone back into its base and returned to the table. "Madison's stuck, too. She can't get back until a helicopter can airlift her out."

Maggie set the dice on the Monopoly board. "Tell me she's not planning to ruin her Christmas cruise to come back here for me."

"No. She's setting up an emergency conference call. Paul and Della, Mrs. Renault and Jimmy, and you and me, Maggie. Grant's on the ship with her. It's all hands on deck in half an hour."

"Is the boat leaking or what?" Warny asked.

"The ship is fine. Madison is fine. Grant is fine."

"Then what's the emergency?" Maggie set her iced tea down. The table looked bare without a gingerbread house. She'd have to make one.

"We'll know in half an hour."

"We'd best get this game cleared up then." Warny started putting the money back into the slots in the box.

Maggie helped him, pausing to ask Ian, "Does she

do this sort of thing often? Emergency conference calls with the entire staff?"

"No. It's rare."

"So just how worried do we need to be about it?"

His eyes sobered. "Madison's never called an emergency meeting without a full-blown crisis attached to it. Typically, a crisis involving someone at the agency."

For her to call one now, when her staff was spread all over the country for Christmas and she was water-locked on the ocean… "Ominous."

"Knowing Madison—" he dropped the metal car into the box "—we should be very worried."

Chapter Four

"Yell if you need me." Uncle Warny retreated to his barn apartment.

Jake rested on his bed in the kitchen beside the door. Maggie sat across the kitchen table from Ian. They both had notebooks in front of them and the phone rested in the center of the table, on speakerphone.

When it rang, Ian answered. "We're here, Madison."

"Good. First, welcome home, Maggie. I'm sorry to drag you into this but none of us can get there because of this foul weather and something's come up that can't wait. Frankly, I need your help."

Madison wasn't just serious and bearing bad news, she was scared. Maggie hadn't seen that often, and she hated seeing it now. "You've got it. What's come up?"

"I'll leave it to Ian to fill in the blanks. The upshot is that a few months ago, there was a security breach at the Nest."

Maggie stifled a groan. Only Madison knew discussing the Nest in front of Maggie would be acceptable. If Paul or Ian had to find out, this isn't the way she would have chosen. "Madison, what are you doing?" Paul sounded as shocked as Ian looked.

Confusion riddled Madison's voice. "What?"

No one answered.

"Oh, no." Some light had dawned for Madison. "Maggie, you haven't told him? How could you not tell Paul?"

"What hasn't she told me?" Paul asked.

"Later. I promise." Maggie avoided Ian's eyes. "Go ahead, Madison."

"No." Ian raised his voice. "Not a word, Madison— not about that. You know why, so no excuses. Isn't Maggie in deep enough trouble without adding a security breach to it?"

Maggie frowned at him. "Stop, Ian. Madison isn't doing anything wrong." This was going to go over like a lead balloon. "Does everyone on this call have the necessary clearances to avoid this discussion being a security breach in any way, shape or form?"

Madison didn't hesitate. "Yes."

Maggie had hoped to avoid making Paul aware of her continued active-duty FBI status, but the situation was what it was. Resigned, she began. "What I'm about to say doesn't leave this group. I'm not an outsider— don't ask me to explain, I won't. What I will tell you is that my clearances are current and intact and I know the Nest exists." Ian stared at some distant point on the ceiling. "Paul, you can shoot me later. For now, go ahead, Madison."

Paul's voice elevated. "What do you mean, you're not an outsider?"

"I can't answer you." Maggie laced her hands atop the table. "Think, brother dear. Would Madison breathe a word about the Nest in my presence if I didn't have the necessary clearances?"

"But you can't. You'd have to still be active…" His voice faded into a groan.

Maggie didn't utter a word. Didn't blink or breathe or meet Ian's gaze, though she felt the weight of his on her. At the moment, he wasn't any happier with her than Paul.

"We will discuss this, Margaret Marie Mason."

She winced, betting they would. Paul wouldn't take the news well that she was not only still active with the agency but also still a subject-matter expert to the military. Profiling consultant. Limited exposure, of course, but he'd never known that. "Go on, Madison." With luck, Madison would hurry up and start—

Ian didn't let her. "After Utah, you promised him you'd quit."

"I did," Maggie confessed. "And I intended to keep to it, too. I just got delayed by Crawford."

Madison interceded. "Next time, if you don't want me to out you, give me a little notice that you're breaking your promise."

"I didn't break my promise," Maggie insisted with a sniff. "I just delayed enacting it a little."

Ian rolled his eyes back in his head, mouthed, "Wrong."

She sent him a frosty glare.

"Save it for later. Mrs. Renault will blister her ears for you—or Ian can do it. He's right there and handy." Madison seized control. "Back to the matter at hand. A few months ago there was a security breach at the Nest. Nothing has changed on its status, Maggie. It's still classified and as unmentionable as Area 51, though a few more people have been brought into the need-to-know loop. Access to the facilities is still restricted, and most assigned to the base are not aware the Nest exists in the woods on the base, much less aware of the underground bunkers.

"The Nest has underground bunkers?"

"Yes, Jimmy, it does," Madison told the youngest member on her staff. "But they're not of interest to us at the moment."

Ian seemed surprised by that news, as well. Maggie wasn't, but held her tongue.

"Since the breach, there's been an active investigation to determine who leaked classified information to the press," Madison said. "General Talbot and Colonel Dayton insist that either Paul or someone on staff at Lost, Inc., is responsible."

No one said a word, but the gravity of the situation didn't escape Maggie. Paul would never do that, of course, but then neither would Ian, Madison or Mrs. Renault. Maggie didn't know Jimmy or Madison's new employee, Grant Deaver, well enough to vouch for them.

"When we were active duty—" Madison's voice crackled, the storm wreaking havoc with the phone "—we all were stationed at the base and had access to some part of the Nest. Maggie, we've already established that none of us know the mission there, including Mrs. Renault."

Her husband had been the base commander, before he'd died at his desk, and General Talbot assumed command.

Madison's tone grew more intense. "As for supposed

motive, we all have reason to not be enamored with the government."

Taking a sip of iced tea, Maggie absorbed the data, slotted it, falling back into the profiling routine as familiar to her as breathing. Madison had been a POW, left behind and reported dead. Ian had lost Beth. Della's son had been the victim of a man suffering PTSD while she was deployed to Afghanistan. Paul fought for veterans' rights routinely through his organization, Florida Vet Net.

She muted the phone and asked Ian, "What's the short-take on Jimmy?"

"His buddy Bruno took an IED to save him. They didn't have the right gear, but the honchos sent them on a mission headquarters deemed critical anyway. Bruno died. Jimmy didn't."

Anger and survivor's guilt, like Ian. She unmuted the phone. "Madison, why are Talbot and Dayton looking outside the base for the leak? Odds are it's someone—"

"General Talbot is up for a congressional appointment. If he gets it, Colonel Dayton gets command of the Nest. If the leak is one of their own, they can kiss their promotions goodbye."

"Got it." Maggie did, and yet she had a hard time reconciling the kind-eyed man and the colonel who'd helped her escape from Nashville with men who would frame innocents. "Would Talbot do that, Mrs. Renault?" She knew more about everyone than anyone in all of North Bay, including Miss Addie at the café.

"He is his career and has nothing else," Mrs. Renault answered. "If he thought it was over, he might."

Her disappointment was evident. She resented having to consider it a possibility. Understanding that, Maggie asked, "What about Dayton?"

"I don't know."

Translated, that meant, Mrs. Renault had an opinion but wouldn't voice it without evidence to back it up. Not good news. But, to be fair, Talbot and Dayton weren't necessarily out of line. Everyone here did have a bone to pick with the government. Would they pick it? That was the question, and on that the jury was still out. Maggie's instincts said none of them would, but she'd worked too many cases where the unlikely had happened. In battles between ambition and honesty, truth was often the first casualty. Talbot and Dayton would move every mountain to save their jobs and get those promotions. "Okay. So what exactly is the development, Madison?"

"A reporter asked Talbot some point-blank questions."

"Reporters do that. I'm sure if the general didn't want to answer them, he deflect—"

"He's dead, Maggie."

"The reporter is dead?" Her gaze collided with Ian's across the table.

"His body was found a few hours ago on an abandoned dirt road about a quarter mile from the highway on 85. I've emailed everyone a map."

"Bullet to the head, right?" Jimmy asked Madison.

"Car bomb, I'm told, but the forensics are problematic. Apparently, the car was moved to its current location after the explosion."

"Why was it moved?" Maggie asked. "Was that the security breach?" A perimeter breach shouldn't cause this kind of stir, but with a congressional appointment and a command on the line…

"It's significant," Madison said. "Pull up your email. Subject line is Pace."

Ian did on his cell and showed Maggie the screen. It was a photo of a dark-haired man in his early thirties with a wide forehead and a sharp nose.

"That's the reporter, David Pace. He signaled Talbot and Dayton that the breach had occurred."

"How?" Maggie asked.

"By asking them for verification of something at the base."

Surprise streaked through Maggie. "That's the breach?"

Ian stepped in. "Not him asking about the base, Maggie. He specifically asked if the Nest existed, and if it did, for what purpose."

Inside Maggie, alarms blared. "Just like Beth."

Ian shot her a look. "What?"

"That's what Beth was doing at the time she was murdered—investigating something at the base." Surprise joined the alarms. "You didn't know that? How could you not know that?"

"I didn't know it," Ian said. "You know military spouses are told not to bother their soldiers with anything at home they don't absolutely have to bother them with. If they're not focused on the task at hand in a war zone, the results can be catastrophic." Ian stilled and the stunned mumbling ceased. "How did you know it?"

"Beth and I were check-in buddies. We talked several times a day. The last time we spoke, she was agitated. She'd been to see Talbot and Dayton about something she was investigating for the station—"

"What station?" Ian asked.

Maggie lifted a hand. "The TV station where she hoped to work."

Ian sat stunned. "Beth worked at a TV station?"

Beth really didn't bother him with things going on at home. "Well, she was trying to, which is why she was investigating something at the base. Getting the job depended on the outcome of her investigation. Anyway, she was agitated because the meeting hadn't gone well. In fact, Dayton told her to back off and never mention it again."

Ian dragged a hand through his hair. "You'd think she'd have said something…"

Maggie shrugged. "Like you said, spouses are instructed not to bother their soldiers with things going on at home. They can't control them and it causes them to sliver focus. In a nutshell, you were gone and she was trying to do something constructive with her time, Ian. She hadn't yet gotten the job, so there was nothing solid to tell you yet. No big deal."

"It might have been a very big deal. She's dead and now this reporter, David Pace, is, too."

Madison shared the station information with them. "Sorry to dump this all in your laps, but there's nothing the rest of us can do to get there until the weather clears. Detective Cray is my point of contact. Ian, call him with anything you get. He'll call you with anything new on Pace."

"Got it," Ian said, still sounding a little dazed.

Inside, he was reeling. It showed in the tension in his face, the rigid set of his jaw. "We'll keep you posted, Madison."

Maggie ended the call, double-checked to make sure it disconnected. "You okay?" she asked Ian.

"Yeah." He swallowed hard. "In the morning, we'll go talk to this station manager."

"Okay." Maggie frowned. "I'll pull his name off the net."

"Madison will email it, if she hasn't already. She always does a written report." Ian stood up. "It'll say you've been doing military consults, too, won't it?"

Not at all surprised he'd deduced it, she nodded.

"I'm going to head out to the barn now. You get some rest."

She nodded. The evening had been great, but boy had it turned bitter now. He needed some time to himself to process this news about Beth. That he'd missed a stone to turn unnerved him. Likely, he'd be chewing himself up for it the rest of the night.

"Guard her, Jake," Ian told the Rottweiler then moved toward the door, stopped and turned around, then walked back to her.

Standing beside the table, he just stared at her a long minute. It was hard not to speak or flinch, but he needed a minute to reconcile something going on in his head. A war raged in his eyes. "I'm blown away by this news about Beth. I can't believe you knew it all along and didn't tell me."

"I would have told you if I'd known you didn't know it. At first, talking about Beth was too painful, and then you said you'd tracked her movements from when you left until she passed. I had no reason to think you didn't know about the station."

He frowned. "You surprised me with the military consults—I didn't know you did that—but you wouldn't have kept anything about Beth from me. Not intentionally."

"No, I wouldn't have." She let him see the truth in her eyes.

"For the first time in a year, I have a new lead. Thank you, Maggie." He kissed her, clearly intending a quick brush of their lips, but when their mouths touched something happened. Something warm and wonderful and welcome. Something sudden and startling that drew them closer, made them linger, and it felt so…right.

Ian abruptly released her and pulled back. Surprise rippled in his eyes. "I didn't…expect…"

She'd felt it—that grounding, that balance—and she hadn't expected it, either. "I know."

"You, too?"

Her heart raced. She nodded. "Fluke?"

"I don't know." He frowned.

"Should we find out?" She wanted to know. Needed to know.

He curled his arms around her, pulled her close and kissed her again. She didn't think, just reacted, and kissed him back.

When their mouths parted, she felt weak and breathless. She'd wondered what kissing him would be like. Now she knew, and it was better than she'd dreamed. So much better, it couldn't happen again.

He drew back. "Not a fluke." Abject misery lit in his eyes.

Certainly, it reflected in her own. "Definitely not."

He backed away. "Welcome home, Maggie."

"Uh-huh." Too stunned to do more than mumble,

she just stood there leaning hard against the back of her chair and watched him walk out the back door.

Now *what* was this electricity between them all about? When had their relationship shifted? How could it shift and neither of them even know it?

The next morning, Ian acted as if nothing happened. Taking her cue from him, Maggie didn't say a word about that kiss or ask a question during breakfast. After they'd eaten, she and Uncle Warny cleaned the kitchen while Ian spoke on the phone with Detective Cray and reviewed the report on Pace.

"Are you ready to get going?" Ian closed a small notebook and tucked it into his shirt pocket. "We have an appointment in an hour. The station manager's name is Brett Lund. That is the same station as Beth's, right?"

Maggie grabbed her purse, checked to make sure her weapon and her new phone were inside. "It is if the station is WKME, yes."

Worry settled on Ian's face. "It is."

Maggie hooked her purse strap on her shoulder. "Are you thinking that these cases are connected?"

"It's a possibility. I'm not sure yet."

"Neither am I. Beth and Pace on the same assignment made it appear so, but why would the manager wait three years to reassign the story? And Beth never specifically mentioned the Nest, just the base. So this could be coincidental."

"It could." Ian took the last sip from his coffee cup. "Hopefully Lund will talk to us."

"He'll be reluctant. He just lost an employee."

"He'll get over it. I lost a wife."

Uncle Warny rubbed at his neck. "If you two want

to get there in time for your appointment, you better stop yapping and get moving."

Wordlessly, Maggie and Ian pulled a security check on the Ford Expedition, mindful of Crawford's penchant for car bombs and well aware from Dayton that he could already be in the area. True, there'd been no alerts on the security system, or any calls from the task force warning her, but with Crawford all that meant is one must be even more mindful.

Buckled into her seat, Maggie waited for Ian to say something about kissing her. But he didn't speak a word about that or anything else, and frankly she didn't know what to think about it. She kept waiting, but to no avail. About five miles from the station, she couldn't take the silence anymore. "Did you gain any new information from Detective Cray?"

"Yes, I did. Sorry. I should have told you. I'm just a little preoccupied." He looked genuinely contrite. "The coroner hasn't issued a formal report yet, but from visuals, he says Pace's death wasn't due to the car bomb."

"What was the cause of death?"

"Uncertain, pending the outcome of his examination."

Maggie frowned. The man was hedging. "What does he think was the cause of death?"

"Apparent suicide." Ian looked skeptical.

"You obviously don't agree. Any particular reason?"

"A couple of them." Ian spared her a glance. "But the main one is that when they found Pace—inside a car gutted by an explosion—he wasn't burned and he had on an unusual pair of shoes."

"So he was placed in the car after it exploded?"

"Had to be postdetonation."

Why would someone do that? "What was unusual about his shoes?"

"They were neon blue."

"Okay. And that's significant because…"

"Della's stalker wore neon blue shoes."

"A lot of guys do." Hadn't she just seen a pair in Dayton's bag on the plane?

"You don't understand. The neon blue shoes helped nail Jeff Jackson as Della's stalker."

"Ian, I'm sure any physical object's been used in a crime somewhere by someone."

"Detective Cray says Jeff denies involvement in many of the attacks on Della and Paul, but the neon blue shoes were found in his hotel room. Blue shoes were spotted by witnesses in several of the bombings and in the fire that burned down Della's cottage." He twisted his lips. "I know what you're thinking."

"What?"

"That jails are full of people claiming to be innocent."

She had been. "They are, Ian."

"We know some things Jeff did do. But this with the shoes isn't sitting right." Ian's gaze shifted to the rearview mirror. "Maybe Jeff isn't Mr. Blue Shoes."

"Mr. Blue Shoes?"

"The guy who pulled the bombing attacks on Della and Paul."

That was a leap she couldn't make. "Cray caught Jackson with hard evidence—"

"That was the shoes. They could have been planted."

"There's no evidence of that, and Jeff Jackson did pull the stunt with the ambulance that nearly killed Paul and Della."

"True. But there's also no evidence—none, Maggie—that Jeff knew anything about explosives, yet bombs were used against Paul and Della multiple times." He draped an arm over the steering wheel. "I'm telling you, something feels...off."

"Okay." She trusted his instincts. They had proved sound. "We'll keep that in mind. When Pace's body was found, he had on blue shoes." It could be something or nothing. They needed more information to know. "It isn't like they're rare."

"Men's blue aquatic shoes?"

She nodded. "Even Dayton has a pair." Catching Ian's odd look, she explained. "I saw them in his bag at the airport, when he was transferring my weapon."

"When we're done here, maybe we can go talk to Jeff Jackson, and get Grant Deaver busy pinpointing where Talbot and Dayton were at the time of Pace's death."

"Good idea—not that either will be directly involved, but maybe we can connect someone to them who could be."

"My guess is they were in Nashville—with you."

"Wouldn't that be an airtight alibi?"

"Yeah, I guess it would." Ian pulled into a parking slot in front of WKME and cut the engine. "One other thing you need to know before we go in there."

"What?"

"Cray believes David Pace was inside the Nest's perimeter fence—soil samples taken from residual evidence on his clothes."

Surely he wouldn't be killed for that. Jailed or fined, maybe, but murdered? Not likely...except for Beth.

Maybe Pace had refused to back off asking questions about the Nest. "I'll make a note of that, too."

Ian looked at her as if he wanted to say something more but couldn't quite make himself do it. She smoothed her black slacks, tugged at the sleeves of her red sweater, unsure if she wanted to push for questions or answers she might not like. But if she couldn't talk to him freely…well, there was no one left. "What?"

"I owe you an apology, Maggie."

"For what?"

"I should never have kissed you. I'm not sure why I did—the second time, I mean."

The urge to cry hit her hard and fast. Not expecting it, she had a hard time burying the swell of emotion that rose with it. She couldn't show it, of course. If he regretted kissing her and she did show it, she could wreck their relationship. Burying her own feelings on the matter, she asked, "What kiss?"

He frowned. "Now you owe me an apology."

She smiled. "You can't have it both ways."

"Were you really unaffected, because it sure seemed like you were kissing me back."

"I was?" That got to him. And it should. She'd been affection-starved for nearly four years. Of course she was affected. That didn't mean she was crazy enough to do it again, especially not with a man who apologized for kissing her, and even more important, not with Crawford on her heels. Ian could end up dead.

"You were, and you know it."

Maggie opened the door and stepped outside. If she stayed in the SUV, she'd have to admit the truth or lie, and though this little discussion left her ego pretty battered, she couldn't make herself lie.

Ian slammed his door and pressed the remote lock until the horn beeped. "I can't believe you won't just admit you liked it."

She slid him a sideward look meant to melt steel. He apologized and then wanted her to admit she liked it? Not in this lifetime. "Maybe I didn't." She started across the lot, heading for the sidewalk.

He caught up near the station's glass front door. "Of course you did."

"If I did—and I'm not saying I did, mind you—I wouldn't read much into it, Ian. I've been alone a long time. It doesn't take much to get my attention." That should shake his cocky attitude. "But keeping my attention is a whole different matter." *Thank you, Madison McKay.* If not for remembering that about her, the thought wouldn't have occurred to Maggie.

He gave her a slow smile that snatched her breath. Before her eyes, it melted under a heap of worry. "You liked it."

Seeing that the possibility troubled him, she hiked her chin. "It was nothing. Like I said, what kiss?" She nodded. "Now hush and get the door."

They cleared security and an escort led them into a corner office on the second floor. A woman with blue contact lenses—no one had eyes that blue—came out from behind her desk and ushered them into the inner sanctum where Brett Lund sat behind a very large oak desk littered with enough files to fill a two-drawer cabinet.

In his midforties, Lund was graying at the temples and nearly bald on the crown. His rumpled gray suit told the tale that he'd been at the office all night, likely staying close awaiting informational updates on David Pace to come in or cross the wire.

"Good morning." Lund stood up and extended his hand, introduced himself and then seated them in his gray leather visitors' chairs. Returning to his own seat, he rocked back. "I accepted this meeting, but I have no idea why you want to talk to me. Is this a professional visit, Dr. Crane, or a personal one?"

"What's the difference?"

The starch in Lund's voice doubled. "Frankly, if you're here on behalf of Lost, Inc., I have nothing to say to you. If it's personal, I might."

"Then let's make it a personal visit." Ian clasped the arm of his chair.

"I'm assuming you're here about David Pace. If so, and you read the paper or heard the news, then you know what I know."

"We're not here about David Pace." Ian's gaze narrowed. "We're here about my wife, Beth."

The starch wilted. Lund tried to reclaim it. "If this is about your wife, then why—" he swiveled his gaze to Maggie "—are you here?"

Already, he was in cease-and-desist-and-admit-nothing mode. "Mr. Lund, these are serious matters. Lives have been lost. Let's not diminish the seriousness of that by playing childish games," Maggie said, already weary of his evasion tactics. First, they were elementary, and second, he was lousy at implementing them. Time to throw a few flames and see if he fanned them. "I know for a fact Beth Crane was working for you. I know that you hired her as an investigative reporter—"

"On a trial basis."

"On a trial basis," Maggie conceded, "and I know she was working on an assignment—"

"I hadn't yet given her any assignments."

Defensive. He knew far more than he wanted to share. Creating distance, self-preservation instincts kicking in. Oh, yes. He wanted to disassociate. But that was not going to happen. "Beth was neck-deep in a personal investigation. She brought her findings to you, and based on those findings, you agreed to hire her pending the outcome of her investigation." Maggie frowned at him. "You asked why I'm here. Simply put, the reason is because I know the truth. Attempting to placate me with half-truths and/or omissions won't work." She dipped her chin and studied his eyes. "Under the circumstances, I'd think you'd have better judgment than to opt for trying them."

He stopped rocking. Stilled. "What circumstances?"

Maggie played a hunch. "First Beth and now David Pace, and you ask me what circumstances?" She grunted. "Mr. Lund, surely not. To do that would make you either incompetent or deliberately deceptive. I don't believe for a second that a man achieves your position being either. Now, let's be logical and efficient. You can talk with us or with Detective Cray. Your call."

Lund had the grace to flush and sank back in his seat. No starch left, he now sat limp.

Ian's glance at her revealed an admiration of her skills. He shifted focus to Lund. "What exactly was Beth investigating?"

Lund darted a look at the office door, as if for reassurance that it was closed and what he revealed would remain private. "The Nest."

Ian stiffened and so did Maggie. There's no way

Beth or Lund should even know the Nest existed, and
no way Maggie or Ian could admit knowing about it
or even ask him for information about it. "And what
was Pace investigating?"

Lund aged ten years before her eyes. "The Nest."

Ian's grip on the chair arm had his knuckles white.
"Was Pace's death suicide?"

A long moment passed with Lund chewing his lower
lip. "That's what I'm being told, but it's just preliminary findings. Final's not confirmed yet."

"Do you believe the preliminary findings are true?"

Lund's jaw locked. He glanced away, paused and
then swiveled his gaze back to Ian. "I have a wife and
two kids, Dr. Crane." His eyes clouded, turned dead-
pan flat. "The truth is whatever the authorities tell me
is the truth."

Two reporters dead… Maggie understood Lund's
position. Beneath the veneer lay turmoil. Turmoil and
raw fear. "Why did you wait three years to assign Pace
to the investigation?"

"The file was misplaced." Lund shrugged. "It just
resurfaced."

Rage simmered in Ian. Maggie felt it radiate from
him like a furnace blast.

"Stop. My wife is dead and you dare to sit there and
lie to me. You owe me more. You owe her more." He
paused and leashed his tone. "You knew drug-seeking
thugs didn't invade our home and kill her. You knew
it was this investigation, and you were afraid you'd
be next."

Maggie agreed with Ian, watched closely for Lund's
reaction, taking special note of his body language. It
rarely lied.

He stiffened, pursed his lips, blinked hard and fast. "I've given you two leeway out of respect for your wife, Dr. Crane." Lund stood up. "But now this meeting is over."

Ian stood and reached over the desk for Lund, clasped him by the shirtfront. "Tell me the truth!"

Lund sputtered and stretched, pressed a button on the lip of his desk, no doubt summoning security.

"Ian, no." Maggie wedged between the desk and Ian. "Let him go." She looked up at him, saw the moment what he was doing registered in his eyes. "Ian, let him go."

He opened his hand, spread his fingers wide and then stepped back. "You knew or suspected Beth was murdered for this investigation and you still sent in Pace. He has a wife and kids, too. Did you think about that? Did Pace know about Beth, or did you send him in blind?"

"I have no idea who or what Pace did or did not know. Now, get out of my office."

"With pleasure," Ian said. "Expect a visit from Detective Cray. You can explain yourself to him. Don't look so worried just yet. Not reporting what you know about Beth's death and admitting you sent David Pace into harm's way blinder than a bat will be easy. It's the other explanations you'll have to give that you need to worry about."

"You threatening me?"

"Don't be absurd."

"What other explanations?" Lund shot Ian a haughty look. "To whom?"

"To David Pace's family...and to your own." Ian leaned over the desk. "Everyone in North Bay and beyond is going to know what you did, Lund—and what you didn't do. I wonder how your wife and kids are going to feel about you then."

He paled and glared past Ian's shoulder to the security guard entering the office. "Get them out of here—and don't let them back in."

The guard looked confused, focused on Ian. "Hi, Doc."

"Jesse." He nodded. "How's MaryAnne?"

"Fine. In the grocery store when we ran into you and her back was hurting—you were right. Her doc checked her out and it was a kidney stone. She's fine now."

"I'm glad." Ian spared Lund a hard look filled with disdain.

"Get out!" Lund bellowed. "All of you get out of my office!"

Jesse reacted first. "I'll walk you out, Doc."

"Thanks." Ian headed toward the door. "You remember Maggie Mason, don't you?"

"Paul's sister. I sure do." He smiled at her. "Good to have you home, Miss Maggie."

"Thank you." She was glad to be home, but in all the hours she'd dreamed of her homecoming, it had been nothing like this.

Jesse opened the station's front door. "Sorry Mr. Lund treated you like he did."

"He's under a lot of stress."

"Yes, sir. He's been terrorizing the whole station since he heard about Mr. Pace." Jesse's face turned ruddy. "I'm afraid I can't let you back in, but if you need anything, call me. I'll help you if I can."

"Thank you, Jesse."

Maggie and Ian stepped outside and she paused on

the sidewalk to study him. *Rattled, devastated* and *outraged* all came to mind. She held out her hand. "Best let me drive."

He didn't argue, just passed her the keys and got in on the passenger's side of the Expedition then slammed the door with a lot more force than was necessary.

"Time for extreme action," Maggie mumbled to herself on her walk to the driver's side of the SUV. *Lord, I could use a little help here.*

She got in and cranked the engine, looked over and saw a billboard for Shady Pines cemetery.

Of course.

Ian called Detective Cray, filled him in on what they'd learned from Lund, requested a meeting at the jail with Jeff Jackson, learned Jackson hadn't yet been transferred to the state correctional facility so Ian could drop in anytime, and warned Cray that Lund wouldn't be cooperative about sharing anything he knew for fear of his life and the lives of his family members.

A part of Ian understood that fear and respected it. After Beth, how could he not? But inside, he was furious. Two years, he'd searched for answers full-time, and he'd continued searching for her killer since he'd hired on at Lost, Inc. He understood now that drugs hadn't been involved but he had a hard time wrapping his mind around the fact that Lund knew or at least suspected Beth's murder had been tied to her investigation and he'd remained silent.

All this time wasted on wild-goose chases. What kind of investigator was he, anyway? Maggie had been back less than twenty-four hours and already she'd made more progress than he had in three years. And the way she'd handled Lund…impressive.

"You okay?" Maggie asked.

Lost in his own thoughts, Ian forced himself to shift his attention to her. "Not really."

She nodded and cut the engine. "Come with me."

Only then did he realize she'd stopped—and where she'd stopped. "Why are we at Shady Pines?"

"Beth is buried here." Maggie left the SUV and waited for him outside.

Ian got out and closed the door. "I know where she's buried, Maggie. I put her in the ground. What I want to know is why we're at the cemetery right now."

She tilted her head. "I couldn't come to her funeral. I knew about the station but didn't realize there could be a connection between it and her death. I had no reason to believe anything other than what the police concluded about a drug addict breaking into a doctor's home seeking drugs. No one did…except Lund. Maggie twisted the car keys in her hand. "I did know the colonel told her to back off but many things go on at a military installation. I didn't know she knew about the Nest. Anyway, I need to tell Beth I'm sorry."

That took the wind out of his sails. "You have nothing to apologize for. I failed her. Not you."

Maggie's eyes looked haunted. "She was my friend." She swept the air with a fingertip. "Which way?"

He nodded right. "Second row, third grave."

"Come with me." Maggie's eyes were dry, but her voice sounded thin and reedy.

His wouldn't, so he kept quiet. Inside, he felt like a jumbled mass of snapping livewires and crackling electrical shocks.

Maggie stood before Beth's grave, gently stroked the headstone, the embedded copper angel so like the medallion Beth had worn all the time. Long minutes passed where Maggie apparently was having a silent conversation with Beth inside her mind or she was praying. He didn't know which.

Finally, she bent down and touched the petal of the fresh yellow carnations in a vase on the grave. "It's lovely that you still send her flowers, Ian." Maggie looked at him and smiled through a face drawn and tense. "Do you need a few minutes alone?"

"No, she's heard it all."

"Why are you angry?" Maggie looked up at him.

"Lund knew."

"He suspected something, yes. But he didn't know, and he didn't want to be buried next to Beth, or worse, he didn't want to see his wife and kids buried next to Beth."

"After Pace, he had to know. But he said nothing to Cray."

"He doesn't want to die." She turned to face Ian. "I've been in that position. I understand his fear."

"You would have told me."

"I think I would have, but I don't know. I didn't tell Paul how close Crawford had come to killing me."

"That's different, Maggie. You were protecting Paul."

"Maybe. But I was terrified if I said anything, I'd make him a target again. So I didn't. Maybe it's that way for Lund, too. That's all I'm saying."

"Do you think he knows who's behind the killings?"

He believed Pace had been murdered. So did she. "No, I think he doesn't know, which is why he's even more afraid. If he knew, he'd report the person to diminish the threat. He doesn't know."

Anger roiled inside Ian. "You think Dayton and General Talbot are involved?"

"Maybe. Honestly, doubtful. It's too obvious. They'd be more subtle."

"I agree." Frustration flooded him.

"But it's too soon to tell." Maggie placed a hand on his sleeve. "Ian, you need to let go of the anger."

"Impossible."

"Essential." Maggie stroked his sleeve. "It clouds your mind, erodes your peace. Beth is dead, Ian. She doesn't want or need your anger."

"How do you know what Beth wants or needs?"

Maggie covered his lips with her fingertips. "Because if I were murdered, I'd want those I left behind to live and love and laugh. I'd want them to be happy and enjoy their lives. To know they were so filled with rage they were—"

"Stuck?"

She nodded. "It would break my heart."

"I don't know how to stop," he whispered. "Anger is all I have left."

"No, it's not." Maggie stepped closer. "You have me." She wrapped her arms around his waist and rested her head against his chest. His heart thudded against her ear.

Warmth. Comfort. He closed his arms around Maggie, let holding her fill his senses. The anger in him weakened, countered by compassion and caring. It didn't dissipate, just faded, there but not as potent or all-consuming. Once again with Maggie, he was the lucky one.

He turned his head. Glimpsed something behind the headstone. What was it? Stepping around, he saw the object propped against the slick marble and stiffened. "Maggie, get to the SUV. Do it now."

"What?" She reached into her purse automatically and withdrew her gun.

Ian quickly scanned the cemetery but saw no one else. Saw nothing out of place. "Take cover."

"From what?"

He grabbed her by the arm and rushed back to the SUV. "Go, go, go!"

She fumbled but keyed the ignition, threw the gearshift into Reverse and hit the gas.

Gravel spewed, the tires spun and grabbed, and she braked hard, then switched to Drive and stomped the gas pedal. "What are we running from?"

Finally, Ian spotted him. Little more than a speck hunched down behind a tomb, he wore all black—except for his neon blue shoes.

A bullet whizzed past the SUV and sent bark flying off an oak lining the road. The sound roared through the cemetery, echoing off the graves.

Maggie fishtailed through the gravel to the main road and hit the pavement going sixty.

"Who was that?"

"I suspect it was the real Mr. Blue Shoes." Ian dialed his phone, reported the incident to Cray, finishing with, "We're getting Maggie back to the ranch. We'll email you statements." He then hung up.

Maggie frowned. "I saw the shoes, too."

"What about in Illinois?" Ian asked. "You said you watched him make his way across the yard. Did he have on blue shoes, then?"

She tried to remember but couldn't. "I don't know. I was so focused on the gun in his hand, I didn't look at his feet. The gun and the mask and that he was in all black. That's all I recall."

Ian unzipped his jacket and the sound brought a flash of a memory to her mind. One of Dayton moving her weapon bag to bag on the airplane. Slowing to the limit, she headed toward the police station. "Ian, yesterday on the plane, Colonel Dayton switched my gun from my bag to his."

"I remember. He returned your weapon once we cleared the terminal."

Maggie nodded. "But that's not what's significant."

"What is?"

"When he put my gun in his bag, I saw a pair of neon blue shoes."

He processed that. A link between Mr. Blue Shoes and Talbot and Dayton, or a coincidence? "You're sure it was Dayton's bag?"

"Yes. Well, no. Not really." She pulled alongside a green truck at the stoplight. "General Talbot actually carried it. But he handed it back to Dayton after he'd cleared security." Uncertainty flooded her. "It could have belonged to either of them."

"So Mr. Blue Shoes could still be either of them— or Crawford, or someone else entirely."

"Crawford?"

"He's good with bombs."

They worked through the time line and on the dates Blue Shoes had been active here, Crawford hadn't been active during those same times against Maggie. "Surely the man hasn't decided to take on all of North Bay to get back at me."

"Maybe it isn't just about you anymore," Ian said. "Paul survived, too. You said he hates loose ends, and you and Paul survived him." Ian frowned. "Where are you going?"

"To the police station. I want to talk to Cray about all this."

Ian motioned her to take a left at the corner. "They closed the old pass-through by the theater." It was shaped like a castle. "You have to go around it now. It's a kids' park."

Maybe Crawford was Blue Shoes. Maybe he was taking revenge on North Bay that she and Paul hadn't died. "Why are you not telling me everything, Ian?"

He turned and looked at her. "What?"

"You didn't see the man wearing blue shoes until later. What did you see first—when you told me to get to the SUV?"

"Park over there." He pointed to an empty slot.

When she had, she turned off the engine and removed the key. "I'm not moving until you tell me."

Regret filled his eyes. "You're right. I'd hoped you hadn't noticed and I could wait to tell you after we were back at the ranch. But, as usual, you're too smart for your own good."

"Smart enough to know you're stalling."

He clasped her hand, covered it with both of his. "There was something propped against the back side of Beth's headstone, Maggie."

"What?"

"A black rose."

Chapter Five

Detective Cray walked out of the police station with a package tucked under his arm. "Ian." He nodded, and then smiled at Maggie. "Maggie Mason, it's good to have you home."

"Thank you." She smiled back. After the warmth of the SUV, the air felt cool and she wrapped her jacket tighter around her.

"I am worried that your arrival wasn't a little more... quiet." He dipped his chin. "Madison called and gave me a heads-up that you were here in case Crawford showed up. So did Della, who didn't know that Paul had already called."

They were worried. With good cause. So was she. "Crawford could be here already."

Cray held up a finger, walked away from the building toward a little greenbelt area filled with benches, motioning for them to join him. "Safer to talk out here. The walls in there have ears."

Maggie had run into the same situation too often to ask questions. Some liked being a contact point for the media. It made them feel important. And no matter how careful others tried to be, there were always leaks. She studied Cray. He had aged well. Late forties, graying ever so slightly, in decent shape, and he lacked the hard edge most in his line of work acquired as a self-defense mechanism. When you deal with the dark side of people all the time and wade through the trenches with them and their victims, it's tough not to get hard. She admired him for fighting it.

Ian stood back to the brick building and scanned the lot, clearly still uneasy because of the shot fired at the cemetery. "What is it that you don't want overheard?"

"Pace was murdered. That's not yet official, but if the coroner comes back with anything else I'll be shocked."

No surprise there. "You have officers at the cemetery now, right?" Maggie asked. When he nodded, she went on. "You need to call them and let them know to photograph the back side of Beth Crane's headstone."

"Why?" he asked, perplexed.

"There's a black rose propped on it."

"Crawford." Cray's brows furrowed and his breath escaped, fogging the cold air.

Maggie glanced from Ian to Cray, waited for two uniformed officers to exit the building and walk past them. "This hasn't been made public, but Crawford has left me a black rose twice before. He also left one for his second victim."

"I thought it was a dozen."

He'd been briefed. "That's only after he kills them. The single rose is before." Was it intended for Ian or her? Had to be Ian. She hadn't planned on going there until she'd seen the cemetery sign.

His concern etched lines deeper in his face, dragged at the corners of his mouth. "This isn't good news."

It wasn't. But he hadn't yet heard the worst of it. She shot Ian a questioning look.

Cray missed it and asked, "Did you see the shooter out there?"

"From a distance," Ian answered, stuffing his hands into the pockets of his jacket. The tip of his nose was pink and the stiff breeze had his eyes watering. "Enough to know he was dressed in solid black, wearing a mask and he had on neon blue shoes."

Cray's eyes widened then disappointment filled them. "I was afraid of that. I'm so sorry." Cray let his gaze wander, shifted the package from one arm to tuck it under the other. "After you called, I pulled the blue shoes from the evidence room and went to see Jeff Jackson. Prison's overcrowded so we're stuck with him until they free up some space."

"We hoped to talk to him, too."

"Not necessary, Ian." Cray frowned. "He's been calling Della every day, swearing he had nothing to do with the bombings and that the shoes weren't his. Frankly, we didn't pay a lot of attention to him. We found them in his hotel room, so why would we?"

"But you are now," Ian said. "What happened?"

"I took the shoes to his jail cell and asked him to try them on." Cray's expression turned grim. "He was relieved to do it."

"They didn't fit." Maggie stifled a gasp.

"No, they didn't."

Ian looked at Maggie. "Crawford could be Mr. Blue Shoes." He frowned. "Do you know where he was during the time Della and Paul were under attack?"

"If I did, he'd be under arrest."

"No incidents during that time?"

"I ran the dates, remember? No activity with me until two days after Paul said the situation here was resolved. Well, when he thought it was resolved for the first time. There was a time gap, and then Ian told me Jackson had been arrested. I was in Illinois then."

"Where were you the first time—when Paul thought the situation was resolved but it wasn't?" Ian asked.

"Fleeing Montana." She'd had to leave in a hurry then, too. Abandoned all her gorgeous big sky landscapes. She swallowed a sigh.

"That's what prompted your move to Illinois? An incident that happened after Paul and Della's problem was believed resolved but wasn't?"

She nodded. "I came home from the grocery store and found a black rose attached to a canvas on my easel with a pushpin. I grabbed my paintbrushes and left."

Cray listened with obvious interest. "Are you telling me that there have been no sightings or activity on Crawford during the time that Blue Shoes was active here?"

"I'd want to double-check the dates before officially verifying, but we ran them once already and found nothing. So I don't believe so. If one was active, the other wasn't."

Awareness gleamed in Cray's eyes. "You let him chase you so he won't kill others." Worry of the worse kind settled in. "Maggie, he's a mastermind killer—"

"Yes, he is, and actually, just him chasing me isn't accurate, though it happens." She sniffed against the cold settling in on her. "I'm always trying to find him, too." The shot at the cemetery fired again through her mind. "Though once again it seems he's found me first."

"Or someone wants you to think he has," Ian countered, rubbing his jaw. "Either way, we need to get you back to the ranch, where security is tight."

"He had no way of knowing I would be at that cemetery this afternoon."

"He could have suspected it," Ian said, then shrugged. "We stopped and bought flowers. If we were spotted…"

"True." That sat easier on her shoulders than Crawford targeting Ian.

"Either way, you two watch yourselves."

Ian nodded at the detective. "We'll post you on anything we find out."

"About Lund." Cray seemed more than reluctant to say what he must. "I'm sorry, Ian, but we won't be finding out anything from him."

Ian grunted his disgust. "He's lawyered up."

"No, it isn't that."

"Then what is it? Is he refusing to talk?" Maggie knew how to tackle that problem. Reluctant didn't mean impossible, just hostile.

"He can't talk." Cray grimaced. "The call came in while you two were on the way over here." He hardened his voice. "According to Jesse, the station security guard—"

"We know Jesse," Ian said.

Cray nodded. "Not long after you left his office, Lund took a phone call. His door was closed and neither Jesse nor Lund's secretary know who he called or what was said, but both of them heard Lund's muffled, heated voice. It wasn't a pleasant call. We're looking into the phone records now to find out who was on the other end."

"Why not just ask Lund?" Ian asked.

"Can't." Cray swallowed hard, bobbing his Adam's apple. "Word from the feds—they're primary on this because of the Pace incident, our guys weren't even allowed on scene—is when Lund got off the phone, he put a bullet in his mouth."

Ian squeezed his eyes shut.

Maggie shook. Hard. "I'll keep him and his family in my prayers."

"Can you drive?" Maggie asked Ian.

"Sure."

Still shaken about Lund, she passed the keys. "We need to stop at the grocery store."

"Okay." Gauging by the set of his jaw, Ian wasn't crazy about the idea. "I'm assuming it's important?"

Fishing her phone from her purse, she dialed and answered him simultaneously. "Very. I need all the stuff to make a gingerbread house." He looked at her as if she'd lost her mind, and she frowned to let him know that she hadn't missed it. "It's five days until Christmas. It's a tradition."

"I know, we spent hours on the phone while you were making the last couple. But I'm not sure it's a good idea to linger anywhere away from the ranch until we find out who put that rose on Beth's grave or took a shot at us, Maggie."

She held up a wait-a-minute finger. "This is Sparrow," she said into the phone. "It's possible Gary Crawford is in North Bay, Florida. Could be a copycat—probably is—I can't be sure at this point. I'll email details to the task force within the hour. Right now, I need satellite imagery." She tilted the phone and lowered her voice. "Ian, get me the coordinates for where they found David Pace's car."

He nodded, and she went on. "A reporter here purportedly committed suicide, but his car was bombed. He wasn't burned and he had on neon blue shoes that are significant to another case. His boss, the station manager, put a bullet in his mouth just after questioning. And a few hours ago, a man took a potshot at me at a cemetery. He left a black rose on a headstone significant to our case, and he had on neon blue shoes, which is significant to the other case." Maggie paused but didn't hear anything coming from the other end. There was nothing uncommon about that. "I want imagery of these coordinates—" She took them from Ian, relayed them, then added, "Extend out ten miles in all directions. I believe the car was moved after the explosion—no residual evidence of it exploding at the scene—and I'm positive the victim wasn't in the car when it exploded. He wasn't burned." She again paused. "ETA?" she asked, seeking an idea of the estimated time of arrival of the images.

A pause, then the speaker, who could have been man or woman, said, "Five hours, thirty-two minutes."

"Thank you." Maggie hung up and stowed her phone.

"It takes us weeks to get satellite images." Ian grunted. "I'm impressed."

"Don't be. We're not that efficient. I went commercial."

"So do we. It still takes weeks."

"One of the few perks of playing cat and mouse

with a serial killer. When you say you need something, people assume you need it right now to survive. Unfortunately, you usually do."

Ian held his silence though his expression darkened. He parked in the Publix parking lot and they went inside. Maggie grabbed a cart and began stuffing items into it. "Do you like cornbread or bread stuffing?"

"Either. But herb-seasoned is my favorite."

"With sausage and apples?"

He nodded.

She smiled. "Me, too."

"How do you switch gears like this?" Ian pushed the cart while she dumped items into the basket. She attacked the supermarket like a telemarketer on speed dial. "You don't seem rattled. How can you not be rat— you don't think it's Crawford. You seriously think a copycat shot at us."

"I think it's highly likely." She grabbed a box of graham crackers, debated, then snatched a second one and dropped them in the buggy. "But honestly, when you're running all the time, you get used to acting anyway. You don't wait until later on anything because you never know what later is going to bring. To have any kind of life, you have to snatch what you can when you can." She shrugged and dropped two boxes of powdered sugar into the basket. "For me, this is normal."

"I'm so sorry." He followed her and they checked out. When he'd loaded the groceries and gotten into the SUV, he muttered, "I knew running was rough on you. I knew at times you got close to him and he got close to you, but I guess I didn't have a real understanding of what that meant in actual life terms and what it's been like for you until today."

"I'm glad you've been spared." She smiled. "Hey, let's get dinner at Miss Addie's Café and bring it home. Uncle Warny loves her lemon meringue pie."

"Call and tell her what you want." He passed her his phone. "She's number two on speed dial."

Maggie grinned. "Who's number one?"

"You."

Her heart lurched. It shouldn't be reacting with a thrill that she rated important to him—he was sorry he'd kissed her—but that seemed to matter only to her logic. Her concerns about Crawford didn't weigh in with sense, either. Or his concerns about Beth. "Ian, do you think maybe one day…" She couldn't make this man-and-woman personal. She almost did, but she couldn't. It just wasn't fair.

"One day, what?"

"Nothing." She wrinkled her nose at him. "I was being silly, dreaming things I have no right to dream."

"I know what you mean," he confessed. "I do it, too."

She studied him, but even her training didn't help decipher that remark. "It's a shame we can't run down to the courthouse and get a license for it, isn't it?"

"A license to dream?" he asked.

"Yeah. Wouldn't that be something? Bet they'd issue a million of them a week. Hey—" she pointed "—you're passing up Miss Addie's."

He hit the brakes. "Sorry." As soon as he parked, he rushed inside and came back out carrying three paper bags full of food. He stowed them in the back and then got in. The hint of a smile curved his lips. "You must be hungry."

"Starved." She laughed. "I love Miss Addie's cooking. I wanted everything, so actually I restrained my-self."

He laughed out loud. "If this is you restrained, I can't imagine what it's like when you cut loose. We won't need to cook again until Christmas."

"Good."

"Miss Addie said next time you're in town, you better come in to see her."

"I should have gone in today, but if I had, we'd be there for hours. We have to get back to the ranch before dark."

His gaze shifted to the dash clock. "If traffic is light, we'll make it. You should call Madison and give her an update."

Maggie reached for her purse. "Paul first. I want to know if he's popped the question." Her stomach fluttered. "Della will say yes, won't she? I mean, they look happy."

"They are. But when have you seen them?"

"In the photos on the piano." Maggie frowned. "You know my parents were crazy about each other, but Paul and me, well, we were mostly inconvenient."

"You've told me they weren't exactly candidates for parents of the year."

"No, they weren't that." She let out a humorless laugh. "They did what was necessary but we were out-siders. Their world was closed to the two of them." If not for Paul, she'd have thought that was her fault. He made sure she knew it was just their way. "It's bothered me for a long time that my parents never took photos of Paul. When I got old enough, I did, but there were dozens of me that he took and only a few of him. Now the whole piano top is covered with photos of him and Della and Uncle Warny and me. I love that."

"You love seeing Paul happy."

"I do." Her brother had made her being happy his priority in life. She was grateful for his sacrifices and the care he'd taken to make sure she'd grown up secure and loved.

"Don't worry. She'll say yes. Della Jackson is head over heels in love with your brother." Ian gave Maggie's hand a reassuring squeeze. "You're a good sister."

"I'm not. But I am so glad about Della. On the phone it's hard to tell, and it's really important to me that Paul be loved." She craved that for him. "You know that without him my childhood would have been miserable, right? But it wasn't. He made it magical."

"Your parents were here."

"Even when they lived here, they weren't here, Ian. Well, not for Paul and me."

Ian stiffened. "I heard they flew in after the Utah incident." When she nodded, he added, "Did they really go back to Costa Rica while you were still in ICU and Paul was in the hospital?"

She nodded again. "Paul was banged up pretty badly and I was clinging to life by a thread, but as soon as Uncle Warny arrived, they said he would watch over us. They had to get home." Her tight jaw quivered. Maybe he wouldn't notice. "Commitments, you know."

"I thought they had an emergency." Ian looked over at her.

"They did. Their social schedule had been disrupted for a week. For them, that's an emergency." Her resentment of that—their social activities rating higher with them than Paul and her—reverberated in her voice. She didn't bother to try to hide it. The minute she left for college, they had taken off to Costa Rica. They'd vacationed there many times and loved it.

"I'm so sorry. I had no idea."

"Family secret. No one knew, or ever did, though Madison figured it out. When we were kids, she was always at the ranch. Paul couldn't hide the truth from her, but he saw to it that no one else knew. I'm still not sure why he covered for them, but he did."

"If you were profiling, what would you conclude?" Ian turned off the radio. "I'd think he'd be angry and bitter and let everyone know."

"If it had been just him, he might have. But—it took me a while to figure this out—Paul didn't do anything for them. He did everything he did for me. My darling brother didn't want me to feel as if I wasn't loved or that my own parents didn't care about me."

"Makes sense, yet I'm hearing a but in your voice."

"You are astute, Dr. Crane. There is a but." She warbled her eyebrows. "The truth is, they didn't love or care about either of us. Paul and I were tolerated. Our parents pulled us off the shelf when it was convenient and shoved us back on it when it wasn't. It mostly wasn't." She swiped her hair back from her face. "I was lucky. Paul made sure I had all the love and support in the world. He was the one who did without—at least, until Uncle Warny showed up. Paul was in his teens then." A lump rose in her throat. "That's why it's so important to me that he be happy now."

"You love him."

"I do. I'm ashamed to say it, but for years I had no idea no one else loved him. I was little and clueless, but once I realized that…" Her throat again thickened, and her voice grew husky. "Well, I've tried to let him know ever since."

Ian flashed her an enigmatic smile. "Between you and Della, I'd say that you can rest easy. He's loved by two special women. That makes him a lucky man."

"Is Della a hugger?" Maggie asked, relieved and curious and eager to learn more. "I'm a hugger. Paul's a big hugger. He needs hugs."

"She's a hugger." Ian smiled. "I am, too—just for the record."

"I know. You even hug with your voice."

"Excuse me?" He turned off the pavement and onto the ranch road. Plumes of dust rose up behind him.

"When we talk on the phone. You hug me with your voice. It's lovely."

A strange look she couldn't interpret flashed across his face. He stopped the SUV at the gate, punched in the code and then ran through the biometric scan.

The broad black metal gate swung open.

Maggie watched to make sure it closed all the way behind them. When it had, she pivoted to look ahead. What she expected to see wasn't there. Where was Jake? He always came out to meet her. And Uncle Warny? And why was Thunder still in the exercise yard? "Slow down, Ian."

He slowed to a crawl. "Why?"

"Something's wrong." Dread dragged at her belly. She pulled her weapon from her purse, scanned the pasture, the woods, between the trees and thick foliage abutting the road.

The house looked fine from the front, but as they rounded the back toward the garage and barn, Ian hit the brakes. "Oh, no."

In the broad yard near the back porch, both Jake and Uncle Warny lay on the ground.

"Leave your lights on." Darkness was settling in, overtaking dusk, and thick shadows lay everywhere. Maggie rushed out and took off running, terror spiking her already pounding pulse. They weren't moving. *Why weren't they moving?*

Flat on his back, her uncle lay with his arms crossed over his stomach, his baseball cap pulled down to shield his face.

And in his hand, he held a black rose.

"Maggie, answer me." Ian repeated. "Is he breathing?"

Shaking hard, she lifted the cap, bracing for what she might see. But Uncle Warny looked normal. *Thank You, God.* She lifted a hand, pressed her fingertips against his throat, checking his carotid, and found a pulse. "He's breathing. Is Jake?"

Ian was on the phone. "Yes, but we've got a complication."

Maggie tried to rouse her uncle. He didn't wake up, but he did snore. She did a quick first-aid scan. "He's been drugged, Ian."

"Jake, too."

She shot a look past the huge fir, twenty yards away, to where Jake lay. And why had Ian, a doctor, gone to the dog rather than to her uncle? "What's the complication?"

"There's a bomb collar on Jake's neck."

"Back away. Do it now, Ian." Panic flooded her. "Crawford loves bombs." She shouldn't have come back here. Now he was going to kill Jake, and if Ian didn't move, he'd die with him. "Move!"

Ian sprinted over to her. "I've called out Major Beecher. He's a bomb squad specialist at the base. He and his team are on the way." He ran a quick check on Warny. "Pulse and respiration are fine." Lifting his lid, he checked one eye and then the other. "He seems okay. Drugged to the rafters but, for the moment, okay."

Relief washed through her, but her gaze slid to Jake and fear rushed right back.

Waiting for Beecher was the longest half hour of her life. "Crawford had to do this." While they'd stopped by the café to pick up food, he'd made a beeline from the cemetery to the ranch. "He'll wait until the last minute, you know." On the ground beside her uncle, she held his hand and fixated on Jake. "That's what he does. He waits and waits until you think you're going to make it, and then, boom, he strikes. Your world explodes and nothing is ever again the same."

"Let's hope not."

"Paul loves that dog. So do I." She couldn't cry, she couldn't allow herself to be that weak. She had to be strong, detached and to think. "Why did I come home? This is my fault. If I'd just kept running—"

"You'd be dead, Maggie. He would have caught you in Nashville and we'd be responding to the call telling us they'd found your body." Ian's voice was flat and firm. "You didn't collar or drug Jake or Warny or put that rose in his hands." Ian looked to where the rose lay in the grass beside Warny's hip.

"No, but I knew he would come after me. I knew he'd follow me home, and I came back anyway. That was a selfish, stupid thing to do."

"Getting yourself killed would have been a stupid thing to do. Coming home was smart, your last resort."

She repeated that to herself over and again, trying to convince herself it was so, determined to believe it. But if it was true, why didn't it rouse that sense of knowing in her that it was? Why did it feel so self-serving and hollow and empty?

Finally Beecher and his two-man team arrived, diverting her attention from her guilt and misery. Dressed in bomb gear, they got a grip on the situation from Ian, and then approached the dog. Jake still lay unconscious, as motionless as he'd been since they'd found him. Beecher examined the device, the team mumbled among themselves, and then Beecher removed his headgear. "It's not hot."

Clammy and shaking, Maggie shuddered a deep sigh of relief. Her whole body collapsed inside as if pounded boneless and limp. "He'll be okay then?"

Beecher removed the collar, took another intense look at it. "He'll be fine." He lifted something off the ground and tucked it into a clear evidence bag and then tucked the bag into his pocket. Looking to the first of the other two on his team, he issued the order. "Thompson, go check Warny."

"Yes sir, Major." He double-timed it over to Maggie, dropped down and began running through emergency medical procedures. He pulled blood and did some field test with a smear.

"Can you tell what it is?" Maggie asked.

"Not without a thorough toxicology, but my best guess is it's a common sedative." He spared her a glance. "I've seen results like this before."

"Ian's a doctor," Maggie said, glancing at him pacing a short distance away. He was reporting in to Detective Cray—and likely to Madison and Paul, though Maggie hoped not, since they were stuck where they were. No sense in worrying them even more about something they couldn't do a thing about. "He says they were sedated, too."

"We'll know with what when I get the reports." Thompson rolled Uncle Warny over onto his side. He stopped snoring and his eyes fluttered open.

"Maggie?"

Relief gushed through her. "Yes, Uncle Warny?"

"This ground's hard."

"Yes, it is."

He squinted up at her. The beam of light from Beecher's response vehicle's headlights sliced over his body. "Why am I on it?"

Pushing herself, she forced her tone light, hoping he'd take a cue from her and stay calm. "Apparently you decided to take a nap."

"I'm sure as certain I did not. I was exercising Thunder—and it was morning, now it's not."

"He's fine," Thompson said, and then reached into his black case for something she couldn't see.

Maybe, but he looked droopy-eyed and confused. "How'd I get here?" Uncle Warny asked her.

Maggie stroked his rugged face. "I was hoping you could tell me that."

"Last thing I remember is holding Thunder's reins. Jake barked and…that's it." He pivoted his head and glared at Thompson. "Who are you and why are you checking my heart with a stethoscope?" He shot a hard look at his niece. "Did I have a heart attack and you're not telling me?"

"No," Maggie said. "Lieutenant Thompson is with Major Beecher. They're checking to see what happened."

"Which would be easier if you'd be still for a minute, sir." Thompson ruffled the hair low on Warny's neck. "There it is." He turned and called out, "Major Beecher, I found the entry-point wound."

Beecher joined them, stared at a little red pinpoint of blood dotting the back of Uncle Warny's neck. Darkness settled in, and he pulled a flashlight from a zippered pants pocket and shined its beam on Uncle Warny's neck. "Get a few photos."

Thompson snapped a few shots with his cell phone, then stowed it in his pocket.

Beecher frowned at Maggie. "The good news is he'll sleep tonight and most of tomorrow, but there shouldn't be any long-term residual affects."

How could he know that about residual effects from a single prick-point of blood? "What are you seeing on his neck that I'm not?"

Beecher held her gaze and lowered his voice so only the two of them could hear. "Something I've seen many times but I've never seen used against Americans on American soil. I can't say anything more than that. I can say there is some bad news."

Ian stood within hearing distance, but pretended to be as deaf as a stone and he avoided her eyes. He knew what had been used on Uncle Warny and Jake and he was as gagged as Beecher and unable to tell her. That could be for only one reason. Whatever had been used had *military application* written all over it. What else could warrant a gag order on Beecher *and* Ian? He'd been a civilian for over three— Ah, wait. Beecher hadn't deduced residual effects just from the pinprick on her uncle's neck. It'd been that *and* whatever he'd picked up and stashed in his pocket in that evidence bag. "What's the bad news?" she asked Beecher.

"Whoever did this is a professional with access to assets not typically seen in the civilian sector."

Definitely military assets. Talbot or Dayton? Her gaze locked with Ian's, asking the unspoken question.

"Not necessarily," Ian said, brushing at the grass clinging to his knees. Nightfall had taken hold and only the light from the headlamps in the SUV and in Beecher's response vehicle lit the dark. The tall fir rustled off her right shoulder, and the brisk wind ruffled Ian's hair. "Production and manufacturing are handled by civilians."

Maggie processed that. Crawford could have bought it, stolen it or hired on somewhere to get personal access. With the Black Beauty rose, Crawford had to have done this.

Uncle Warny grunted. "Maggie girl, could you get me off this cold ground. My bones are about frozen solid."

Ian and Maggie flanked him and helped him up. "Ian," Warny said, "can you get Thunder into the barn? He's gonna be stiffer than a rigor corpse, being out in the cold this long."

"Go on, Ian. I'll get Uncle Warny inside." She looked beyond him to Beecher. "Would you carry Jake for me? His bed is in the kitchen."

"Sure, Maggie." Beecher's forehead crinkled in a deep frown. "We've been briefed on what you've been through for the past three and a half years. I'm sorry that after all that you're having a lousy homecoming."

Not half as sorry as she was. Of course, she was the reason it was lousy. She shouldn't be here. Exactly what she had feared would happen was happening. She had to fix that.

And to pray hard Crawford wouldn't keep coming after her family anyway.

Standing in his Rhino ATV on the far side of the creek, he watched the activity near the ranch house through the binoculars.

He knew every inch of this property. Knew all about the security and surveillance—the Mason land was under camera observation 24/7. But provided he didn't get careless or do anything stupid, the only ones who'd know he had been here were the birds and squirrels. He'd been preparing for this day for a long time, a contingency to his contingency plan, though honestly he had hoped not to be forced into implementing it. Few would believe it, but he actually liked Maggie Mason. He respected her courage and the lengths she would go to, to protect her family.

Something he couldn't say for his own.

As long as she stayed away from North Bay, everything had been fine. He'd monitored every email she'd saved as a draft, every one she'd sent, and listened to every phone conversation she had. Her switching phones hadn't created even a minor blip. As soon as she reported in, he had her. He'd gotten to know her very well in the past three-plus years. The constant exposure to what she said and wrote made it easy to determine the way she thought, her strengths and weaknesses, and likes and dislikes. Without giving him that advantage, she might have caught him. She was sharp, quick and blunt and honest. Rare traits in women—at least, in the women in his life. He loved testing her, pushing her to the limits to see how she'd react. Impressive. Very impressive. But then she'd ruined it all. She'd come back home and that…changed everything.

She had been so caught up in the cat-and-mouse game she hadn't realized there was more she knew that Crane didn't know. Information about his wife's activities at the time of her death that, in his hands, could be problematic.

Now she had shared it, and she and Crane were acting on that information together.

That, coupled with finding a printed email draft from Maggie to Crane at Crane's house, had forced his hand. She was even better than he'd thought. Setting up a fake email account. Never transmitting messages through it. Just the two of them signing in to it under the same ID and password, reading drafts. He hadn't expected her to adopt terrorist tactics, and he should have anticipated the possibility. That he hadn't even considered it annoyed him. She was the mouse, not the cat. The hunted, not the hunter. But apparently she hadn't gotten the memo on that. She pursued as often as she was pursued, and she'd gotten far too close.

Dangerously close.

Then she'd come home. Anger churned in his stomach. At the airport in Nashville, he'd modified his plan. David Pace had to go. His records and Beth's had to be destroyed. Ian Crane definitely had to go. And, of course, now Maggie had to go, too.

He doubted that news would surprise her. She'd documented in one of her FBI reports the aversion to loose ends, and from the body of knowledge she'd generated on her adversary, she had to know that the time for game playing was done. Even if she hadn't drawn that conclusion on her own, she had been given fair warning. The roses said it all.

Black Beauty roses. Rare and, like him, not found in nature but created by man. They symbolized death, impending doom and a perilous journey, which, of course, was why they had been chosen. She knew that—she'd looked it up. Just as she knew that they also symbolized distaste or disdain between rivals, which is why they'd been chosen specifically for her. Most of the killings weren't acrimonious. Her adversary simply liked to kill. But there were exceptions, and those exceptions were always warned. Like his second victim.

Authorities thought only his second victim and Maggie had gotten the single roses. But Maggie actually was the fourth, and she'd been gifted with several. Yes, indeed. She'd been entertaining, very resourceful, particularly for a woman he'd once severely injured and kept under duress. Yet the season for play, like all seasons, had to end so a new season could begin.

The killing season.

Still, he would miss her—and that likely would surprise her.

He watched her walk the old man into the house through the back door.

Five days. Start your Christmas countdown now, Maggie. Don't delay.

In five days, you'll be dead.

Chapter Six

After dinner, Warny went upstairs to Paul's room and within minutes was sawing logs. Jake hadn't awakened long enough to eat, only to get a dog treat left for him on the floor near his bed, and he crashed again before he got half of it down. He was snoring, too, though not nearly as loud as Warny.

Ian and Maggie cleaned up the kitchen. She worked quickly, efficiently, and mindful of Dayton's warning, Ian watched her for signs of PTSD but saw none. She seemed calm and, for all purposes, normal—far more normal than he. Every nerve in his body was raw and snapping. He was edgy and on full alert. The last time he'd felt like this he'd been in the zone in Afghanistan. But Maggie acted as if it were a normal day. She'd eaten well, talked with Paul and Della and then with Madison, and she'd even joked with them. How she did it, knowing Crawford was in North Bay or close by, Ian had no idea.

Now she had the tabletop covered with ingredients—powdered sugar, eggs, boxes of graham crackers and bags of gumdrops, candy canes and peppermint rounds. "What are you doing?"

"Making a gingerbread house." She wrapped a tray in shiny foil and smoothed it down, crimping the edges around the tray. "I usually make the gingerbread, but it's been a rough day. Graham crackers will have to do this year." She stuffed icing in a Ziploc bag with a plastic tip punching through its bottom corner, and then beaded a line of it to glue together two crackers. "When I was little, Paul and I used graham crackers for the walls and roof all the time." A hint of a smile curved her lips. "I wasn't yet allowed to use the stove." She glanced up at him. "Can you hold that wall up so I can put the roof on?"

Ian stretched over and held the wall crackers vertical. "Maggie, are you in denial?"

"About what?"

"Crawford."

She paused, and then started buttering icing onto the next cracker, shingling the roof. "He's impossible to deny, don't you think?"

"I do, which is why I'm wondering how you're managing to act so normal, when today has been anything but. First the connection with Beth and David Pace, then Brett Lund killing himself, and then Crawford or Blue Shoes—*somebody*—taking a shot at us. We could have been killed today but—"

"We weren't."

"But we could have been."

"Ah, I see." She bit into her lower lip, focusing on attaching the first of the roof crackers. "Dayton was wrong. I don't have PTSD, Ian. After Utah, I had to get a psych evaluation before I returned to active duty."

She pressed the cracker down, reached into the package for another and then buttered it. "I guess it does seem odd to you that I can feel normal or do normal things, but it's not odd to me." She paused, the knife midair, and looked at him. "When you live like I've been living, you take the good whenever you can find it, and when a crisis is over, you let go of it. You assess and see where you were weak, seek ways to strengthen, and then put it on the back burner where it belongs."

"So fast?" She made sense, but he had doubts. "How do you process so much in such a condensed period of time? You're moving at warp speed."

"I have no choice. It's cope and deal with it…at warp speed…or get run over."

"Run over?"

"It's harder to hit a moving target, Ian. If you don't move on quickly, you won't be prepared when the next crisis hits. You'll still be looking back instead of ahead." She adjusted another roof shingle. "Don't military doctors take tactical training?"

"Yes, but even in it, processing took days, sometimes weeks."

"Do that with Crawford, and you'll only need to do it once. While you're processing, he'll be killing you."

Her time alone had been horrific. He'd known it, and she'd been open in discussing some of her trials and challenges, but he hadn't grasped her situation having impacts like this. "Do you think Crawford will come here again?"

"I think he'll strike again. But whether or not it'll be here, I don't know. No history on that. Typically, I'd be running again now." She reached for another cracker. Seamed it into place. "I haven't had such a close encounter and stayed put." She opened a new package of crackers. The cellophane crackled. "I shouldn't stay put now."

His chest went tight, his stomach knotted. "Don't you dare run on me, Maggie."

"I'm not." She slid a long cracker out of the torn package. "I considered it, but without a guarantee he'd leave Uncle Warny and you alone, I can't." She put the last cracker on the roof. "That die was cast when I came home." She blinked then stood to put the "snow" on the roof. "I regret it now, but done is done, and—"

"Things are what they are." She wouldn't run. Should he be happy or more worried? Unsure, he watched her work.

"Why don't you check the security monitors then prepare to gumdrop?" She shot him a warning look. "I put the candy canes around the door."

He smiled. He couldn't help it. "How about you put one on the left, and I'll do the one on the right?"

She twisted her mouth, tilted her head. "I guess we could negotiate. But it's going to cost you. I've always done the candy canes."

"Oh-oh. Negotiate. I've seen you do that. It's not pretty." He rubbed his jaw. "What are the damages apt to run? I have a feeling I'm going to get soaked or hosed or worse."

"Oh, you are." She grinned. "We'll start with you telling me about your Christmases when you were young and see if that's worth amending the tradition."

Pleasantly surprised, he grunted. "I can handle that." He went to check the monitors. In a ten-by-ten room just off the kitchen near the back door, they covered an entire wall. He studied each of them, saw one oddity but nothing out of the ordinary, and then returned to the kitchen.

"Everything looks okay," he told her. "But I'm curious about that clearing on the far side of the pasture—the one on the hill near the creek."

"Because it's clear and the rest we keep natural?"

He nodded.

"I cleared it." A wistful look crossed her face. "I was getting ready to build a home there when all this started with Crawford."

"I'm sorry," Ian said and meant it. Maggie loved this land, and he doubted she could be content anywhere else. So she'd dreamed of building her own home here, and Crawford had stolen that from her along with everything else.

She had a pile of red gumdrops set apart from the others, and snagged one and put it in her mouth. Scooping a handful of green, yellow and orange ones, she dotted the roof. "You do the back side and tell me about your Christmases."

"They were good. Loud." He popped a green gumdrop into his mouth. "All my mom's family lived close, and everyone congregated at her mother's house. Between the kids, spouses and their kids, there must have been thirty of us, plus whatever strays Gramps brought home. He couldn't stand the thought of anyone being alone on Christmas."

"Compassionate man. As we both know, being alone on Christmas is horrible." She paused decorating the house. "You still miss him."

"I do." He'd passed away the year before Beth. "We did everything together—except play golf."

"He didn't like golf?"

"He loved it." Ian grinned. "We went to his club and played once. I was nine. The manager said he'd give Gramps a year's worth of green fees if he wouldn't bring me back."

"What did you do?" Maggie tried not to smile. "That's awful."

"It was terrific. I hated golf. Pretty much messed up their greens." His face burned. "Gramps took offense, but before he could refuse the manager's offer, I negotiated a better deal."

"He was going to leave the club." She laughed. "You fixed it where he had to stay."

"Free green fees for two years." Ian chuckled. "I got bad marks from Gramps on golf, but great ones on negotiating."

"Ian." She shook her head. "How'd you get the manager from one year to two?"

"I said I planned to get good at golf even if I had to play every day."

She laughed harder.

So did Ian.

She stopped and squeezed his hand. "I'll bet you were Gramps's favorite."

"I think at times we all were. He made time for each of us, so we had his full attention. We all felt special." Ian clasped her arm, resting on his shoulder, looked up into her smiling face and sobered. "Maggie, you've done the impossible."

"What?"

"News today about Beth, all this with Crawford and Blue Shoes, and yet you've managed to make me laugh."

"I like it." She smoothed his sleeve and backed away.

"Me, too." He stilled, leaned against the table. Guilt settled in on him. Beth was dead. Dead, and he sat here laughing. "Does that make me an awful person?"

"No, Ian. It doesn't." Maggie unwrapped a candy cane. "Do you know the story of the candy cane?"

"They used to use ribbon to decorate barbershop poles to mimic candy canes?" He shrugged. "That's the only story about them I've ever heard."

"Oh, Ian." She made a *tsk-tsk* clicking sound with her tongue against the roof of her mouth. "You slept through Sunday school."

"We never talked about candy canes in Sunday school."

"Well, isn't that a shame?" She tilted her head. "It's a very cool story."

"So are you going to tell it to me, or do I have to run a web search?"

"I'll tell you." She unwrapped a candy cane and frosted its back side as she talked. "A candy maker created a hard white candy and shaped it like a J for Jesus. Some say it's used to shepherd the lost and, when they go astray, He hooks them and brings them back into the fold, so they call it a Shepherd's hook." She pressed the candy cane into place, framing the left side of the doorway on the gingerbread house. "Its being white is a symbol for Mary and the virgin birth of Christ— pure and sinless—and the three red stripes represent two things. These two thin ones represent Christ being scourged, and the thick one is to remind us that Christ bled on the cross to give us eternal life." She studied the candy. "Some put green in them and don't stick to the traditional three red stripes, but I don't buy those. The stripes have important meanings, so I always look for those that follow the tradition." She passed him the second candy cane.

Knowing now how important placing the candy canes were to her, Ian paused then drew back his hand. "No, you go ahead."

She smiled, lifted his hand and placed the candy cane gently in his palm. "Frame the doorway, Ian. If you frame it, you know it's there, and then you can walk through."

His mouth went dry. This symbolized far more than the doorway to a gingerbread house. It symbolized acknowledging God's place in his life. He believed; he'd always believed. But from the time of Beth's death until now, he'd been angry with God, blamed Him for allowing her death. Yet in the simple story of a candy cane, he recalled how much Christ suffered, and it made him feel petty and small. Remorseful and contrite, too. It reminded him how much he was loved and how great a sacrifice had been made for him. His heart beat fast and hard and his pulse throbbed in his ears. *I owe You an apology.* "Don't let me mess it up," he told Maggie.

"You won't," she promised. "You can't mess it up."

He seated the candy cane to the right of the door, positioned it just so, nudged it a tad, then sat back to take a look. "Is that right?"

At his side, she bent down and eyed it. "Perfect."

Maybe she was overly stressed anyway. "Maggie, it's not perfect. The whole gingerbread house is listing twenty degrees. The snow on the roof would be heavier on the north side than the south, you ate all the red gumdrops, and my candy cane is stuck on crooked."

She laughed and hugged him hard. "Not the gingerbread house, Ian. You." He smelled so good, like soap and fresh air, and the urge to kiss him hit her suddenly and hard. Before she could stop and talk herself out of it, she kissed him, stunning them both, and started to pull away.

Ian pulled her closer, cradled her against his chest and kissed her again.

A long moment later, he looked deeply into her eyes and whispered, "I'll never again look at a candy cane and not remember your story."

"I know." She stroked his face. "Gauging by your expression, I'd say you'll remember a lot more than that."

Too tender! He shielded himself from his response to her remark, and added, "I'll never again see a gingerbread house without remembering tonight, either." He studied her eyes, the gentleness in them. "I have a whole new appreciation for your traditions."

"So do I."

Her cell phone rang and she sobered, stepping over to the kitchen bar and answering with it on speakerphone. "Hello."

"You can run. You cannot hide."

Maggie shot a look at the clock on the stove. Straight-up midnight. "Coward." She punched the disconnect button.

Ian stood, joining her at the counter. "What was that about?"

Dread flooded her eyes. "It means, in this game of cat and mouse, I'm the mouse."

"It was Crawford." Ian frowned.

She shrugged. "We knew he was here."

"We suspected it. Him, Blue Shoes, one and the same or a copycat—we had a lot of possibilities. But now we know it's him." Ian reached for the phone. "I'll call Detective Cray."

"You can call him, but it's a waste of time. I've run locators on every phone call like that I've gotten. Some are near wherever I am. But many of the others, especially lately, have been from bizarre places—Iceland, Germany, Iraq. Places I know he can't be."

Ian stilled.

Maggie noticed. "What?"

"We have contact points in all those places."

She leaned a hip against the kitchen counter. "Contact points? What are you saying?"

This development wasn't what he'd hoped to find. It was his worst nightmare. "I'm saying, run the locator on this call."

"I guess you'll get around to telling me what's on your mind soon enough." She phoned the call in to the agency, made her request and then waited for a woman to process it.

Finally she came back on the line. "Fussa."

"Fussa? Where is that?" Maggie asked.

"In the Tama area."

Ian offered his answer. "Western Tokyo."

"Add it to the interim report, will you? I'll submit the final later. Thanks." Maggie hung up. "Tokyo. See what I mean? It's crazy. He can't drug my uncle and Jake and then a few hours later be on the ground in Tokyo. It's not physically possible."

"No, it's not." Ian pulled out his phone.

"What are you doing?"

"Following a hunch." Ian got online on his iPad and keyed in a search. In short order, he sucked in a sharp breath. "Yokota is there."

"What's a Yokota?"

"A military base." Ian let her see his worry. "All the other non-local-to-you places you've been called from—do you have a list?"

"Yeah."

"Get it," Ian said.

She parked a hand on her hip. "Are you going to tell me what you're on to here?"

"I think we're going to find all of the nonlocal locations of these calls are ones with US military installations."

"You are aware that I do profiling consults with the military."

"That's the only way you'd know about the Nest." He nodded. "But those consults explain you calling others. It doesn't explain Crawford calling you from those locations—"

"You think he's somehow routing the calls through the installations." She slapped her forehead. "I can't believe I didn't pick up on that before now."

"We don't know it yet."

"I know it. Crawford's not tracking me through the FBI—we thought there could be a leak there. He's tracking me through my military connections. But how?"

"Have you been keeping them *and* the agency informed of your whereabouts?"

She nodded. "Have to or I'd lose my security clearances, and without those I can't get anything done."

"Okay." Ian stood up, paced between the granite bar and the table, his reflection catching in the polished surface. "Then this development raises a question we need to answer. How is Crawford gaining access to military routers? Is he military? A civilian contractor? A consultant? Is he in the Intelligence realm? He can't just be hacking into their phone systems. There's got to be a legitimate connection or they'd have shut him down long ago. They haven't. And that raises another question."

"What other question?"

"Is Crawford really Crawford?" Ian looked her right in the eye. "Or is he Mr. Blue Shoes pretending to be Crawford?"

"Or Crawford pretending to be Mr. Blue Shoes."

Ian stilled, parked a hand at his hip. "Maybe they are one and the same."

The next morning, Maggie and Ian had breakfast with Uncle Warny and then he left the table. "I'm going to the barn to check on Thunder. If he's half as stiff as I am this morning, poor fella's gonna need extra walking time to loosen up."

When he'd gone, Maggie and Ian verified the listing of call locations. Not one location lacked a military facility, and while the agency couldn't trace the calls specifically to the facilities, common sense led her boss to the same conclusion it had them.

Maggie reported their findings to the task force handling the Crawford cases but withheld military notification. If General Talbot or Colonel Dayton were involved, the last thing they needed to know was that she and Ian had made the military connection.

Ian again checked the monitors and rejoined Maggie when she got off the phone. "Madison," Maggie told him, "thinks Crawford could be military. She doesn't think he and Blue Shoes are the same person because

Crawford has been too actively engaged in trying to kill me. They've been tied up with their duties here."

"Doesn't mean they aren't sending an emissary, who might or might not know who he or she is working for, Maggie." Ian poured himself a fresh cup of coffee.

"Maggie!" Uncle Warny came rushing in with Jake fast on his heels. "Somebody's been messing with your car."

She stood up. "What do you mean?"

"There's flowers on it. I'm supposing you didn't put 'em there." His face looked piqued. "I went out to walk Thunder and saw 'em stewed out all over the thing—roof, hood, everywhere."

"Black roses?" she asked, her heart racing.

"Yup." His chest heaved.

"You sit down and rest up, Uncle Warny." She reached for her handbag, retrieved her weapon. "Don't you go out there, Maggie girl. Wait for the police."

"I can't wait. He could be setting bombs. We have the horses, the barns, our vehicles. The longer we wait, the more danger we're in."

"She's right." Ian met her at the back door. "Keep it locked, Warny, and keep Jake with you."

The old man nodded. "Watch out for her, son."

It was cold out. Gray and dismal. Maggie's breath frosted the air. She lifted the front of her sweater to cover her mouth and muffle her exhaling from view. The huge fir stood strong and green in the middle of the yard. It'd always been her favorite tree. She'd had tea parties near its broad base, and played dolls there and played ball with Paul. Before she'd left here, they'd decorated it for Christmas every year. If there was time, it'd be a good project for her and Ian.

She scanned the pasture, then the woods and finally the bank of the creek. No reflections of anything shiny or any mirror, no sounds of any four-wheeler, or signs of movement beyond a few squirrels.

Ian joined her at the fir. "I don't see a thing out of place."

She looked across the expanse between them and the garage. The barn was beside it. The animals didn't sound disturbed. That helped settle her nerves.

Ian stepped out into the open, walked closer to her car.

"Stay away from it. Crawford loves to bomb cars."

"I know." He kept moving.

She caught up to him, checking her peripheral. The cold had her eyes watering, but still no odd sounds intruded. No strange movements caught her eye. The wind crept over them, as if it, too, remained guarded. The black roses lay on the hood, the top, the trunk. "He was here."

"He's gone now."

"Yes." She had to agree. She sensed nothing, and with her honed instincts and Ian's in agreement, she felt certain he was long gone. But that he had been on the ranch again and the security cameras hadn't picked him up had her insides quivering like gelatin. Jake hadn't barked. The horses hadn't whinnied. No alarm had triggered. That was just odd. Jake could still be off from the sedative, but the horses? Paul's stellar security system? The only explanation was that Crawford had come onto the land through the woods and creek rather than through the road or gate.

"What?"

She couldn't make herself look away. So many roses. "He's never done this before."

"Done what?" Ian still held his gun in his hand, but reached up and zipped his jacket.

"Put so many roses in one place. He usually just leaves one."

Ian stepped into her line of vision. "Do you think the number is significant?"

"It is to him." She finally broke her gaze and looked at Ian. "But how? I have no idea."

"What is his pattern?"

"One to his second victim. One to me twice in the past, then one in Illinois on the porch. One at the cemetery on the back of Beth's grave, one on that dud device he put on Jake and one in Uncle Warny's hand. That's a total of seven. All single roses." She mentally shifted through his file, his habits, taking another view on the obvious and the subtle. "This just doesn't fit, Ian."

"Wait." He inched a little closer to the car. "They're not all roses. They're petals."

Dread dragged at Maggie. "Count the stems." She couldn't see those on top of the car. Being taller, Ian could.

"Four stems." He backed away from the car, returned to Maggie. "Eleven roses."

"Definitely doesn't fit." She looked up at him. "Let's get out of the open. You can't trust that he isn't within shooting distance."

They returned the way they'd come, hugging the house to the fir by the creek, then back through the opening to the back door.

Inside, Ian holstered his gun at the small of his back then peeled off his jacket and hung it on an unused hook.

"Everything okay?" Warny yelled out.

"Except Crawford's been here," Maggie called back. "We saw no sign of him, though."

Maggie put her jacket on the hook beside Ian's. Their sleeves touched. She liked the way they looked side by side. She shouldn't. But she did. Just as she shouldn't like him putting himself in danger to look at the car with her. When you've seen the carnage Crawford's left in his wake, facing him without fear is impossible. Yet having Ian with her helped. At least, it did in one way. She wasn't facing the monster alone. In another way, it made it harder. She endangered Ian, and she shouldn't rely on him in ways that demanded he risk his life. He didn't owe her that kind of loyalty.

"Glad to hear that varmint ain't on the ranch." Warny shuffled toward the door.

"No." Maggie blocked his path. "You can't go out there right now."

"Why not? You said he ain't here."

"I said we didn't see him. He's a marksman. He could be a long way away and still shoot."

Ian interceded. "I've called Cray. He's sending a unit out to take the statement and Beecher is coming to run a bomb check."

Maggie frowned. "Poor guys are getting a workout with us, aren't they?"

"His team's clocking in hours on readiness training. Beecher's fine with it, Maggie. Cray's probably chugging antacid."

"Can't blame him for that." She washed her hands at the sink. Squirted soap and rubbed them hard, turned the tap so the water was as hot as she could stand it. Any time Crawford was involved or close she had that icky slimy feeling. It wasn't logical, of course, but it was relentless.

Ian grabbed an apple from the bowl of fruit on the counter. "You said that this doesn't fit Crawford's pattern. Why?"

"In the past, he's always only left one rose until after his victims were dead. Then he's had a dozen delivered to their graves. Until today, he's never left multiple roses, or given anyone living more than one."

"Maybe he don't see you as a victim, Maggie girl." Uncle Warny rubbed at his neck.

"If he didn't, he wouldn't have given me a rose at all." She tilted her head, snagged a bite of Ian's apple. "Crawford just doesn't breach patterns. He works in consistent numbers. Some would say he's crazy, but he's not. He just has a very different way of seeing and processing things. To him, his reasoning is clear and logical, and through four killings, he's remained consistent and methodical." She searched her mind. "He could be waiting to deliver the twelfth rose after he kills me. That would be in line with his patterns, but to leave multiple stems on the car…that doesn't fit."

"What does the twelfth rose mean—when he delivers 'em to the graveyard?"

"That he's done," Maggie said. "I'm almost positive now it means he's completed his mission and saved them."

"Saved 'em?" Uncle Warny's eyes stretched wide. "But his victims are dead and buried."

"I know." Maggie pursed her lips. "I'm not sure why—the specific reasoning varies case to case—but to him, he isn't killing these people just to kill them. In his twisted mind, he's protecting them from fates worse than death. Death is their escape. So to him, he's saving them."

"He's out of his mind."

"Yes, he is." Maggie rubbed her face. "It's kind of like a cracked mirror, Uncle Warny. You still see everything in it, but not in the same way you do when the mirror is intact."

Ian looked more disturbed. He finished the apple. Tossed the core. "So he deliberately breaks the pattern and he's not saving the last rose until he—I can't say kills you, Maggie. I just can't." Ian shuddered. "Then what else is he doing? What else could the twelfth rose mean?"

"Maybe it's a different signal or a sign of some other sort. That'd be consistent with him." Maggie looked from Jake, napping on his bed, back to Ian. "Maybe he's signaling there's something else to be found."

Warny grunted. "Or someone." He slid his gaze to Maggie.

"I'll check with the agency," Maggie went for her cell. "Make sure we don't have another victim."

Ian nodded toward the security room. "I'll check the surveillance tapes."

Thirty minutes before midnight, Maggie started tensing up. If Crawford had been signaling there was something else to find with the absence of the twelfth rose, he'd surely phone to jab at her for not finding it—whatever it happened to be.

It wasn't another victim. At least, not insofar as the agency could tell. No reports had come in, and considering the weather socking in nearly everyone in the entire country, that didn't surprise her.

"You're pretty deep in thought there."

Maggie sat in the living room, staring at the empty corner where the tree should be. She started at the sound of the man's voice, then recognized it as Ian's and smiled up at him. "Waiting for the other shoe to drop."

"The midnight call?" He sat down beside her.

She nodded. "The agency had nothing to report. Neither did my military liaison."

"I didn't see anything on the tapes, either." Ian lifted her hand, gave it a reassuring squeeze. "Maybe the missing rose wasn't a signal."

"Oh, it was, Ian." She looked over at him, his warm breath fanning her face. "I just don't yet know for what."

They ran through some possibilities and then some outside possibilities, but found nothing.

Ian frowned. "Why do you keep staring at that corner of the room?"

"The tree should be there. It's not." She gave him a bittersweet smile. "I guess I just wanted…"

"The kind of Christmas you've had at home in the past? Before Crawford?"

He always understood. She nodded. "There's no tree, no decorations inside or outside. Paul and I always strung lights on the bushes out front and framed the porch and wrapped lights around the columns. We did the back porch, too, and decorated the big fir tree in the yard. This year…nothing is decked out for Christmas."

"The table is," Ian said softly. "The gingerbread house is there."

"Yes, it is." She leaned her head against his shoulder. "I'm being silly."

He hooked her chin with his thumb, stroked it and looked deeply into her eyes. "No, Maggie. You're many things, but you're not silly."

He was going to kiss her. She saw it in his eyes, felt it in the slight tremble in his hand. Could he hear her heart racing? Could he see how much she wanted his kiss?

She tilted her face into his hand.

"Maggie?"

"Mmm?" Words were beyond her.

"I need to kiss you." His fingertips grew gentler still. "I know you don't want me to, and I shouldn't want to, but I do and… I'm going to kiss you, Maggie."

Before he could change his mind, she turned and their lips met, caressed. No gentle kiss, this. This kiss claimed and then consumed, spoke of longing and wanting and loving. Spoke of emotions felt to the core but unexpressed in years of notes and cards and calls that lasted hours and filled dark, empty nights. This kiss bombarded the senses, the emotions, and bonded souls, and when it ended, it left them breathless and staggering, wrapped in each other's arms and feeling that it was there they belonged.

He looked into her eyes. "I won't apologize."

"I'd be devastated if you did."

"I won't feel guilty, either." He stroked her hair back from her face.

"There's no need, Ian." She looked up at him, forced her voice steady. "We both loved Beth. She's gone now, but we're not. I can't believe she wouldn't want us to be…" A worry flitted through Maggie's mind and took root. "Is this about me, or because I was close to Beth?" She didn't want to think it could be about Beth, but until he'd kissed her, she'd seriously doubted Ian was ready to move on. In fact, she'd been certain he wouldn't be ready to move on until he solved Beth's murder. Was she setting herself up for heartbreak? Oh, after all they'd both been through, the last thing either of them needed was heartbreak. This could be about Beth. Because Maggie mourned her, too. Because they'd shared that grief and those bonds. Was it? How could she know for sure?

His expression clouded. "It's about us—you and me."

"Are you sure?" He sounded sure, but was he really?

He hesitated a second. Just long enough to raise doubt. "Yes, I'm sure."

He didn't sound sure. He wasn't. How could he be? She had doubts. Surely his were stronger. But he thought he was sure, which definitely made him not sure.

He let out a frustrated sigh. "I have real feelings for you and they're deep. I never thought I'd feel this way about a woman again."

Was it her, or the memories of Beth he relived through her? That had to be it. Had to be. Her heart squeezed, a hard ache filling it. "You don't want to hurt me, I know that. But we've always been honest with each other, so I have to ask. Are you being honest with yourself?"

"I care about you. A lot. You've no idea how much. That isn't new, but it's different, too, and feeling as if it's all right to express the difference…that's new."

"Since the cemetery?" Maggie was getting a grip on this. "Since we went to Beth's grave?"

He nodded. "And since you reminded me she didn't need me anymore."

"Ian, that doesn't mean you need me." A substitute? A lump rose in her throat. Constantly compared with the love of his life? No, she couldn't do that. With Crawford, she shouldn't do anything. And she shouldn't forget it.

"It's not like that." He frowned. "Look, I might not have it all figured out yet—what this is growing between us—but I know what it isn't, and it isn't that. I do need you, Maggie."

She shouldn't push. She really shouldn't push. "Because..."

"Because you make me feel again."

She brushed the backs of her fingers along his jaw. "What do I make you feel?"

No hint of a smile touched his lips or his eyes. Nothing but a serious, sober, almost regretful pleading he couldn't verbalize. "Everything."

This wasn't about Beth. The truth came as clearly as Christmas. "You make me feel, too. You shouldn't. Not because of Beth. I believe she'd want us happy and I think she'd be glad if we could be happy together." Beth would want them to be loved.

Ian had loved Maggie for a long time. It had been clear in everything he had said and done. She'd loved him, too. She thought about it, and she was right. But it was different now in a way that probably made them both kind of panic. There was a big difference in loving and being in love. Were they falling in love? Was that the difference? What was happening?

She didn't dare ask. With Crawford, she couldn't help but not be okay with falling in love.

Ian looked at her, silent, his thoughts clearly as turbulent as her own. She couldn't reassure him. She couldn't reassure herself, though she wondered, what if there were no Crawford? What if it were just Ian and her living a normal life? Would them falling in love be okay then?

She grimaced. What difference did that make? That wasn't their situation.

Refusing to answer her own question, not daring to answer her own question, Maggie sighed and stood up. "You know what I think?"

"What?"

"I think we should not worry about us and what's happening. We should just trust that it'll work out like it's supposed to and we should focus on something else."

"I don't have it in me to take leaps of faith anymore, Maggie."

She blinked hard, buying time to think. Ian had to work through his anger with God and put this faith crisis behind him, but that was a journey and conflict between him and God. Only they could repair the broken trust. *Please, let it be sooner rather than later.* "I want to put up the tree and decorate the house, Ian. I want a merry Christmas."

Ian stood up. "Then let's go get a Christmas tree."

Maggie brightened. "Really?" When he nodded, she squealed and hugged him. "And shopping. I need to buy gifts and—"

"Hold on." He laughed. "We have four days."

"Three shopping days." She wrinkled her nose. "But we can start now. We'll pull the stuff out of the attic and—"

The phone rang.

Maggie checked the mantel clock. "Midnight."

"Don't answer it."

"I have to. He'll do something horrible." She retrieved her phone from the kitchen and answered. "Hello."

"Did you find the twelfth rose?"

Crawford. "Was I supposed to?" Her hand shook. She broke into a sweat.

"Not yet."

"Then I guess today was a draw."

"Hardly." He snorted. "Maggie, Maggie, Maggie. You're so predictable. Cute all bundled up in your white coat and boots, but predictable."

Panic shot through her body. She had been wearing a white coat and boots today. He'd seen her. "How does it feel to have to watch from a distance all the time, too scared to show your face?"

"Scared?" He laughed, cackled. "Trust me, Maggie. My face is the last thing you want to see."

"Quite the contrary. I'd love to see it."

"Sure you would. Through the site on your gun, maybe."

She stiffened. "That would work."

"Who knows? The opportunity might arise. For now, I have a message for you."

"A message?" She looked at Ian, confused. Crawford had never talked to her like this.

"You can run. You cannot hide."

The line went dead.

She hung up the phone, looked into Ian's expectant face. "He saw us at the cemetery or here—maybe both. He mentioned my white coat and boots."

"So he called to let you know it was him at the cemetery?"

"No, he had a message for me."

"What was it?"

"I'm the mouse." Her resentment of that showed in the way she punched the face of her phone, dialing. "Reporting it to the agency."

"You can bet he was local. The call might not be but the man was."

"Definitely." She reported the exchange, then waited for the locator to track the call.

"Sparrow?" the unidentified woman said. "He isn't local."

Maggie glanced ceilingward, resentful and confused. "Where is he?"

"NORAD."

"The NORAD that's tracking Santa?"

"One and the same."

"Where is it?"

"Colorado Springs."

"Thanks." Maggie disconnected, saw that Ian already sat at the kitchen table keying in a search on the laptop. "Petersen Air Force Base."

Maggie thought a long moment. "Maybe Talbot or Dayton is pretending to be Crawford. It'd be really convenient to do whatever and blame him for it."

"That could explain why he's breaking patterns." Ian looked over at her. "It's not really Crawford."

Logical conclusion, but her experience did have its perks, and her certainty was one of them. "That explains nothing. Crawford could be routing the calls pretending to be Talbot or Dayton. He's incredibly resourceful—and even more clever. He'd see humor and irony in framing one of them for his crimes." She let out a heartfelt sigh. "It's Crawford, Ian."

"He could be setting them up. But with the deviations from his patterns, we don't know that."

"I do." How she knew, she couldn't honestly say. But she felt it down to the marrow of her bones. "I've had years of this kind of parsing with him. Ordinarily, I'd say the only person on the planet who knows him better is his mother, but she was his first known victim. Seven years ago, two days before Christmas, he beat her to death and tied twenty pound lead weights to her feet."

"Lead weights?"

Maggie nodded. "He does that to all of them so they 'stay put.'"

"Why did he kill her?"

"If I knew the answer to that, he'd be caught and in jail." Maggie rubbed at a little pounding in her temple. "From all I've pieced together, she wasn't around much. Single mother and, according to him, a very hardworking woman."

"You'd think he'd admire that."

Had he? Had he admired her so much he killed her to spare her from having to work so hard? She'd thought so at one time, yet that never felt quite right. What was wrong in it niggled at the fringes of her mind, but it still hadn't come into focus. "It's hard to tell. He's caustic and takes sarcasm to new levels. He could love or hate her for it. I'm not sure." She rubbed her temple harder. "That's the thing with Crawford. He always double-talks and he does so in such a way that it rings true, but then he takes the opposite position and what he says still rings true."

"Is he sarcastic when he's lying or when he's being honest?"

"Random." She thought a second more. "That's deliberate, of course. Clever confusion."

"I hate it that you've been going through this for so long on your own. We've talked about it, but it's different, being with you and seeing it happen and the impact firsthand."

"It is, and it's totally selfish of me to be glad you're with me—it's definitely not in your best interest—but, forgive me, Ian. I am glad. This has been...incredibly hard."

"You're the understatement queen." Ian curled his arms around her. "What can I do?"

Inside, she shook. "You can hold me." She let him see her vulnerability. The constant fear she carried with her every minute of every day that she tried to hide from everyone else, including most often from herself. "Just hold me."

"Oh, Maggie." He opened his arms. "Come here."

She walked into them, felt them close around her. The comforting feel of his heart beating against her face. A shuddery breath escaped her. "This is better."

"Better than what?" He held her tighter, buried his face in the side of her neck.

"Being alone after he calls." She slipped her arms around Ian's waist and moved closer still. "I hate being alone after he calls."

Ian pressed a kiss to her crown and then whispered, "You're not alone anymore, Maggie. Those days are over."

They were over. But were they over for a lifetime? Or just for now?

That she couldn't answer.

Yet she had experience at living in the moment. She'd done nothing but live moment to moment for over three long years. She didn't need to know about tomorrow to appreciate his gift today. And because of her experience, she recognized that gift for the rare treasure it was, and so rather than feeling doubtful or pensive, she let the wave she did feel wash over her.

The wave of gratitude.

Chapter Seven

Christmas music floated up the stairs.

Startled by it, Maggie sat up in bed and heard Uncle Warny singing "The First Noel." Ian chimed in. He had a good voice. Smiling, she got up, showered quickly and dressed in jeans and a teal sweater, then rushed downstairs to the lyrics of "Jingle Bells."

At the foot of the stairs, she saw them setting the tree up in the empty space near the piano. The scent of evergreen wafted to her. She inhaled deeply, relishing it.

"Ah, Maggie girl. Morning." Uncle Warny motioned. "Come look and see if you think this scraggly bush will do for a proper Christmas tree."

She left the steps and joined them, already smiling, then examined the tree. It was perfect. Six beautiful feet of fat branches and long needles just waiting for lights and bulbs and traditional decorations.

"Well?"

"It obviously didn't come from the attic." She looked at an array of red and green plastic boxes littering the floor that held all the decorations. "Where'd it come from?"

"I picked it up this morning," Ian said. "I thought a fresh tree would help you get your merry Christmas."

Touched by that thoughtfulness, it wasn't lost on her that Ian needed a merry Christmas, too, and he certainly hadn't had one since Beth's death. They were both overdue. "Well, it's gorgeous. Naked, but gorgeous." She smiled. "I think it'll be a fabulous tree."

"I'll get some coffee for you, Maggie girl. You fight with those tangled up lights and get them on the tree."

She frowned. "You know I hate doing the lights." She sent Ian a hopeful look.

"Sorry." He shrugged, the front of his shirt dusted with flour and splatters of…something gooey. "I'm on baking duty. Snickerdoodles."

Snickerdoodles? "You're joking me."

"No, unfortunately, I'm not."

"But—" Ian didn't cook much. He never had.

"Warny shoved your grandmother's cookbook at me and said they were your favorite. If I could learn to practice medicine, I could bake a cookie. I figured he had a point, so I'm giving it a shot—and making no promises whatsoever they'll be edible."

The stove timer went off.

"That's my cue." Ian rushed from the living room to the kitchen.

Maggie followed him. "The lights can wait a minute. I need food and coffee." Looking at the total disaster in the kitchen—was every single dish used to make a batch of cookies?—she needed lots and lots of coffee.

Uncle Warny shoved a filled cup in her hands. "We had cereal this morning so we could get moving. That okay, or you need something hot?"

"Cereal's great." She took the box and then filled

a bowl with something that resembled tree bark and nuts and splashed on milk. Jake was fairly dancing. "What's he so excited about?" Paul always saved Jake a bite. But dancing for tree bark? Not happening. A bone? By all means.

Uncle Warny passed her a spoon. "We've been eating the broken cookies. Getting rid of the evidence." He nodded at the breakfast bar, and lowered his voice. "Ian needed a little practice run at getting 'em off the cookie sheet and on the paper."

She glanced over. The bar was covered in wax paper with curling edges and tons of snickerdoodle cookies lined up like little soldiers. But there were a lot of gaps in that formation. "Uh-huh." Ian was a surgeon. No way would he mess up that many times learning to use an egg flipper. She sent her uncle a knowing look. "How many have you broken so you could munch more?"

"Maybe a dozen," Uncle Warny confessed, his cheeks turning ruddy. "But that's for me and Jake together." He waved a finger between his chest and the dog.

"Of course." She ate a bite of cereal, which not only looked but also tasted like tree bark, and watched Ian lift the cookies from the cookie sheet to the wax paper. No problem whatsoever. "He's a pretty quick study."

"He's eager to please you." Uncle Warny's voice warmed and his eyes glossed. "He's a good man, Maggie girl."

"Yes, he is." She took another bite of her cereal, swallowed and bit her lip to hold off a smile. Never before had Uncle Warny given any man his stamp of approval. Not James Parker in tenth grade, not Donald Greer in college. He'd gotten a snort, which proved to be about what he should have gotten. But Ian and his devotion, his eagerness to please, had gotten approval. That warmed her heart.

The Christmas music stopped. Maggie stilled, instinctively reaching for her gun.

"It's okay." Ian stayed her hand. "Warny, you want to handle the CD?"

"CD?" He grunted and hauled himself to his feet. "My boy, these ain't no newfangled CDs. They're honest-to-goodness albums. Been around here for years and years." He lumbered toward the living room and yelled back, "Jake, don't you snitch that cookie."

Maggie whipped around and saw Jake snitch a cookie from the edge of the bar. "Oh, you are so busted."

Ian laughed. "Warny put it on the edge so Jake could get it."

Maggie wrinkled her nose, the tension draining from her body, and whispered, loving the twinkle in Ian's eyes, "I know."

They spent the rest of the morning baking cookies, decorating the tree, stringing lights along the front porch and draping the netted ones on the bushes, and wrapping the front porch columns. Swags of fresh-scented pine hung in low-slung ropes along the mantel with huge red bows on each end and dead center. The Nativity set was in its place atop the piano, and the photos had been bunched closer together to make plenty of room.

"Where's baby Jesus?" Ian asked, studying the aged set.

"He doesn't get into the manger until Christmas Eve, when he's born."

"My grandfather used to do that." Ian smiled.

Maggie's heart skipped a full beat. "I'm so glad you're enjoying remembering your traditions, too."

"I am, Maggie." He looked away, studied the tree. "I missed them. Who wouldn't? But it just didn't seem right to celebrate—until this year."

Her breath hung in her throat. "Everything's different now, isn't it?"

"It is." He didn't seem troubled by that. "Can we put a twig of mistletoe right here?" He pointed to the light fixture in the ceiling just inside the entryway at the front door. "We always did that at home."

"Absolutely." She dragged the stepladder over and hung it. "Look okay?"

Ian held the ladder steady. "Looks great."

"Ian Crane, you didn't even look at it." She rocked the ladder and grabbed his shoulder to steady herself.

He cranked back his head. "I see you standing under it, which means you owe me a kiss, Maggie Mason."

She laughed. "Indeed I do." Bending, she claimed his lips.

Uncle Warny grunted. "Jake, my boy, I think we might just see mistletoe hanging all over the place this year." He let out a soft chuckle.

"Woof!"

"All right then." Warny lumbered back into the kitchen. "You flea-bitten hound. I told you not to snitch that cookie." His voice dropped. "Here you go, boy. Now this is absolutely the last one…"

"Got your weapon ready?"

Maggie nodded at Ian. Crawford had likely long since been gone, but one didn't assume anything about him twice. They stepped out the back door. "We still have to decorate the fir." Maggie glanced at the tree in question on the way to Ian's SUV.

"It's special to you?" Ian walked beside her.

She nodded. "And to Paul. Our mother had a perfect tree. Every ornament and bow and bit of garland had to be hung just so. No self-respecting icicle dared to crimp out of place on her tree."

"Let me guess." He lifted a fingertip. "You and Paul weren't allowed to touch it."

"Touch it? She barely allowed us to breathe in the same room with it." Maggie grunted, cautiously scanning the woods, down toward the creek. "Uncle Warny brought Paul and me three big boxes of decorations and told us to decorate the fir. It could be our tree." She smiled at the fond memory. "So we decorated the fir our way."

"Your uncle is a special man."

"He knows what matters." She smiled. "Paul called while you were on the phone with Madison. The weather's finally broken. They can't get out yet, but with luck, they'll make it home by Christmas."

"That's great news." Ian brightened. "It can't be your best Christmas unless Paul's here."

Ian cared and he was trying so hard to make the holiday special for her. It wouldn't be the best Christmas without Paul, but it would be good. She wanted it to be special for Ian, too. "After the last few years we've both had, being here, together…it's going to be a great Christmas."

"It is, isn't it?" He looked away, and then said, "Maggie, would it be okay if we brought Beth some flowers after our shopping today? I mean, would that bother you?"

"Of course not." She automatically checked the vehicle for explosives with Ian.

"Clear."

"Clear." She climbed into the SUV.

"You're sure. I don't want you to feel—"

"I loved her, too, Ian. I'm sure."

He nodded, opened the driver's door. "She loved poinsettias."

"White ones, not red." Maggie recalled. "We'll shop and pick up one, then run it out to her. And afterward, I think we deserve a special treat." The decorations looked beautiful, the ranch smelled of cookies and home. Perfect…except for Crawford's interference.

Ian slid in beside her. "What kind of special treat?" He cranked the engine. It roared to life. "Wait. Let me guess. Whatever it is, it's at Miss Addie's Café, right?"

She nodded enthusiastically. "It's Friday. During the season, she has Christmas cakes every Friday."

"I hope one is carrot cake. I haven't had a good carrot cake in…a long time."

"Ooh, me, either." Maggie clasped his hand. "Beth made the best I've ever eaten. But don't tell Miss Addie. Her icing is really good—and she does bake them—but Beth's had something that isn't in Miss Addie's. I have no idea what it was, but it was delicious."

"It was her secret ingredient. Anytime anyone asked, she'd say, 'That's the love.'"

Maggie smiled. "It probably was."

"Definitely," Ian said, "and a dash of vanilla nut. But don't tell."

"Your secret is safe with me." She crossed her heart. "I'm surprised Beth told you."

"She didn't." He gave her a wonderful mischievous look. "I peeked."

Maggie laughed, lush and deep. "Shame on you."

"I'm awful, but I never told another soul."

"Ian Crane, you just told me."

"That's different."

"Why?"

"Because you're the other half..." He faltered. "It just is," he said, then quickly changed the subject. "You having carrot cake at Miss Addie's, too?"

She didn't dare make too much of it. His other half, he'd started to say, but he hadn't. He'd stopped himself, and she couldn't afford to forget that. Still, her heart could long to hear the rest of it. It could...even if it shouldn't. Even if longing for his love was absolutely the last thing she should do. Her head understood the logic in that perfectly. Her heart didn't. Either by choice or stubbornness, it felt what it felt, and while she wouldn't let herself think the word, apparently her heart had no reservation in feeling it. That had to be squelched...she supposed. Didn't it?

"Carrot cake?"

"Sorry, I drifted."

"I'll say. So...?"

"Nope, no carrot cake this time." Maggie rubbed her tummy. "Red velvet." She feigned a swoon. "Miss Addie's red velvet cake is simply the best anywhere in the country."

"Mmm, with an endorsement like that, it's going to be hard to resist."

"It's a tough call. Oh, but her key lime pie. Mmm, I love her key lime pie."

"Stop. You keep this up, and on the way back we'll have to stop at the weigh station like the trucks."

"It's hard, Ian." She fished in her purse for her sunglasses. The day had turned even drearier, but the glare was as bad as the sun. "I've missed…everything." She seated the glasses at the bridge of her nose. "I'm home and… I'm home."

He lifted their clasped hands to his lips and pecked a gentle kiss to her wrist. "So we're shopping, doing flowers and having cake—and maybe just a sliver of key lime pie." Ian grunted. "It's beginning to feel a lot like Christmas."

"It is." Maggie's throat went thick. "Thank you for that, Ian."

"Thank you for that, Maggie."

He squeezed her hand and drove to North Bay.

"Miss Addie!"

Ian hung back and watched Maggie wrap the frail Miss Addie in a bear hug. Gracie, her seven-year-old granddaughter, stood beside him, absorbed in the exchange.

The two women both talked at once, and every head in the place turned to see what had them in a ruckus.

Then Gracie saw her face. "Maggie!" She flew into her arms, jumped and wrapped her legs around Maggie's hips.

Maggie caught her, squealed and spun in a circle. "Oh, Gracie! You're so big." She squeezed her, and then eased her head back. "Let me see you."

Gracie lifted her precocious chin. "It's the same. Hardly changed at all."

"Oh, but it has, Gracie." Maggie studied her carefully. "Your cheekbones are higher and your skin—you've been eating your growing food. You're so beautiful."

"I'm not. I don't have all my teeth." She spread her lips, revealing a gap where a front tooth had been.

"The new one's on the way. Another month and you'll be stunning." Maggie's eyes softened. "You look so much like your mother."

"She ain't dead, Maggie."

Maggie knew she wasn't dead, but she didn't know what Miss Addie had elected to tell her granddaughter about her mother. Maggie had found her six months ago in Atlanta, living between a shelter and the streets, strung out on drugs. She'd tried to get her into rehab, but the woman wanted no part of it. Knowing it wouldn't work without her cooperation, she'd called Miss Addie and given her the report on her daughter. Maggie cast a glance at Miss Addie. "That's good news, I'm sure."

"It's great news," Gracie confided. "Gran doesn't cry as much anymore. But we still pray for her every day."

"That's wonderful." Still, Miss Addie didn't send the first signal. Maggie wasn't sure what to say or do.

Ian appreciated her caution. He'd not been a parent but if he had, he'd like that kind of care exercised with his kids.

Maggie stroked Gracie's hair. "We don't have to talk about it if you'd rather not."

"I ain't talking about her at all except to tell you she ain't dead. Gran says that's the Christian thing to do, in case you're praying for the wrong thing."

"Ah, well, your Gran is very smart about these things, so we'll just listen to her on it."

Gracie twisted her mouth to say something, decided against it and nodded.

"So sit down, sit down." Miss Addie fluttered, her apron splattered with tiny wet spots. She'd clearly been in the kitchen all day.

Maggie put Gracie down and took a seat at the table. Ian sat across from her.

Miss Addie clasped his shoulder. "You're looking good, Ian. I'm glad to see it."

"Thank you." He smiled. She'd been nagging him for months to quit scowling and find something in his life to be joyful about. He hadn't done it. He'd tried but couldn't find his way until he'd watched Maggie. Then he realized that hiding behind the past and the hurt was being a coward, and Beth would hate that. So did he. That's a lot of what had his feelings so jumbled up about Maggie. It felt like love, but it could be the absence of nothing. When you're feeling nothing, and all of a sudden you're laughing and excited and even needing the company of a beautiful woman, and you're noticing so many wonderful things about her you hadn't noticed before…well, it confused him. He wasn't too proud to admit it. It felt like love. But was it?

Maggie was right. They did love each other. But it sure felt a lot like falling in love, too. Standing, holding that ladder, looking up at her hanging that mistletoe…

Heaven help him.

"Ian." Maggie leaned over and touched his hand. "The menu. Miss Addie's asking what we want."

He smiled. "Sorry, Miss Addie. We've been on a marathon shopping run. I'm dragging."

"From shopping?" Gracie looked stunned.

"Well, I baked cookies, then we decorated the tree and the house and everything else—"

"Except the fir," Maggie interjected.

"Except the fir," he conceded. "Then we went shopping."

"Oh, my." Miss Addie touched a hand to her face. "You're with one of the two shopping queens. Back in the day, when Maggie Mason and Madison McKay went shopping, every storekeeper in North Bay celebrated. Nobody can outlast those two shopping."

Didn't surprise Ian. "And I'm out of practice."

"So let's get you some hot coffee to warm your bones and…what kind of food?"

"Dessert." He lifted the menu.

"We're torn," Maggie said. "I've missed everything. Ian wants carrot cake, I want red velvet, but I really want key lime pie, too."

"Oh, hon. Wait. You remember the year you turned thirteen and I made you a queen cake?"

"What's a queen cake?" Gracie asked her gran.

Miss Addie's eyes twinkled. "When you turn twelve, I'll tell you. But—" she looked at Maggie "—it just so happens Adeline Cray was in with her Rebecca, and she turned thirteen today, so I baked one."

"Oh, I love it." Maggie bounced in her chair. "Now I have to pick one!"

Miss Addie sniffed. "Long as you been gone from home, girl, no, by gum, you don't. You leave it to me." She winked and then disappeared into the kitchen.

Gracie waited until Miss Addie couldn't see her. "Maggie, my mom's on drugs. That's why she stays away. I hate drugs, and I'm mad at her for it."

"Mad at her?" Ian asked.

"She loves them more than us."

"She doesn't—" Maggie started.

"Gracie," Ian interrupted. "You know I'm a doctor, right?"

She nodded.

"Your mom loves you. She's what we call an addict."

"Ian, I don't know if Miss Addie would approve—"

He ignored Maggie. "Her body has gotten used to the drugs, and now if it doesn't get them, she gets really, really sick."

"I didn't know she got sick."

"If she doesn't get the drugs into her body, she does. We could help her with that, if she'd let us, but that's a hard thing to do when you're sick. It doesn't mean she doesn't love you, honey. It means she's fighting a war inside her body, and right now she's losing."

"But she won't always lose, right?"

"I hope not." He clasped her shoulder. "The truth is, sometimes people win and sometimes drugs do. We just have to hope this time your mom does."

"I'll pray."

"That would be…" He stopped, thought it through. "Prayer is the best hope there is for your mom, Gracie."

"Dr. Crane?"

"Yes, Gracie?"

"Will you pray for my mom, too?"

Ian could feel Maggie's eyes boring through him, but his answer would be the same either way. "I will, Gracie."

She smiled. "You, too, Maggie?"

"Every day, sweetheart."

"Maybe with us all praying it'll work. Gran does, too. That's four of us. God can probably hear four of us."

"Well," Maggie said, propping her chin on her hand, her elbow on the table, "my uncle Warny says God hears every single prayer a child says. They're special to Him, and He always, always hears them."

Gracie thought about that. "He would know 'cause he's old. Old people know lots of stuff."

"He's always known a lot of stuff." Maggie nodded.

Miss Addie came out carrying two mugs of steaming-hot coffee and a platter. "Gracie, get Maggie and Ian some water, hon."

"Yes, ma'am." She started to move. "Oh, wait. Maggie, tomorrow night you and Dr. Crane have to come to our Christmas program at church. I'm gonna be Mary."

"You are?" Maggie asked. She'd been an angel for three years and wanted to be Mary so badly she couldn't see straight. Another important development Maggie had missed with this last move. "What time?"

"Six o'clock. You'll come, won't you?"

"You bet we'll be there, won't we, Ian?" Maggie looked at him with such hope. "Gracie being Mary is a huge, huge deal. She's worked hard for this for a long time."

"That is a very big deal." He gave her a solemn nod. "We wouldn't miss it, Gracie."

Smiling ear to ear, she fairly floated to get their water.

"Wonderful." Miss Addie set a tray down in the center of the table. "Another problem solved." She dropped her voice. "She's pretty peeved at her mother."

"Mmm."

"It means a lot to her that you'll be going to see her be Mary, Maggie."

"Wouldn't miss it, Miss Addie," Maggie repeated. "I know how long she's wanted this."

"That she has." She clicked her tongue to the roof of her mouth. "I fixed you two a sampler. Three little pieces of everything." She backed up. "You can both try everything and then fight over who gets the third piece of whatever." She laughed.

Maggie squealed and hugged Miss Addie. "I just love you."

"We love you, too, dear heart." Miss Addie sniffed. "About time you got yourself home." She gave Maggie a hard pat, and then backed away. "Now, eat yourselves sick."

To laughter and lighthearted banter, they tried.

He sat alone at a table just inside the door, listening and watching the exchange. She looked straight at him.

Slightly, he dipped his chin.

She visibly relaxed, nodded back, and then returned her attention to the kid.

Maggie wasn't a mother, but she had listened to the child and given her all of her attention. So had Ian Crane. And he'd been honest but compassionate in talking to the kid about her mother's drug addiction.

They weren't too busy. Otherwise occupied. Or present but not really there.

His stomach churned. He had to stop. He couldn't see them this way. Their concern for the kid couldn't be real. What did they care about her or her mother?

And Maggie sitting there throwing around *I love you* to that twig of a woman, Addie, as if it meant nothing. Those words were sacred. How dare she toss them out as if they were cheap junk?

His ears perked. So they'd be at the Christmas program tomorrow night, would they? The wheels in his mind started turning, spinning fast, then suddenly stopped. Well, so would he.

And come Christmas, news of what happened would be on every channel nonstop all day.

Merry Christmas, Maggie Mason.

With this slight revision in his plan, it was critical he get back to the ranch before they did. He dropped a few bills on the table and then eased out the door.

Chapter Eight

Maggie walked into the packed church beside Ian, who remained patient while she greeted people she hadn't seen in ages. Still, she didn't want to push it. He hadn't been inside the church since Beth had died, and he likely wouldn't be in it tonight if Gracie hadn't pulled his heartstrings.

She'd worried about him maybe changing his mind until he'd declared that there wasn't time to decorate the fir and get into town in time for the program. Only a blind woman would have missed the hint that he hoped decorating the fir was more important to her and they could skip the Christmas program, but Gracie would be so disappointed. They had to go, Maggie had insisted. The last thing that child needed was another adult breaking promises to her.

That had gotten Ian into a navy suit that did amazing things to his eyes and had an equally amazing effect on Maggie's heart rate.

She was in real trouble on that front, and she knew it. When or how she wasn't sure, but Ian Crane had her full attention, and it didn't seem likely that all the rational reasons in the world for keeping her distance because of Crawford were going to do a thing to convince her heart to shield itself. *It is what it is, and things are what they are.*

Ian led her to seats near Miss Addie. "The decorations look really pretty, don't you think?" he said.

"Gorgeous." Maggie felt almost giddy. At home for Christmas, in her own church's gathering room, with her own friends and Ian. She looked at the Christmas tree, listened to the adult choir sing "Joy to the World" and then "It Came Upon a Midnight Clear." They continued singing songs while people filled the seats. Maggie looked at the children, the happy and expectant faces of both them and their parents, and saw a family with three children, one of whom was an infant. They looked adorable, all dressed in green. A little sigh escaped her. A family. Her heart hitched. One day... For now she didn't dare to dream. The agony of Crawford coming after her was horrific. But imagine if he were after her child. Her heart couldn't bear it. Yet tonight she wasn't running, or alone in a strange house indulging in her annual Ben & Jerry's ice cream and hot bubble bath pity party because she was isolated. Tonight she was home with people who knew and loved her, and they were celebrating Christmas. She and Ian, in church together, celebrating Christmas. Peace and contentment filled her. Sometimes life was just so good.

"Maggie! Maggie!" Gracie ran up to her, her head covered in a long white cotton scarf and her robe covering all but the tips of her toes. "You came!"

"Ian and I told you we would."

Gracie gave her a gap-toothed smile. "But you really did it."

Relief that she hadn't given in to temptation and stayed home to decorate the fir had her knees weak. "Of course." Gracie's arm was bent. She held something behind her back. "What are you hiding?" Something for her gran, probably.

She smiled and whipped out a black rose. "It's for you."

Maggie went on full alert. So did Ian.

"Where did you get that, Gracie?" Ian asked before Maggie could.

"The man gave it to me. He said to give it to you and to tell you that you look pretty in red."

Crawford was here! "What did he look like?"

Gracie described him. Shorter and heavier than Ian, brown hair, tanned, wearing a black suit and a red tie.

She looked at Ian. "I saw Detective Cray and his wife three rows up, center aisle from the door. Clear the church." Maggie touched Addie's shoulder, interrupting her conversation with Liz Palmer, sitting on her right. "We have to get everyone out of here. Quickly."

Addie's gaze collided with Maggie's and she nodded, answering the unspoken question. She gained her feet. "Liz, start evacuating—right now. Orderly, so we don't scare the kids."

"Gracie, go with your gran."

"But I have to get back—"

"Go with your gran right now."

She frowned but went, and Maggie headed for the front of the stage, grabbed the mike and forced a calm into her voice she didn't feel. "Attention. Attention, everyone."

The low rumble quieted and a hush fell over those gathered.

"A situation has arisen and we need to vacate the premises immediately. Please don't linger, just use the nearest exit to you and walk outside and wait across the street until the authorities—"

The pastor came running up to her. "Maggie, what are you doing?"

"—clear the premises and tell us we can return. Go now, please. Hurry, but be safe and orderly…just like in the fire drills at school."

"Maggie Mason, if this is a prank…"

She covered the mike with her hand and shot the pastor a hard look. "The serial killer who loves bombs and is trying to kill me is here. We have to vacate the building to make sure no one gets hurt."

His mouth dropped in a big O.

Ian and Detective Cray, several people she recognized as volunteers with the fire department, and General Talbot and Colonel Dayton ushered people out the doors.

Maggie started searching, automatically calling Ian on her cell. When he answered, she asked, "Did you call Beecher?"

"He's here. His equipment is not. The team is on the way with it."

"Get them across the street, Ian." She couldn't see him and could barely hear him over the din of raised voices and screaming kids. "Keep people out of their cars and away from the parking lot. It'd be just like Crawford—"

A huge explosion rocked the walls, set her ears to ringing.

"Maggie! Maggie!"

She dropped to a crouch, looked around. "It's not in here. I'm fine."

"The parking lot's on fire!" a man yelled.

A series of secondary explosions ripped through the air. Screams flooded the gathering room, carried inside from outside the church.

"He got the cars," she told Ian. "That's just one round. There's a second one somewhere—I'm betting in here." The gathering room had cleared. She started scanning, looking for a device.

"Get out of there, Maggie."

"He always works in twos. Always, Ian. There's a second bomb somewhere."

"You can't find it if you're dead. Evacuate now."

He was running, trying to get to her. Her heart sank. "Don't come in. Please don't. I love you, Ian. I can't live with knowing I'm the reason you're..."

"Leave it to Beecher to find. Do you hear me, Maggie?" Panicked. Terrified.

Nothing along the edge of the stage. Nothing in or under the piano. Nothing wired into the potted plants decorating the stage, or in the festive tree strung with popcorn and handmade ornaments. "It's here. I know it's here."

She dropped to the floor, lay flat on her stomach. "I have to go. I need the flashlight app on my phone." She hung up. Punched the screen to pull up the app and flooded the underside of the rows of chairs with light.

Nothing.

She stepped onto the stage. Examined the life-size crèche. Checked the statues of the animals. The manger. She reached for a handful of hay and saw the device. Called Ian. "I found it. It's in the manger." Bold red numerals flashed. "Beecher's got three minutes and twelve seconds."

"He's on the way."

"Anyone hurt?"

"No. No, but, Maggie, will you please get out of there?"

"When Beecher gets here. I have to make sure no one else comes in."

"But, Maggie—"

"He's here." She hung up. "Beecher, up here!"

He ran over to her, followed by the same two team members who had been at the ranch. One was Thompson. She didn't know the name of the other one.

Beecher scanned the device. "This one is hot. Go outside, Maggie."

"Can you disarm it?"

"Yes." He spared her a glance. "Go! You're slowing us down."

Maggie ran out of the building and into a plume of black smoke. Two cars in the parking lot had exploded. She found Ian. "You're sure no one was hurt?"

"I'm sure." He looked over at her. "What's going on inside?"

"Beecher said he could disarm it. I saw plastics. Probably enough C-4 to take down the building."

"That's what Crawford wanted."

She frowned, her jaw trembling. "Yes."

Ian wrapped an arm around her shoulder. "We're fine. They're all fine. No one was hurt."

"He wanted to kill as many of us as he could, Ian."

"But he didn't."

"But he wanted to, and he could try again."

"Yes, he could. And if he does, we'll deal with it.

Right now, let's get everyone farther away from the building."

"Miss Addie's Café's parking lot," Maggie suggested. "Upwind from the smoke."

"Let's move."

People moved surprisingly fast. They were loud, nervous, wary, but working to calm down the children and account for everyone.

The fire department put out the fire on the cars, and the smoke started clearing. Finally, Beecher surfaced with his team and they evacuated the device on a tank-looking truck that had a police escort. Maggie nudged Ian to look. "Where will they take it?"

"Probably to the base." He noticed her shaking and wrapped an arm around her shoulder. "It's all going to be okay, Maggie."

"I ruined the play for the children."

"No, you didn't. Crawford did." Ian dropped his voice. "Gracie said that the man left in a black car. She watched him drive away before she came inside. So he's not here anymore."

How had Ian known she feared Crawford had stood beside her and she hadn't known it? When had he learned to read her so well? "We need to get details from Gracie right away."

"As soon as the police are done."

"We know," Ian said, "that Blue Shoes isn't Talbot or Dayton."

"We do?" It was Crawford. It had to be Crawford.

"Gracie would have known either of them. They're in Miss Addie's all the time. She didn't know the man who gave her the rose."

They were, and she didn't. Unfortunately, the description of the man she'd shared didn't fit them or Crawford. Had to be a disguise. And his blue shoes had been spotted out behind the ranch several times. Paul had chased him on a horse, but Blue Shoes escaped on a four-wheeler. They couldn't be dealing with an unknown.

Pastor Brown found her. "I'm sorry, Maggie. I should have listened immediately without questioning you." His balding pate caught the light from a streetlamp and reflected a sheen. "The children could have…"

"They're fine, Pastor. We're all fine."

"But, Gran, baby Jesus isn't in the manger," Gracie told Miss Addie. "We can't do this another time. Tomorrow's Christmas Eve."

The children were all upset that the program had been ruined. Guilt swamped Maggie.

Pastor Brown heard Gracie and turned. "Ian, has the church been cleared?"

"The gathering room has, but not the rest of the building."

"Come with me." He motioned for Ian to follow.

"Where are you going?" Maggie asked.

"To get the crèche and manger and the rest of the Nativity. We're going to have this program right here in Miss Addie's parking lot."

The children squealed their delight.

A few other men took off after Ian and the pastor, and they soon formed a line that shifted folded chairs into the parking lot. In less than thirty minutes, even the decorated tree was in place—everything but the stage, which didn't seem to bother the children a bit.

Their tears stopped.

Their long faces turned to smiles.

And their Christmas program was now about to begin.

"I should go," Maggie told Miss Addie. "Tell Gracie I'm sorry she didn't get to be Mary on the stage."

"Go where?"

"This whole mess of their program is my fault. I should leave so they can enjoy it."

"Absolutely not." Miss Addie took on the same tone she used to scold Gracie. "You park yourself in that seat right there, Maggie Mason."

"But—"

"But nothing. We're people of faith, girl. We stand together. You leave now, what kind of example are you setting for the children? That when one of us is in trouble, we all turn tail and run, or shun our own? Is that what you want them to think?"

"Of course not." Maggie gasped. "But he could come back."

"If he does, we'll know it," Liz said. "Gracie got a good look at him and we're spreading the word. We're watching for him now."

"You're sure, Miss Addie?"

"Absolutely certain." She patted the seat next to hers.

Maggie looked at Ian.

"I agree with them," he said.

Maggie smiled, sat down and soon the program began. One of the three kings lost his turban. A shepherd tripped over a cow and kissed the concrete, but he jumped up and warned his mom with a raised hand to stay away, he was fine. Maggie watched them reenact the Christmas story with wonder and delight. When the piano would have been played, all the audience hummed and the children sang.

Ian looked at her and smiled. "You're bemused."

"Totally," Maggie whispered and watched Gracie, her little face so serious, her voice so earnest, carry across the hushed crowd. Ever so gently she put the baby Jesus in the manger. Her reverence and care humbled Maggie. "Gracie's just the best Mary ever," she whispered softly to Miss Addie.

"She's worn out a doll practicing."

Maggie smiled and watched.

Ian clasped her hand. "Thank you, Maggie."

She looked over at him. "For what?"

"Making me come tonight." His warm breath fanned her face. "I'd forgotten how terrific these people are. Now I remember."

Ian had reclaimed his church family.

A lump rose in Maggie's throat and she smiled. Crawford intended to cause tragedy. Instead the opposite had happened. His twisted cruelty had brought their community closer, and because it had, the children wouldn't be leaving church tonight traumatized but all aflutter at their special Christmas program held in Miss Addie's Café's parking lot.

God promised that what others intended for harm, He'd turn to good, and He had.

"Talbot and Dayton—"

"It's not them. It's Gary Crawford, Ian. Gracie's description is generic, but not one thing points to anyone else." The only question in her mind was if Crawford killed David Pace and maybe even Beth.

Oh, but she hoped he hadn't. Ian could forgive Maggie many things, but the serial killer after her killing his wife simply because she was Maggie's check-in buddy? That would be too much for anyone to forget, much less accept or forgive.

A pang of regret threatened the spark of hope in her heart that somehow a way would appear for a future with Ian. She couldn't see a way, not so long as Crawford was alive, but if he'd killed Beth, then even his death wouldn't set Maggie free, and it sure wouldn't endear her to Ian. He'd hate her forever—and she couldn't blame him.

Any hopes for more between them seemed doomed and foolish. She stiffened. From the start, she'd known they would be, and she'd warned herself over and again not to fall in love with him. Not to ruin a perfectly good friendship—a special friendship—that if lost would leave her wanting and mourning.

But her heart hadn't listened. And now with Talbot and Dayton cleared…it looked more and more as if Crawford had staged all the challenges in North Bay. Well, except those actually caused by Della's ex.

And because the possibility of Crawford's guilt rang true deep down inside and stood up to the test of her skilled instincts, to Maggie, the magical night suddenly seemed dimmer. Dimmer and sadder and lonelier, though she sat surrounded by people she knew and cared about and some she loved.

And that truth left her wondering.

Where would Crawford strike her next?

"It's after five, Maggie girl." Uncle Warny fussed with his tie. "You ain't planning on going to the Christmas Eve service?"

She sat at the kitchen table, her chin braced with her hand atop the table. "No, I'm not going."

"Why not? You always loved the Christmas candlelight service. You ain't sick—"

"I'm fine." She staved off a sigh. "I think I've caused enough excitement at church already. They should have a peaceful service on Christmas Eve."

"Ah, I see." Uncle Warny let go of the tie, which was decidedly crooked, and sat down. "Fix this thing before I choke myself to death, will you?"

Maggie stood up, tried adjusting his tie, gave up and started over.

"I figure you ain't meaning to snub the folks here, though by hiding out at home that's exactly what you're doing, sweet pea."

"I'm not a coward." She glared at him. "I'm trying to not get them killed."

"Nobody got hurt last night."

"If Luke Sampson had gone back to his car for Elizabeth's sweater a minute sooner, she'd be a widow this morning." Maggie's stomach soured, tensed. They had two little ones at home.

"Luke's fine. Elizabeth's fine. Their kids are fine. Everybody's fine." He looked deeply into her eyes, hesitated for a long moment, then said, "Maggie, I admire what you been doing, trying to keep Paul and me safe, but that Crawford is right about one thing. You can't hide. And, to my way of thinking, you can't run anymore, either."

"What do you suggest I do, then?" She pulled the tie sharply, smoothed it down and then returned to her chair and plopped down. "I don't have a lot of options."

"I suggest you pray."

She looked over at him. "I do, Uncle Warny. All the time. Mostly that he doesn't murder anyone else. And that I get to live another day."

"I say put on your Sunday finest then, and let's go hunting."

He wanted her to hunt down Crawford. "I have hunted him. And hunted him and hunted him." She shuddered. "He could be anyone."

"Maybe you're right." He stood up. "Maybe it's best you stay put here until we know his face." He gave Jake a dog biscuit, then paused and looked back at Maggie. "Ian's a good man, Maggie girl. I hope you don't get no foolish ideas about protecting him by shutting him out of your life." He rubbed at his neck. "That'd surely hurt him in the heart, and I believe it's been home to enough pain already. Just something to think about."

She wanted to rebel. How painful would it be if he learned Beth was dead and it was Maggie's fault?

But she didn't. She sat silently and watched her uncle leave for church.

She should go decorate the fir. She should, but Ian was napping and doing it alone…her heart wasn't in it.

The phone rang.

She checked caller ID. It was Paul. She punched the button. "Hey, big brother." Surely he had to almost be home. They'd been reporting progress, and they couldn't be that far away.

The static in the phone was awful. She could barely hear him. "We're… Better tell Warny to shut up the barn… A bad storm…blowing through."

She made a mental note to check the weather report to find out the specifics of his warning. "I'm catching most of what you're saying, but not all of it," she told him. "I'll check the weather. When will you get here?"

"After… Storm is dropping slush and it's freezing up. Roads are deadly."

Disappointment bit her hard. He wouldn't make it home for Christmas. "Maybe you'd better find some-place safe to wait it out until the storm passes, Paul. It's not worth it."

"Let you know…when…stop."

"I think you said you'd let us know when you stopped. Call if you can. Just be careful. People down here have no idea how to drive on icy roads." There'd be a string of wrecks a mile long before morning.

The line went dead.

She hung up and turned, saw Ian standing in the doorway, soaking wet. Definitely not sleeping. "What happened to you?"

"I locked down the barn and took care of the animals. A bad storm is coming."

"From the looks of you, it's already here." She grabbed a towel and brought it to him. "I'll snag something of Paul's for you to wear while your clothes are drying."

"Thanks."

She ran up to Paul's room for jeans and a shirt, and then returned to the kitchen with them.

He shot her an apologetic look. "Sorry about the fir."

"What about it?"

"We didn't get it decorated."

"It's okay." Not much about this Christmas at home was turning out as it had played in her mind. But that didn't mean it was awful. A lot of good had come from what had happened. It was just the possibility of Crawford and Beth weighing heavily on her mind. If nothing else, in these past three years of running, she'd learned to be flexible and adapt without drama. She'd had no choice and no one around to notice. Not much sense in engaging in drama when you're alone. God saw it all, of course. But He wasn't impressed with self-pity or with displays of drama. So she'd just stopped that—and wondered what merit Madison and she had seen in it as teens.

Ian lifted his arms, one higher than the other, then shifted them. "Monopoly or popcorn and a movie?"

Maybe the movie would do her good. Get her mind off herself and her troubles. "Movie." She smiled. "A Christmas one."

"Let me guess." Ian rubbed his chin, feigning deep consideration. *"It's a Wonderful Life."*

Her jaw dropped. "How did you know that?"

He smiled and his eyes twinkled. "You've watched it every year since you were in third grade, Maggie. It doesn't take Christmas magic to know…"

She stilled. "Do you remember everything I tell you?"

"Don't you?"

Her face heated. "I don't know. But can we not test it tonight?"

He swung an arm around her. "No tests. Just a quiet, no-stress evening eating popcorn and watching a movie."

A sigh of relief shuddered her shoulder. "Wonderful."

"Somebody's at the gate." Maggie heard the alarm. Ian was already out of his seat and headed toward the monitor room. When Maggie stepped in, he told her, "It's Detective Cray."

"Buzz him in."

Ian stretched, tapped the buzzer and on the monitor Maggie watched the gate swing open. He drove through then up to the house, using the back door as everyone did.

She passed him a towel on the back porch. "Boy, it's really coming down out here."

"Worse, the roads are freezing up." Cray swiped at his face with the towel. "Thanks."

"Why are you all the way out here? Have the wrecks started already?"

"Not yet, but we're on alert for them." He blotted his face and took off his coat, then hung it on a peg out on the back porch. "Dripping. Sorry about that."

"Don't worry about it, Detective." Maggie urged him inside. "Come on in. It's cold out here."

His hands were red and raw from the damp cold. "If you run warm water over your hands you'll feel better quick. I'll get you a cup of coffee."

He moved to the sink. "Is it decaf? I've had a potful already tonight."

"It's decaf." Ian filled a mug and set it at the table. "Sit down."

Maggie sat across from him, between the two men. Ian was as perplexed as she, gauging by his pensive expression. "So what's wrong?"

He hesitated as if torn. As if he intended to share something but had second thoughts about it now that he was here.

"Detective?" Maggie tilted her head. "Are you okay?"

"No, Maggie, I'm not. I'm in a dilemma. I shouldn't

be here. I shouldn't tell anyone what I'm about to tell you. But if I don't and something happens... I won't forgive myself. Ever."

Ian stiffened. "If it can cause harm, you've got to share it."

Maggie interceded. "It's not always that easy, Ian. Not when the news is official." She looked at Cray. "You're here about something official, but you're here personally, off the record and the clock."

"Yeah." Some of the tension fell from his face.

"Okay. So as a person, you've discovered something that could be problematic for us. For me. That means Crawford."

"Yeah."

He hadn't found him. He hadn't identified him. She'd have gotten that information through the agency. So it had to be local—the reporter. Where was that investigation? "You got new information on David Pace."

He didn't answer.

"Is that a yes, or a no?" Ian asked Cray.

"It's a yes," Maggie told Ian, then swiveled her gaze back to Cray. "Did you get the final report back from the Coroner?"

Again, no answer. Cray sat still as a stone statue.

"That's a yes," Ian said, clearly seeking confirmation.

Maggie switched hats. "Detective, confidentially I'm notifying you that I'm still an active agent with the FBI. I've been undercover, and staying undercover is crucial to my survival. Confidentially, I'm telling you I have reason to believe there's a connection between the murders of David Pace and Beth Crane. Confidentially, I'm telling you that whatever information you have in your professional capacity that you withhold could impede my investigation. You see—" she braced "—I believe Gary Crawford killed David Pace."

"Crawford killed Pace?" Cray asked, a little confused. "Why do you think so?"

"I can't prove it but Crawford is extremely clever, warped and vengeful. He'd be thrilled to see the general or the colonel blamed for murder. Setting up two upstanding, respected officers and watching them fall from grace. He'd love that—"

Cray interrupted. "And you're undercover?"

"Yes," she said. "I'm counting on your total discretion so you don't get me killed."

"I understand." He nodded slowly, still absorbing. "If you're active, then I have no ethical conflicts sharing information."

"No, you don't." Precisely why she'd told him. If in an ethical dilemma, whatever information he had must be important. "So what did you risk treacherous roads getting here to tell us?"

"A couple hours ago, I got a message to call the coroner. Not his usual telephone call. He sent his grandson to my house to summon me."

"Very odd."

"He didn't want me to come to his office. He asked me to come to his house." Cray frowned. "So I went."

"And?" Maggie asked.

"He said he'd been visited by Daniel L. Ford from Homeland Security. Ford told the coroner what to say and insisted he forge the David Pace report—it was a matter of national security."

Maggie's mind tumbled and reeled, mixing this in

with all she knew about Crawford, his patterns, his history, his methods.

"Did the coroner do it?" Ian asked.

Cray nodded. "But he wanted me to know the truth…in case there was a connection."

"To what?" Ian asked.

"My death, Ian," Maggie said. The puzzle pieces slammed into place. He hadn't tracked her through her FBI connections but her military connections. Crawford hadn't stopped coming after her because he feared her profiling skills or because she was a loose end. He kept coming after her because he feared Beth had told him about her investigation of the Nest. That fit. "Homeland Security, you said?"

Cray nodded.

It did fit, but maybe she'd been wrong. This sounded more like Talbot or Dayton. "Did the coroner say what really happened to Pace?"

"He wasn't shot." Cray sipped at his steaming coffee. "There wasn't a mark on him, and the blue shoes didn't fit him, either. Too big. Pace had an embolism."

"A blood clot?" Ian sounded skeptical. "Then why the explosion? Why burn his car and make sure he's not burned? Why move the car and Pace's body to stage a crime? This makes no sense."

Maggie chewed on her lower lip. "Unfortunately it makes perfect sense." She risked a glance at Ian. "The embolism didn't just happen. It was inflicted."

"It was." Cray nodded. "The coroner was stumped at first. No fat from the marrow of a broken bone. No tumor."

"Only one thing left, then," Ian said. "Air bubbles."

"That's what the coroner thought. But Pace had no

history of deep vein thrombosis and no needle marks in the usual places."

Maggie frowned. "Did he check between Pace's toes?" If his shoes were off and replaced with the neon blue ones, between the toes was a likely place.

"He did," Cray said. "Nothing."

Ian sighed. "What about the roof of his mouth? Or under his tongue."

Cray set down his cup, looked at Ian. "How'd you know that? Pace wasn't a druggie. Medical school, military or what?"

"Military." Ian held Cray's gaze. "It's a tactic we saw a lot in the Middle East."

"Well, it was used here." Cray looked from Maggie to Ian. "Under his tongue."

"So Pace was murdered with air," Maggie said. "And Homeland Security—" She stopped midsentence.

"What?" Ian asked her.

Maggie gripped the ledge of the table. "Did you say the Homeland Security agent was named Daniel L. Ford?"

Cray nodded. "Yeah."

Shock pumped through her body. "He was Crawford."

"What?"

"Shh, wait," Ian told Cray. "Why is he Crawford, Maggie?"

"His mother. Her maiden name was Ford. And her first name was—"

"Danielle," Ian finished for her. "Does the coroner have a surveillance photo of him?"

Cray pulled a photo out of his shirt pocket. "This is him. I came hoping maybe one or the other of you would recognize him from your previous careers. I had a gut feeling something was wrong."

He had no idea how much. Maggie looked at the photo and into the face of the man trying to kill her. So many emotions rocketed through her body, if not seated, she would have staggered. He was an ordinary-looking man. Not handsome, not ugly, not strong and formidable-looking. He didn't look like any of the powerful, brilliant, elusive things she knew him to be or at all like his mother. He looked like a quiet, gentle man who lived down the block maybe, or— "Oh, Ian. He was at Miss Addie's. I saw him when we were there for dessert."

"He fits Gracie's description. But if he was at Miss Addie's, wouldn't Gracie have remembered him from there?"

"She's a child. Maybe or maybe not. You know how unreliable even adult eyewitnesses are."

"Wait. Are you saying this is Gary Crawford?" Cray asked.

"Yes." Ian studied the photo. "And apparently, he's also Mr. Blue Shoes." He shot a look at Cray. "He did put the blue shoes on Pace."

"Somebody did, posthumously."

"So nothing that's happened was Talbot or Dayton," Ian said. "It was all Gary Crawford."

"Looks that way to me." Cray grunted. "Hard to believe someone who looks so normal is so twisted, isn't it?"

"It always is," Maggie confessed, screwing up her courage to say the one thing she wished with every fiber of her being she didn't have to say. "Ian, you know that if Crawford is Blue Shoes and he did all he's done, then it's highly possible he was also responsible for Beth's murder."

Ian's gaze collided with Maggie's. Pain flashed through his eyes. "That's pretty much a given, Maggie. Beth was your check-in buddy. Your one daily contact. He went after her to isolate you."

Her throat swelled and regret flooded her. Regret and guilt. "I'm so sorry, Ian. If I could—"

"No." Ian reached across the table and snagged her hand, squeezed it hard. "No, you didn't do this."

"But if it hadn't been for me, Beth—"

"Maggie, don't. This is Crawford's fault. He killed Beth. He killed Pace. And if given half a chance, he'll kill you. Put the blame where it belongs. On his shoulders. Not yours."

"You can forgive me?" she asked. He couldn't. How could he?

"You haven't done anything, and Beth would be the first to say it."

Relief washed over Maggie. Relief and sorrow. "I'm sorry anyway, and I was so afraid you'd never be able to forgive me…"

"Don't be." Ian gently squeezed her hand a second time. "I don't blame you, Maggie."

The urge to cry nearly brought her to her knees. She fought it with everything in her. If she cried now she'd never stop. She'd fall apart at the seams and Crawford would win.

Jake sprung from his bed to his feet. A low, throaty growl rattling in his throat.

"What's the matter, boy?" Ian stood up. "Maggie, check on Warny."

She grabbed the phone. He'd insisted on staying

in his apartment in the barn with the animals in case they were uneasy about the storm. "The line's dead."

"Use your cell."

"Here, use mine." Cray passed her his phone.

She dialed the barn. It rang and rang. "No answer."

Jake still stood on alert, still growled and bared his teeth.

Ian rounded the edge of the table and checked the security monitors. "Maggie, when did Warny decorate the fir?"

"He didn't." Her mouth went dry. "He was at church."

"Somebody did."

Her gaze collided with Detective Cray's. "Crawford." She headed to the monitor room.

The fir was alight and beautifully decorated with ornaments and tinsel blowing in the wind. Even through the rain, it looked gorgeous. And beneath it lay dozens of packages, all wrapped in shiny paper. Green, red, blue and gold and silver.

Cold chills swept up Maggie's spine, firing every nerve ending in her body at once.

"What are all those packages under it?" Cray asked.

Her voice came out stilted, stiff. "From the wires sticking out of the boxes, I'd say bombs."

"Definitely Crawford," Cray said.

Maggie agreed.

As they watched the twinkling lights, the tree exploded.

Chapter Nine

Jake barked, fierce enough to split eardrums, batted at the door and it opened. He took off out of it like a shot.

"Jake!" Maggie shouted at him. "Come back here!"

But Jake was giving chase. And he did not come back.

Maggie grabbed her coat. Ian stopped her. "Oh, no. You're not going out there. Not now."

Cray was on the phone, summoning reinforcements.

Maggie tried to pull free of Ian. "But Jake..."

"Maggie, you can't." Ian met and held her gaze. "Have faith."

"I'm glad you're back in touch with God, but He does help those who help themselves."

"Just stay put until backup arrives. Please." Ian grabbed her by the shoulders. "I can't lose you, too. Okay? I...can't." The struggle in him settled. "You need to notify the task force."

He was right.

Fifteen minutes later, a rain-drenched Jake appeared at the back door.

And in his mouth he carried a neon blue shoe.

"Wearing one shoe, he's still here." Ian moved Maggie away from the back door.

Her cell rang. She grabbed it off the kitchen counter and connected the call. "Mason."

"Merry Christmas, Maggie."

Crawford. "Why did you blow up my fir?"

"Because you loved it. Decorated it every year, I hear."

No emotion. Maybe for the same reason as Beth. To isolate Maggie from all she loved. She factored that into his psychological profile. Rushing sounds snagged her attention. Running through crackling leaves. He was still on the ranch or in the woods adjacent to it where he'd been glimpsed several times. "You lost a shoe. Must be uncomfortable—cold feet on the bare ground. Lots of twigs out there."

"You should be thanking me, not worrying about twigs or my feet. I took your fir, but I let your mutt live."

He had. Why hadn't he shot Jake? "I'd thank you if you'd stop killing and leave me alone. Why can't you do that?"

He cackled. "Scorpions sting because they're scorpions. The world made me what I am, Maggie. You should know that by now."

"If you believe that, then you're wrong." Agitated, she paced the kitchen. "You choose who you want to be. We all do." No more crunching. He couldn't be in the woods. He had to be on the ranch itself. If he were on the road, there'd be street sounds and there weren't any.

"My mother—"

"Was no worse than mine," she interrupted. "You were ignored because she was working all the time.

She neglected you. Didn't attend all your events at school, make your lunches and all that. Well, guess what? Neither did mine. And unlike you, my father was here, too, and he didn't do any of those things, either. You use your mother as an excuse to kill and trash people's lives. But it's just an excuse to do what you want to do."

"You know nothing about my life."

"I know a good bit about your life, Daniel," she said, disclosing that his identity was no longer a secret. The officers in charge of his mother's murder had made notes on her young son. "You were small for your age. You got teased and beaten up. You blamed her for that, too. And—"

"Blamed her? I saved her!"

Hence the roses. His way of mourning his loss, but serving the greater good by setting the woman free. Classic, but no. No, his patterns weren't wholly consistent. "You killed her to put her out of her misery— or so you say. But that's not the truth. You killed her because you blamed her for your misery. You blamed her for all that happened to you."

Bells sounded in the distance. Church bells. He was on her homesite! The place on the ranch where, when all this started, she'd been about to build her home.

"Don't you dare judge me. Don't you dare."

Maggie shook all over. This could be the wisest choice or the dumbest move she'd ever made. But a knowing settled inside her. She had to follow it. "You can run. You cannot hide." She punched the screen to disconnect the call.

Ian and Cray looked at her as if she'd lost her mind.

"I know where he is." She grabbed her coat, slung it on.

"Down by the creek." Ian grabbed his coat, shoved his arm into his sleeve. "Where I caught a flash of him before on the ATV."

Maggie didn't answer. She couldn't. Ian would put himself in harm's way. Cray, too. She had to protect them. Crawford wouldn't stop. He'd never stop. He'd tag them loose ends and kill them, too.

"Cray and I will go," Ian said. "You check on Warny. He's still not answering his phone."

The barn was closer to her homesite, and it would keep Cray and Ian a safe distance away. "Be careful."

Once again, she would face Gary Crawford alone.

Maggie dipped her chin against the driving rain, torn between going to the barn to see about her uncle and getting to the homesite before Crawford got too far away to track.

If Uncle Warny were harmed, she wouldn't be able to leave him, and she would lose the chance to stop Crawford from killing again. Warny would tell her to go after Crawford.

Trying to move as quietly as possible—even the rain didn't drown out the sounds of snapping twigs under her feet—she made her way to the edge of the homesite and paused at a magnolia, using its wide trunk as cover. Scanning, she spotted him, limping from the site toward the woods.

She reached under her coat and pulled her gun from its holster at her waist. Her hands shook. She shook all over. Rushing her steps, she intercepted him. "Crawford! Stop right there." Hunching low to the ground, she prepared in case he turned and fired.

Only one hand was visible, and it was empty, but what caught her attention were his feet: one bare foot and one blue shoe.

Thank you, Jake.

Rising up, she moved in, began shouting through the rain, reading him his rights.

"Something's not right," Ian told Cray. "There's no sign of anyone down here."

"She was wrong." Cray shielded his eyes from the icy rain to look at Ian. "We better get to the barn and see about her and Warny."

"She's not at the barn." Ian's jaw went stiff. He'd assumed Crawford was at the creek because he'd glimpsed him there before. She hadn't lied. Just let him assume. Fear rippled through his body. "She's protecting us. She knows where he is, and it's not at the barn." Where would Crawford go?

"Where then?"

"Somewhere that means something to her. He blew up her tree because she loved it, right? He'd be somewhere that matters."

"Something signaled her where he was."

Had to be sound. Sound...the church bells. "Her homesite."

"What homesite?"

"The site Maggie had cleared to build a home before Crawford started up." Ian moved. "Let's go."

"Surely the woman isn't confronting him on her own. Surely— That's exactly what she's doing, isn't it? She stayed away to protect her family. Now she's protecting you."

"And you. And if she's still alive, I'm going to make her wish she wasn't for doing it, too." Ian rushed his steps. "Oh, please, God, let her still be alive."

Maggie tripped over a stump and nearly went down.

A second was all Crawford needed. He whipped out a weapon, drew down on her. "Well, now we have a little dilemma. You have a gun. I have a gun. Who'll shoot first?"

On her stomach on the cold ground, she kept a two-handed aim on him. If she tried to get up, he'd shoot. She had no choice but to stay put. "I thought you'd be taller."

"What?" He chuckled. "Never mind. I thought you'd be smarter. It's been difficult to lead you every step of the way, Maggie."

"Not every step. For a while, I thought so, but that's just not true. I held my own against you just fine."

"A little credit is due, but you are, after all, the one on your belly in the dirt."

He had a point. "Why did you kill Beth and David Pace?"

He paused a long second and then shrugged, rain pelting his black trench coat. "Scorpions do what scorpions do."

"Glib, but not the truth. It wasn't related to me." The truth hit her. "It was because of your Homeland Security work." He couldn't afford for his connection there to be exposed. That's how he'd tracked her. Through those connections.

"Was it, now?"

It had to be. "I thought it was because Beth and I were check-in buddies, but it wasn't. It was about the Nest and keeping your affiliation to it secret."

"Tsk-tsk. You're not supposed to talk about that place." He grunted. "So little respect for rules, Maggie. I'm shocked."

"You know all about the Nest. You've been there—actually, you've seen parts of it that I haven't. And you're going to shoot me." She tried to lull him into complacency. "I want to know the truth. Are you even capable of telling the truth anymore?"

"Maybe they asked questions I didn't want to answer. It could be just that simple." He laughed. "You're not surprised that I know all about the Nest. Interesting. It is an enormously huge project, of course. Anytime you get that many people involved, it's impossible to prevent leaks." He stepped closer to her. "People just aren't as concerned as they once were with personal integrity or honor, are they? Hugely disappointing, that."

He was definitely out of his mind. "You routed your calls to me through the installation there. Which means you had access."

He feigned a sigh. "You're boring me now, Maggie."

"Ah, yes. The urge to kill again has been building hasn't it? You're almost out of time. You're deep into your two weeks."

"Well, at least you picked up on that pattern. You've missed quite a few."

Maybe she had. She didn't think so, but maybe she had. "Why do you do it?"

He glared at her, rain sliding in sheets down his face. "Because I can."

"You're never going to stop, are you? You're so full

of rage that you're never going to stop." She shook her head. "Don't hand me that scorpion nonsense. You love to kill. Do you realize how sick that makes you?"

"Sick enough to know I wouldn't be standing here in the rain unless I was sure I'd be able to walk out of here." He glanced around. "This is a nice site for a home. Too bad you'll never build one here. But maybe Paul will bury you here."

"If you think I'm afraid of dying, you're wrong."

"Of course. I am." He spread his lips in a sneer that was supposed to pass for a smile. "You know where you're going. God and Jesus and all that."

"Death has never frightened me," she admitted. "It's life that strikes terror in my heart. Apparently, in yours, too."

"Spare me your psychobabble. I'd rather be shot."

"That creates a problem."

"Why?"

A calm flooded her deep inside and somehow came through in her voice. "I don't want to kill you."

"Right. And you say I'm crazy?" He snorted. "You want me dead. Don't lie, Maggie. I know you better than you know yourself. You want me dead and buried so you know I'll never bother you or anyone else again."

"At one time I did, but not anymore." Her hands were numbing. She had to get up. She risked rolling into a sitting position. When he didn't shoot, she pulled up to her knees, then to her feet. "I do want you to stop killing." She swiped her hair back from her face. "I want you in jail. Every day for the rest of my life, I want to know that you're there. That your life is as alien to you as you made mine to me."

"Me? In jail?" He aimed at her chest. "That is not happening." He issued her fair warning. "Kill or be killed, Maggie Mason."

He meant it. *Oh, God, please.* She didn't want to kill him. She didn't—

She glimpsed Ian and Detective Cray through the trees. She had to stall Crawford. Keep him talking. "You're not going to kill me. You kill to save people." Ian moved closer. A few more seconds. That's all he or Cray needed. Just a few more seconds. "This isn't saving me, it's saving you."

"Saving you?" He harrumphed. "After all the trouble you've been?"

Ian eased into place behind the thick trunk of an oak. Cray squatted in a clump of palmettos. "Trouble I've been. You stole my life."

Ian and Cray exchanged hand signals and Cray raised up. Maggie's heart seemed to stop, time suspended. Simultaneously, they lunged.

Crawford went down. The gun in his hand fired. Maggie dropped and rolled aside. A stray bullet shattered a branch above her head and it toppled to the ground.

"Let go of me. Now!" Crawford's screams split the sounds of rain, penetrating the blood gushing through her on an adrenaline surge.

Ian jerked Crawford to his feet.

"Kill me. I got your wife. Kill me."

Ian struggled with it. He wanted to kill Crawford, and for a second, Maggie wasn't sure which way he'd go.

"No," Ian said. "No, you live. You live a long, long time and you think about all the lives you've destroyed." He turned to look at Cray. "Cuff him and get him out of my sight before I change my mind."

Cray cuffed Crawford and he and an armed Warny escorted him to Cray's car. As they walked away, Cray called in the capture. The FBI task force would no doubt be waiting for Crawford when he arrived at the station.

Ian eyed Maggie. "Are you all right?"

"I'm fine."

"You sure?" Ian asked. "He didn't hurt you?"

He'd hurt her every day of her life for over three years. "No, not this time."

"Why didn't you shoot him?" Maggie asked Ian. He had to have heard Crawford admit killing Beth.

"I nearly did. But vengeance isn't mine and killing him wasn't necessary. He'll pay for his crimes."

"You heard that he's connected to the Nest."

Ian nodded. "Through Homeland Security." Ian clasped her arms. "You're really okay?"

She nodded, wrapped her arms around Ian and held on tight.

Ian kissed her hard, and then glared at her. "I'm pretty ticked off at you. You led me on a wild-goose chase down to the creek."

She couldn't deny it.

"You knew where he was because you heard the church bells on the phone with him."

She nodded. "That's why I chose this as the site for my home. Every night, you can hear the church bells here."

"You lied to me, Maggie."

"No, I just didn't tell you—"

"That's a lie by omission, and you know it." He frowned. "You've got to stop that."

She clutched his shirtfront, stroked his face. "I couldn't put you in his path, Ian. Not Beth and then you. I love you."

"I love you, too." He kissed her again, pulling her close. When their mouths parted, he warned her, "But if you ever do anything like that again, putting yourself in that kind of danger, we're going to have a big problem."

Bluster. He was scared for her. Still shaking. But he loved her and he'd forgiven her. Maybe there was a slim chance he'd fall in love with her after all.

"Unit's on the way to escort Cray in with him," Warny said. "Could take a while because of the roads. They're iced up pretty bad."

"We should stay with Cray. He could try something—Crawford, I mean."

Her uncle stepped out from a thicket of bushes, his shotgun in hand, wearing a camouflage slicker. "He's staying put, sweet pea."

Ian frowned at Warny. "You had your gun?"

"I usually have my gun. Rattlers out here and all."

"Why didn't you shoot him?"

"She was handling it. Three years of running... I figured Maggie needed to take care of him herself." Uncle Warny gave Ian a sidelong look. "If I needed to, I'd a shot him."

Maggie saw straight through that bit of business. Uncle Warny hadn't shot Crawford because of Ian. Ian had been ripped to shreds inside at not being there for Beth when she needed him. He needed to be there for Maggie, and Uncle Warny knew it.

She didn't mention that, but Ian would figure it out. Tomorrow, maybe the next day, the truth would hit him.

"Well." Warny hiked his gun on his shoulder. "I'll

feel better if we stick close to Cray until his backup gets here."

The three walked over to the patrol car near the ranch house and joined the detective, then talked about everything that happened. Maggie slid her gaze to the hunched heap kicking up a ruckus in the back seat of the patrol car. Gary Crawford was going to jail for the rest of his life. His reign of terror was finally over.

And Maggie still didn't dare allow herself to shed a single tear.

"Do you know, this is the first midnight in three years that I haven't dreaded hearing my phone ring?" Maggie looked at Ian seated beside her on the sofa. They'd been Christmas tree gazing in total silence for nearly an hour, absorbing all that had happened and how quickly their lives had changed.

"I'm glad." Ian's arm lay stretched over her shoulder and he absently rubbed the sleeve of her silky blouse with the tips of his fingers. "It's been a long couple years for us both, but mostly for you."

"We've had our challenges." She leaned her head into his shoulder and chest. His heart beat slow and steady near her ear.

"Yes, we have." He started to say something, stopped and fell silent.

"No more cookies, buddy." Uncle Warny's voice carried through to the living room from the kitchen.

"You know that means he's giving Jake another one, right?" Ian asked Maggie.

"I know." She smiled, looked up at Ian. "I'm so glad you're here."

The look in his eyes warmed. "So am I." He glanced

at the tree, then back at her. "Maggie, I need to know you're not blaming yourself for what Crawford did to Beth. You shouldn't be. I know you loved her."

A lump rose in Maggie's throat. "I did. So did you. If I could trade places—"

He pressed his fingers against her lips. "No. It was her time or it wouldn't have happened." He paused a second, then another. "It's time for both of us to move on now. To be at peace with all this."

She was so ready for peace. "Can we do that?" she dared to ask. "Together, I mean?"

"I sure hope so because I can't imagine my life without you."

Don't make more of that than there is. Being in his life doesn't mean being in his heart as more than close friends. Loving, yes. In love, no. No, it didn't mean that to him. "Me, either." She swiped her hair back from her face. "But things are different now. You're not caught in that awful place of not knowing what happened and I'm not running, praying I won't get caught and Crawford won't kill again. It's a new start for both of us."

A strange look crossed Ian's face, one she couldn't decipher. Before she could ask, he changed the subject.

"It doesn't look as if anyone's going to get back for Christmas."

"Paul and Della are trying." If the icy roads didn't land them in a ditch, there was a chance they'd get home.

Ian looked back at her. "Madison, too, with Grant, but it's not looking promising for them. Passengers on the ship are lined up, trying to fly off. Rough seas have made that cruise anything but fun."

She reached for his hand on his thigh. Laced their

fingers. "Would it be so awful if it was just the four of us—Uncle Warny and Jake, you and me?"

"It wouldn't be your merriest Christmas." He drew back to look her full in the face. "I'm still ticked off at you, you know."

"I know." She sat up. "But what was I supposed to do, Ian? Put you right in the path of a man who would kill you for the kick of seeing me devastated by it?"

"You'd be devastated?"

"Don't be ridiculous. I love you. Of course I'd be devastated." She lifted a hand. "I couldn't send you to him and watch him kill you or try to kill you. I'd rather he shot me."

"Well, put yourself in my shoes. I love you, too, you know."

"I know. And I'm sorry you're upset, but I won't lie and say I'd do anything different. I couldn't—not and live with myself." She sniffed. "Just so I'm clear, you did decide not to shoot him. It was your choice. So why are you still ticked?"

"He had a gun aimed at you. He could have shot you, Maggie. Then you'd be gone, too." He grunted. "Good grief, can't you see why I'd be upset about this?"

"That's been established, and no, actually, I can't."

"Well, give me a few days to get my heart back in my chest and I'll explain it to you."

"All right." She agreed, but she wasn't sure if that was a conversation she should eagerly anticipate or dread.

The thing about serial killers is that, once they're caught, they'll confess to anything. Whether or not they're guilty, they'll take blame and claim credit on all they can to elevate their stature, their inflated sense of self-importance, the fear of them in others.

Gary Crawford, aka Daniel L. Ford, had been no exception. He'd taken blame and claimed credit for murdering David Pace, Beth Crane and so much more that was possible for him to have done, including acts against Maggie's brother, Paul, and his fiancée, Della Jackson, but he hadn't.

And that suited the real Mr. Blue Shoes just fine.

Actually, it was better than fine. Because Crawford worked for Homeland Security and had access to the Nest and had actually been there on multiple occasions in his official capacity, which was highly classified, he made the perfect fall guy for the security breach that put the promotions essential to him at risk. The Talbot congressional appointment was looking good. The Dayton command of the Nest appointment was looking good, and maybe now with the security breach investigation officially closed, the promotions would go through quickly.

That didn't just suit the real Mr. Blue Shoes—it made him deliriously happy. He'd gotten away with murder, and now no one would ever know the truth, because Crawford had claimed responsibility. Inside, Blue Shoes laughed. *Brilliant plan. Absolutely brilliant.*

He walked into Miss Addie's Café and took a seat at the table in the corner near the door and then waited. With the exception of Paul and Della, the staff from Lost, Inc., had returned to North Bay and should arrive momentarily for a "Crawford capture" celebration lunch. Blue Shoes would be celebrating with them… they just wouldn't know it.

Maggie and Ian arrived first. Mrs. Renault, Madison's assistant, came in with the youngest investigator, Jimmy. They were all seated at a long table when Madison and Grant came in. She looked elated and he looked exhausted.

Now what was up with him? Blue Shoes could well imagine. Being stranded on a ship with Madison McKay for five days when she was bent on getting off it…the man had done well, remaining upright.

Miss Addie served him a slice of key lime pie with extra whipped cream, just as he liked it, refilled his coffee cup and then dropped a pat to his shoulder before joining the group.

They didn't have a clue. None of them. They were sharp—some of the best he'd ever commanded—but still, even combined, they hadn't outsmarted him. He took a bite of pie; let the sweet and tangy flavors roll around on his tongue. True, a slight element of luck had broken his way. But tricking all of them…?

Crawford was a clever dog. A killer through and through either bent on enhancing his legacy or using Beth Crane's murder as a final way to create strife between Maggie and Ian. Even a blind man would know they were in love.

It'd been ridiculously easy to position Crawford to take the fall, of course. The one thing that had concerned Blue Shoes was witnesses to his phone call to Brett Lund. Lund's secretary and Jesse, the station's security guard, could have been problematic. She could have recognized his voice. But lucky for her, she hadn't. Still, who could have predicted the station manager would wig out over connecting David Pace's and Beth Crane's deaths to the Nest and kill himself?

But Blue Shoes was nothing if not flexible. No one

made it to his position without learning how to sidestep a couple of land mines. Now any authority could look all they liked. Officially, on the record, that phone call never came into the station. Oh, Lund's secretary and Jesse knew a call had come in, but the records proving it had been successfully eradicated. The coroner had responded exactly as planned, had told Cray the truth, and Maggie and Ian had pegged Crawford with the murders. So that, too, had worked out exactly as planned.

Which had left Blue Shoes with one challenge. The security breach.

At the moment, the Lost, Inc., team blamed that on Crawford, too. It'd been easy to plant him in the system as an operative for Homeland Security. All it had taken was a few well-placed records that could disappear as quickly as they had appeared—after he'd taken the legal hit for tracking Maggie Mason's every move for three years, breaching his chain of command. Tying Crawford to the Nest put those records in a need-to-know classification that would be seen by few, but would resolve the matter in the minds of many.

Satisfied, Blue Shoes sat back in his seat, sipped at his coffee and then took another bite of the tart pie. Oh, yeah. Crawford was the perfect fall guy. And he was a killer, after all, and as crazy as a loon. The world was better off with him tucked away in prison until he died. Even if at some point in the future he elected to dispute his connection to Homeland Security or to the David Pace or Beth Crane murders, or he later denied putting the neon blue shoes on Pace after his death on the Nest's perimeter, who'd believe him? No one.

But, as Blue Shoes stared across the crowded café

to the stunning blonde he loved to hate, there was still a problem. Madison McKay.

At some point, stalling tactics would fail and the beautiful owner of Lost, Inc., would get the satellite images of the base Maggie had requisitioned be sent to Madison. When she did, she'd know far too much about the Nest. She'd see the amount of construction going on and she'd know that no one outside the direct command could do what Crawford purportedly had done—regardless of what the records showed. She'd be a problem.

Which meant she had to go.

Congressional appointments and base commands didn't come along every day, and no one, not even Madison McKay, would be allowed to get in the way of them. He wanted that job. He'd sacrificed for two decades and earned that job, and he was going get it.

He'd handle Madison McKay. She'd be dispatched soon enough.

But today was for celebrating. He polished off the last bite of pie. They were none the wiser and considered everything all tied up in a perfect little bow.

Merry Christmas to me.

"What's the matter, Maggie?"

Leaning against Ian's shoulder, she took her gaze from the lit Christmas tree in the corner of the living room and risked a look at him. "It's been three days. I keep waiting for you to explain, but I'm torn. I'm not sure it'll be an explanation I want to hear so I'm…"

"Worrying."

She nodded.

"Me, too," he confessed, sliding a hand down the

thigh of his slacks. "If I knew how you'd react… I guess that's why you're worried, too. You don't know what's coming."

"Exactly."

"It's simple but complex, Maggie."

"Your faith crisis?"

He shook his head no. "I see the error of my ways on that. It's Beth."

Her heart nearly stopped. "You do blame me for Crawford killing her."

"No, I don't. It's just that I loved her with all my heart. You know I did."

She nodded. And he didn't love her. She had been a substitute for Beth, because she'd loved her, too.

"When she died, I thought I'd die, too. I'm ashamed to admit how many times I wished I would, but I did, Maggie. It hurt so deep, in places I can't even name. I never thought one body could hold that much pain."

"But you did hold it."

He nodded. "I felt so guilty for failing her. So guilty that she was such a good wife and she was dead and I was a lousy husband and I was still alive. It didn't seem fair to take joy in anything, to want or need anything, to care about anything—or about anyone."

"Survivor's guilt—"

"Is only part of it." He paused and focused on the tree, as if emptying his heart like this was too difficult to do while looking at her. "We've been there for each other since Beth died. Grief brought us closer. Well, grief and a need to share whatever was left of us with someone who got what we were going through. But both of us were shells, Maggie. I was because of Beth, and you were because of Crawford." Ian clasped her hand. "Do you know how many nights your emails got me through? It was as if you had this special gift. You knew when I was at rock bottom, and somehow you got me through it. I still don't know how you did that."

"I didn't know I did." What did all this mean? "So what you're saying is that you love me out of gratitude but it's nothing more than that?"

"I do, but no. That's not what I'm saying. I think we started out loving each other out of gratitude, but long before you came back home, things started to change, and when we took that first walk on the ranch—you were barefoot and it was cold out—things really started changing then. And I felt so…"

"Guilty," she speculated. "Because you were alive and feeling again and Beth was dead."

He nodded yes. "But at the cemetery, when you reminded me she didn't need me anymore, that's when my whole world—and my attitude—shifted."

"What exactly do you mean?"

"It occurred to me that Blue Shoes could have killed you and if he had…" Ian's voice faded.

"What?" She waited, but he still didn't answer. "Ian, what?" she asked again.

He looked at her. Pain shimmered in his eyes. "I realized it would hurt as much as losing Beth."

"Because…?" Maggie didn't dare make the leap to what she prayed he was saying. She didn't dare.

He dipped his chin so they sat nearly nose to nose. "Because I love you and I'm in love with you, Maggie Mason. In that moment, I knew it, and it scared me half to death."

Her mouth went dry. "I can see where that'd be

daunting. But intense situations often trick us into thinking we're feeling emotions that—"

"I know that. Which is why I told you to give me three days. I didn't want to hurt you and I don't want to be hurt. I had to be sure what I was feeling wasn't just because of our circumstance, that it was real."

And he'd discovered it wasn't, which is why he hadn't brought it up. Her heart shattered. Why, oh, why, had she pushed him into talking about this? Why?

"You look upset." He sighed. "You don't want me to love and be in love with you?"

That question wasn't expected. "I want to know where you stand now." At least, she thought she did. Did she have the courage to hope? "Was it real, Ian? Do you love me and are you in love with me?"

He cupped her face in his big hands. "I am. Maggie, I am so in love with you that even without a license to dream, I'm dreaming."

Her heart soared. "You are?"

He nodded.

"What are you dreaming?"

"Of you and me together for the rest of our lives. Of us building a beautiful house on your homesite where we can hear the church bells every night and raise a family and be deliriously happy."

Maggie couldn't breathe. Didn't dare breathe. Maybe it was adrenaline. Maybe it was the shock of everything that happened. "Are you serious?" Her mouth went dry. "You're dreaming my dreams and you're honestly in love with me?"

"I am—and don't try to tell me I'm not. I have been for a long time. I was just confused. When a man never expects to love again discovers that he already does and he didn't know it, it is confusing." He sobered, his voice dropping an octave. "So are you going to keep me in suspense the rest of my days or tell me—am I dreaming alone?"

"Oh, Ian." She hugged him hard. "Of course not. I'm in love with you, too."

"I hoped."

"You did?" She'd been too terrified he wouldn't love her back to risk hoping.

"I know the exact second I dared to hope."

"When?" She couldn't believe it. Her mind just wouldn't wrap around it. All she wanted was within reach.

"The moment I realized you'd sent me away from Crawford and you were facing him alone. You were protecting me because you'd taken me into your heart, because that's what you do." He dipped his chin. "Don't ever do that again, by the way. Whatever we face, we face it together."

Bemused, she couldn't find her voice but settled for a nod.

"I was scared to death he'd kill you before I could tell you."

"Or before you could wring my neck for letting you go to the creek."

"That, too." He smiled. "But I am really glad you didn't die."

"So am I. Spares your arm—from throwing rocks at my grave every day." Maggie tilted her head and received his kiss.

"Ahem." Uncle Warny cleared his throat. "Sorry to interrupt you two, but you ain't sitting under no mis-

tletoe, so this smooching ain't official, and I got me
a surprise for you I figure you'll want to be seeing."

"But we exchange gifts in the morning." Maggie
didn't understand. They'd officially held off exchang-
ing gifts until everyone who'd been stranded had time
to shop.

He grunted. "You'll be wanting this gift right now."

From behind him, Paul walked in and held his arms
open.

Squealing her delight, Maggie sprung up off the sofa
and flung herself at her big brother. They hugged long
and hard, and Maggie saw Uncle Warny dabbing at
his eyes with the edge of his red-and-white bandanna.

Della let out a delicate sniff. "Hi, Ian."

He watched the reunion, his gaze fixed on Maggie.
"Welcome home, Della."

Paul put Maggie down on the floor and she hugged
Della then grabbed her hand. "Let me see." She shot
her brother a warning look. "Paul Mason, there'd bet-
ter be…" Maggie let out another squeal of pure delight.
"Oh, yay! You're engaged. I'm so happy. Ian! Ian, look.
She's wearing an engagement ring!"

Congratulations were shared and accepted amid
laughter and smiles and heartfelt joy.

Paul hugged his sister again. "It's over, Maggie. Finally, it's over."

"You know?" How was that possible? He'd been
without phone service…

"As soon as I heard he was in custody on the radio,
I knew what had happened."

"Not exactly, Paul. But I'll fill you in on the details,"
Uncle Warny said. "Let's get you and Della something
hot to drink. Me and Jake was sipping us some hot

chocolate. It ain't as good as Della's, but it'll do when it's freezing out."

Paul stilled, stared at his sister. "It's almost too much to take in, isn't it? It being over, I mean."

Crawford had ruled her life and affected Paul's for such a long time. "It's over," she assured him and tugged Ian close, then wrapped an arm around his waist. "And it's just beginning."

Paul looked from her to Ian and back again. "What does that mean?" Paul frowned. "Maggie, you're crying. But you never cry unless…" He shot a warning look at Ian.

"Oh, no." Uncle Warny sighed like the dying. Even Jake made tracks for the kitchen. "I'm outta here. When she gets going, I can't stand it. Maybe if she cried more often it wouldn't be as bad, but rare as it is, it rips this old man's heart to shreds."

"It's okay, Uncle Warny," she assured him. "These are happy tears. I'm…happy." Maggie smiled. "We're all here and together and—"

Paul looked totally lost. "That makes you cry?"

Ian laughed, closed his arms around her and held Maggie while she wept. "Of course it does," he told Paul.

"I'm missing something here." Paul scratched his head.

"Well, when you get it, come tell me and Della and Jake. We'll be in the kitchen."

"Silly cowards." Maggie laughed through her tears. "It just means that I'm getting my merry Christmas."

"Go get some hot chocolate, Paul." Ian winked. "I'll take care of her until she's normal again."

Paul crossed his chest with his arms. "That could take a while."

Ian nodded. "About a lifetime, I figure."

Paul's eyebrows shot up. "Seriously?"

"Oh, yeah."

"Well, all right. Congratulations." Paul looked at his little sister. "Welcome home, Maggie."

She nodded, sobbed, soaking the front of Ian's shirt.

He rubbed circles on her back. "It's okay, honey."

"It's not okay. It's wonderful. I thought I'd never know anything wonderful again, and now everything I ever dreamed of is right here and it's…it's…"

"Wonderful." Over her head, he motioned to Paul to go on.

Smiling, Paul slipped into the kitchen.

Ian pressed his lips to her crown. "You cry, Maggie. It's safe to cry now. You can be weak and vulnerable and it's okay. I've got you now, and I'll be strong for us both for a while and you can finally rest."

"You understand even that—that I couldn't cry or fall apart because if I did…"

He cupped her face in his hand. "Of course, I understand."

Sheer relief washed over her face. "I do love you, Ian."

"I know."

She sniffed. "You're going to have to quit that, you arrogant thing. Say I love you, too."

"It's not arrogant." He cupped her face in his hands. "You have no idea how much it means to me to know you love me." He kissed her forehead, the edge of her brow. "Let me enjoy it just for a while."

That admission changed her whole way of thinking.

"Okay." She settled in, her arms around him, his arms around her, and let her emotions settle. The Christmas Countdown was over, and its gifts truly had just begun.

* * * * *

Dear Reader,

In some way, all of us have experienced doing without to give to someone else. Maybe a friend in trouble, maybe a loved one at risk, or maybe someone hungry on the street. We willingly chose to deny ourselves for their benefit.

That's the heart of Maggie Mason in *Christmas Countdown*. Maggie loves her home, her family and her life, but when a twisted soul threatens it and her, she forfeits all but her life to protect those she loves. Yet for three long years, the twisted soul continues to torment her. It seems things get worse, not better. I say seems, because we too often discover what we see is only a part of the bigger picture and in that bigger picture is something very good. So it is for Maggie.

She does what she has to do and keeps walking in faith. And in her darkest hours, she keeps reaching out to a friend as isolated and alone and wounded as she is—Dr. Ian Crane, a widower craving an elusive peace.

Together they discover that when you dare to care, love can find a way to blossom and grow...and heal.

That's the story of Maggie and Ian. It moved me deeply, and I hope it also moves you.

May you and yours have a joyous Christmas!

Blessings,
Vicki Hinze

WE HOPE YOU
ENJOYED THIS

LOVE INSPIRED® SUSPENSE BOOK.

Discover more **heart-pounding** romances of **danger** and **faith** from the Love Inspired Suspense series.

Be sure to look for all six Love Inspired Suspense books every month.

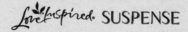

www.LoveInspired.com

SPECIAL EXCERPT FROM

The final battle with the Red Rose Killer begins when he kidnaps Captain Justin Blackwood's teenage daughter.

Read on for a sneak preview of
Valiant Defender *by Shirlee McCoy,*
the exciting conclusion to the Military K-9 Unit miniseries,
available November 2018 from Love Inspired Suspense.

Canyon Air Force Base was silent. Houses shuttered, lights off. Streets quiet. Just the way it should be in the darkest hours of the morning. Captain Justin Blackwood didn't let the quiet make him complacent. Seven months ago, an enemy had infiltrated the base. Boyd Sullivan, aka the Red Rose Killer—a man who'd murdered five people in his hometown before he'd been caught—had escaped from prison and continued his crime spree, murdering several more people and wreaking havoc on the base.

"What are your thoughts, Captain?" Captain Gretchen Hill asked as he sped through the quiet community.

"I don't think we're going to find him at the house," he responded. "But when it comes to Boyd Sullivan, I believe in checking out every lead."

"The witness reported lights? She didn't actually see Boyd?"

"She didn't see him, but the family who lived in the house left for a new post two days ago. Lots of moving trucks and activity. She's worried Sullivan might have noticed and decided to squat in the empty property."

"Based on how easily Boyd has slipped through our fingers these past few months, I'd say he's too smart to squat in base housing," Gretchen said.

"I agree," Justin responded. He'd been surprised at how much he enjoyed working with Gretchen. He'd expected her presence to feel like a burden, one more person to worry about and protect. But she had razor-sharp intellect and a calm, focused demeanor that had been an asset to the team.

"Even if he decided to spend a few nights in an empty house, why turn on lights?"

"If he's there, he wants us to know it," Justin responded. It was the only explanation that made sense. And it was the kind of game Sullivan liked to play—taunting his intended victims, letting them know that he was closing in.

He needed to be stopped.

Tonight.

For the sake of the people on base and for his daughter Portia's sake.

Don't miss
Valiant Defender *by Shirlee McCoy,*
available November 2018 wherever
Love Inspired® Suspense *books and ebooks are sold.*

www.LoveInspired.com

LISEXP1018

Love Inspired

Wyoming Christmas Quadruplets
Jill Kemerer

Save $1.00

on the purchase of any
Love Inspired® or Love Inspired®
Suspense book.

Available wherever books are sold,
including most bookstores, supermarkets,
drugstores and discount stores.

Save $1.00

on the purchase of any Love Inspired® or
Love Inspired® Suspense book.

Coupon valid until April 30, 2019. Redeemable at participating retail outlets in the
U.S. and Canada only. Limit one coupon per customer.

52616033

Canadian Retailers: Harlequin Enterprises Limited will pay the face value of
this coupon plus 10.25¢ if submitted by customer for this product only. Any
other use constitutes fraud. Coupon is nonassignable. Void if taxed, prohibited
or restricted by law. Consumer must pay any government taxes. Void if copied.
Inmar Promotional Services ("IPS") customers submit coupons and proof of sales
to Harlequin Enterprises Limited, P.O. Box 31000, Scarborough, ON M1R 0E7,
Canada. Non-IPS retailer—for reimbursement submit coupons and proof of
sales directly to Harlequin Enterprises Limited, Retail Marketing Department,
Bay Adelaide Centre, East Tower, 22 Adelaide Street West, 40th Floor, Toronto,
Ontario M5H 4E3, Canada.

U.S. Retailers: Harlequin Enterprises
Limited will pay the face value of
this coupon plus 8¢ if submitted by
customer for this product only. Any
other use constitutes fraud. Coupon is
nonassignable. Void if taxed, prohibited
or restricted by law. Consumer must pay
any government taxes. Void if copied.
For reimbursement submit coupons
and proof of sales directly to Harlequin
Enterprises, Ltd 482, NCH Marketing
Services, P.O. Box 880001, El Paso,
TX 88588-0001, U.S.A. Cash value
1/100 cents.

5 65373 00076 2 (8100)0 12391

® and ™ are trademarks owned and used by the trademark owner and/or its licensee.

© 2018 Harlequin Enterprises Limited

LICOUP44816

SPECIAL EXCERPT FROM

*With her family in danger of being separated,
could marriage to a newcomer in town
keep them together for the holidays?*

Read on for a sneak preview of
An Amish Wife for Christmas *by Patricia Davids,
available in November 2018 from Love Inspired!*

"I've got trouble, Clarabelle."

The cow didn't answer her. Bethany pitched a forkful of hay to the family's placid brown-and-white Guernsey. "The bishop has decided to send Ivan to Bird-in-Hand to live with Onkel Harvey. It's not right. It's not fair. I can't bear the idea of sending my little brother away. We belong together."

Clarabelle munched a mouthful of hay as she regarded Bethany with soulful deep brown eyes.

"Advice is what I need, Clarabelle. The bishop said Ivan could stay if I had a husband. Someone to discipline and guide the boy. Any idea where I can get a husband before Christmas?"

"I doubt your cow has the answers you seek, but if she does I have a few questions for her about my own problems," a man said.

Bethany spun around. A stranger stood in the open barn door. He wore a black Amish hat pulled low on his forehead and a dark blue woolen coat with the collar turned up against the cold.

The mirth sparkling in his eyes sent a flush of heat to her cheeks. How humiliating. To be caught talking to a cow about matrimonial prospects made her look ridiculous.

She struggled to hide her embarrassment. "It's rude to eavesdrop on a private conversation."

"I'm not sure talking to a cow qualifies as a private conversation, but I am sorry to intrude."

He didn't look sorry. He looked like he was struggling not to laugh at her.

"I'm Michael Shetler."

She considered not giving him her name. The less he knew to repeat the better.

"I am Bethany Martin," she admitted, hoping she wasn't making a mistake.

"Nice to meet you, Bethany. Once I've had a rest I'll step outside if you want to finish your private conversation." He winked. One corner of his mouth twitched, revealing a dimple in his cheek.

"I'm glad I could supply you with some amusement today."

"It's been a long time since I've had something to smile about."

Don't miss
An Amish Wife for Christmas *by Patricia Davids,*
available November 2018 wherever
Love Inspired® books and ebooks are sold.

www.LoveInspired.com